Blood Echo

by Tessa Dawn

A Blood Curse Novel
Book Eleven
In the Blood Curse Series

Published by Ghost Pines Publishing, LLC
Volume XI of the Blood Curse Series by Tessa Dawn
First Edition Trade Paperback Published November 14, 2019 10 9 8 7 6 5 4 3 2 1
First Edition eBook Published November 14, 2019 10 9 8 7 6 5 4 3 2 1

ISBN-13: Paperback (general) 978-1-937223-40-3
paperback (Amazon) 978-1-699020-42-5
Printed in the United States of America
ISBN-13: eBook 978-1-937223-41-0

This is a work of fiction. All characters and events portrayed in this novel are either
fictitious or are used fictitiously. Any resemblance to actual persons, living or dead,
business establishments, events, or locales is entirely coincidental.

Ghost Pines Publishing, LLC

For Julie Bibby

∼ Thanks for all the inspiration!

ACKNOWLEDGMENTS

Credits and Acknowledgments

Ghost Pines Publishing, LLC, *Publishing*
    Damonza, *Cover Art*
    Lidia Bircea, *Romanian Translations*
    Reba Hilbert, *Editing*

Passing Mentions

The Flintstones – An American animated sitcom produced by Hanna-Barbera. Original broadcast: September 1960.

One of These Things – The Sesame Street Book & Record; song written by Bruce Hart, Jon Stone, & Joe Raposo; album released 1970

THE BLOOD CURSE

The Blood Curse

In 800 BC, Prince Jadon and Prince Jaegar Demir were banished from their Romanian homeland after being cursed by a ghostly apparition: the reincarnated Blood of their numerous female victims. The princes belonged to an ancient society that sacrificed its females to the point of extinction, and the punishment was severe.

They were forced to roam the earth in darkness as creatures of the night. They were condemned to feed on the blood of the innocent and stripped of their ability to produce female offspring. They were damned to father twin sons by human hosts who would die wretchedly upon giving birth; and the firstborn of the first set would forever be required as a sacrifice of atonement for the sins of their forefathers.

Staggered by the enormity of the Curse, Prince Jadon, whose own hands had never shed blood, begged his accuser for leniency and received four small mercies—four exceptions to the Curse that would apply to his house and his descendants, alone.

Ψ Though still creatures of the night, they would be allowed to walk in the sun.

Ψ Though still required to live on blood, they would not be forced to take the lives of the innocent.

Ψ While still incapable of producing female offspring, they would be given one opportunity and thirty days to obtain a mate —a human *destiny* chosen by the gods—following a sign that appeared in the heavens.

Ψ While they were still required to sacrifice a firstborn son, their twins would be born as one child of darkness and one child of light, allowing them to sacrifice the former while keeping the latter to carry on their race.

And so...forever banished from their homeland in the Transylvanian mountains of Eastern Europe, the descendants of Jaegar and the descendants of Jadon became the Vampyr of legend: roaming the earth, ruling the elements, living on the blood of others...forever bound by an ancient curse. They were brothers of the same species, separated only by degrees of light and shadow.

PROLOGUE

Gwendolyn Hamilton hugged her knees to her chest as she perched on the large, uneven boulder and watched the team of vampires—*yes, vampires!*—continue to inspect the old cobblestone well. Her captors were an unlikely crew: Braden Bratianu, the tall, muscular, good-looking hero who had rescued her from The Fortress; Kristina Silivasi, Braden's girlfriend or companion—Gwen wasn't quite sure what the redhead was to Braden, other than extremely possessive over every inch of his hard-cut body; Deanna Dubois, who was a stunning beauty with a generous spirit to match; and Deanna's mate, Nachari Silivasi, who honestly defied common words.

Nachari was extraordinary.

The kind of gorgeous that stole a woman's breath, made her lose her words and stutter, and caused her heart to skip a beat every time he spared her a glance.

Yeah, he was that damn beautiful...

And, in truth, all of them had been nothing but kind, generous, and accommodating to Gwen since the moment they had taken her in at the brownstone. Kristina had bought a host of new clothes and shoes for her "boyfriend's" houseguest; Braden and Nachari had bent over backward to make Gwen feel at home; and Deanna had gone so far as to redecorate one of the luxurious guest rooms just to suit Gwen's personal taste—as if the panoramic mountain views from the private balcony and the deluxe adjoining bathroom, with its decadent rain-shower and hammered-copper clawfoot tub, were not enough already. Gwen was living in the lap of luxury, and she was being treated like a queen. It was almost enough to make her forget her predicament...

Almost.

Not quite.

One simple truth remained: Gwen was still being held captive, against her will.

Nearly seven weeks ago, Gwen had been abducted from a ski resort and taken to a brutal fortress to be sold as a high-end prostitute and used as a human slave. Fortunately, she had been rescued thirty-two days later, but her rescuers had been a horde of vampires.

Vampires!

Immortal, blood-sucking creatures of the night.

Not only were they real, but they were living in Dark Moon Vale, and for some inexplicable reason, they refused to let her go. Yes, they were treating her kindly, and yes, they expressed regret for having to keep her "a little bit longer"—whatever that meant— but from all Gwen had learned and overheard, they could erase her memories of the entire event, fill in the time-gap with something far more pleasant, and deposit her safely back at home in Denver, where she could get on with her life and her post-graduate plans.

She could go back to her friends—they had to be worried sick.

She could reunite with her parents, and Lord knew she

missed Mark and Mary Hamilton more than words could express.

Yet and still, here she was, her rear end planted on a rough, dirty rock, watching a group of ungodly beautiful creatures circle around a well like it contained the secrets to the very universe in its depths. Braden was taking samples from the stones and the water. The wizard, Nachari, was doing heaven-knows-what with his fingertips and some creepy spells, and the women—Deanna and Kristina—kept asking questions about invisible doors, portals, and the interior of the structure reeking with the smell of vampires, according to some girl named Zayda. And much to Gwen's chagrin, there was a whole lot of talk about something that sounded a lot like...*werewolves*.

No.

Just no.

Gwen refused to let her mind entertain the thought of *werewolves*—she had more than enough supernatural freakishness to process as it stood.

Just then, Nachari Silivasi placed his fingertips on a pale, wheat-colored stone that sat atop the well, and began tracing the dark gray mortar all around it. He had done this a dozen times already, outlining stone after stone—but this time, he absently glanced over his shoulder at Gwen, and the stone began to sizzle: The wheat-colored rock turned molten red, an electric charge filled the mountain air, and a high-pitched whir vibrated through the canyon.

The vampire drew back his hand.

He stared fixedly at his fingertips.

And then he blew what appeared to be icy shards over the singed flesh in order to cool it.

He touched the stone again.

Nothing happened.

He let his hand fall to his side, and he glanced once more at Gwen—

Nothing happened.

He placed two fingers on the rock, locked his gaze with Gwen's, and *pop, sizzle, flash!*

Flames, electricity, another buzzing sound.

He withdrew his hand with a quickness—his fingertips were literally on fire, but he didn't bother to put them out.

"Shit," Gwen murmured, standing up on the rock. *What the hell was happening?*

"Gwen," Nachari said in that smooth, cocky tenor. "Come here for a minute."

Gwen shook her head so briskly her ears began to ring.

He pitched his voice an octave lower. "Gwendolyn, come to me."

Deanna and Kristina backed away from the well, even as Braden drew closer, and Gwen's feet, defying her better judgment and willpower, began to inch their way down from the boulder. "No," she spoke out loud, trying to regain control over her body. "Stop, stop, stop!" She dropped onto her butt and scooted down from the rock. "Stop it, Nachari!" she shouted, realizing he was using some sort of compulsion.

His amazing forest-green eyes softened. "Shh. It's okay. Come. Take my hand." He extended the limb that wasn't burning.

"I'd rather not," Gwen squeaked, her voice betraying her terror. Up until this point, the vampires had never exerted their power over her, and Gwen didn't like it one bit. Nachari crooked his fingers, and her feet kept right on shuffling. "Please, Nachari. That well freaks me out."

"It's just energy," Braden offered, trying to smooth over the situation. "What'd you get your degree in, again? Integrative Physiology? So you took a whole lot of science, right? Think of it this way: Nachari's just doing a controlled experiment, but neither one of us is going to let anything hurt you."

Gwen felt her face flush and grow pale, as if all the blood was draining out of it. "His fucking hand is on fire," she argued. "And he doesn't seem to give a shit."

Nachari smiled, and despite her fear, her heart went pitter-patter. "I'm blocking the nerve impulses right now—can't feel a thing. Trust me, Gwen; it'll only take a moment."

Gwen's eyes shot nervously from Nachari to Deanna, from Deanna to Kristina, and from Kristina back to the wizard. They were all as surprised as she was—no one knew what the hell was happening with this well. Against her better judgment—and well, because she had no real choice in the matter—she slowly padded her way to Nachari and reluctantly took his free hand.

He held hers gently.

He rotated the trunk of his body toward the well.

And he placed the full palm of his burning limb on top of the stone in question.

There was an eerie moment of silence...stillness...hushed anticipation.

And then a neon bolt of lightning lit up the heavens, followed by a thunderous explosion, an echo so enormous it shook the stones loose from the cylinder before crackling outward in waves across the valley.

Another bolt of lightning shot up from the well—*not down from the heavens*—and the pure electrostatic discharge radiated outward in a horizontal circle, wave after wave of lethal energy coursing sideways through the air like a burning scythe chopping wheat from a field.

Nachari threw Gwen to the ground, dived beyond her body, and leveled Deanna and Kristina before the wave could hit them. Braden lunged on top of Gwen's back and shielded her body with his heavy torso. The once high-pitched whir became a piercing, deafening drone—a never-ending, cascading echo across the valley—as the group hovered beneath the fire line waiting for the sudden mystical storm to pass.

"Build a holding cell, Braden!" Nachari shouted from the other end of the well. "Draw carbon from the living organisms around you and bond each atom covalently to four other atoms." Even as he spoke, his hands were working furiously, and a thin, sparkling dome was beginning to form over the vampire and the two other women.

Braden arched his back, pushed up on his biceps, and raised his body a few inches off Gwen to call out to the Master Wizard. "A holding cell or a restraining cell? You want me to construct it out of *diamonds*? Nachari, that'll neutralize our power! It'll leave us completely defenseless!"

"I've already called out to Marquis. When the storm is over, he'll come and unlock the barriers; but yes, you need a multiple layered cell, constructed from the strongest element possible. Build it to contain and restrain—nothing in, nothing out. Braden, the only energy surge I've ever seen like this was from Napolean Mondragon, when he was harnessing the freakin' sun. This storm is being created by a vampire, and whoever he is, he's drawing from my power—he's a thousand times stronger than you or I. If you don't build that cell, you and Gwen will die."

Thump-thump.

Thump-thump.

Thump-thump.

The vampire's arcane heart beat in his chest at a steady, even rhythm just as it had done for decades...centuries...millennia.

He was aware of no one.

He was aware of nothing.

He had not been aware for over twenty-eight hundred years...

At least not until now—not until he felt a subtle prick of magic piercing his blood-starved organ: the sensation of familiar power; the taint of another wizard; the pulse of a singular woman's heartbeat.

Destiny...destiny...destiny.

His *destiny?*

The word was as odd as it was unfamiliar, yet it rang inside his ears.

And then something—someone—connected the circuits: her eyes, his power, a stone from the well.

All fell silent, yet again.

Then another connection, stronger still: *her eyes, his power, a stone from the well!*

Fabian's eyes blinked open, only to find darkness above, below, and all around. All the world was dark and dank; water and mud; earth and clay. The circuit closed once more, and this time, it was teeming with electricity, sorcery, and power: an undiluted pool; an unrestricted chain; a pure, untainted channel to the source that fed his heart...and awakened his timeless soul.

That wizard.

And that girl.

Thump-thump; thump-thump; thump-thump—his heart sprang to life, and he let out a thunderous roar, releasing a millennium of anguish, confusion, and famine! He was starving all the way to his core, the hunger gnawing, bone deep. His muscles spasmed in agony, and his skull began to throb.

Blood.

He needed blood.

He needed *her blood*, and he needed it now.

And then his power flowed back into him like water breaking through an ageless dam, and he sent the full breadth of it lambasting forward, exploding through the grave...the mud...the sand...

The well.

Fabian Antonescu, the most infamous wizard to have ever been born to the union of a celestial god and a human mate, was lying at the bottom of a simple archaic well.

He was...

He was...

He was no longer in Romania, leading the convoy of warriors, a secret group of mercenaries, through the Transylvanian Alps. He was no longer holed up in the southern Carpathian Mountains, hiding Ciopori and Vanya from their bloodthirsty brother, Prince Jaegar. He was no longer changing, suffering, wishing for his final death, along with his loyal followers, as claws and fangs and power beyond imagining assailed them...changed them... made them into something else.

And he was no longer in that rotting ship, being tossed about at sea.

He was...

He was in North America, awaiting Prince Jadon's return.

No!

He was lying beneath a well.

Starving.

Ah, yes...yes...*yes!*

He was Vampyr.

His hunger overcame him, and he called to the four cardinal winds. He tunneled one hand into the dirt and extended his grimy fingers, reaching for that wizard's power, the one who had spoken to the stone, and he suckled on the magick like a newborn babe, growing stronger, more determined...more alive.

He threw back his wild hair and embraced the elements all around him, gave vent to his feral nature, and became the untamed storm, lashing out in all directions. And then he exploded from the belly of the well, emerged into waning sunlight, and recoiled from the unbearable glare of the light.

Where was she?

That woman...

His woman!

The one who would feed him her blood?

He scanned his surroundings like a stalking predator, sinking down onto his haunches as he prowled.

Domes.

There were two carefully constructed domes...

Carbon.

Intricate bonds.

Powerful, magical weaving...

He tossed his head back and laughed.

Flicking his wrist in the direction of the nearest conical structure, he sent an explosion of diamonds scattering across the mountain, then reached inside the collapsing rubble and snatched the female by her arm. Her legs kicking and dangling beneath her, he drew her to his mouth, sank his fangs deep into her convulsing throat, and groaned in exquisite pleasure.

Ah, yes...

Blood.

Release.

Destiny.

Still drinking to his heart's content, he wrapped a firm, unyielding arm around the female's waist and dove back into the well.

CHAPTER ONE

G wen Hamilton let out a shriek of pure, unadulterated terror as the conical dome above her exploded into thousands of pieces; a large, powerful, grimy hand shackled her bicep; and her torso dangled in the air, her legs kicking and squirming frantically beneath her. The memory of the Aspen ski lodge and her subsequent abduction—being kept as a human slave in that hideous fortress—flooded the prefrontal cortex of her brain, but she didn't have a chance to grasp it beyond one initial, overwhelming instinct: *Not again!*

Dear God, please; not again!

She was prepared to fight for all she was worth—surely the Dark Moon Vale vampires would help her, wouldn't they?—but she didn't have a moment to catch her breath, nor to follow that train of thought: Spikes...nails...some ungodly sharp implement pierced the flesh of her throat, and she gasped in shock, staggered by the intensity of the pain.

Oh God, those were fangs—not nails or spikes!

And she was somehow in the arms of a foreign vampire, a supernatural monster, who was groaning in pleasure even as he tightened his forearm like a powerful, unyielding clamp, constructed of iron, around her waist: grasping...bracing... cleaving her to his rock-hard chest.

And then the entire world went topsy-turvy.

The sky flipped upside down; the ground seemed to undulate beneath her; and vertigo assailed all five of her senses.

She was flying...

No, she was diving...

She was traversing a pool of dank, murky water; tunneling downward into noxious smells; tumbling through swirling eddies of plants, earth, and algae; drifting...sinking...into cold, wet oblivion.

The vampire's forearm tightened like a vise, knocking the wind right out of her, and her arms and legs flailed like a child's, a newborn babe falling from a crib. Without conscious thought or reason, she jerked to the left, twisted her torso in a circular motion, and grasped desperately at her captor's arms—she had to encircle his shoulders before she sank or floated away. If she didn't cling to the monster, she would surely founder and drown.

Gwen didn't know how long she could hold her breath, but she knew she had to try. She bit down hard on her upper and lower lips and told herself not to panic. Surely, vampires couldn't breathe under water—surely, the monster would seek air soon— because if he didn't, then Gwen was as good as dead.

Humans could not sustain life under water!

No sooner had the thought entered her mind than the vampire began to tunnel sideways.

He removed three or four stones from the side of the well as if they were nothing more than plastic bricks—a block of flimsy Legos to be snapped apart by a child's thumbs. He scattered several more in earnest, and then he began to dig.

Swiftly.

Earnestly.

At a furious pace.

His free hand was crooked like a blade as he swept it, again and again, in a scooping motion, deftly excavating an emerging trench...faster and faster...until a steady drone vibrated in the water, buzzing and humming like a churning engine. And then he began to twist like a cyclone, spinning his body—and Gwen's —around and around in dizzying circles, one hand acting as a drill-bit, still excavating the earth, the other functioning as a shield, protecting his captive's head from flying and splintering debris.

They must have tunneled—and traveled—a mile or more, burrowing their way through the earth until, at last, they turned upward, shot through the surface, and emerged in a dark, cryptic cave.

The moment the vampire withdrew his arm, Gwen scampered like a spider to the wall of the cavern, ducked beneath a low, rocky outcropping, and tucked her knees to her chest. Gasping for air and hugging her stomach, she finally let her fear... and her anger...get the best of her: *"What the actual fuck!"* she shouted.

Fabian Antonescu released his hold on the human woman.

The odd, beautiful, frightened female who dressed in strange clothing—and heavy trousers—like a man. And then he remembered...*ah, yes*...he remembered...

Blood.

Release.

Destiny.

The power of another wizard grounding energy to the well.

The overwhelming need to seize her, claim her, taste her, to rise from the watery grave and awaken the ancient memory...or perhaps it was inborn instinct...driving him unerringly to the old, familiar cave.

As quickly as the lucid thoughts came, they vanished.

His canine teeth throbbed in his mouth as the last remaining essence of the female's life-force snaked down the back of his throat, and his hunger began to rise anew. He tilted his head to the side, narrowing his pupils into thin, vertical slits in order to see clearly in the darkness—the overwhelming, all-encompassing darkness—and watched as the human female scampered beneath a low-hanging ledge.

He sniffed the cavity for traces of dung or recent carrion, evidence of a lurking carnivore, lest his own prey scamper into the waiting jowls of another predator, unknowingly. Satisfied that they were alone in the cave, he tried to reach for his magick...for his understanding...to divine where he was, why he had stirred from his slumber, what had just happened to his body...

How had he come to be in that well?

"*What the actual fuck!*" the female shouted.

And Fabian recoiled from the sound.

Nonsense.

Gibberish.

The words had no meaning.

He closed his eyes and sent his power outward, seeking, reaching, as he peered inside her mind.

Of course...

English.

An odd, bastardized form of English.

Nonetheless, he couldn't make naught nor reason of it. "*Veniti inainte!*" he commanded in his native Romanian tongue. *Come forth...come forward!*

She didn't obey.

Perhaps she couldn't see in the darkness; perhaps she couldn't hear from beneath the craggy ledge.

He waved his hand through the void in front of him, conjuring the elements and commanding the ether to do his will. A small flicker, like that of a single candle, alighted in the dark, vacuous space and hovered in midair. And then the flame sputtered, as if bowing in reverence, and Fabian nodded.

The candle became a torch.

The torch became a blaze.

And the blaze took on the reflection of orange, yellow, and gold.

Too much light!

He recoiled...

He had spent far too much time in darkness to adjust to such noxious glare—with the wave of his hand and a flick of his fingers, he dialed it down to dark honey, ambient red, and blue.

Better.

Much better.

Then he lowered the blaze to the cavern floor and circled the palms of his hands in a smooth, graceful arc, directly above it— the flames spread out into an oblong circle and began to sway, crackle, rise, and ebb. There was no wood or kindling to sustain the conflagration, so he ordered the carbon atoms all around him to offer their essence in a continuous dance with the air, only he didn't call them *carbon atoms*—they were simply one of a dozen energies he had manipulated since he was a child. He wasn't sure how he knew this—but *he knew.*

The fire dancing, the cavern warming, he turned his attention back to the female and repeated the command once again, this time in her familiar English. "Come forth!"

She jolted, tightened her arms around her knees, and shimmied even farther back beneath the angular ledge.

Fabian snorted as his ire got the best of him. "*Numele meu este Fabian Antonescu, cel mai puternic vrajitor care a trait vreodata, si vei face voia mea.*" He repeated the refrain in English:

"My name is Fabian Antonescu, the most powerful wizard that ever lived, and you will do my will." He paused, before adding, "You shall obey me."

The odd, insubordinate female began to wail like a distraught, wild banshee.

And that's when the wizard rose to his feet, cloaked his shoulders in a long, flowing tunic made from—*and of*—the fire, and growled an unmistakable warning.

CHAPTER TWO

N achari Silivasi rolled onto his back, still safe within the diamond-encased holding cell, but he couldn't say the same for Braden and Gwen—

What the devil had just happened!

He turned toward his *destiny* and reached for her hand. "Deanna, are you okay, my love?"

She shook out her hair and slowly sat up. "Yeah...*yes*...I'm okay."

"Kristina!" he called next, eyeing the redhead with concern as she crawled along the ground, searching for a missing shoe. "Sister, are you hurt?"

Kristina grumbled beneath her breath, spit some pine needles out of her mouth, then reached for her missing heel and slipped it back on. "No, I don't think so...what the hell?" She spun around, placed both palms against the interior of the dome, and squinted to see out the enclosure. Her eyes grew wide with fright. She pounded against the barrier and let out an ear-piercing shriek. "Braden!" She pummeled the dome with her fists. "Nachari, his holding cell is gone!" She rolled onto her back, tucked her knees to her chest, and started kicking the top of the barrier.

Stomp! Stomp! Stomp-stomp-stomp!

She kicked, and she shouted.

She shouted, and she kicked.

"Braden! Oh my gods, what happened to Braden?"

"Whoa!" Nachari crooned, softening his voice to conceal his own distress. "Slow down...ease up...you can't unravel a holding cell by stomping it."

She made temporary eye contact with the Master Wizard, then went right back to stomping the conical dome.

"Kristina..." Nachari restrained her legs, and then he dropped his tone to a deep, silken tenor and spoke with command in Romanian—no, she hadn't mastered the ancestral language, but she would have to grow quiet to listen. *"Liniste,"* he whispered, which meant *be quiet. "Fi linistita,"* he commanded. *Be still.* "Kristina, this is not helping Braden." And beyond that, all her frantic, chaotic energy was making Nachari's inner panther restless—every instinct in his body wanted to release the lethal cat, bound from the cell, and stalk the foreign vampire who had leached from Nachari's magical essence.

Kristina panted to release some tension.

She drew in a steady, deep breath of air and finally stopped screaming.

Then she crawled onto her knees and braced both hands on her hips, at last growing calm. "I'm okay...I'm *okay.*" She scooted to the edge of the cell and peered out once more. "Where are they, Nachari? Braden and Gwen? The holding cell is in a million pieces."

Concealing his rising concern, the Master Wizard closed his eyes, muted his emotions, and reached for a private, telepathic bandwidth in order to search for his acolyte: *Braden? Can you hear me?* He spoke clearly and evenly. *What happened, son?*

Where are you? When his entreaty was met with silence, he told himself not to panic—the boy was likely rattled, maybe injured, maybe wandering about the mountain in a state of confusion, but it was highly unlikely that he was dead. Nachari added a heavy layer of compulsion to his next command: *Say something, fledgling—speak to me now.*

Gwen is gone, Braden mumbled. His psychic voice sounded ragged.

Son, are you okay?

One heartbeat.

Two heartbeats.

Three heartbeats passed.

Then, *Yeah, yeah...I'm not hurt or anything, just a little shaken up.* Another delay as eerie silence lingered on the line. *Nachari, I couldn't stop it...I couldn't stop* him. *I promised Gwen that we'd protect her. I told her that neither one of us would let anything hurt her, but there was nothing I could do. That vampire...his power...the way he blasted out of the well—*

I know, Nachari interjected. *It's going to be okay. You did everything right; you did as you were told. Where are you now? Are you somewhere safe?*

Yeah, Braden said. *I think he's gone. I'm on the other side of the well, just surveying the damage. I think I must have shifted into the form of an eagle and flown to the other side of the hill when the dome exploded, maybe a few seconds after the vampire took Gwen.*

Nachari shut his eyes. He could hear the guilt, remorse, and fear in the fledgling's psychic voice, and he understood it intimately; after all, they had both been responsible for their human ward—they had both been honor bound to protect her. *Did you see what happened? Did you see which way he took her?*

No idea, Braden whispered. *He exploded out of the well like a rocket, dropped down onto his haunches like a freakin' hyena, and then he flicked his wrist at our dome—like the sight of it seriously annoyed him, or maybe it actually humored him—and the whole freakin' cell exploded. Nachari, he snatched Gwen so fast, I barely knew what was happening, and then before I could react, he dove back into the water.*

Nachari's eyes shot back open. *He dove back into the water—you mean into the well? With Gwen?*

Yes, Braden answered. *That's what I'm trying to tell you. He took her back into the shaft...back underground...back to wherever he came from. But I can't feel his power...or register her presence... there's no longer any energy, any imprint, coming out of that well, not a single ripple in the water. It's like they freakin' vanished into thin air. Nachari, I have no idea where they've gone.*

The Master Wizard analyzed Braden's words, trying to come up with a theory or a rational explanation, but the more he turned it over, the more confounded he became—nothing about the situation made any sense.

And then a gruff, no-nonsense bark shook him out of his reflection. "Back away from the perimeter, Nachari!" Marquis Silivasi's angry, commanding brogue. "What in the name of Lord Draco," he grumbled as he towered over the remaining holding cell and glared inside.

One look at the Ancient Master Warrior's expression, the tension in his shoulders, and the furrow in his brows, and Nachari backed away as ordered.

Big Brother was not there to play games.

He was dressed in his dark leather duster; his right hand was cloaked in a cestus; and his phantom blue eyes were gleaming blood red. "One minute I'm sitting on the bank of the river, behind the house with Ciopori, and the next, I'm getting this flurry of shit: You're telling me you're building a cell made of diamond—a cell that's going to sap your power and trap you inside—and then half the Dark Moon valley is shaking. A bolt of lightning the size of a small city pierces an otherwise clear blue sky, and then World War III breaks out in the heavens—thunder, explosions, and an echo that sent half the water in the river onto the bank. Next thing I know, I can hear trees falling, rocks sliding, and the crackling of fire, miles away. If this was some sort of wizardly experiment—you and Braden trying to open that damn portal or playing with some spell in that damn Blood Cannon, that creepy-ass book of black magic—I swear, I'm going to kick your ass, little brother."

Nachari waited patiently as the warrior ranted and raved, all the while unraveling the holding cell—membrane by membrane, carbon by carbon—uncoiling the powerful magick that had built the supernatural dome. When at last the sparkling walls fell away, Nachari rose to his full, graceful height and sighed. "Brother," he said pointedly, "this wasn't about the portal, and it wasn't about a spell. An ancient vampire flew out of that well"—he gestured absently at the disheveled, cobbled structure, at least a quarter of its stones now strewn about the mountain—"and as he ascended, he extracted my power—siphoned my magick—like he was simply draining water from a faucet. He destroyed Braden's holding cell with the flick of his wrist, snatched Gwen off the ground, and dove back into the water. *That* was the echo you heard. *That* was the storm you witnessed. *That* is what—and who —caused all this destruction." He swept his arm in a wide, circular arc, allowing the Ancient Master Warrior to take in the devastation. "If we hadn't built those cells when we did, the wave alone would've taken our heads, and somehow, I just don't think it would've been any great feat for that Ancient to have extracted our hearts if he wanted them."

Marquis recoiled and took a generous step back, but before he could speak, Braden Bratianu finally joined the other vampires and sidled up to the Master Warrior. "Hey, Marquis," he said in a hushed, solemn whisper. "Nachari's telling the truth

—I've never seen anything like it. That dude was hella powerful, and he looked wild as hell!"

Kristina's bright blue eyes clouded with moisture as she rose from her knees, stepped toward the three huddled vampires, and studied Braden in earnest for the very first time: His jeans were tattered and covered in muck; his boots were missing, and his feet were bleeding; his chestnut brown hair was littered with fragments—rocks, pine cones, and remnants of gemstones—and his smooth, tan skin was beleaguered with cuts. She gulped. "Bray, are you all right? You don't look so good."

Marquis held up an implacable hand. "Later," he mumbled, his tone brooking no argument. "There'll be time for pleasantries later."

Deanna nestled beneath Nachari's arm, even as Braden took Kristina by the hand. "I'm fine, Red," he whispered, pulling her close. He pressed a tender, chaste kiss to the top of her head, and for the first time...ever...she didn't object.

"Tell me about this vampire." Marquis scowled, scanning the mountain like a hawk. "Was he a Dark One, one of the elders, perhaps an evil twin from the house of Jadon who somehow eluded the sacrifice—someone who might have escaped the Curse?"

Nachari shrugged. "Wish I knew, Master Warrior. Braden, what color was his hair?"

Braden let out a drawn, ragged breath. "I dunno, but it was wild...wild as hell... I didn't see any black-and-red bands, but then, Ian, Julien's twin, was from the house of Jadon—he was a dark twin who knew magic, and he was able to mask his hair as blond for a while."

Nachari nodded, growing ever more pensive. "But why take Gwen? Why the human girl? Why did his power come alive when I looked at her?"

Marquis furrowed his brows. "What the heck are you talking about?"

Nachari sighed. "Before the storm, before all hell broke loose, we were studying the well, collecting samples, when I started to trace a random stone. At first, nothing happened, but then I glanced at Gwen—"

Once again, Marquis held up his hand. "Permission to view your memories, Master Wizard. We don't have time for this shit."

Nachari blanched, but then he quickly recovered. *Okay,* he thought, *tactless as usual, but at least the Master Warrior had asked for permission.* "Do whatever you need to do," he said.

Marquis inclined his head, closed his eyes, and just like that, the vampire was inside, beyond the gray matter—dissecting white matter—extracting information, playing back each memory like a video-recording: fast-forwarding when expedient, rewinding when necessary, recording Nachari's knowledge as if it were his own. Finally, he blinked and took a generous step back. He turned toward Braden and cocked his brows. "Son, you had a completely different vantage, a very different experience. I need to hear what you heard and see what you saw."

Braden smiled, although his eyes looked wary. "Permission granted, Master Warrior." He tried to sound both formal and brave as he released Kristina and stepped closer to the vampire.

Marquis didn't waste any time.

He repeated the process in half the time, and then he cursed beneath his breath in Romanian. "Nachari, heal Braden's wounds, then take your *destiny* and Kristina to Kagen's clinic." He appraised both women with a keen, watchful eye. "They don't look like they're injured, but I'd rather be sure—one never knows when dealing with magick." His expression hardened, and his voice grew resolute. "Bring Father and Nathaniel into the loop—I'm going to share both sets of memories with the valley's sentinels, and we're going to need to call in the tracker. Let's all meet back up in thirty minutes, and we may as well start where we're going to end up—at Napolean's manse. Maybe the king can shed some light on this vampire; maybe Julien can track his flight. Who knows, but he definitely poses a risk to the house of Jadon, and the sentinels will want to react accordingly. Thirty minutes. Napolean's manse. And watch your fuckin' back in the meantime."

Nachari was not about to debate...or object.

He understood Marquis' reasoning—and the Ancient Master Warrior's need to take charge—even if his list of *"next steps"* was fairly obvious: Yes, the tracker was going to have to hunt like a demon, try to locate the ancient vampire...try to recover Gwen. And yes, the sentinels would have to protect the vale. Keitaro, Nathaniel, and Kagen would be intimately involved, if for no other reason than their family was involved...the vampire from the well had struck too close to home.

And as for Napolean Mondragon?

The thought gave Nachari chills...

The power that had come out of that well.

The storm that had cut through the valley.

The magick...the might...the chaotic energy.

Nachari wasn't willing to go so far as to believe this vampire was as powerful as Napolean, but of one thing he was absolutely certain: If they did find this Ancient, if they managed to locate Gwen, Napolean Mondragon was the only living soul strong enough to bring her home.

And even then, the king might need the assistance of sorcery —of all the house of Jadon's wizards...

Yeah, Marquis had made the correct—if not obvious—call.

CHAPTER THREE

Gwen gasped, shrank back, and slammed her head against the rim of the ledge, stifling her screams in mid-wail.

Oh.

Holy.

Shit.

No. No. No-no-no!

That wasn't just a growl—it was a primitive, bestial snarl—and the vampire clearly meant it as a warning—*freakin' hell*, he was wearing a blazing, supernatural fire like a blasted superhero's cape!

A fire he had built with his hands.

Stoked with his magic.

And painted over like some dark Picasso, changing the primary colors.

The male had barked some foreign command—*veniti inainte!* —but Gwen had no freakin' idea what that meant. And then he had ordered her to *come forth*—as if she would dare—before making the world's most terrifying introduction: *My name is*

Fabian Antonescu, the most powerful wizard that ever lived, and you will do my will—you shall obey me.

Oh, no-no-no-no-no!

She couldn't obey—whatever he was. This creature was nothing like Nachari or Braden.

He was the essence of nightmares, the inspiration of legends, some sort of demon, warlock, or sorcerer, in addition to being a vampire: *My name is Fabian Antonescu, the most powerful wizard that ever lived...*

Humble much?

This brute was incredibly arrogant—and dangerous. He was obviously accustomed to everything and everyone bowing down before him, and for whatever reason, he had emerged from that well like a mythical phoenix, broken through Braden's barrier like it was nothing more than papier-mâché, and bit Gwen in the neck, guzzled from her vein, like she was his own personal human spigot.

She still had the throbbing, open wounds to prove it.

And now...

And now he wanted her to obey him—*you will do my will.* That was never going to happen.

Still, it might be wise to at least show a little deference...a little fear... There was no reason to further incite him. Trembling like a leaf, Gwen unwound her arms from her knees, placed her hands palms down in the dirt, and slowly scooted forward on her bottom. She ducked to make sure she cleared the ledge this time, and she kept her eyes submissively averted.

Her only hope—her only prayer—was that if the creature intended to kill her, he would be merciful enough to do it quickly.

Painlessly.

Maybe he would siphon her blood until she died of exsanguination, and she would somehow sleep through it, pass out before the agony grew unbearable. One thing was for certain: This was nothing like being held captive in The Fortress, however horrendous that nightmare had been. At least at the Giovanni compound, the guards had been mortal, the enemy had been human. At least Gwen had possessed a chance to use her brains and her wit to contend for her life in the end. At least she had stood a fighting chance, no matter how slim...

There would be no surviving this.

She couldn't outfight him, outlast him, outthink him, or outpower him.

For all intents and purposes, he was invincible, and she was virtually defenseless.

A bitter tear of helplessness streamed down her cheek as she summoned every ounce of courage she could muster, rocked forward onto her hands and knees, and closed the remaining distance, crawling. Halting two to three feet in front of the mystical campfire, she sat back on her heels, straightened her spine, and raised her chin in order to meet the vampire eye to eye. Humility and submission was one thing—she had given the creature his due—but if he wanted to dispatch his quarry, then he needed to look her in the eyes: At least she could force this indomitable wizard to slay a person instead of an object.

He blinked three times, his fiery cloak now undulating behind his shoulders, and his haunting stare met hers; only she didn't feel empowered—or emboldened. Her heart nearly seized in her chest. And now, as he stood illuminated by so much firelight, the male was even more captivating...extraordinary...and petrifying, all at once.

Gwen had never seen anyone—or anything—like him.

His indigenous clothes were antiquated and tattered, yet still somehow regal: His real shirt was nothing more than a plain ivory tunic with sleeves attached to the shoulders, a hole cut into the neck, and a leather thong dissecting the waist. His trousers fell just beyond his knees. They were made from some loose-fitting cloth and appeared to be cinched at the top and the bottom. Both garments were relics from a bygone era, and needless to say, they were drenched with water—and he wasn't wearing an under-garment.

Gwen gulped.

Yeah...

He was definitely superhuman.

She wanted to look away, but she couldn't.

Despite her modesty and her terror, there was also a sense of morbid fascination, and then a singular comparison flashed through her mind...

Zeus.

That was the only word that could adequately describe him: the god of sky and thunder from Mount Olympus, descended in human flesh and standing before her, reanimated in a twenty-first-century cave. Only, this ancient deity must have been glazed in burnished bronze because his coloring was nothing short of remarkable: Despite the soil and the grime still coating his hair and tunic, his entire *being* was emblazoned in shades of rust and gold. His almond-shaped eyes were an antique, burnt copper, each pupil rimmed in raven black and framed by two silken brows. His chiseled, angular features were the stunning hue of copper—they were perfectly symmetrical, etched into high, copper cheekbones, and imperial above a strong, defiant jaw. His full, sculpted lips were drawn into a frown, a timeless expression that one might almost call a scowl, yet the visage screamed *power* and *majesty*, more than anger or contempt. And his hair—that wild, thick, golden-bronze hair—it was dotted with crisscrossed locks of blond and interspersed with tendrils of burnt red. It fell at least six inches beyond his shoulders: wavy, untamed, and a dozen different lengths. For lack of any other portrayal, the wizard wore the mane of an archaic lion.

He shifted his weight from one foot to the other, his eyes still locked with Gwen's, and the subtle display of might and power—his muscles, his physique, his entire bearing—was not to be upstaged by his peculiar coloring: The vampire was cut like a statue.

Gwen's throat convulsed, and her stomach fluttered, even as she continued to study his outline: Every hard-cut muscle was clearly defined; every tendon and striation was accentuated. Every valley and ridge was pure perfection, and standing there like a timeless artifact, a deity from another dimension, he had to be at least six-feet-four...maybe five.

She felt the urge to scramble to her feet and run.

To hell with awaiting her fate!

But then her eye caught the flicker of a pale blue flame that was glowing like a lantern, illuminating a birthmark: a small, heart-shaped blemish etched subtly into the flesh of one shoulder and visible beneath a tear in the sleeve. For a moment, she was struck by the irony of the emblem—the birthmark was so simple...*so benign*...so organic, so at odds with the harshness of his aura, the power that emanated from his very pores, and the lost, feral look in his eyes.

Who are you? she thought. *And where did you come from?*

But she didn't dare utter a word.

She just knelt on the ground, frozen in front of him, as he studied her carefully in turn.

"*Cum te numesti?*" The vampire's voice filled the cavern, his tone still carrying a savage lilt.

Gwen shivered and shuffled back.

He stepped forward, and she jolted, her eyes darting frantically—up and down, back and forth—between the flames on the ground and the blazing cloak of fire still whipping about his shoulders.

"*Cum te numesti?*" he repeated. And then he grasped the

emblazoned cloak, removed it from his shoulders as if it were merely made of cloth, and flicked it into the fire, where, once discarded, it blended seamlessly into the original flames.

Gwen couldn't believe what she was seeing, yet the smallest glimmer of hope alighted in her chest:

Was that a conciliatory gesture?

Was the vampire offering an olive branch?

Had he removed the cloak to lessen her fear?

She lowered her eyes in a show of deference—or maybe just to shield her mind from such an audacious, paranormal display—and folded both hands in her lap. "I'm sorry," she whispered softly, "but I don't understand your language."

If he understood her words, his expression didn't show it: He brushed his hair behind his shoulders, extended one arm to the side, then swept it outward in a graceful arc, moving the fire beneath it—*yes, the fire obeyed his command; it may as well have been an extension of his fingers*—and just like that, there was no longer an obstacle between them.

Oh shit, Gwen thought as he took several steps forward, sank down onto his knees, and loomed like a mighty oak above her. "*Cum te numesti*: What...is...your name?" He spoke each word carefully...slowly...like he was trying them out for size.

Gwen started.

Holy shit!

He had really been listening, and he was actually *trying*—he was attempting to speak to Gwen on her level. "Gwendolyn," she answered warily, once again meeting his gaze.

He tilted his head to one side—he seemed to do that a lot. "*Destinul meu*," he grunted, his eyes taking on a faraway look.

"*Destinul meu?*" she parroted, hoping for another translation.

"My *destiny*," he grunted.

"Oh, no," Gwen shot back. She had heard the word once or twice in the brownstone, but she wasn't entirely sure what it meant. "My name is Gwendolyn...*Gwen Marie*...but everyone just calls me Gwen."

He made a guttural noise in the back of his throat, then reached out to finger her hair; and that was it—that was all—the moment Gwen lost her composure.

The proverbial straw that broke the camel's back.

Gwen flinched like the vampire had struck her, slapped his hand to the side, and flipped over onto her hands and knees to scurry away like a frightened mouse.

He snatched her by the ankle and tugged.

She kicked back at his face with her heel.

He grabbed both ankles, one in each brawny hand, and flipped her over like a human pancake.

She stomped at his face in earnest, clawing at the ground with her hands, trying desperately to gain purchase...to scramble backward...to break free of the vampire's hold. "Stop!" she shouted, and then she whimpered, "Please...please, just stop. Stop!"

He snarled—another one of his warnings—and she flung a handful of dirt in his eyes.

Bad move.

Really bad move.

He descended over her body like a swarm of locusts swooping to devour a field, and in a matter of seconds—less than that, really —he had both her arms stretched over her head and both her wrists pinned in one hand. He anchored her body to the cool cavern floor with the weight and mass of his torso and fisted a handful of her hair.

Gwen writhed, twisted, and grunted, desperate to break free, but her every effort was futile.

One terrorized look into his burnt-copper gaze, and she knew she may as well stop struggling...stop grunting...stop hoping.

Fabian Antonescu was no longer there.

The male who had asked for her name; the wizard who had removed his fearsome cloak; the vampire who might reason or listen...or care...was lost in a feral haze. The simple truth of the matter: Gwen's captor wasn't sane. He was more like a rabid animal than a man, and she had just incited his beast.

"Fabian." She tried his name, hoping to break through the fog.

No reaction.

"*Fabian*," she tried again.

"Cease!" he grunted, his canines descending. "Light cleaves to light, and darkness cleaves to darkness." He was speaking in English, but it made no damn sense! "The raven...the hawk...the blood of the ancients..."

And with that, he lowered his mouth to her throat and sank his teeth—once again—deep into her sore, pulsing jugular.

CHAPTER FOUR

Napolean Mondragon paced around the conference room, eyeing each of his servants in turn—his brow was deeply furrowed, his back and shoulders were tense, and his jaw was set in a thin, hard line. Keitaro Silivasi and his four beloved sons were seated along the southern side of the oval mahogany table, their backs facing the front of the manse. The Olaru brothers were perched like restless lions bordering the opposite section, each balanced on the edge of their seats. Saber Alexiares and Julien Lacusta had chosen to stand in the east, leaning against the thick, paneled wall that divided the room from the king's private office, and Braden Bratianu was seated next to Ramsey, closest to the head of the table...closest to Napolean's empty chair.

The king could not stop pacing.

Thinking...

Wondering...

Hoping...

That Kristina, Deanna, and Brooke were having luck in the public Hall of Justice, the chamber that held the ancient tomes of the Vampyr race, where the *destinies* were researching the historic annals, trying to find a similar psychic storm; probing for a reference to colossal-sized lightning and blazing sonic echoes; combing through the house of Jadon's genealogy in order to uncover a wild, missing twin...a dark, ancient child of the Curse who had somehow eluded the sacrifice.

But something in the king's gut told him they wouldn't find anything, at least not in so far as a missing sacrifice was concerned. The events that had recently transpired had antiquity written all over them: King Sakarias, the Old World, and the ancient castle of Napolean's homeland. It somehow just screamed, *Romania*!

That kind of power.

That level of sophistication.

Such mastery of the elements—and the arrogance required to reach out and take it.

Napolean had seen similar things as a boy, when he had walked down streets of cobbled stone and intermingled with the original progeny of gods and men, when he had lived among kings and princes and almighty wizards...when he had...when he had...

When he had...

Oh gods, when he had lived among kings and princes and almighty wizards.

His stomach lurched, his hands curled into fists, and his black-and-silver banded hair nearly crackled with energy as he turned to face Nachari. "Master Wizard," he commanded, "describe his powers again, and not what you saw—tell me what you *felt*."

Nachari's deep green eyes darkened with purpose as the vampire rested both elbows on the table and leaned forward as if into his thoughts. "Milord, I'm not sure if I can adequately describe it. I'm not sure if I know how to put it into words."

"Try, son," Keitaro urged him, placing one hand on his beloved son's shoulder.

Nachari nodded. "It all happened so fast, and then we were hunkered down...hiding beneath the veil of the holding cell...but before that moment, before he emerged, when I was tracing the stones in the well, it felt like my finger had become a conduit for electricity, at least every time I glanced at Gwen. The air was humming, my skin was tingling, and then just as miraculously, the flesh was burning. But that wasn't it...that wasn't it." He ran his hand through his thick, wavy hair, and the king could see how hard he was concentrating.

"Go on, wizard. You say he drew from your power, leached from your magic—did it feel like a tap on your mind? Like that subtle sensation—or even harsh interference—when another male enters your thoughts...opens a bandwidth...or takes from your blood? Did it feel like when you feed your *destiny*, when you release your venom? Or was it something altogether different?"

Nachari shook his head, and his brows creased in consternation. "It wasn't anything like that, milord—it was a thousand times more intrusive, more powerful, more insidious. It felt like my heart was being ripped from my chest, like my blood was being siphoned from every artery, at once. It felt like my breath, my very core, had been stolen from my lungs so someone else could breathe them in. And the craziest thing, perhaps the most unsettling realization, is it didn't feel like he was trying very hard. I could sense that he was only using a fraction of his power. It felt like he was seconds away from draining my anima, extinguishing that spark that keeps me alive...emptying my corpse like a gourd filled with liquor. He was just drinking, milord, taking one sip at a time, imbibing on whatever he wanted."

Marquis Silivasi shifted restlessly in his seat. Ramsey stopped chewing on his toothpick, and the remainder of the males grew deathly quiet.

Napolean Mondragon pinched the bridge of his nose, and then he took several strides closer to Braden. "Son," the king said, "describe him again, every detail you remember from his physical appearance."

Braden gulped and began to recite the same characteristics he had already shared fifteen minutes earlier: wild, twisted, maybe golden hair—it was hard to tell when it was wet—dark, strange-colored eyes, maybe copper or bronze, but definitely rimmed in black; and a tall, powerful, muscular frame, maybe six-foot-five in height. "Do you want me to try to project a hologram? I think my memory is only in bits and pieces. It happened so fast, and we were scrambling to—"

"Stop." Napolean raised his hand to silence the lad; they weren't getting anywhere with this line of questioning. Marquis Silivasi had already viewed the boy's memories, and he had shared them with the sentinels and the tracker. Although the images were cloudy, and some of the impressions were muted or jumbled, the king was quite certain the sentinels had gone over it...again, and again...and again. Drilling the boy a dozen more times was not going to spark any clearer information, and the king was weary with tales of wild hair and wild eyes. He was looking for something...different.

Something that might demark time or place, something more clearly identifiable.

And then his jaw grew slack, and his brows shot up. "Son, you never mentioned what the male was wearing." He turned toward Marquis, the sentinels, then Julien. "None of you did. You said he was dirty...grungy...he had come out of the water, and he was covered in mud and filth; but none of you described his clothing. Was he naked? Was he cloaked in any sort of protective armor? Could he have been wearing any jewelry? Were there any visible tattoos or unusual markings?"

Julien Lacusta cleared his throat, and the guttural bark almost sounded salty. "With all due respect, my king, I am the valley's tracker. I've gone over the memory two dozen times—there's just an impression of ivory, like a slab of color, from his collarbone down to his knees. His shoulders...you can't see beyond the mud...definitely no jewelry around his throat or ears. If he has any markings, if he's sporting any tattoos, they're not clear in the image the young vampire shared."

"I concur," Santos added. "He may have been wearing some sort of belt...or a thong...beneath his ribs, but the algae...the memory...it's just dark green and brown."

At this, Braden shot up in his chair, his back stiffening and his countenance lightening. "Oh, shit," he burst out, turning to eye Marquis. "You took my direct memories—the pictures in my head —but you didn't dabble in my thoughts." He lowered his gaze and stared at the table. "I know it was a sign of respect—you didn't want to glimpse my fear or witness my panic—you just wanted to get at the facts, but I did have a thought, an impression, when he first came out of the water, in that immediate millisecond when he was coming right at us, like something about his clothes was all wrong. Like he had just stepped out of a period movie: you know, those ones where the guys wear some sort of knickers and tunics, instead of real shirts? Like he should've been wearing a pirate's eye-patch, and he should've had a sword tucked into his belt."

"Then he *was* wearing a belt?" Napolean asked.

Braden held both palms upward in a dubious gesture and sighed. "I dunno...I don't know. But what I thought in that moment, the second I saw him, was yeah...an ancient pirate with knickers, a tunic, and a leather belt."

Napolean closed his eyes.

Knee-length knickers.

An ivory tunic.

And a leather belt—the boy had just said *leather*, and the clothing he described was from another time.

Napolean tuned out the room and tried to concentrate, to go back...back...far back in time, until, at last, he had conjured the visage of an ancient village and a humble, one-room domicile: until he had retrieved the memory of his own handsome father getting dressed in his ceremonial finery.

The Mondragons had neither been wealthy, nor elite, despite their prominent progeny, and their shifts felt more like gunny-sacks than silk—they would not have been dyed to look ivory. Nonetheless, Sebastian Mondragon had worn one such garb to the Harvest and other religious rituals.

Content that the image was fixed in his memory, Napolean sent it out as a hologram, projecting the visage behind a glowing back light hovering above the conference table. "Is this what he was wearing—at least, was it similar?"

Marquis rocked forward in his chair and grunted. "I could see that outfit...superimposed...it fits with the outline Braden gave us."

"Yes," Saxson drawled, leaning back and thumbing his chin warily.

Santos nodded, and Ramsey harrumphed.

Saber popped his neck. "In the Dark Ones' Colony, the library where we kept the physical and digital historic annals, where we also stored the likenesses of the ancient monarchs— Prince Jaegar, Prince Jadon, my mate, and Princess Ciopori— there were paintings that looked like that."

Braden Bratianu smiled. "Looks a lot like a pirate's outfit to me. Feels a lot like my first impression."

Julien's keen, moonstone gray eyes seemed to sharpen. "It's almost exact," he grunted. "If you look at the lines in the shoul-ders, the way the sleeves are cut in, then look at the murky, ivory background in Braden's hazy memory: The brown...the mud... near the top of his shoulders—that's stitching—that's where the sleeves were attached. And the lighter gold, just beneath the throat, that isn't dirty cloth; it's his golden-colored skin. The neck hole has been cut out." He leaned back in his chair and crossed his arms. "Besides, stop looking with your eyes for a second, and use your sense of smell. Every fabric has a different scent. And these two cloths—they're not just the same color; they were made from the same material. And unless my senses aren't as sharp as I think they are, my guess is they're equally aged."

Napolean's heart thumped heavily in his chest. "Come again, tracker? Are you saying what I think you are: You can pick up the scent in my memory—and in Braden's—clearly enough to discern the age of the garments?"

At this, Julien declined his head. "Permission to enter your mind, milord—I need to experience the memory, firsthand, without the interference from the hologram. Am I sure? Eighty... maybe ninety percent, but if you allow me to—"

"Permission granted," Napolean barked.

And then he waited while Julien examined the memory.

One, two, three seconds passed before the most skilled tracker the house of Jadon had ever produced backed out of the king's hippocampus and nodded. "Give or take a decade...maybe two...the cloth is from the same era."

Nathaniel Silivasi whistled low, beneath his breath, even as Kagen, his twin, just shook his head. "So, what gives, milord?" Nathaniel asked Napolean. "Who is this Ancient? What are you thinking?"

The king strolled quietly to the head of the table and lowered his weight into the finely upholstered seat: kings and princes, and almighty wizards; ancient, wild eyes and hair; knee-length knickers—*no*, ivory trousers—with a matching tunic, bearing sewn-on sleeves and a hole cropped out of the neck.

The power of an ancient god.

The sky...

The thunder...

The majesty of lightning...

All his to wield and command...

No, the male could be no other than the progeny of the celestial god Hercules and his human mate, Arylia; the greatest wizard to have ever lived; the High Mage who had served King Sakarias and, ultimately, his sons and his daughters too, the latter having been his reason to travel to Dark Moon Vale..

At least a millennium earlier.

"His name is Fabian Antonescu," Napolean said with awe, "son of Fortino Antonescu and Koryn Anne Rosa, High Mage to the royal king Sakarias and his noble queen, Jade. I was just a boy when he lived in Romania. I was only ten at the time of the Curse. And, needless to say, we didn't travel in the same circles, but even as a lad, I heard the legends..." His voice trailed off and he regarded Nachari circumspectly. "Master Wizard, you were wise to build the holding cell out of diamonds, and Braden, you were wise to retreat. He could have slaughtered both of you, as well as your beloved companions, in a matter of seconds, but it would seem he wanted the girl."

Nachari nodded solemnly, then waited on his king.

Braden grimaced, shook his head, and let out a slow, deep breath.

"Nachari," the king continued, "I am assuming you have taken Gwen's blood—I know you and Braden have been acting as her wards. Am I right to conclude that you secured a way to track her, if necessary?"

Nachari leaned back in his chair and nodded. "Yes, milord. I can track the human female."

"Good. *That's good.* At least I hope it's good. One way or another, I want to know if she's alive. I want to know where Fabian has taken her...where the ancient wizard is hiding. How is he living...how is he existing...and how great is this threat?" He held up two fingers, lest the wizard act too fast, then trained his noble gaze on the newest sentinel in his private inner circle. "Saber..." The dragon's coal-black eyes met his. "I am going to need you to awaken your mate and summon her to the manse. And Marquis"—he shifted his attention to the Ancient Master Warrior—"I would have you do the same. Vanya and Ciopori are the only souls yet living who can provide any insight into this wizard's state of mind: why he would endanger his fellow vampires from the house of Jadon, what he might want with the human girl, and what the hell he could have been doing all this time that would lead him to leap out of a well."

The hairs on the back of the king's neck stood up as he struggled to process the myriad layers of the problem: "A king is only as wise as his counsel, and we need to understand what we're dealing with before we seek to locate Gwen." He shuddered to think that the girl might be dead...or that Fabian might be coming for the princesses next. "Assuming that Miss Hamilton is still alive, it is not as if we can simply take her back. Based on Braden's description—how Fabian behaved at the well—I think it unlikely he would give her up." He paused to consider his next words more carefully. "No, we not only need the princesses' insight, we may very well need their celestial magic."

As his last words lingered and his heart filled with dread, he turned toward Ramsey, Saxson, and Santos. "I know that Saber will wish to stay close to Vanya, and I have no objection to the same. Just as we all know Julien will be instrumental in any tracking expedition we embark upon. That said, I will leave it to the three of you to divide the remaining responsibilities: At some point, once Fabian has been located, I will need you to cordon off a wide area, to keep *all* in this valley away from his travels...or escapades. No one in the house of Jadon is to approach or go near the Ancient until we figure this conundrum out."

CHAPTER FIVE

W hat time was it?
    Two AM; three AM; maybe four?
    Where was she?
And why did she feel so weak?

Gwen rolled from her back onto her stomach and tried to slide off the bed—she needed to use the bathroom—only, her leg didn't fall off a mattress, and her cheek didn't slide off a pillow. Rather, she ended up banging her knee on the cold, hard ground and dragging her mouth through the dirt.

Oh...

Yuck...

What the hell?

And then the memory came back like a wrecking ball, slamming squarely into her chest and jolting her into full, waking consciousness: Fabian. The vampire. The mystical fire. Trying to fight him off as he pinned her to the ground.

Blood.

Feeding.

The ache in her neck.

She was still in that damnable cave, only the fire had gone out, she was enshrined in darkness, and she had to get out...or perish. The scent of distant, fresh dew on mountain grass wafted to her nostrils, even as her ears perked up, and she tuned into her sense of sound: rustling leaves, perhaps quaking aspens; an owl hooting in a faraway tree; other than that, only deafening silence. It had to be the middle of the night...

Oh Lord, where was he?

Could he possibly be sleeping?

Or had lady luck finally shown Gwen some favor and sent Fabian out of the cave...maybe hunting...nocturnal shapeshifting...wandering around aimlessly, attacking helpless animals—she really didn't care just so long as he was gone.

She spun around on her hands and knees, blinking furiously like a ninny, straining to see in the dark. And then she heard the low, guttural snarl coming from the back of the cave.

No.

No!

No-no-no!

Why couldn't Gwen catch a break?

Exhausted, defeated, and distraught, she slammed a clenched hand against the ground, and then she fisted her own hair and began to weep. To hell with it—she wasn't that strong. She was cold. She was tired. She was hungry, thirsty, and filthy. And for heaven's sake, she still needed to pee!

"*Destinul meu?*" The vampire's deep, satiny voice.

Gwen choked back a sob. *Oh, shit! Be quiet*, she told herself. *He's using those foreign words again...the ones that sound all sweet and endearing, right before he pounces and tears out your throat. Just be still...and quiet...and maybe he'll leave you alone.*

"*Destinul meu,*" he said again, only this time it was more of a statement—he knew exactly where she was, and she knew the utter futility of resisting his supernatural supremacy.

"I'm here," she mumbled, resenting the very air she was breathing.

"Gwendolyn," he entreated, "my *destiny*, come." A light began to glow around his fingers as he quirked them in a come-here gesture.

Yeah, Gwen thought. *Come. Sit. Stay.*

Feed me; humor me; live, if I allow it; die when I say.

She absently rubbed her throat before scooting along the floor of the cave—and then she noticed an odd, lumpy pile of myste-rious *stuff* stacked next to the vampire's leg. She sat crisscross, about three feet away. If he wanted her closer, he could drag her by the ankle—it wasn't as if he hadn't done it before.

The vampire cleared his throat and fixed his piercing, copper gaze directly on Gwen. "I wish"—his voice sounded like it had been ground to broken glass, and he paused to try again. "I would ask your forgiveness"—he was speaking in English again!—"for my occasional...bouts...of boldness." He closed his eyes like he was really concentrating—perhaps he was searching for words— and then he added: "I'm not entirely...present...or rational."

Gwen gulped.

And then she swallowed her temper: *occasional bouts of boldness?*

Did he mean regular episodes of brutality?

He waved his hand in a semicircle, and the glow from his fingers created a backlit halo, illuminating the corner of the cave like a lantern. "You are hungry, no? Thirsty? Cold." *Was the vampire reading her thoughts?* He reached into the sundry pile, fisted something furry, then tossed it unerringly into her lap.

Gwen squealed and jumped back!

She clutched her stomach, quelled her trembling, then stared down at the—

Dead, crusty rabbit...

"A rabbit!" she shouted, losing her cool. "You brought me a fucking rabbit?" She flicked it away like it was covered in maggots and tried to banish the heebie-jeebies. "It still has the fur on it!" she cried. "What the hell do you expect me to do with a rabbit?"

He tilted his head to the side and frowned, and that's when she noticed the obvious—her shirt was absent, her jeans were missing, and her trembling shoulders were bare and exposed. Well, no wonder she was practically freezing! The rabbit had been resting on a naked inner thigh, and Gwen was wearing nothing more than her bra and her panties—*how had she missed this before?*

"What did you do with my clothes?" she squealed, her stomach roiling in waves of nausea. She was beginning to feel lightheaded. In fact, Gwen was about to faint. *What did you do to me?* she wanted to whisper, but she couldn't bear to hear the answer.

This time, the corner of his upper lip quirked up, like he was trying to replicate a smile. "I washed them in a stream that meanders beyond a waterfall—'tis also where I found the rabbit." His cadence was unnatural, if not a bit robotic. "Then I placed them beside the fire while you slumbered, and I watched you as you slept. I studied your dialect—took various linguistics and phrases from your memory—until the fire eventually burned out. You see, I replaced the elements of magic with kindling, pine needles, and juniper—it infuses the garments with a fresher scent."

Gwen was truly at a loss for words.

So, he had pinned her to the ground, sucked her blood until she'd blacked out, then stripped her of all but her underwear. He had scampered off into the forest to a meandering stream— beyond a waterfall—before washing her clothes in a river. Then he had returned with some kindling, pine, and juniper—some prehistoric version of fabric softener—before returning to the cave to stalk her, read her mind, and ultimately, sulk in the dark.

Oh, and one shouldn't forget the fucking rabbit.

No, Gwen had no rejoinder for that one.

She watched, dumbstruck, as he reached into the pile a second time and retrieved her soft, cotton T-shirt. It didn't look worse for the wear, but when he reached a third time for her blue jeans, she almost gasped out loud.

What-the-actual-hell-was-that?

He was displaying the denim creation like he had just fashioned a diamond necklace, but for the life of her, Gwen couldn't figure out what it was.

The waist was still there.

Well, sort of.

But there were strips of material wound through the belt loops.

And the longer she studied it, the more it became clear: He had ripped the legs of her jeans into pieces, laced the strips through the material hanging from the belt loops, and then more or less woven the fabric in and out until it had formed a crude, interwoven dress. The freakin' Neanderthal had turned her pants into a miniskirt! Despite her trepidation, she lunged forward, snatched it out of his hand, then quickly shimmied back where she could study it in the shadows.

"The...dress...displeases you?" He sounded irritated.

Gwen barely knew how to reply. "Oh, no, not at all." She spat the words with heavy sarcasm. "If I were planning to camp in a cave, indefinitely, I would certainly pack a miniskirt! Great for climbing, and crawling, and sleeping in the dirt—who the hell would prefer a pair of blue jeans?" She shimmied into the garment and huffed: "But at least it's clean...and smells like juniper."

He sniffed and waved his hand through the air. "Gwendolyn, I care not that your family is indigent."

She coughed. "Excuse me?"

He frowned.

"No, really," she urged, "please explain." *This one was going to be priceless.* When he didn't reply, she challenged him further, no longer caring that he could rip her throat out. "My family isn't indigent, Fabian. I didn't grow up poor."

He furrowed his brows and scrutinized her features. "You do not hail from a meager upbringing? The...Hamiltons...are not impoverished? Yet your father is forced to dress you in trousers?"

She literally felt the tips of her ears grow hot.

The Hamiltons?

The Hamiltons!

What? All two hundred thousand of them, worldwide?

"My *father* doesn't dress me at all," she practically snarled.

He flicked his fingers in a dismissive gesture. "'Tis just a matter of speech, Gwendolyn. He provides what he can for the family, does he not?" Before she could answer, he shook his head. "It is of no matter, the state of your upbringing. Should the shadows ever recede, should we ever get out of this cave... together...I will see to it that you dress like a lady. You may have whatever you like."

Dumbstruck had risen to stupefied.

And stupefied was quickly approaching dazed!

His English was getting better and better, but his words were nothing but gibberish.

That wasn't entirely true—

They were shocking, ominous, and terrifying at once: *Should the shadows ever recede...should we ever get out of this cave... together...*what the hell did that mean?

Gwen bit her tongue and resolved to ignore him—it would do her no good to pull a tiger by the tail, even if that terrifying tiger had her cornered and she was swiftly losing her mind. She pointed at her T-shirt, held out both hands, and waited for the vampire to place it in her palm.

He tossed it in her lap.

"Nice throw," she murmured beneath her breath. *Great toss,* she continued, but only in her head. *That was almost as clean as the rabbit bank shot!* She kept the defensive sarcasm to herself. *Oh, Lord, she was really cracking up...*

The tips of his fangs descended from his gums, and all humor instantly vanished.

In fact, Gwen's reasoning and her clarity returned in a millisecond: She pulled the T-shirt over her head and smoothed the hem over the top of the skirt. *Keep your freakin' mouth shut, Gwen, and don't look him in the eyes. Just focus on the only thing he's said that truly matters—he left the cave while you were sleeping...*

He left the cave while you were sleeping!

And if he did it once, he might do it again.

Shut up, and try to stay alive...

Silence permeated the space between them, even as Fabian continued to watch her like a hawk. Finally, after what felt like an eternity, he reached into the pile and retrieved a hollowed piece of wood. The center had been carved into a cavity, and the hollow was several inches deep. Gwen's heart skipped a beat as she finally put *two and two* together—the cavity was filled with fresh, sparkling water, and she wanted it so badly, it hurt.

He motioned her forward with the crook of one finger. "Drink," he snarled, as he extended it outward.

Gwen's instinct to survive was stronger than her revulsion: Despite the fact that he was a snarling tiger, his fangs poised and ready to bite, her raging thirst drew her forward. She scooted along the ground, ever so slowly...*cautiously*...the hem of her skirt riding up on her thighs, until she was practically sitting in his lap.

And all the while, her eyes remained fixed on the hollow and the life-giving water.

He placed the tip of the gourd against the rim of her mouth, and she grasped both sides of the container, tipped it until the liquid flowed, and greedily guzzled the contents. She drank until the last drop had been swallowed, and then she slowly raised her lashes and met the wizard's eyes.

Oh...

No.

Not again...

He was changing...growing feral...displaying clear signs of primitive bestiality.

His copper irises were gleaming red, and he was staring at her mouth like a hungry, carnal animal. His deep, burnished pupils were fixed on a drizzle of water as it trickled from the corner of her mouth, beaded along her bottom lip, and dribbled down to her chin. He reached out and brushed it away with his thumb. Gwen froze for the space of several heartbeats.

"Thank you," she finally whispered. She lowered the bowl and set it on the ground. "For the water...for your kindness...for washing my clothes. And thank you for bringing me a rabbit." At this point, she would've said anything to distract him, to draw his gaze away from her mouth, and to erase that feral longing...

And then it hit her—*the rabbit!*

Oh Lord, she had almost forgotten the crusty bunny—the kill had been a peace offering, a gift, the caveman equivalence of a half-dozen roses. She wasn't sure if she could successfully redirect him—or if she would only incite his savage instincts—but it was worth the old college try!

She spun around swiftly and pointed toward the lump. "Fabian, could you please build another fire?" Her tone was delicate and even. "I'm starving, I'm cold, and I'd like to cook that bunny." She glanced at him askance, pretending not to be utterly terrified, and then she gestured toward some kindling in the pile. "Could you make some sort of spit...or spear...maybe some kind of skewer"—she had no idea which word would resonate—"something I could use to cook with?" And then out of nowhere, an antiquated term came back to her—a male of high rank in a feudal society: "Please, *milord*: I am so very hungry."

He studied her eyes, her cheekbones, and her lips—and then he cupped her jaw in his powerful hand. "I've treated you harshly—it was not intended."

She closed her eyes and nodded, too afraid to even breathe.

This was good.

Wasn't it?

If nothing else, it was progress...

If the vampire was aware of his cruelty, then he might be able to control it. If he was sorry for his...harshness...then he might actually have a conscience. "It's okay," she lied, reopening her lids and forcing herself to maintain eye contact. "You seem to be feeling...better now. You no longer seem as agitated."

He chuckled, and it was a wicked sound: hollow, distant, and deeply tormented. "Am I not?" he murmured. "As agitated." His eyes glazed over, the blood-red gleam darkening into far-away embers. He reached out to finger a lock of her hair, brushed the side of her cheek with the backs of his fingers, and lowered his gaze to her breasts. A moment later, he raised his eyes again; this time, fixing them squarely on her jugular. "I will build you a fire to keep you warm, and I will skin the rabbit and cook it for you. The next time I hunt, I will bring you a more...palatable...fare, and when the sun rises, I will take you to the waterfall to bathe. Will this please you, Gwen?"

Letting me go would please me more. She kept the rejoinder to herself and bit her lip, instead.

She wanted to hope, but she didn't dare.

The vampire's fangs were still extended, and he was dipping

his head—lower and lower—resting the tips of his fingers along the nape of her neck, while tracing the fall with his lips. His canines were way too close for comfort, way too close to her vein.

Please...

Just this once...

Not again.

She stiffened, and then her bladder contracted—holy hell, it was about to burst!

She grabbed both of his wrists in a firm, unyielding grasp and wrenched them away from her neck. "Fabian!" She tried to startle him. "I have to pee...*right now.*"

He jerked back, and his golden-bronze, silken brows furrowed in consternation. "What is this word? You have to do *what?* I know not the meaning of this outburst."

"I have to empty my bladder," she repeated.

* * *

Fabian stood watch in the woods while Gwen relieved her bladder, the shadows in his soul growing deeper...and deeper.

The girl didn't understand.

The odd human woman.

Not if she thought she could manipulate him with quiet words and kindness, cut through his darkness with her light. Not if she thought she could call him *milord* and magically vanquish his demons.

She had no idea how lost he truly was.

The extent of Fabian's confusion; the power in her blood; the loss of time, memory, and sentience—how he moved in and out of the fog like a specter.

When he had awakened in the well, there had been no conscious thought, no awareness of period or place, just hunger, stark and raw.

Destinul meu.

Destinul meu!

My *destiny,* floating on the wind.

The thunder, the lightning, the need to take her—the others, hiding in their piteous diamond domes—Fabian had acted out of instinct, pure and primal, when he had snatched the girl and taken her back into the water...when he had fed from her vein until his starvation had abated and his vision had eventually returned.

Yes, his power had come back, though it had likely never been gone. He had called to the four cardinal winds, after all, and commanded the powerful storm. But the fates had not returned his understanding, and his judgment had not been clear. He had tunneled through the mud, traveled to the cave; he had been led, instinctively—unerringly—by some sort of inner compass.

Some sort of imperious directive.

And now he had her, the strange human woman, and the compass continued to guide him sluggishly: *Hide her in the dark, feed from her vein, place her in a mystic sleep, and return to the meandering spring. Fetch water and food; tend to her dress; extend an olive branch—offer kindness—you speak Romanian, Latin, English, and French; retrieve the dialect from her mind if you must, but seek to win her trust. She has answers. Information. She knows where you are, what period you now live in—she knows the current customs and the green-eyed wizard from the house of Jadon. You may need him...you may need him...you may require his awesome magick.*

But did the female know the truth beyond the fog?

Did she know of the raven...or the hawk...or the vials filled with blood?

Did she know of the Millenia Harvest Moon and what was coming?

The power; the scourge; the epic battles?

A pain like that of an axe splitting wood assailed the back of his skull, and he retreated from the notion like a son of Jaegar fleeing the sun—

A son of Jaegar?

Where had that thought even come from?

For in truth, Fabian had flashes of awareness, not comprehension. He had moments of clarity, not blocks of time. He could emerge from the fog for an instant, here and there, before the darkness, once again, swallowed him. And in all actuality, he was as likely to drain the human female as to learn from her—her fresh, enchanted blood was all that brought him solace for a time —a short, transient, precarious sum of time.

He was as apt to slay her as to care for her, as likely to ravage her body as romance her. He had left her hungry, thirsty, terrified, and cold—he was in no position to look after anyone, not if he couldn't break through the fog and *remember*...

Celestial Gods, why couldn't he remember!

Everything.

The Curse.

The ship.

The females in his charge?

Sleeping for centuries, dreaming all the while, traveling through an endless night with a piece of his disembodied soul veiled in the body of an immortal hawk...or hidden in the breast of a raven...a vial of sacred blood—no, two vials—grasped within his talons. Light cleaves to light, and darkness cleaves to darkness...

Ahhhhhh!

The unbearable pain assailed him again, and just like before, he retreated from the memory.

Gwendolyn was returning from behind a grove of trees—he could see her feminine outline.

Destinul meu.

Destinul meu!

This odd human woman was his *destiny*.

How did he know that? What did it mean?

No matter; he just needed to focus and take care of her. He had to keep it together, just a little while longer.

CHAPTER SIX

It was nearly three o'clock in the morning, and Nachari was still waiting to track Gwendolyn's blood—he had yet to even try. Deanna had returned to the brownstone, hours ago, to relieve the nanny and look after Sebastian; Kristina had headed to the farmhouse to watch Nikolai and Lucien; and the queen had retired to bed.

Meanwhile, Marquis and Saber had gone to retrieve their original celestial mates. Wary of Fabian's presence in the valley, they weren't about to let them travel alone—and Nachari couldn't say that he blamed them. Apparently, the initial shock had been enormous, a mixture of regret, disbelief, grieving, and excitement. Needless to say, the princesses had needed some time to process the shocking turn of events: to speak to each other alone, sort through their emotions, and regain their composure before they could address the vampires at the manse.

And even then, they had both appeared extremely rattled.

And then the history lesson had begun...

Much of it was familiar from Nachari's time at the Romanian University, but the detail, the descriptions, the living accounts and remembrances; the women's tales were as enchanting as they had been bone-chilling.

Fabian Antonescu was now the oldest living being in the valley, more ancient than Napolean, Ciopori, or Vanya. In fact, he had actually been born twenty years before Prince Jadon and Prince Jaegar, and he had served King Silvano before he had served King Sakarias, the latter being only five years older than Fabian.

As a child, the wizard had been born to a noble family, sired from a long line of powerful mages, and he had studied alchemy in the royal palace, at first, tucked away in the castle's undercroft, a vaulted crypt or cellar, beneath the lowest levels, where he practiced his craft and learned from his elders. Later, during the reign of Sakarias, he had been elevated to High Mage and relocated to the castle's oratory, a chamber attached to the royal chapel, nearest the Great Hall and palace life—he had always communed with the monarchy, and he had always commanded their respect...and their fear.

At least until Prince Jaegar had risen to power, and the High Mage had opposed his tyranny, choosing to align with a band of rebel warriors and mercenaries instead; to hole up in the Transylvanian Alps as their leader and to take guardianship of Ciopori and Vanya soon after they had escaped the castle.

Fabian had secured passage for the princesses on a ship to North America, nine months after the Curse, in 799 B.C., and undoubtedly, his magic had played a pivotal role in both navigating and securing the vessel—human pilgrims would not make the voyage until 1620 A.D.

Arriving in May of the same year, he had acted as their ward: protecting them, feeding them, leading them to what was now Dark Moon Vale, until at last, he had placed them in an enchanted sleep in order to await the return of their brother, Prince Jadon. According to Ciopori, the High Mage had been horribly vexed by Jadon's delay, and he was often forced to leave the girls alone in order to fly as a vampire, to survey the coast—to watch, again and again, for the arrival of the remaining Vampyr males. His food supply was scarce, though not nonexistent: a scattering of ancestors, the descendants of Paleo-Indians, had inhabited the strange, distant land for centuries, their progeny believed to have crossed the Bering Strait many millennia earlier.

Yet and still, Fabian had to hunt and toil.

He had to find food for Ciopori and Vanya.

He had to find blood for himself.

And he was thus far new to the scourge of his kind, still adjusting to the rigors of the Curse. His greatest fear was of the native beasts—that the women might be set upon by a wild animal, or worse, that Fabian, himself, might harm them whilst swept away in bloodlust. The enchanted sleep had been an agonizing decision, but he had been confident in his skills as a wizard: He knew he could keep them alive, and he knew that Prince Jadon could awaken them. The two had already made a *worst-case-scenario* pact, and to that end, Prince Jadon had taken Fabian's blood, and Fabian had procured a vial of Prince Jadon's. It was one of two cryptic amulets the High Mage wore around his neck, should he ever need to imbibe it.

However, what happened to the male was another story, still yet to be told.

Upon awakening in the twenty-first century, the princesses had assumed Fabian had died. Though Prince Jadon had never shown up, the cursed, banished males of his house had indeed followed Fabian to North America, for they had long since chosen the Rocky Mountains as a final destination, following many distant and arduous explorations, not long after the Curse. They had chosen the Rockies for their similarity to the Transylvanian Alps, and because relocating to such a faraway land would ultimately appease the Blood. Between 801 B.C., when the females had escaped the castle, and 799 B.C., when they had sailed to the new, foreign land, Fabian had kept in contact with Prince Jadon, though the princesses did not know how: perhaps through clandestine meetings; perhaps through their new telepathic skills; perhaps he had done it with alchemy or through the use of a scrying mirror...perhaps he had communed with their souls.

The point was: the first of the males from the house of Jadon had arrived in 791 B.C., eight years after Princess Ciopori and Princess Vanya, and Prince Jadon had not been with them. The history from there was well-known to all—they studied it extensively at the University—and Fabian Antonescu, the infamous wizard who had served two generations of the Demir monarchy, was not mentioned from that point forward. His legend was anchored in Romania, and had it not been for Marquis Silivasi awakening Ciopori from her sleep, the house of Jadon would still be none the wiser—they would've never known what happened to the royal daughters, either.

Nachari knew that the lapse in time—and information—deeply bothered Napolean.

He was their king.

He was their leader.

He was sworn to protect them, and he had all but created the *house of Jadon*: its laws, its mores, its legacy.

Napolean was the only reason the lighter Vampyr had survived.

And now, he was struggling with a ghost from the past—

They all were.

But for the sake of the gods, the king had only been a child: *ten years old* at the time of the Curse, *nineteen years old* when he arrived in Dark Moon Vale. He could not be expected to know everything...

"Will you be able to see through the girl's eyes?" Princess

Vanya leaned forward in her chair, beside Napolean, and grasped Nachari by the arm, presumably in an effort to pull him out of his musings. "Is there any chance that you will get a look at the High Mage?"

Ciopori swept the balls of her thumbs beneath her lower eyelids, brushing away another pair of teardrops. "Can you tell us if he's well, if he's injured...or seems lost? I still cannot believe he would harm the girl."

Marquis put his hand over his mate's. "Not now, my love." He spoke tenderly. "I know you have questions, but now is not the time to seek answers. Nachari's goal is to locate Gwen. From there, we will play it by ear."

Saber shifted restlessly, from his perch at the back of the room—he was standing in front of the eastern wall, leaning against the panel, with both arms crossed over his chest and one leg bent, his right foot flush with the millwork, and for all intents and purposes, the male looked angry. Something about the whole situation just wasn't sitting right with the sentinel.

Nachari flashed a warm, reassuring smile at Vanya, then Ciopori, hoping to reassure them both. He was exhausted and anxious, eager to get on with it, but he understood their angst: Fabian may as well have been a second father to the females, and he had been missing—presumed dead—all this time. The princesses had never insisted that the house of Jadon comb the forest, the meadows, the canyons, or the waterways in search of the High Mage's remains. *But hell*, they had lost their parents, their brothers, their civilization; they had lived through the slaughter of their ancient sisters; they had been awakened from slumber *after 2,800 years*; and so many vampires had died since the Curse. At the end of the day, they had accepted Fabian's loss as one of many, *many* others. "At this point," Nachari told them, "I am just hoping to pinpoint the girl's location."

Napolean cleared his throat. "Are you ready, son?"

Nachari stood up from his position beside Keitaro, who was on his left, and Nathaniel, who was on his right. He made fleeting eye contact with Saxson, who was seated directly across the table, near the middle of the long, mahogany slab, and he nodded his head. While tracing one's blood was instinctive for a vampire, Nachari intended to project a hologram of all that he saw...or sensed...so the entire room could witness the psychic tracking. Instantly, every male around the table sat to attention—those standing grew tense and alert, and the women wove something... curious...in the air with their hands—but Nachari didn't have time to start another round of questions. "I'm ready," he said, and then he went right to it.

He closed his eyes, took several deep breaths, and began to focus his attention.

His awareness...

On Gwen's hair, her eyes, the slope of her throat...her pulse as it thrummed in her veins.

He flashed back to *feeding*, the first night she had arrived at the brownstone, until the memory became vivid and clear. Gwen had been under compulsion, none the wiser, and the feel of her blood, the scent of the plasma, the texture as it snaked through his fangs had been distinctive: strength, vigor, indomitable will...

Nachari had tasted the female's rare courage.

His awareness deepened.

His heartbeat quickened.

Until he could actually hear the faint *pitter-patter* of foreign platelets traveling through his veins.

Gwen's essence.

Gwen's anima.

Gwen's singular footprint in the universe...her spiritual essence, coming to life.

And then the hologram began to glow: Gwen at the well, sliding off the rock. Gwen being snatched by the arm and hauled from a broken holding cell; water—cold, deep, and murky—then mud, the sense and feel of tunneling up, through the earth.

And then, at last, a dark, quiet cavern: a fire, a sundry pile of objects, the carcass of a rabbit cooking on a spit—Gwen was sitting by a fire, staring up at the High Mage!

Nachari gasped, and the hologram shuddered.

The male's visage was as stunning as it was captivating.

"She's alive," Nachari said out loud, not addressing anyone particular, and then he focused his energy in a different manner —he backed away from the fire and channeled all his intention into entering Gwen's body through the third-eye chakra. Once there, he meandered until he was lodged behind her retinas and intercepting the electrical impulses going to her optical nerves.

In other words, he was seeing through Gwen's eyes.

Where are you? he asked internally, hoping to stir the energies. *Where is this cave you find yourself in?* Longitude and latitude each had a vibration, as did one's position within the meridians.

His head fell back as he felt the moon's tug on the earth and the tides, and he zeroed in on the celestial data: west of the Red Canyons; southeast of Santos' hidden lake; close to the border of Dark Moon Vale, where it intersects with the Snake Creek River. Gwen was in the heavily forested canyon, about thirty-five miles from the old sacrificial chamber, the one once used by the Dark Ones. She was less than five miles from the old stone well.

Which cave?

Which burrow?

Which tunnel did you go through?

Nachari continued to focus his questions and intent.

And then, all at once, the table shook, the hologram sparked, and the lights in the conference room went out. *"Tu indraznesti sa-mi vanezi destinul!"* the ancient mage snarled in the cave: *You dare to hunt my destiny!*

Nachari jerked back, trying to retreat from the two burnt-copper orbs now glowing in the darkness: The formidable, angry vampire was staring right at him, and Fabian was seeing Nachari, both in the cave, and in the manse. "Fabian," Nachari whispered. He might as well try speaking...try reasoning...the powerful High Mage had already caught him. "I am not here to harm her; nor am I here to harm you. You are welcome in the house of Jadon, my brother. We are only trying to locate your cave."

The fist that closed around Nachari's throat felt more like an iron vise than ancient fingers, as the stunned Master Wizard shot off the floor, kicked wildly at the conference table, and sent his leather chair flying backward, behind him.

The Ancient One tightened his grip and released his fangs, and then he tore through the Master Wizard's throat with his claws, punctured his chest, and grasped his heart. "Stay away!" he bellowed, sounding half rabid and half amused. "And let this be a warning to all who might come for me...*or mine*...that this is what awaits them when they get here."

He seized the organ and wrenched back with his fist.

CHAPTER SEVEN

One minute, Gwen was sitting by the fire, waiting for the rabbit to finish cooking—Fabian had taken her to use the bathroom, refilled the makeshift gourd with water, and even collected a pile of pine needles to help her build a sleeping pallet later—when all of a sudden, his eyes had widened, his pupils had narrowed, and his mouth had curved downward into a vicious snarl.

"Tu indraznesti sa-mi vanezi destinul!" he had shouted, glaring at Gwen like he wanted to kill her. He had cocked his head to the side like he was listening to something—perhaps hearing voices—and then he had lunged at her so quickly, she had never seen him move.

He'd snatched her by the throat, raised her off the ground, and closed his fist around her larynx, squeezing for all he was worth.

At first Gwen had gasped.

She had kicked and tried to fight.

But then she had simply dangled her arms and allowed him to do his best.

No, she wasn't stupid.

And no, she wasn't ready to die, but the oddest thing was: She couldn't feel a thing—there were simply no sensations, no pressure, and no pain.

She was hanging in the air, suspended by his fist, yet her airway was not constricted, and she wasn't in any pain.

And that wasn't even the half of it, the strangest part...

He released his claws and dug them into her neck—he literally put his hand right through her—and from the trajectory of his forearm, the angle of his elbow, it was clear that he had punctured her chest as well, yet still...no blood, no pain, and no gore. His wicked fangs were gleaming in the firelight, and he was reaching for her heart to dislodge it; yet all she felt was an odd, funny tingle—like the tickle of a feather—as his claws seized her organ.

And then he practically foamed at the mouth: "Stay away! And let this be a warning to all who might come for me...*or mine*...that this is what awaits them when they get here."

He yanked back his arm, and she fell to the floor.

She didn't have a single scratch on her.

* * *

"Nachari! What the *fuck*?" Marquis' angry bellow.

Keitaro lunged toward Nachari's chest, both palms extended outward, even as Napolean Mondragon shifted into some preternatural, molecular vortex, dived into the Master Wizard's mouth, and tunneled down his throat.

Nachari jerked and gagged, but he didn't have time to spit the king out.

He felt a tear on his aorta, the High Mage seizing his heart, and immediately shifted into his panther. The mystical hand fell away as the black cat twisted, clawed at the Ancient's face, and roared in pain and fury.

Fabian responded immediately by conjuring a magical cat of his own, and while the large, savage snow leopard was terrifying and fierce, Nachari knew the beast wasn't real. It was an illusion, a projection, a feat of extraordinary sorcery, but *damnit all to hell*, it felt like flesh, bone, and blood.

The massive cats lunged in the cave and met in midair, trading brutal swipes, vicious bites, and merciless tears to the throat. The panther pounced on the snow leopard, but it faded like a mirage, suddenly re-emerging on the black panther's back. The leopard's claws dug deep; it locked its jaw on the panther's neck, and then the bestial apparition shook its enormous head furiously from side to side, emitting a primal snarl.

Flesh ripped.

Blood gushed.

And bones popped like brittle twigs.

And then Napolean Mondragon, the king of the Vampyr, took over the black panther's body, directing Nachari to wrench free from the leopard's lethal grasp.

Nachari's jugular tore in the process, but Napolean wouldn't let him be.

The panther came up clawing, biting, and locking its jaw around the circular protrusion in the snow leopard's snout—and then the panther bit down and crushed the leopard's bones, ivory fangs gnashing against ivory.

The snow leopard grunted, jerked back its head, then transmuted back into a vampire.

And that's when Napolean, in the body of the black panther, forced Nachari to retreat.

The black panther loped away from the Ancient, bounded to the mouth of the cave, and leaped off the high, rocky ledge, summersaulting into the night. And all the while, the king was manipulating, weaving...unraveling ghostly threads...freeing Nachari's soul from the clutches of the ancient mage and the power that had allowed Fabian to seize Nachari through the blood-link he shared with Gwen.

Just like that—they were back in the manse—Napolean catapulting out of the panther's body; the panther shifting back into a vampire; and the dazed Master Wizard swaying in front of the conference table.

Nachari's legs gave out. His knees buckled beneath him, and he hit the floor with a *thud*, but not before catching a glimpse of Napolean and regarding the king with awe: Everyone knew Napolean Mondragon could thrust his soul outside his body, travel through space and time—*even kill with his ethereal form.* The legends in the house of Jadon abounded. But it was also well-known that the feat cost him dearly: in strength, in exposure, in vital life energy. Yet, the king hadn't hesitated to follow Nachari, to leave his corporeal body and risk his life to free the youngest Silivasi brother from the lethal clutches of Fabian.

Nachari must have been bleeding profusely because he couldn't organize his brain to say, *thank you.* His vision was fading, the ceiling was spinning, and Keitaro was shouting something at Kagen. And then Nathaniel sped away in the direction of the kitchen, the sentinels surrounded Napolean, and Marquis straddled Nachari's body.

"I've got his legs." *Was that Julien Lacusta?*

"Braden, clear out those damn chairs!" Marquis commanded. The Ancient Master Warrior slid one hand beneath Nachari's upper back and cradled his neck with the other, and then the two giant males lifted Nachari from the ground and set him gently atop the conference table.

"*Perseus!*" Nachari cursed as Marquis grasped the wizard's chin, tilted his head, and struck his throat so swiftly that the vampire's incisors burned as they sank in. And then Marquis started pumping venom into Nachari with such intensity—at such a high volume and with so much velocity—that Nachari's body began to jerk on the table. It felt like his insides were boiling from acid.

"I've got 'em!" Nathaniel returned—*from the kitchen?*—and tossed something at Kagen that looked like a set of knives, several silver blades in a velvet-lined box.

"Napolean's venom?" Kagen asked Nathaniel.

"He's filling the bowl right now."

"Good," Keitaro barked, rushing to the side of the table. He reached down and ripped Nachari's T-shirt. "Start working on that damn aorta, *now!*"

"What...the...hell?" Nachari slurred his words. "I'm fine. *I'm good.* I'm just a little dizzy."

Braden stepped up to the table next, and his burnt-sienna eyes were glazed with moisture. He reached for Nachari's hand. "Hey, Master Wizard"—his voice betrayed a quiver—"don't worry about it, okay? Just hang in there...you know...stay with us, Nachari." He choked back a sob as he voiced the last few words, and that's when Nachari finally got it: *Holy shit*, this was really serious.

"This might hurt a little, baby brother." Kagen's placid tone.

Then *sweet mother of Auriga*—Nachari jackknifed off the table.

"Hold him down," Keitaro commanded.

Marquis braced Nachari's shoulders, and Nathaniel held his legs, even as the former continued to administer venom.

And then Kagen began to slice through the Master Wizard's sternum with one of the knives from the kitchen...

Nachari was immediately catapulted back to the Valley of Death and Shadows—those days and days of inescapable torture —and he tried to focus his mind elsewhere, anywhere but on the pain. Somewhere in the background, one of the sentinels was offering Napolean his blood, and even further away, muted and distant, Ciopori—*or was that Vanya?*—was speaking into a cell phone, talking in hushed, hurried whispers, and Nachari thought he heard her say, *Deanna...*

Shit.

Just shit.

"Father?" Nachari couldn't see him.

"I'm right here, son. What the hell did you do—tussle with a coven of warlocks?" He chuckled softly, but the sound was hollow; the humor didn't resonate in his words.

And then the door to the conference room flew open, and Arielle Nightsong-Silivasi rushed in. She hurried to the table, thrust a surgical bag at Kagen, and stepped toward Nachari with a syringe in her hand.

"Whoa...wait...I don't like needles." Damnit, he was still slurring his words.

"Needles, porcupines, spiders, or snakes." Nathaniel's silken drawl. "Go to sleep already, little brother. We'll see you in a few."

Another poke.

A slow injection.

The faint sting of serum, nothing nearly as bad as the venom, and then the sweetest sound he'd ever heard: Deanna's elegant voice flowing through their private telepathic bandwidth...

I love you, Master Wizard—please come home soon.

And then all the world went black.

CHAPTER EIGHT

Fabian stumbled back, fell to the ground, and swept his hands through his ragged, wild hair.

What the hell was that?

He was out of air; his nose was broken; his chest, face, and throat were clawed and bleeding; and for a moment, he had not been able to fend the panther off.

Blessed Borealis, that green-eyed wizard—he had traced Gwen's blood from a previous quaff and tracked her to Fabian's hidden cave. That wasn't anything special or extraordinary. However, the vampire had not stopped there. He had burrowed into her consciousness, settled inside her vision, and gazed right at Fabian as if he were standing in the cavern. And when Fabian had confronted him, torn through his throat, punctured his chest, grasped his still-beating heart, the wizard had shifted into a panther!

And not an apparition.

Not a conjured animus, but a real, live, breathing feline, who had fought like a demon. Indeed, Fabian had the injuries to prove it, but the oddity did not stop there: Somewhere along the way, when Fabian's snow leopard had the cat by the neck, a power beyond reasoning...beyond reckoning...rose up in the dying cat.

The beast tore its own jugular yet came up fighting with a force that was beyond a mere vampire. Yes, wizards had exceptional talents, but this had been altogether different: There was a harnessed power, a celestial authority, a thinly veiled mastery of the elements—nay, the solar system—that the beast had not even reached for...yet.

Thank the gods, the panther had retreated.

And Gwendolyn—*great lords, where was Gwendolyn?*

She had to have witnessed everything. Well, she would not have seen the green-eyed wizard, or the black panther, but she would have seen the struggle: Fabian lunging, rolling, pouncing like a leopard; grunting, panting, and bleeding.

She would see his injuries now.

He scanned the cave, the berth by the fire, and the low-lying ledge she liked to hide beneath.

Nothing.

Where the hell had she gone?

He closed his eyes and sighed. The green-eyed wizard wasn't the only one who had taken Gwen's blood—and he wasn't the only one who could track her.

Ah, yes, the incalcitrant female...

She had taken advantage of the half-invisible battle, slipped out while Fabian was fighting, and shimmied down the side of the mountain, avoiding the perilous ledge.

She was running through the forest.

Sprinting in the dark.

Heading right for the valley Fabian had seen in his dreams, surveyed in his sleep through the eyes of the raven. She was heading straight for the Red Canyons and the black-and-red-haired demons that, at least in his dreams, frequented the arroyo.

The High Mage struggled to his feet and fought against the

fog—the blood of the panther was staving it off—the battle had afforded Fabian clarity...sanity...and the swallows of blood he had gulped had bought him time.

Maybe minutes.

Maybe an hour.

But not much more.

Soon, the darkness would swallow him, once more, and the fog would return.

He released his incisors and filled both palms with a viscous, vampiric substance, swiftly coating his wounds with venom, and then he reached for a memory...a long-ago memory...how to call forth and release his wings outside of the dreamscape, outside of the raven or the hawk.

Yes, he was Vampyr...

He could transport—or fly—but the former skill was still rather murky.

He would rather take his chances in the skies.

* * *

Gwen's lungs were on fire. Her side was aching, and her heart was pumping so hard it sounded like it might beat right out of her chest. She had always been in good shape, athletic by nature, but she had never run so fast or so far.

She didn't dare try to wrap her mind around what she had seen in that cavern.

Fabian Antonescu was batshit crazy.

Pure and simple—the vampire had been hallucinating.

Only...*only*...whatever battle he was waging inside tore at his flesh, battered his bones, and caused blood to spurt out in rivulets from his veins.

It was beyond creepy.

It surpassed *supernatural.*

This whole damn valley was inexplicable...and terrifying!

And that's when the dense forest skylight went out.

At first, Gwen thought her sight had left her—something horrid had happened, and she had suddenly gone blind. The forest was dark as pitch already, but this was altogether different—the scant beams of waning moonlight had vanished.

She careened to a halt, throwing both palms against the bark of an aspen tree to halt her trajectory, then blinked several times, trying to restore her vision.

Why can't I see?

Her existing terror rose to panic.

And then the sky began to light up again, like small, individual torches, blazing one by one.

She scrubbed her eyes with her hands—*what the hell was wrong with her eyesight?*—and shifted her gaze to the pale yellow moon.

No, not yellow, but a deep shade of rose.

Then burgundy...maroon...deep blood red!

She gasped, leaned back against the tree, and stared up at the heavens.

The stars were moving, realigning—the torches were dancing —until they had formed a clear, recognizable constellation: Corona Borealis.

What the actual hell?

Her left wrist started burning, and she sank to the ground, encircling her knees with her arms and burying her head in her lap—this was more than her feeble mind could process.

All of it.

The past ten or so hours; vampires and wizards; Fabian's endless antics; and now her eyesight...and the sky. Surely she was living in a never-ending nightmare—she had fallen down a rabbit hole or been swept up in Dorothy's tornado. Gwen was stuck in a bizarre, fairy-tale nightscape that just kept getting stranger and stranger...and stranger.

As if on cue, she heard a scattering of footsteps: toes and heels crushing leaves; the sound of somebody approaching...

No, not *somebody*, but several *somebodies*.

She jerked her head up, leaned forward to listen, and strained her eyes to see.

What in the world?

Three teenage boys, maybe sixteen or seventeen, wandering about the woods at four or five o'clock in the morning?

This shit just kept getting better and better.

And then the teenagers drew nearer...

The guy in front had long, straight hair, and from the looks of it, it was half red and half black. The guy right behind him, following from the middle, had more of a typical teenage hairstyle, the front longer than the back and swept over in an arc. Yet, once again, the strands were red and black. And the last guy; he had very little hair at all, almost a skull trim, but the hint was there—shadows of crimson, patches of black.

Gwen shot to her feet and backed against the tree, thrusting both palms upward and out, in a defensive gesture. Something about these guys was all wrong. And not like the night, not like the sky, not like the nightmare she had been living until now: the Fortress, the well, and Fabian.

These boys weren't crazy or out of their minds.

They were clear as day and focused on Gwendolyn. They were darkness personified...evil...soulless. It was in their eyes, their postures, and the way they advanced. Every heartbeat or two, they would glance at the sky, turn to each other, and make facial expressions, but they didn't mutter an audible word. It was almost as if they were speaking without sound. Then just as quickly, their eyes would dart forward, and the corners of their mouths would turn down in a scowl.

They were going to tear Gwen's heart out.

She just knew it.

And that was only if she were lucky.

Pure, unadulterated terror seized her soul, and she covered her ears and screamed.

And then the males lunged, the night exploded, and everything happened at once: A torrent of falcons rained down from the sky, dozens and dozens of screeching fowl with wingspans as long as Gwen's arms. Their faces were horrid, twisted, and demonic—devils, gothic monsters, hideous beasts, and deformed apparitions—and fire and blood streamed out of their beaks.

The teenagers ducked and ran, backpedaling as fast as they could, even as the birds coalesced into the silhouette of a man and hovered in the air between Gwen and the trio. The silhouette began to twist like a cyclone, streaming down from its perch in the air—it plucked Gwen from the tree and spun her around to face the twofold apparition.

Flesh.

Blood.

Viselike arms surrounded Gwen's shoulders and wrenched her backward.

And just like that, Gwen was caught up in the air, tucked beneath the wings of a familiar vampire...nestled closer than breath or blood to *Fabian's* heart.

CHAPTER NINE

THE DARK ONES' COLONY

Salvatore Nistor stared into the dim gray glow of his otherwise crystal cube as it continued to flash, light then dark, on his nightstand. His nephew, Derrian, was sleeping soundly in his crib—the boy would be two years old in exactly two months—on the other side of the craggy lair, and Salvatore prayed the damnable object wouldn't wake him.

Part of the globe's behavior made sense—it was signaling the sorcerer to look at the sky, to record the fact that there had been a Blood Moon, and another vampire in the house of Jadon was somewhere out there claiming his *destiny*.

Yeah, yeah, so what was new?

The cycle had gone on for ages.

But there was something peculiar in the globe as well, something that made no sense: bits and pieces; quick, random flashes; strange, cryptic objects...and birds. One moment, the cube was projecting a falcon; the next it was projecting a hawk. Three seconds later, it flashed like a strobe light, presenting raven after raven, after raven.

Then a vial of blood.

Then a pair of copper eyes.

Then it settled back into dim, hazy gray.

If only the sorcerer could buy a new cube—this antique relic was on the fritz.

Pound. Pound. Pound.

Frantic fists knocking at the door to Salvatore's lair...*at nearly five o'clock in the morning?*

Who the hell!

"He won't open his door," a young male cautioned.

"He has to," another argued. "It's too important."

"What if he's angry, and he strikes us dead?" Still a third voice outside Salvatore's compartment.

Salvatore flicked his wrist in the direction of the heavy wood-and-iron panel, slipping the antique lock from its joint. "Enter at your own risk," he drawled in a heavy Romanian accent, just to give the boys a fright. "Try not to get dirt on my marble floors and stay away from the crib." He strolled to a large, nearby davenport and took a seat.

The first of the three vampires had long, straight hair; the second was trying to be more fashionable with a flip toward the front; and the third may as well have been bald, for the length of his hideous skull trim.

"Who are you?" Salvatore bellowed. "And why do you dare to disturb my chamber this night?"

The long-haired vampire raised his chin, squared his shoulders, and led the pack, even though his knees were visibly wobbling. He took several brave strides forward, toward the davenport, then dropped to his knees and bowed his head. "Your excellence," he said reverently, "we are here because of your esteemed seat on the council, and my name is Anton."

The second vampire—the one who wanted to be a model—shuffled forward, far more quickly, knelt beside his friend, and hugged his stomach. He looked like he was about to vomit. "My father named me Sven," he whispered. "We came to you, instead of Milano, Sergei, or Demetri, because of your magical powers... your sorcery."

Now this caught Salvatore's attention, but it also left him a bit perturbed—there was yet one more member of the Dark One's Council, the illustrious chairman, Oskar Vadovsky. "And why didn't you seek out Oskar? He is both powerful and influential in the house of Jaegar—why choose to disturb *my* peace, instead?"

The third fledgling swept his hand over his head, joined his brethren on the floor before the davenport, and looked Salvatore straight in the eyes. "We were out hunting when we saw the moon and heard a human female in the forest, near the Red Canyons. We went closer to investigate, thinking she was easy prey, and this crazy flock of falcons came out of the sky! Only, their faces and their throats—"

"Wait," Salvatore interrupted. "Did you say *falcons*?"

"Yeah," the third teen interrupted.

"I didn't get your name."

The third teen gulped. "It's Ozzie," he said. "My sire is—"

"Who gives a shit," Salvatore barked. "Just get on with your story."

The boy—Ozzie—wrung his hands together, and Salvatore could see that they were unusually pale. In fact, as he looked closer at the boy's complexion, his entire pallor was sickly and green. He listened to the young vampire's heartbeat: It was slow... waning...hardly beating, unlike his terrified friends'.

"The falcons breathed fire and blood," Anton offered, "and as we were running away, they coalesced into the body of a male— the biggest vampire we've ever seen—and shot into the sky. The vampire took the girl we were hunting, but we didn't look back."

Now this pissed Salvatore off.

He had passed *perturbed*...lapped *annoyed*...and landed at downright pissed. "You fled from the apparition?" He scowled.

"You ran from this vampire and came to me?" He reached out a hand, curled his fingers inward, and squeezed with all his might, constricting the vampires' hearts—perhaps they would find greater courage in the future. "Know this," he snarled. "Whenever you are out in the open; whenever you interact with another of our kind—be it a vampire of light or a vampire of darkness— you represent the house of Jaegar and all three of your sires. The sons of Jaegar are not cowards, boys! We do not run from anyone."

Anton began to shake in his boots, even as Sven visibly puked in his mouth. And Ozzie—the sickly fool—toppled over.

Salvatore released their hearts.

He rose from the davenport, took several graceful strides forward, and snatched the nearly bald vampire by his scalp, lifting his head to stare into his eyes—and that's when he saw the boy's neck.

Two deep, perfect puncture wounds stamped directly over his jugular.

Two steady trickles of blood flowing along the length of his throat.

"This apparition," Salvatore said, "this vampire you describe: He fed from Ozzie's throat while you were watching? Yet you somehow left that out of your tale?"

Sven shook his head furiously, back and forth. "No, Your Majesty—"

"Just call me Salvatore—where the hell do you young ones get this shit?"

Sven groveled in apology. "No...Salvatore...the vampire...the thing...never touched him. He never touched any of us." He lowered his voice in shame. "We ran too fast."

Salvatore harrumphed.

Now this was very interesting...

He studied Ozzie's neck a second time, then listened for the whir of his blood snaking through his veins. There was nothing. No sound. No pulsation. For all intents and purposes, the boy was drained dry. And if his buddies didn't act swiftly, he was going to die on the floor of Salvatore's lair, a victim of exsanguination.

Well, Salvatore thought, *he won't exactly die—his heart and his head are still intact.*

Still, the boy needed blood, and he needed it immediately. Whoever this vampire was—and the thought was, oddly, orgasmic—he was a very great practitioner of magick, indeed. He had fed on Ozzie and drained him dry, from a distance. He had somehow imbibed Ozzie's blood through sorcery. This did not sound like Nachari Silivasi, nor Napolean Mondragon, the all-powerful king. Yet they were the only two vampires Salvatore knew of who even approached such levels of skill.

"Your companion has been leeched; he is near death from blood loss. Feed him, then get out of my lair," Salvatore snarled. "Go back to your familial clusters and get some sleep. Your council is now aware of the...anomaly."

As the boys scrambled to slit their wrists and pour the thick, crimson substance down their cohort's throat, Salvatore glanced askance at his cube: a falcon, a hawk, a series of ravens; a Blood Moon, a vial of blood, and a pair of copper irises...

Perhaps the cube had a little life left in it, after all.

And Salvatore had a mystery to solve...

For surely there was something more important in the omens than the fact that a son of Jadon would soon be getting his rocks off.

* * *

Napolean Mondragon took a deep, cleansing breath as he walked the perimeter of his mansion and surveyed the Corona Borealis Blood Moon.

The High Mage had known.

Even before the omen.

Somehow, Fabian had just sensed that Gwen was his *destiny*.

What manner of power did this male possess?

It was a stupid question: *They had almost lost Nachari.*

The Ancient had almost taken the youngest Silivasi from the house of Jadon when no one was looking...or expecting it...anticipating his power or his animus. But Napolean was king—he should've seen it coming. There was no excuse for such a lapse in judgment.

He rubbed his brow and bowed his head. "Thank you, Andromeda, for showing me the correct reaction." Had he not left his body and inhabited Nachari's—had Napolean waited ten seconds longer... He couldn't finish the thought.

Nachari was safe in Kagen's clinic, surrounded by his family, Braden, and Kristina. He was in his *destiny's* arms, and he would heal completely over the next twenty-four hours.

The sentinels were home with their mates as well, as were the princesses and Julien Lacusta.

Napolean's orders—he would not shirk his duty again.

It was up to him to figure this out, to devise a plan, and command his loyal subjects like a king who was worthy of their veneration. Yes, he was weakened from the astral travel. He would need to hunt and *feed* before the sun came up, and eventually, he would need to sleep...a lot. But he could deal with all that later, once he at least had a game plan. Right now, he needed to figure this out.

He glanced at the stars for the umpteenth time, awed by their beauty, yet reminded of their meaning: After all this time, Fabian Antonescu was alive, and the gods had seen fit to give him a *destiny*. Hell, Braden Bratianu had pulled her out of the basement ductwork at The Fortress, and the neophyte had somehow known that he needed to keep her, bring her back to the valley... that she belonged in the house of Jadon.

And that meant so did Fabian...

He was meant to come home.

Napolean shook his head and repressed a feral snarl: Yeah, but Nachari Silivasi belonged here too, and Fabian would have killed him if he could have. He might have killed all of them that day at the well: Nachari, Braden, Deanna, and Kristina. The male wasn't sane, nor was he friendly.

And his powers—

Napolean crossed his arms and stared at a haphazard pile of pine cones, resisting the childish urge to kick them into the cosmos. He didn't want to acknowledge what he was thinking, the fear that deeply unsettled him: Fabian Antonescu might be more powerful than the king.

Napolean shook his head and waved his hand in a dismissive gesture.

Cowardice was unbecoming.

Besides, Napolean didn't exist in a vacuum—he had warriors and wizards and healers at his side. He had the fiercest damn sentinels the earth had ever seen. He had Julien Lacusta, whose latent power was strong enough to level a village, and he had Keitaro Silivasi and his powerful sons—each one strong enough to take on an enemy, alone. No, Napolean could best Fabian if he marshalled his resources, if he could get him out of the wilds and bring him back to the manse...

If he could find a way to cut through that inky darkness and bring the male back to his rational mind. Perhaps Vanya and Ciopori could play a pivotal role, although Saber and Marquis would balk—they had seen what the Ancient had done to Nachari, and they weren't likely to offer their beloved mates as ambassadors, interpreters...or royal bait.

As it stood, Keitaro would object as well—he would not readily agree to the king's burgeoning plan.

But it was of no matter.

Napolean's word was law.

And he knew what had to be done.

Fabian could not stay out there, running free and wild, terrorizing Napolean's *house*—and his ilk. A pang of shame sliced through Napolean's heart, and he gasped as he caught the error. "Forgive me, dear prince; it was a momentary lapse. I've never forgotten—and I will never forget—our legacy is the house of *Jadon*, not Napolean. We are all alive because of your wisdom and your humility...because you begged the Blood for mercy and made your followers pledge our loyalty...because you rose up from the ash and bile of the Curse and directed us to a new homeland, beyond the shores of Europe. Because you fought your brother, Prince Jaegar, when he was hellbent on destroying all of us, when he would've never stopped coming...hunting...killing... and utilizing his superior army of cursed souls to wipe our seed from the earth, forever. Oh, my prince, I was just a boy when it happened. Where did you go on that fateful night? That night when Jaegar's loyalists were coming to kill us—those of us who hadn't already died from the Curse, those of us who weren't still feral and consumed by bloodlust—that night when the wind whispered secrets, and you bargained on our collective behalf. Brother against brother. Prince against prince. Vampire against vampire, so the legions might live. Whoever survived the one-to-one combat would rule, uncontested, and decimate the others—Jadon against Jaegar—in order to spare your respective armies, when half of us were still animals, crawling on the ground. But neither one of you ever came down from that mountain." Napolean could hardly speak the words aloud. "Rumor has it you beheaded each other at the exact same moment, and Blessed

Celestial beings, we were lost...and desolate...scattered for hundreds of years."

Napolean sidled up to a moss-and-rock retaining wall, sat on the ledge, and rubbed his hands together to dispel the nervous energy, even as he turned his attention back to the present and allowed the strategy to take form:

Fabian Antonescu was alive, and he was here.

The Ancient had a *destiny*, and stable or not, he was sticking to his female like glue.

And that meant Gwendolyn Hamilton was the key to the mage's future—the most effective ambassador, the most perfect lure. Wherever she went, Fabian would follow, and that meant Napolean needed to appeal to them both: Once he had healed, in twenty-four hours, Nachari Silivasi could pave the way. He could trace the female's blood, yet again; only this time, the house of Jadon would be ready.

Julien would be primed to follow Nachari's coordinates.

The sentinels would go with him and capture Gwen.

While Napolean and Nachari occupied Fabian, the warriors would utilize the decoy to snatch her away from the Ancient and bring her back to the holding cell beneath the manse.

No, it wasn't the ideal location, nor was it a very hospitable way to treat a cherished *destiny*, but Gwen would be more protected in those thick, diamond-encrusted walls than out in the open with the forest at her back. She would be safer with Napolean and his warriors than a mage who couldn't tell friend from foe.

Yes, Fabian could come for her—*Fabian* would *come for her*—but he would have to go through the sentinels first. He would have to go through half the house of Jadon to get her, if not through Napolean Mondragon, himself. He would have to speak with...and reason with...the males of his race, and that would buy them *all* time to figure things out:

And in the interim, Gwen could listen and learn.

While Vanya and Ciopori tried to reach the High Mage—if anyone could get through to him, the princesses could. He had loved them, protected them, cared for them for years...

The king's heart felt heavy as he considered the risks: What would happen if they failed, or the plan didn't work? Gods willing, Gwen would lure Fabian to the manse, and with time—and compassion—his heart might soften...

His mind might heal.

But if something went wrong—terribly amiss—if the Ancient continued to threaten the king's subjects, or worse: If he tried to harm one of the princesses—if he couldn't claim his *destiny* and fulfill the Curse, without destroying half the house of Jadon in the process—then Gwen, Napolean, and all involved would only have to last for thirty days.

For not even Fabian Antonescu, the greatest wizard who had ever lived, could outrun...or outlast...the Blood.

CHAPTER TEN

G wen couldn't stop shivering.

She couldn't stop crying; she couldn't stop wringing her hands together; and she couldn't stop replaying the night's events.

Fabian had flown them to a different cave, a narrow grotto carved out of a canyon behind a rushing waterfall—he had quickly built a fire, wrapped his arms around Gwen's shoulders to warm her, and crooned something foreign in her ear.

Yet and still, Gwen couldn't come back from the trauma.

The invisible fight in the previous cave: Fabian hallucinating, spinning, pouncing like a cat, how close she had come to escaping —fleeing, running, being lost in the woods—the three terrible vampires who had almost torn her throat out. And then there was the moon, the color of fresh blood, Corona Borealis, and the welts on her wrist! The hideous falcons that had rained down from the sky, and Fabian snatching her away from...death.

She couldn't wrap her mind—or her emotions—around it.

"*Destinul meu,*" Fabian whispered, still crooning in her ear. "Be still." He placed his hand over hers and sent a strange, calming pulse into her skin. "Be calm." He brushed away her tears with his thumbs, and she felt a stream of...quiet...settle behind her eyes. "Be well." He placed his palm on her stomach, through the jean skirt, and the butterflies in her stomach settled.

How was that possible?

How was any of this possible?

How was it possible that all his wounds had healed?

And why was he having such a moment of clarity—

When would he revert back to feral?

Gwen knew in her heart it was just a matter of time: Whatever had happened in that canyon, perhaps with those teenagers, whatever had occurred as a result of that red moon was feeding the vampire strength—and lucidity—but she had no doubt, none whatsoever, that he would be back to hallucinating soon. Back to crazy. Back to savage. Back to terrorizing—and *feeding* from —Gwen.

Still, his powers were amazing...extraordinary...and he had managed to still her soul.

If only for a moment, she had to try something different...*do something different*...approach the situation from a new strategic approach. She had to make *something* hopeful happen before he changed back.

Because heavens knew, she could not survive this much longer.

A few more days—hell, a few more hours—and she would be just as crazy and lost as he was.

She spun around, scooted on her butt to face him, and forced her rising fear to retreat, just a little. Summoning courage from a place she didn't know she possessed, she slowly raised her hands and cupped him by the cheeks. "Fabian," she whispered insistently, "speak to me, now. Talk to me while you can. We both know you won't be like this much longer." Perhaps honesty was the superior policy.

He blanched, but his steady, burnt-copper gaze remain fixed on her seeking, light-green eyes.

"What happened in the other cave?" she said. "What were you seeing? What were you doing? Do you even know why you were acting like that?" She traced the bridge of his nose with her forefinger, then quickly pulled it back and settled both hands in her lap. "Your nose was broken—I saw it bleeding—and now, it's just as perfect as ever."

Fabian shook his head. "The green-eyed wizard, he traced your blood. He came into the cave to look around...to find you. I wasn't fighting an absent foe, Gwen. I was fighting to keep you with me. He is a very powerful wizard, indeed—he can shift into the body of a panther. I became a snow leopard to match his prowess, and that was the battle you were witnessing. My nose was broken, my face was clawed, and my throat was torn open by his teeth. But I've since healed my wounds with venom, and I fed on one of the three interlopers. You are right to draw such wise conclusions. I cannot hold this sobriety for long, but I do not know if it's insanity that claims me." His tone grew solemn and stern. "Gwen, my *destiny*, you must understand; I am neither capable of claiming you, of fulfilling our Blood Moon, nor returning you to your people. I mustn't. *You are mine.*"

Gwen shivered all the way from her spine to her toes, but she managed to hold it together.

This was progress...

So many questions swirled through her mind, she could hardly keep them straight or put them in order: Nachari was searching for her? *Oh, God, yes!* She wanted to know more about that, but she didn't dare ask. And they fought as jungle cats—a panther and a leopard—she needed to know more about this magic, this wizardry, how Nachari could see into the cave, and why the fight was invisible to Gwen. But again, she didn't think it was relevant. It wasn't the most imperative information she could seek in this rare, honest moment.

Fabian fed on one of the three interlopers?

The vampires who had attacked her...

She knew what *feeding* meant—she had figured that one out by now—but she didn't comprehend how he could've sucked the blood of one of those teenage vampires.

Again, it didn't matter.

She could always learn more later...

What stood out the most, in her mind and her heart, was that ominous final sentence: *I am neither capable of claiming you, of fulfilling our Blood Moon, nor returning you to your people. I mustn't. You are mine.*

"Fabian," she said evenly, still staring into the bottomless depths of his enthralling eyes, "what do you mean by *fulfilling our Blood Moon*, and why can't you let me go home? How am I yours? Why did you take me? And if it's not insanity, then what is it that claims you? Is there any way to forestall it, to stave it off?"

Her hands still in her lap, Fabian brushed the backs of his fingers over her palms, along her forearms, and up to her shoulders. He drank in her chest, her jawline, and her throat as he continued to trace her collarbone. And then he cradled her neck in both hands, bent forward, and kissed her—just a feather-light touch of lips against lips—and Gwen's heart nearly leaped out of her chest.

Fear.

Intimidation.

But also, entrancement—every nerve ending she possessed came alive.

He repeated the tender gesture on the tip of her nose, then her forehead, and then he slowly rocked back and appraised her with fondness. "You are beautiful, Gwendolyn." His voice sounded hoarse. "And it occurs to me now that if I would have taken you"—he stared brazenly at the swell of her breasts—"believing I was fulfilling the Curse, I would have killed you in forty-eight hours. I am far, far more dangerous than I realized."

Gwen gulped.

"And yet, I will never release you." His burnt-copper eyes were darkening with heat—there were flames in their depths, and the pupils were simmering.

"My body belongs to me," Gwen blurted, not knowing a more tactful way to say it. "You cannot just touch me...or take me... without my permission. Do you understand that, Fabian?"

The corner of his sultry mouth turned up in a smile, and Gwen was taken aback by his visage: He was stunning, pure and simple.

"Back in Romania, when I yet served King Silvano, the maidens would come to my chambers by the dozens—they would sneak out in the night for a chance to be chosen. Sometimes, I only selected one, but other times, I chose several—and none ever left my arms dissatisfied. Quite the contrary, I assure you. I was trained in the art of love...to play a woman's body like a finely tuned instrument. If I touch you...like that...you will grant your permission." He shrugged one shoulder, and his smile faded. "But, either way, you belong to me. And I"—he glanced conspicuously at his groin—"belong to you."

Gwen's stomach was trembling again.

Both from fear...and some inner betrayal...an inexplicable flutter of a different type of butterflies.

She took a slow, deep breath and tried again. "Fabian, will you please answer my questions?"

He nodded slowly, seeming to dismiss the previous subject easier than she had expected. "The Blood Moon is a sign from the heavens, a signal from the celestial gods to let a male vampire know when he has found his *destiny*, the woman he is fated to mate." He held up one hand, ostensibly in the hopes of staving off any premature reaction. "However, I knew you were mine the moment I sensed your energy, the second I heard your heartbeat —you awakened me in that well." He reached out to take her left wrist, and she drew it back, but he was a thousand times faster than she was. "Shh," he crooned, "I do not seek to harm you; I only wish to show you your wrist." He turned her arm over and circled the welts with his thumbs. "Did you glimpse the heavens, my dove? Did you see the stars? Do not these markings on your wrist look familiar?"

Gwen stared down at the itchy, raised stripes, and she instantly noticed the pattern. "Corona Borealis!" she exclaimed with wonder. The same constellation she had seen in the sky.

What the hell?

How did that happen?

This time, his smile was brilliant. "You know your constellations." He inclined his head with approval. "Corona Borealis is my ruling celestial lord, the one who chose you as my *destiny*. And this"—he tightened his grip on her forearm—"is proof that you were chosen to walk this world beside me." Before she could reply, or pose a dozen more questions, he released his grip and pressed on. "Now then, why can I not take you home or release you? Because our fates are linked, and our futures are intertwined. If a male loses his *destiny* before he appeases the Blood, his death will be both imminent...and unpleasant. Why did I take you? This is why. Although none of it was clear...or sentient at the time." His brow drew into a deep, troubled furrow, and he grimaced like he was experiencing pain.

No, no, no, Gwen thought. *Not now. Not now!*

There was still so much she needed to ask him.

Like what the hell was the Blood?

And what did he mean by *appeasing* it?

"Fabian, stay with me—I don't understand. Your words and your thoughts are terrifying. I just—"

"Stop," he commanded, his tone growing harsh. "Your pleading will only make matters worse: Listen carefully, Gwen, and heed my words: Many centuries ago, I traveled to this continent with the two remaining females of my species. I remember this vaguely, but it comes and goes; at times, it is no more than an impression. And I also remember—at least I think I recall—fashioning a similar elixir so I could join them in a long, enchanted slumber. I was waiting...*we were waiting*...for something, for someone, and I could no longer bear the nights of isolation. I didn't crawl into a well! I slept in the ground, and the well must have come later..." His voice was becoming more and more agitated. "The water, the stones, and the dreams. Yes, the dreams! I couldn't escape the grave or the dreaming... And the vials, the blood, the hawk and the raven, I traveled outside my body; I scoured this land in my slumber." He grasped his temples and shook his head, and then he began to rock in place. "The fog will not let me remember. The truth is bound by the darkness. The sin is buried with the truth. If one escapes, the other will follow— my mind refuses to let this surface." He was rapidly slipping away.

Guided by an instinct she couldn't name, Gwen reached out and tunneled her fingers in his hair, that wild, glorious, golden-bronze mane. "Fabian, I don't understand: what words did you want me to heed?"

He blinked several times in quick succession, and his burnt-copper irises flashed red. "When the mage is gone, when the vampire rises, when all that exists in this shell is a beast, do not fight me, Gwendolyn. Do not seek to escape—I know nothing in such moments, but instinct. I *feed* to live, to stay alive, but also to conquer the demons...the fog... When I take your vein, do not panic or struggle. Fear is the most potent elixir. Place your hand

91

on my chest and feel the beat of my heart. Submit to its rhythm... relax into it. Your acquiescence will halt the pain. And know that I am always seeking...searching...trying to catch a glimpse inside the fog. At some point, the memories must return—they have to. Without them, we will both remain lost."

Gwen scrambled onto her knees, grasped him by the jaw, and bore her gaze into his feral soul, her heart beating a frantic rhythm in her chest. "When did you leave Romania?" she inquired.

"What?" He cringed and drew back.

"When did you leave Romania for this continent—what year, Fabian?"

He shuddered. "In 799 B.C."

"And who were the women that were with you? What were their names? *Try to remember*."

He squinted, cringed, and growled.

"Sarah?" She tossed something out there. "Alice? Isabel?" Hell, she didn't know what names they used back then.

"Stop," he snorted, almost sounding offended.

"Eva? Felicia? Muriel?"

"Vanya!" he shouted. "And Ciopori. I have warned you not to challenge me!"

"Good," Gwen whispered. "Fabian, that's good. Now try to listen *to me* if you're able: You left Romania over 2,850 years ago —I don't have time to do the exact math—but you're living in the twenty-first century, the first century of the third millennium in accordance with the Gregorian calendar. You are in Dark Moon Vale, and there are others of your kind who have settled here, other vampires with mates they call *destinies*." She remembered Nachari referring to Deanna this way, more than just a time or two. "Does this have any meaning for you?"

He narrowed his gaze in fierce concentration, and then he muttered absently: "The boy at the well...there were *female*

vampires...the green-eyed wizard is from the house of *Jadon*..."
His voice trailed off, and his features grew livid. "Ah yes, but we
glimpsed the house of Jaegar this night. Light cleaves to light, and
darkness cleaves to darkness. The hawk...the raven...the Millenia
Harvest Moon."

"What about the hawk?" Gwen insisted.

He swiped his hand through the air like a wild animal.

"What about the raven, Fabian! Tell me about the raven.
What about these birds disturbs you?"

"*Birds?*" he mocked. "If only they were *birds*. They were no
more—or less—real than the snow leopard, earlier. Phantoms of
my mind. Ghosts of my creations. Flesh, blood, feathers, and
beaks, conjured from millennia, sleeping. Drink this blood, and
welcome Life. Drink this blood, and welcome Death."

His fangs descended.

His claws came out.

And his powerful, muscular shoulders rippled with rage and
tension.

Then he crouched on his knees and glared at Gwen, his
features twisting into a murderous contortion.

Gwen closed her eyes—she couldn't look at him.

If she didn't die of fright, she might dive into the fire.

And either way, Fabian could move faster...

She bowed her head, a paltry gesture of submission, and
forced herself to crawl onto his lap.

His back stiffened—he was clearly startled—and Gwen
opened her eyes. She stared through his vacant pupils as she
swept her hair away from her shoulder, and then, shaking like a
leaf, she splayed her fingers, pressed her palm to his heart, and
tilted her head to the side.

He struck her jugular so quickly she almost punched him and
bolted, but something stronger...something deeper...kept her in
his lap.

The pain was agonizing as she struggled to find his heartbeat —to feel it, then to hear it, to tune everything else out—and just like that, she was connected to Fabian, and the pain abated as he continued to *feed*.

Gwen rebelled against every impulse in her body.

She defied her reason.

And she ignored her fear.

She placed her left arm around his broad, massive shoulders —her right hand against his cheek—and she allowed the vampire to soothe his madness.

She encouraged the wizard to *remember*...and heal.

Did she have a sudden surge of empathy or kindness toward her captor?

Did she sympathize with his plight, and want him to be whole?

No.

Not at all.

But for the first time since Fabian had taken her, she finally had a roadmap and a burgeoning ray of hope—*Nachari was searching for Gwen, and he had managed to injure Fabian.* More than ever before, she was determined to live...

To survive...

To escape.

And at least, at last, she had found a way to appease the feral beast.

CHAPTER ELEVEN

Saber Alexiares leaned back against a large wooden post in the lofty, majestic living room of his and Vanya's custom-built Gothic Victorian home, just ten miles northeast of the Dark Moon Vale Hot Springs. "Not gonna happen," he growled. "At least not alone, and not with Ciopori as your only backup."

Vanya sighed. "*Dragon*...we don't even know if the king's plan will work: if the sentinels will be able to capture Gwen; if Gwen will be able to lure Fabian to the manse; or if Ciopori and I will have an opportunity to see him. We don't—"

"We do know," he interrupted, "that you...and Ciopori...will not have a chance to meet with Fabian alone. We clear on that, Vanya? Or were you not at the manse when Fabian almost beheaded Nachari—via route of his jugular—and extracted his heart from fifty miles away?"

Vanya grimaced, and then she sighed. "*Saber*, Nachari was a stranger, and Fabian felt threatened—do you recall how you behaved during our Blood Moon? Ciopori and I are like his second family, and I have to tell you—I'm with my sister on this one. I do not believe he would ever raise a hand against either of us, feral or not."

Saber snickered in derision. "Did you hear what you just said?"

"Of course, dragon." Her voice grew clipped. "There is nothing wrong with my hearing or my mind."

"Define feral."

"Excuse me?" she snipped.

"*Feral*. Define it for me, Vanya."

She placed both hands on her hips and glared at him. "I'll do no such thing."

"Feral," he said, "in a wild state or resembling a wild animal. If he were capable of reasoning, of not raising a hand against either one of you, then he wouldn't be feral to begin with. That is one of the most ill-advised things I have ever heard."

At that, Vanya's temper flared. "Who are you calling ill-advised, dragon? I'll have you know, I have 2,831 years to your 801, and I spent much of that time—"

"Sleeping," he interjected, his telltale smirk emerging at the corner of his naturally cruel but sexy mouth. "For all intents and purposes, you're still twenty-one."

She reached for a nearby bronzed statue of an angel and raised it in her hand, testing the metal for its weight.

Saber chuckled: low, soft, and almost sinister. "What are you gonna do with that figurine?"

"Ping you in the head," she warned. "How do you like them *apples*." She was careful to get it right as Ciopori tended to say *oranges*.

"I'm a vampire," he smirked. "I don't like any apples. And Vanya?"

She raised her brows in a haughty expression.

"Not gonna happen."

She huffed. "I heard you the first time, and it's not your call."

He spun on his heels in a fluid, graceful motion, flicked a lock of unruly black-and-red hair behind his shoulder, and began to head toward the archway, out of the living room.

"Don't turn your back on me," she said, "and don't you dare walk away when we're in the middle of a discussion. This conversation is *not* over."

He kept right on strolling—no, sauntering—slinking like a cheetah out on a stroll, with nothing but sinew and muscle, and finely crafted bones, shifting with every forward step he took, *the cocky, hard-headed jackass!*

She flung the statue at the back of his head.

He spun around, caught it, and placed it gently on a nearby end table—a table he had built with his own two gifted hands—and then he turned his back again and continued walking.

"If you walk out of this room, I'll cut you off," she threatened, feeling exasperated, desperate, and mildly aroused. The nerve of him—who did he think he was?

"Cut me off from what?" he said, mockingly. "I don't think so, Vanya. I can smell your excitement from here."

She could've sworn her eyes actually crossed, and her ears were literally burning—she was going to kill the mongrel. "Saber, this is serious," she called after him. "The situation with Gwen and Fabian—Napolean's plan—you don't just get to dictate what happens going forward."

"I know it is serious," he answered, not bothering to look back. "And that's why my word is final. You and Ciopori are not going to meet alone with that vampire." He dragged his palm against the millwork as he crossed the threshold. "And as for anything else that happens, we'll cross those bridges as we come to them."

Vanya thought she saw red.

Or maybe it was just her pupils flashing.

"*Your word is final?*" she echoed angrily, tears welling up in her eyes. "You neither resemble my father, nor my king!" she shouted after him. "I don't think your *word* means Jack Diddly to me."

At this, he turned around in the doorway. "Jack Diddly? Really?" He furrowed his brow. "My father—the Dark One—had his heart ripped out right in front of me. The same was true for my brother, Dane. And as for my other sibling, Diablo; he tried to murder me outside my cave. You and I both lost everything and everyone we devoted the lion's share of our lives to, and we went through hell and then some coming together. And now, you wanna sidle up to some crazy, half-baked, violent mage, who may just be more powerful than Napolean, and take your chances that he'll remember the good times...respond like a loving father. Well, forgive me, princess, if I consider that ill-advised—and that's putting it delicately."

Vanya crossed her arms over her stomach and slowly nodded. "'Tis not your feelings I take issue with, dragon; the problem was in the delivery. At some point, you are going to have to learn: I am your partner, not your enemy. And when matters arise that are disagreeable...or even frightening...you need to turn to me, not against me."

He slumped against the archway and groaned. "Vanya..." His voice grew solemn, and his eyes clouded over. "If something..." He cleared his throat and tried again. "If something happened to you, I wouldn't make it. Do you hear what I'm saying—because that's all I've got—the best I can do. I'm trying to tell you something, the only way I know how. I wouldn't survive it, Vanya. I wouldn't. This vampire...this High Mage...he's not one to toy with. And bad shit can happen, faster than you or I can blink. Believe me, I know. I've lived it."

She took several calming breaths and extended her hand. "Saber, come here."

He shook his head. "I don't want your pity, princess—you know I can't stand that shit."

"I know that, dragon," she whispered. "And that's not what I'm doing...that's not what I'm offering. *Come here.*"

He took three or four steps inside the room before he halted, forcing her to meet him halfway.

Rolling her eyes and forcing a slight but ingratiating smile, she met him in the middle of the space. "My handsome sentinel," she whispered, wrapping her arms around his shoulders. "We will do this together, okay? Play it by ear as you suggested. Whatever happens—and should the time come when Ciopori and I come face-to-face with the High Mage—I will not do anything without consulting you first. But I want you to think about something in the meantime: Yes, animals can be dangerous, even lethal. They can be wild and feral and governed by instinct. But they can also be gentle and forgiving, and fiercely loyal. They have long, deeply imprinted memories that don't have to be conscious, like ours." She smiled and lowered her lashes. "How do you think I fell in love with a dragon? How do you think that wild beast fell in love with me?"

His coal-black gaze turned molten, and his hands trailed down her waist to her hips.

"I know Marquis and Ciopori will have the same discussion. These aren't easy times, and this is a harrowing situation. But you and I can get through it as long as we practice respect. I am not opposed to seeking your *mutual* consent, Saber, but that will never be the same thing as your permission. Do you understand?"

He cupped her jaw in his hand, bent his head to her mouth, and traced her top, then bottom, lip with his tongue.

She shivered. "Do you understand?"

He covered her mouth with his, kissed her until she was breathless, then snaked his hands beneath her dress, tearing the thin layer of lace he found into scraps.

She moaned and panted. "But, do you—"

He encircled her waist with one strong, muscular arm, placed the other hand beneath her bottom, and lifted her from the floor until she was seated, halfway up, against the ornate millwork. Holding her steady, he unfastened his jeans, slid between her thighs, and slowly pushed into her. "Yes, I understand," he groaned against her mouth.

And she could no longer remember what they had been arguing about to begin with.

CHAPTER TWELVE

"**G**ood evening, my dove. It would seem you slept the entire morning, afternoon, and twilight away."

Gwen rubbed her eyes, sat up slowly, and turned around to survey her sleeping pallet.

Where was she?

Oh, yeah, that was right—they were in a new cave behind a waterfall.

And Fabian had just said, *Good evening,* like a normal person. He had just called Gwen, *my dove.*

What gives?

She put her hand to her throat, feeling for the fresh, ragged puncture wounds—at least she remembered that much—but there was nothing but smooth, unmarred skin. "What happened, earlier?" she asked, and then feeling emboldened, she added, "And why are you so...sentient?"

He smirked, but his expression betrayed his discomfort with the topic. "You fell asleep after I fed, so I moved you to your sleeping mat, and then I peered inside your mind while I was still...sentient enough, as you put it...to retrieve a handful of important memories." He held up one hand to quell any rising anger. "Nothing too intimate, Gwen—nothing too personal—just twenty-first century *stuff*." He seemed imminently proud of that last word: *stuff*. Like he had just recited the modern Declaration of Independence—and for him, that would be a modern document.

Gwen gave in to her curiosity. "What kind of stuff?" she asked.

He smiled, actually smiled, then shook his head in wonder. "More than I cared to find," he admitted. "Automobiles, airplanes, telephones—*no, smartphones*—though I can't comprehend how an inanimate object can be smart; bartering markets —*nay, shopping malls*—and appliances that wash one's clothes and dishes. Your world is overwhelming, my dove." He shrugged, seemingly to dismiss the implications, and then he circled back to the most pertinent topic. "I was searching for a more appropriate fare, something you might enjoy more than rabbit, perhaps some parish—a village or a township—where humans gather to break bread, someplace I could frequent to hunt and *feed* to my heart's content. I was hoping to find a way to relieve you of this burden."

Now this got Gwen's attention.

She cocked her head to the side and studied him closely. Though still dirty, his hair had been combed, his eyes were far more alert, and his skin was positively radiant. "From the looks of it," she said, "you found it."

Damnit, why did she always sleep when he left her?

If she could just wake up...

Just once!

He frowned as if he knew what she was thinking, and then he turned his attention back to his outing. "I did find a township called Silverton Creek and a red-and-white tavern called 7-Eleven."

Gwen placed her hand to her mouth and coughed. *So much*

for the twenty-first century, she thought, careful to restrain any mocking laughter. But then her stomach grumbled at the thought of a convenience store.

Did he just say he had found a 7-Eleven?

She straightened abruptly, and her eyes started to water, the thought of familiar food nearly bringing her to tears. "Did you bring me something? Anything?"

He nodded briskly, and his enigmatic eyes nearly shimmered, metallic. "I brought you many things, Gwendolyn."

She was beginning to see a pattern—why he sometimes called her Gwen and sometimes called her Gwendolyn. The latter seemed to be more formal, when he was angry, or when he wanted to use her name as a term of endearment. "Well?" she asked, dismissing the thought. Her mind was still fixed on the 7-Eleven.

He rose from his perch beside a waning fire, strolled to the back of the cave, and returned with two plastic grocery bags filled with gently masked items. "What is this?" he asked, rustling the plastic. "I don't recall this...stuff...from your memories. As I said, I only sorted through a few."

This time, Gwen smiled. "It's plastic. Cheap plastic, actually. We use it a lot, and it creates many landfills."

"Landfills?" he asked.

She shook her head. "Can I explain it later." She pointed at the *plastic*. "What's in the bags?"

Fabian promptly dumped them both in the dirt, and then one by one, he held up the various items, the first being a container of chewable vitamins. "Last night, before you fell asleep, you were wondering about blood loss, concerned about vitamins." He frowned. "I hope to address both issues."

Gwen nodded. "Thank you," she said as he tossed them over.

And then he picked up a six-pack of V8, which made perfect sense when she thought about it—after all, the vegetables were right there on the cans. It was something the wizard could recognize. When he presented three overstuffed packets of beef jerky next, Gwen wanted to jump up and hug him.

Okay, well...*no*.

She didn't want to go anywhere near him.

But she had never been more grateful for anything in her life.

His pupils sparkled with amusement, and his facial expression softened to something tender, warm, and...seductive? "You're welcome," he drawled, and his voice sounded husky. He reached back into the pile, scooped up a comb, a brush, and a bar of soap, and tossed each item in Gwen's direction.

She caught all three, unerringly. "Well, this explains your hair," she said.

His entrancing expression darkened. "You noticed my hair?"

She quickly backtracked. "I, um...no...that's not what I meant."

He nodded slowly and mouthed the words: *Thank you.*

She shivered and looked away, but only for a few seconds—her curiosity continued to get the best of her. "What else?" she asked, pointing toward the pile.

He tossed a carton of Tic Tacs into her lap, and she blanched. "Tic Tacs!" she blurted. "What the hell, Fabian?" It was one thing to kidnap her from the well, whisk her to a hidden cave like he was Tarzan the ape man; it was another, still, to feed from her jugular, take her blood whenever he felt like it—whenever his mind got loopy, and he started seeing birds—but it was something altogether different to insult her, to imply that something... anything...was going to happen between them that would require an entire case of Tic Tacs!

And now that she really thought about it: the whole thing pissed her off.

The first time he did anything even halfway romantic, he ruined the gesture by pointing out the obvious: her hair, her appearance, and her stale cave-breath, something totally outside her control. Hell, despite the fact that they were both disheveled —Gwen probably looked like *who-dunnit?* and Fabian looked like he had been dragged through the paleo era by a wooly mammoth—for the most part, he still resembled a Greek Adonis: His body *never* emitted an odor, and his breath was always perfect.

She bristled inwardly.

Not everyone could be born a vampire.

And then her thoughts struck her, square in the head, like Lizzy Borden's axe: *The first time he did something halfway romantic, he ruined it? Her hair, her appearance, her breath?*

Who gave a shit!

What the hell was Gwen even thinking?

Fabian studied her more keenly than he ought to, his wizardly gaze appraising her thoughtfully, and then he gestured toward the carton of Tic Tacs. "Are those not medicinal nostrums? Are they not healing agents?" he asked. "I thought it might ease some of your various discomforts, the aches and stitches from sleeping on the ground."

Gwen frowned. "Oh. *Ohhh.* No, those are...something else." She forced a faint smile. "Something I can eat."

He nodded, but his countenance remained wary. "Apologies, Gwen. I would *never* insult you. You are exquisitely beautiful to me."

She stared at him like he had pie on his face.

Had Fabian Antonescu—the greatest wizard that ever lived— just apologized to Gwendolyn Hamilton? Something in her chest stirred, or maybe ached, and she quickly dismissed the unfamiliar sensation. "What else did you get?" she asked, staring fixedly at the remaining two items. She couldn't see them clearly in the shadows of the cave.

He lifted a fingernail file out of the dirt, then followed it up with a single Bic pen, extending both curious items in the palm of his hand.

Gwen shifted nervously on her sleeping pallet, a mixture of pine needles, leaves, and wild grass. "You got me a fingernail file?" she said, mockingly. "A fingernail file and a *Bic pen?*" What the heck did he expect her to do with those items?

"As I mentioned before, you were projecting your thoughts— your concerns about vitamins and loss of blood. Last night, outside the 7-Eleven tavern, a caravan of humans arrived in a"— he paused to search for the word—"in a *bus?* It was simple enough to bar the door and spare the women and children: I fed very well on a half-dozen men, maybe more. I have more than enough sustenance to replenish your blood."

"Oh, no!" she blurted, staring at the pen. Was he planning to remove the ink cartridge and the nib from inside the plastic casing, and use the latter as a catheter...as a tube? "If you're thinking what I think you are, the answer is absolutely not. No. *No.* No-no-no." There was no way Fabian was going to stick that pen in Gwen's arm—or worse, her neck, her thigh, or her throat— and try to give her a blood transfusion.

And just what the devil was he planning to do with the fingernail file?

The corner of his mouth curled up in a devious smile. "They didn't have any lancets...any blades...any *knives.*"

She felt the blood rush out of her cheeks, and she knew her complexion had turned pale. She didn't even want to ask what the *knife* was for. "Please, Fabian," she whispered, her voice sounding scratchy, "no blood and no knives, okay? I'm very appreciative of the drinks and the jerky, and the soap will go a long way toward making me more comfortable." She hoped her sudden manners—her cordial approach—was enough to keep his mind off her worries over blood loss. "Do you mind?" she added, pointing at the six-pack of V8.

Fabian slid the case of cans across the cave floor, then followed it up by pitching the jerky onto her pallet. "Eat," he encouraged. "Drink. Once you have had your fill, I wish to fulfill my promise: to take you to the waterfall to bathe." He glanced down at his own filthy tunic and trousers. "I am in need of a good scrubbing, myself."

* * *

Nachari Silivasi drifted in and out of sleep at Kagen's clinic, following his harrowing ordeal at Napolean's manse just sixteen hours earlier. His brother, the Ancient Master Healer, had brought him back to the Dark Moon Vale Clinic just as a precaution: to go over the handiwork, performed on Napolean's conference table, with a fine-tooth comb in a more clinical and advantageous environment, to make sure Nachari's heart and throat healed swiftly and perfectly under constant—and diligent —supervision.

No one was willing to take a chance on Nachari's full recovery, especially when the king wanted the Master Wizard to go back in, seek Fabian and Gwen again, first thing tomorrow morning at eight o'clock. This would allow Nachari exactly twenty-eight hours to regain his strength and replenish his blood loss—twenty-four hours as a precaution, and four extra hours to prepare...

And while he honestly didn't feel like he needed that much sleep, his father and his brothers had insisted. And so the Master Wizard had rested, dozed, and dreamed, his spirit taking over while his body recuperated.

At first, his dreams had been ordinary: Deanna rising in the morning, the sun setting behind the brownstone at dusk, the rustle of leaves in the trees, anchored into the canyon behind the secluded home. And then they had turned more ominous...more instructive...like clues being left for the Master Wizard by a higher, celestial power: Gwen's distinct, narrow footprints cluttering the ingress about the familiar Red Canyons; a strand of blonde hair floating down into a pine tree; the scent of birch, juniper, and spruce rising in the smoke of a fire, intermixed with traces of Gwen's perspiration and pheromones.

Why did this matter?

Julien, of course.

The valley's best tracker would not need to wait for Nachari's signal, for information garnered the next time Nachari traced her blood. As a result of the Master Wizard's dreams—Gwen's footprints, her scent, and a strand of her hair had to be nestled in that particular stretch of forest—Deanna had promptly given Julien Gwen's sweatshirt, her hairbrush, and a detailed, chemical imprint of her body chemistry, and the tracker could now find her in five minutes or less if he started at the Red Canyons and worked his way in. And that meant Nachari and Napolean could concentrate solely on distracting Fabian.

The dreams had given the house of Jadon more than enough to go on, yet the visons had not stopped there.

Somewhere between deep sleep and waking, between delta waves, alpha waves, and beta, the images had become more obscure, yet more insistent: the Dark Moon Vale forest shrouded in a pale yellow Harvest Moon, the ancient mage, Fabian, eclipsing the lunar sphere, and Salvatore Nistor, the dark sorcerer of the house of Jaegar, peering into his crystal orb. And then the orb had exploded into a thousand fragments of glass, and the glass coalesced into the outline of two birds: a glorious hawk with magnificent dark-brown wings, and a midnight-black raven with a stark, onyx gaze.

A gaze filled with madness, vengeance, and contempt.

Nachari had no idea what the night visions meant, and truthfully, Kagen had given him some powerful drugs.

Still, he was wary...and aware.

When Saber Alexiares had been returned to the house of Jadon, after living for eight hundred years with the Dark Ones, he had brought an invaluable secret with him, a trove of hidden treasure: knowledge about the lycans, the land of Mhier, and the fact that Keitaro Silivasi may still be living. The Silivasi brothers had been able to mine that treasure and, at long last, bring their beloved sire home.

Fabian Antonescu had a secret of his own, only it felt more like a trojan horse than a treasure chest filled with gold. At the end of the day, his powers, his feral nature, and his imminent Blood Moon with Gwen might only be the tip of the iceberg...

CHAPTER THIRTEEN

Gwen stood beneath the roaring waterfall, shielding her breasts with one arm, her most intimate...*secrets*...with the other, and shaking from head to toe. She couldn't believe Fabian had possessed the nerve to undress her, or that he expected her to bathe her entire body while he just stood there, behind her...that he had already taken it upon himself to soap and rinse her hair, and the entire escapade was taking place in a frigid, torrential spray. If something didn't give, she was going to turn into an icicle.

"It's too cold!" she called, glancing over her shoulder to plead with her eyes.

He hung his head and shook it slowly. "Apologies, my dove. Perhaps my earlier *feeding*, outside the tavern, is beginning to wear off." He raised both hands, leaned toward her, and she jumped.

"What are you doing?"

The corner of his mouth quirked up in a half glower, half smile, and he slid both palms into the waterfall, about two feet above her head, while closing his eyes. The torrent lost its frosty bite, and then it slowly began to warm...and slow down...until a soothing, gentle, hot stream of water began to sluice over her shoulders and run down her back.

Despite her trepidation, Gwen sighed. "Keep your eyes closed," she admonished him.

His smile broadened. "As you wish."

"Promise me, Fabian."

He chuckled. "You have my vow."

Distrustful that he would stick to the promise, she began to lather her body in earnest, careful not to use too much soap at once—who knew when Fabian would get another bar. The gentle vanilla scent smelled heavenly as it finally washed away the stench from the well, but it felt pasty and dull against her shoulder-length blonde locks, and she wasn't sure if the water was still flowing fast enough to rinse it all out. What she wouldn't have given for a bottle of salon-grade shampoo and conditioner.

And a towel.

What did Fabian expect her to do when the "shower" was over, and her clothes were still drying on a nearby rock? Moonlight wasn't exactly as effective as sunshine.

"Allow me." His voice was thick and husky against her ear. And then he tunneled one hand in her hair and splayed his fingers, gently separating her matted tresses. The water remained warm—and gentle—as he redirected the flow to rinse each parting, one by one, proceeding slowly and systematically while massaging her scalp. "Is that better?"

Gwen gulped.

When he bent to press a tender kiss along the nape of her neck, just above the curve in her shoulder, she squealed.

He chuckled.

And then he traced a line along the very same curve, trailed the tips of his fingers down her shoulders, along her arm, and covered her hand with his. Call it curiosity—call it common sense

—the natural, healthy survival instinct to keep one's eyes on a nearby predator, she couldn't help but subtly twist her body, angled toward his, to watch: her arms still covering her private places.

He took the bar of soap and stepped back—*thank goodness!*—before crossing his wrists, grasping the hem of his tunic with both hands, and peeling it over his head.

Gwen gawked.

She had seen him before, that first night by the firelight, his tunic being drenched and translucent, but up close and personal, completely unclad, his burnished bronze skin nearly sparkled in the moonlight. His stomach quivered, and her eyes followed the motion instinctively. He didn't have ribs; he had an eight-pack, every hard abdominal muscle distinct and defined, over baby-smooth skin and narrowing hips.

Narrowing hips...

Oh Lord, he was hooking his thumbs beneath the cinch in his trousers—

He wouldn't dare!

Not right there in front of Gwen, not when she was already so exposed and vulnerable.

The garment fell away, and Gwen took a generous step back, trying to disappear beneath the waterfall. He lathered the soap in his hands, coated his hair with the suds, then began to rub circles —and lines and swirls—along his shoulders, his chest, then his arms.

Gwen felt awkward...and angry...and extremely uncomfortable. She was having a hard time drawing deep breaths. "Do you mind," she snarled, covering her eyes with one hand, even as her other arm continued to lay at an angle, crosswise over her breasts and lower belly.

He didn't smile or smirk; he just turned around.

Slowly, like a lazy jungle cat.

And then he arched his back, stretched his neck, and let the water sluice through his hair.

Gwen told herself not to glance downward. The last thing she cared to do was watch the batshit-crazy wizard taking a shower, but...but the globes in his ass...were those really gluteus maximus? Because, short of plastic surgery or implants, that kind of definition was impossible. And the curve in his lower back, the musculature in his hips and thighs, to say nothing of his back and his shoulders...

Shit...

He washed, rinsed, then turned back around—and as she backpedaled to create even greater distance between them, Gwen stepped right off the ledge.

Fabian was doing his damnedest not to stare at his *destiny*—after all, she had asked him to look away. Still, he couldn't help but notice that even as she covered her eyes, she left enough space between her fingers to peek at him.

And oh, was she peeking...and studying.

However, he knew he had to be careful—keep a diligent watch on his instincts—suppress the carnal desire to seduce her: The enormous amount of blood he had taken from the caravan of humans was sustaining his sanity for now, keeping the darkness and the fog at bay, but there was no telling what might happen in an hour...or two...and seducing Gwen would require a great deal of time, skillful patience, and energy. Not to mention, he had yet to convert the maiden. One momentary lapse in judgment, one feral slip in consciousness, and he could destroy her in forty-eight hours. A pregnancy was not something to toy with, not when Fabian's demons still haunted him so ferociously, and the darkness would not grant him clemency.

He was just about to reach for his clothes, scrub them with the bar of soap, then clad both himself and Gwen in a magical robe so they could dry off in modesty by the fire, when the odd, enigmatic female stepped right off the edge of the waterfall and tumbled backward toward the rocky basin below.

Fabian's wings shot out of his back, and he dove after Gwen, hurtling at a speed that surpassed the barrier of sound. In silence, he came up beneath her, wrapped both arms around her soft, slender waist, and tugged upward, just as she was about to strike a particularly craggy boulder.

"*Destinul meu*," he breathed in her ear, sighing with deep relief, and then he flew back to the ledge, snatched both sets of their clothing, and sailed back into the cave. One wave of his hand, and the fire was roaring. A second wave, and they were both cloaked in gossamer robes. He laid out their true, corporeal garments as close to the blaze as possible and ran his hands over her shoulders to stave off the chill. "What the hell were you thinking?" he scolded.

Her light-green eyes grew wide with shock. "I wasn't...I wasn't thinking anything," she panted, the terror in her voice so stark. She blinked several times, and her thick, dark-brown lashes coated with crystalline tears.

"Shh," Fabian whispered, drawing her into his arms. "You're safe now, Gwendolyn. There has been no harm. Quiet, little one. Be still." She shivered and laid her head on his chest, and he felt his heartbeat respond to her nearness—was this the first time she had ever relied on him, let go of her suspicion, or at least sought his comfort?

He didn't want to move.

He didn't want to breathe.

He didn't want anything to disturb the moment...

At last, she took several deep, calming breaths and slowly withdrew from his arms. "Thank you," she mumbled, padding toward the fire and warming her hands beside the flames. "For moving so quickly...for saving my life." She cringed. "I really thought I was a goner."

He cocked his head to the side. *A goner?* He was unfamiliar with the term, but he got the gist—she thought she was going to die on the rocks. "Never, beautiful one," he murmured. "Not in my care. You do know I would protect you from anything, don't you? I *will* protect you from anything."

She sighed and continued to stare into the flames. "Anything, but you," she murmured, slowly shaking her head. "From anything, but the fog...and the darkness...and your demons. Whatever it is that haunts you and robs you of your reason." She rubbed her hands together, then extended them again, dropping down to squat in place as if the fire was truly soothing.

Fabian shut his eyes. "Do you really think I could strike out at you in one of my feral states?" He was asking himself as much as he was asking her. "That I would *feed* to the point of extinguishing your life, or that I would be too unaware to come to your aid?" He opened his eyes and stared at her.

She cocked both brows. "I don't know. Would you? Could you? Have you not been brutal?"

He blanched and narrowed his gaze, looking as much *past her* as at her. "How was I brutal, Gwen? When did I strike you?"

She sighed and met his gaze with her peripheral vision. "Fabian..." She was quiet for the space of several heartbeats. "You grabbed me by my ankles and dragged me through the dirt. You flipped me over and pinned me to the ground. You fed until I eventually passed out. If that wasn't brutal, then I don't know what is. You don't have to strike someone to hurt them."

Fabian practically recoiled inside.

He had done all of that—and worse.

Only it wasn't him...it wasn't conscious...it wasn't the male, nor the wizard, but the vampire in the throes of savage madness.

He...

Fabian Antonescu...

Would never choose to harm this woman, yet what she said made sense: If he wasn't aware enough to make such choices, then how could either of them know that he wouldn't harm her—how could she ever come to trust him? And was he even worthy of such trust?

He wanted to be.

Gods knew...

But he had spent so many centuries sleeping in the earth: dreaming, traveling, deteriorating...

And his hunger rose so rapidly—so ravenous, stark, and out of control.

The need to keep the secrets within the fog at bay was always, *always* paramount.

"When I was nine, maybe ten," Gwen said in a whisper, drawing Fabian out of his musings, "my father had a secret. He was a good man, or at least he tried to be—but at some point, he got caught up in gambling." She oscillated one hand in the air as if thinking with her fingers. "Being reckless with money...making bets."

Fabian nodded. He understood this concept, noblemen partaking in games of chance and often forfeiting large sums of gold.

"It wasn't the gambling that I understood so much," she continued, "but the toll it was taking on our family. At first, we just couldn't go out to dinner, and then we couldn't shop for new clothes. After a while, it started showing up in other ways: late mortgage payments, fewer groceries, and having the electricity turned off a time or two." This time, she sighed and rubbed her brow. "My father couldn't always make the rent, put food on our table, or keep enough oil in the lanterns...light the candles." She shook her head. "As I told you before, I did not grow up poor, so it was really evident when he was gambling."

Fabian moved slowly toward the fire and took a seat beside her, careful to remain an arm's length away. He studied her exotic green eyes, noticing how the firelight danced in their shadowy reflection—these were not easy memories to speak of.

"Anyhow," she pressed on, "I later learned that he gambled so much money—lost so much currency—that he had started borrowing from a really bad man, and every so often, that man would come to our house in a long black limousine—a wealthy man's carriage—and speak to my father quite aggressively." She bit her lower lip. "Eventually, it got so bad that the man began to threaten my father, and that's the first time I remember truly feeling fear, knowing it deep down, inside my gut. I don't remember when...or how...my mother found out. I just remember she used to argue with my father, and eventually, she threatened to leave him. That was when my father decided to quit gambling, when he really got serious about making it happen. But by then, he was so far in debt." Gwen lowered her body to the ground, rocking out of her squat, and sat with her legs crossed beneath her, her hands placed gently in her lap. "You have to understand, my mother was a very beautiful woman, and my father was really, really trying, but the bad man —the one with the long, dark carriage—he wouldn't leave us alone." Her shoulders stiffened, and her voice became rote, like she was pushing her next words out by force. "One morning, when I was on my way to school, I looked back toward our driveway and noticed the limousine. My father was already at work, and I remember cringing...feeling fear...wondering if I should go back inside and try to protect my mother. But I was too scared to move, to decide either way, so I slipped behind a nearby hedge of bushes and just watched... I watched as my mother came out the front door, dressed in one of her most beautiful dresses, and I watched as she climbed into the back of the limousine and smiled at that monster of a man. Actually smiled. And then I sat there for hours, too stunned to get up, just trying to figure it out in my head. Eventually, the limousine came back, my mother climbed out, and she turned around to kiss the bad man. She went back into the house, closed the door behind her, and we never saw or heard from him again. The gambling stopped, and so did the bad man's visits. But my mom's secret—the way she had paid for my father's debts—it was almost worse than the betting. It saturated our home in darkness, and it was every bit as thick as your fog."

She raised her chin and looked right at Fabian. "I guess what I'm saying is this: I got lucky. Eventually my parents talked, and they even sought therapy—when people seek a healer of the mind, a wise counselor who can help them banish their demons—and we ended up okay. I got my family back...my life back...and at least what was left of my childhood. But Fabian, I do know this much: those secrets...those demons...those things we keep hidden in the dark, they don't go away, and they don't eventually just fade into the background on their own. Unless and until we bring them into the light, they can haunt us forever."

She turned back toward the fire and sighed. "My dad's affliction almost destroyed our family, and my mother's secret could have destroyed us all. At some point, you're going to have to leave this cave—*the last one, the next one, running away*—and figure out what it is that's haunting you. Who is the bad man in your figurative memory? Why do the raven and the hawk haunt your dreams? What are you running from that your mind won't let you confront? Because until you face it, you can't protect me...or anybody else. You can't even live like a vampire or a wizard. You're just lost in the dark, and I'm lost with you. And all the *feeding* in the world won't chase that away."

Fabian swallowed hard.

He swallowed his rising anger, and he swallowed his wounded pride.

And he swallowed his *destiny's* words.

"Your family," he grunted, his voice sounding hoarse. "They are good now? Your parents are yet together?"

Her expression softened, and she smiled faintly. "They are. And they love each other dearly."

He nodded, at least taking solace in how the story had turned out; although, gods knew, he might later want to revisit this...*bad man.* "And do you think...if I somehow banished my demons...in time, you would come to love me?"

She jolted in place, and he had his answer.

No, Gwen was not looking for a way to love him, or to stay with him. More than anything in the world, she was still looking to escape, an eventuality he could never allow to happen. Still, she was weary of living such a piteous existence, the captive of a male who couldn't even control his...brutality.

He rose from the floor of the cavern and paced to the back of the cave.

His hunger was gnawing at him again, and his vision was beginning to dim.

The fog...the cursed inky darkness...was rising like the morning tide.

"Gwendolyn," he snarled, spinning around. "Sleep, my dove. Take refuge for a time."

Her head rolled back on her shoulders, her lashes floated downward, and her body slumped over in the direction of the fire.

Fabian lunged and caught her just in time.

Curse the celestial ancestors, he had almost harmed her again!

He carried her gently to her sleeping pallet and laid her down on the aromatic, grassy mat—at least the pine needles were softer than the ground. He might be a vampire—*he might be a monster*

—but he would not be as the man who violated Gwen's mother. He would not take his sustenance from her vein again, not when he could return to the township and hunt the local human population at will...and to his heart's content.

He just wished she understood.

He wished *he* understood.

Some demons were far too menacing to confront.

Some secrets were too deeply buried to resurrect.

Some truths were meant to remain untold.

CHAPTER FOURTEEN

ONE HOUR LATER...

Napolean Mondragon was seated on the formal sofa of his private rectory, enjoying the peace and stillness of the night as Brooke and their three sons, Phoenix, Paris, and Parker, settled on the floor by the fire to assemble a new toy castle, complete with a drawbridge, horses, and a dozen armored knights. He had just settled into the thick, embroidered cushions and put his feet up on the ottoman when an insistent drone murmured in his head—a telepathic *knock-knock*, as it were—resounding against his left hemisphere.

Milord. The voice belonged to Nachari Silivasi, and Napolean immediately glanced out the window to appraise the sky: It was nearing ten o'clock, eighteen hours since the Master Wizard's surgery—the king hoped everything was going all right.

Nachari, are you well? Have you been resting, healing? Preparing for tomorrow morn?

Nachari sighed. *Yes, milord. And thank you for asking. I apologize for interrupting your family time, but my king—the girl is alone.*

Napolean sat up straight, planting both feet firmly on the

floor. *Who do you mean, Nachari? Are you referring to Fabian's destiny, to Gwen?*

Yes, Nachari answered. *Off and on, throughout the day, in between sleeping and talking with my family, I've closed my eyes, felt for Gwen's imprint, and simply peeked from a distance through the blood link. I have not approached the couple or made my presence known—I think I learned my lesson the first time— but I have sought to check in, to make sure the female's heart is still beating and the two of them are still in the vale.*

Napolean nodded, pleased with the report. Of course, Nachari would remain diligent, even as his body was healing. *And last you checked, the female was alone... How long ago was this, Nachari?*

Maybe a couple of minutes...five at the most.

Napolean rubbed his jaw in contemplation. *And are you certain the Ancient is away from the girl—he isn't just masking his presence or cloaking his spirit? This could very well be a ruse to deceive you...to keep all of us unbalanced.*

Oh no, Nachari answered quickly, *Fabian's presence is unmistakable. It's hard to explain, but masking it entirely would be a bit like hiding the sun from the sky. Even if you can't see it, you can feel it. Both by the temperature it creates and the ensuing radiation. He isn't within a thousand feet of her—I'm sure of it.*

Napolean considered the Master Wizard's words carefully: So, Fabian had left Gwen's side for a time, most likely to go hunting or scavenging, to bring back necessities for the woman's survival—she was still human after all.

Or maybe she wasn't...

It was of no matter.

The Ancient would not take any chances while leaving her alone: He would surround their settlement with powerful wards to keep out animals or potential intruders, and he would definitely put the woman to sleep, make sure nothing was going to wake her in his absence. *Great Corona Borealis, Julien and the sentinels could get her out of there without another dangerous confrontation, without requiring Nachari to face off with Fabian as a decoy...without the necessity of Napolean leaving his body to provide the youngest Silivasi with backup.*

And Julien already possesses the girl's sweatshirt, hairbrush, and knowledge of her distinct, quintessential chemistry? Napolean asked. *He knows where to start in the Red Canyons, the placement of the footprints in your dream, and he is yet ready to track at my command?*

Absolutely, Nachari answered. *And if I know Ramsey, Saxson, Santos, and Saber, they've already run through the logistics a dozen times. They would not have waited until tomorrow morning to get started on a plan.* He paused as if carefully considering his next words. *I'm not trying to imply that this is the best route to go, or that I've even considered all the unknown variables. I just wanted to make you aware, milord; Gwen is alone right now.*

Napolean knew that it might be best to proceed more methodically, line up his warriors, and prepare each advancement, each potentially perilous action, with razor-fine precision. Fabian Antonescu was not a vampire to trifle with. Yet and still, the opportunity was golden, and serendipity was nothing to scoff at. If the sentinels went in now—and they failed—Fabian would be on to them. He could take the girl halfway across the continent, and the house of Jadon would be none the wiser: They would be forced to go forward, living their daily lives, never knowing if and when he was out there, whether he might one day return or attack someone in the valley. Just the same, Napolean knew Julien Lacusta, and in all the king's centuries of living, he had never known a better tracker. Moreover, he knew Ramsey, Saxson, Santos, and Saber—the vampires were precision on wings and laser-focused. If they had one goal—to get in and out in the blink of an eye, retrieve the female, and bring her back, beyond the ceremonial chambers, to the holding cell adjacent to the watch room, where Fabian could not easily gain access—the males would not fail in their mission.

And if something went wrong?

If Fabian returned at the most inopportune moment...

If Napolean's warriors were forced to fight such a great and imposing High Mage...

Well, *"hiding the sun from the sky,"* indeed. It may be night, and the golden orb might be facing the other side of the planet, but Napolean could still draw from its might. He did not want to face the powerful mage—vampire-to-vampire; lord-to-lord; one ancient celestial progeny to another—but if it came down to it, he would.

Nachari, alert Keitaro, Marquis, Kagen, and Nathaniel. Also get in touch with your fellow wizards: Jankiel Luzanski and Niko Durciak. I want everyone awake, alert, and ready to act in an instant, whether that's somewhere out in the Dark Moon Forest or here at the manse, surrounding the lower chambers. In fact, put Kristos Nastase and Rafael Dzuna on standby as well, just in case we require a couple more warriors. If need be, I will call every male in the house of Jadon to aid in this mission, but I don't think it's necessary...quite yet. I will speak to Julien and the sentinels directly, so be prepared, Master Wizard. I know we wanted to give you at least six more-hours to recuperate entirely, but I want you and Deanna here at the manse, waiting for the female's arrival— Braden and Kristina can call upon her later. Gwen knows Deanna, and on some level, she has to feel she can trust her. I will be counting on your destiny to explain much of what is happening and to provide whatever is necessary for the female's comfort— Brooke will readily assist her. And as for you, Master Wizard, I think it goes without saying: I have no intentions of grabbing this tiger by the tail—inciting Fabian Antonescu—without a skilled magician, my own practitioner of magic, right by my side at all times. So prepare to remain at the manse indefinitely if needed.

With that, Napolean closed the communication—he didn't have a moment more to spare on protocol and pleasantries. *Julien!* he barked next, soliciting the tracker's telepathic attention, even as he waved his hand to capture his mate's gaze and followed it up with a somber wink. "Listen in, my love," he whispered insistently. "I'm about to reach out to Julien and the sentinels, and I won't have time to repeat what's happening. Suffice to say—we're going in to get Gwen right now."

CHAPTER FIFTEEN

Having been summoned by the Vampyr king, Julien Lacusta kissed Rebecca, his little mouse, on the forehead, then slid out of bed. He headed straight to the large en suite bathroom where he slipped on a pair of faded gray jeans, a matching cotton T-shirt, and a pair of heavy black tactical boots. Careful to walk as silently as a large, prowling cat through a jungle, he exited the bathroom, padded through the master bedroom, and traversed the broad, wooden planks in the long, dimly lit hall, peeking in on his son, Jayce Gideon, as he passed the nursery.

Yep, everything at the home front was airtight. Rebecca had already come to expect—and simply roll with—Julien's frequent, spur-of-the-moment, late-night forays, and he would use the remote, created by Santos Olaru and Nachari Silivasi, to trip both the alarms and the wards on his way out the door.

He grabbed a small canvas backpack from the entryway closet—one already containing Gwen Hamilton's sweatshirt, hairbrush, and by default, her chemical imprint—as well as his own familiar tracking gear and well-used battle-axe. He slid the pack effortlessly over his shoulder, his muscles instinctively bunching, as they always did, with both tension and anticipation for the upcoming hunt. Palming the small remote attached to the pack, he triggered the alarms and glanced absently over his shoulder, eyeing the high wooden beams and thick, circular posts—the former, hovering above; the latter, standing sentinel in the entryway foyer—and then he transported directly into the Dark Moon Forest, materializing about five hundred yards southwest of the Red Canyons.

He copped a squat.

He placed both hands, palms down, in the dirt.

He stood back up and sniffed the air—countless dry, damp, and aged scents—analyzing, sifting, categorizing, and discarding... keeping only those olfactory imprints that pertained to Gwen. Then he spun around in a 360-degree arc as he began to scan the soil, the bushes, the rocks, and the trees, his moonstone-gray eyes emitting soft red beams as he toggled between supernatural and infrared vision, recording everything he saw, sensed, and felt.

Nine paces forward.

He angled to the left.

He held out his hands—palms down, yet again—and copped another squat.

Yeah, there it was...

Right beneath his fingertips: two female footprints exhibiting bilateral variation. Not only did the size and depth of the prints give the gender away, but the swipe of the left heel, the backward brush of the right toes...the female had been backing up...backing away, hurrying to escape from something.

Julien followed the pattern to the base of an aspen tree—Gwen had placed her hands on this tree; she had leaned back against it—his eyes shifted unerringly to a delicate, quaking leaf, curled in the shape of a spade, and he saw a minute follicle dangling over the stem, two centimeters long, maybe three, of a shed blonde hair. He didn't need to check Gwen's brush to match the strand to the human female's follicles—*it was Gwen's all right.*

He rubbed the strand between his thumb and his forefinger, then turned his attention back to the ground, back to the retrograde footprints.

He wouldn't need to follow them like a human hunter. The energetic vortex was still in the air, which was something human's didn't get. Despite their fairly advanced knowledge of science—a force in motion remains in motion with the same speed and in the same direction, unless acted upon by a counterforce—they still believed that "hauntings," the lingering presence of spectral activity, indicated a malevolent force that was trying to harm them, a ghost hoping to frighten them away, when much of the time these kinetic sightings were energetic cinemas, movies playing on a circular feed, quantum energy repeating a familiar pattern...over and over...like a broken reel of film.

No matter.

Julien could track Gwen's initial, then lingering, fear as well as Fabian's flight, which had been seeped in a vortex of rage as he'd scooped the human girl up in his arms and carried her away, heading...heading?

Northeast.

Five minutes, maybe seven, and Julien would be at Fabian's cave—he would have a set of precise coordinates to send to the sentinels and the Master Wizards.

Shrugging his shoulders to release some tension, he glanced up toward the heavens and sent out a celestial prayer: *Lord Hercules, if it pleases thee, please don't let Fabian return too soon.*

* * *

"Wards, brother." Niko Durciak leaned into the threshold of his housemate's bedroom, murmuring the obvious to Jankiel Luzan-ski. He braced both forearms against the upper doorframe and flashed his signature million-dollar smile, the one that always made his twin dimples stand out. "Nachari traced the girl's blood from the clinic," Niko continued, "just a subtle sneak peek, nothing intrusive, but he found her alone in the cave. The tracker is already in the forest, and the king says, *Now*. Nachari's headed to the mansion to help Napolean deal with the girl and intercept Fabian, should the need arise. You and I? We're unraveling Fabian's wards, checking the cave for any mystical traps."

"Shit," Jankiel murmured, rubbing the sleep out of two light-gray eyes that tended to sparkle like quartz—except for when the vampire got serious, like right now—then the soft gray orbs turned smoky and turbulent.

Odd, Niko thought, his mind meandering as it often did: *two Master Wizards, sharing a domicile, each with gray eyes; one, the light crystal hue of a quartz; the other, the hard, granite palette of pyrite.*

And then there was Julien Lacusta, the tracker, eyes the color of moonstone...

Also gray...

So triple grays, heading into an ancient mage's cave...

Coincidence?

Maybe.

But maybe not.

As a practitioner of magick, nothing went unnoticed to Niko Durciak; he listened to all six senses intensely, and something in his sapient soul said, *Not on purpose, but a sign just the same...a mark of divination: Nothing is black or white with this ancient vampire, this infamous High Mage from a time long gone. He's mired in the shadows, locked away from the light. Everything we're dealing with is shades of gray.*

"Got some sort of epiphany?" Jankiel asked, eyeing Niko sideways even as he sat on the edge of the bed, laced up his boots, and folded the hems of his faded blue jeans over the laces. He stood up, snatched a long-sleeve, pullover hoodie from an adjacent hang-around-chair and slipped it over his head.

"Nah," Niko answered. And then feeling the need to be a little more formal, he repeated: "No."

Jankiel raised his dark, honey-brown eyebrows, the stiff, clean arches that matched his chin-length hair, and one corner of his mouth quirked up in a smile. "All gray eyes," he murmured.

Niko chuckled. "Yes."

"Yeah," Jankiel pondered aloud, "this Ancient is shrouded in secrets, Niko, and it's not just the obvious—the fact that he ascended out of a stone well after all these centuries, the fact that he lived before, during, and after the Curse. This guy has secrets rooted to Dark Moon Vale."

As if they'd done it a hundred times before—and truth be told, they probably had—Jankiel fell into an easy, quiet step behind Niko, following him out of the suite and into the sleek, marble-tiled hall. They rounded the corner in silence, entered the foyer, and opened the entryway closet, snatching satchels full of cryptic objects and talismans...dusters and weapons...stone and wooden containers, inscribed in archaic symbols and filled with dried, sacramental blood.

"When we enter the cave," Niko said solemnly, "we're gonna have to move swiftly. I'll clear the first three cardinal directions: north, south, and east. You take the latter three—west, above, and below."

The two Master Wizards exited the heavy glass-and-titanium front door, and Niko turned around to set the wards and alarms with his handprint. The polished white-granite manor house, set tastefully amongst elaborate gardens, modern fountains, and a meandering lap pool that wound around the entire manor, would remain safe and sound on the easternmost edge of Dark Moon Vale until the two Master Wizards returned.

Hopefully...

Prayerfully...

Having aided their king in recovering Gwendolyn Hamilton and setting a trap—or at least providing an extremely tempting lure—for Fabian Antonescu.

And may the celestial gods be merciful, Niko thought, even as he locked on to an incoming telepathic transmission—Julien had just successfully tracked the girl to the cave, and he was broadcasting images and coordinates to all the relevant vampires. *Please let Fabian be reasonable...sentient...at least capable of regaining lucidity.* Because there could be nothing more invaluable, more life-changing or inspirational to a Master Wizard than an opportunity to at some point meet, and learn from, the greatest mage that had ever lived.

"You got it, Niko?" Jankiel's sonorous voice.

"Yeah, I've got it," Niko replied.

"Then may Lord Aquarius"—Jankiel's ruling deity—"and the power or Lyra"—Niko's governing lord—"give us strength, wisdom, and perfection of purpose."

"I'll second that," Niko said.

And the two vampires vanished from view.

CHAPTER SIXTEEN

Arms folded across his chest, feet a shoulder's width apart, Saber Alexiares stood behind the roaring waterfall, outside the cave where Fabian Antonescu had been keeping Gwen Hamilton, and scanned the crevasse below like a hawk or, rather, a sentinel, to be more exact.

Ramsey, Saxson, and Santos Olaru had started out maybe eight, possibly ten steps inside the cave, in front of Saber, eyeing the High Mage's dwelling like three amped-up predators while waiting for Niko Durciak and Jankiel Luzanski to clear away the wards. *And damn,* Saber thought, a low, unwitting growl emanating from the base of his throat, *it was a good thing they all had the Master Wizards with them.* Saber had almost stepped right into a psychic bear trap of sorts, dead center, toward the entrance of the cave. The way Niko had reacted when he had spun around, dropped into a squat, and thrust both palms outward, sending Saber flying backward before his feet hit the ground—some kind of wizardly magic, Saber figured. The damn thing would've likely snapped Saber's ankle in half, maybe severed his foot from his body.

As if the invisible bear trap had not been enough, the cave had then filled with fog—and not the ordinary, thick, vaporous gray cloud that just happens to touch the ground. This stuff had swirled and undulated, risen up like the crest of a wave or the head of a cobra—and appeared to look around...to slither about. Ramsey, Saxson, and Santos had backpedaled out of the space like three pubescent human boys in a grisly haunted house —*screw it!*—planting their proud warriors' feet firmly at the cave entrance, next to Saber instead, and refusing to budge while Niko and Jankiel hurried through one spell after another, trying to clear the viscous mist.

The harder the Master Wizards worked—the faster they conjured spells, each magician acutely aware that they were up against time—the more weird and noxious shit appeared: spiders that could leap several feet at a time and stand up on the back two of their eight spindly legs; sinkholes opening up beneath the wizards' feet as they shuffled about the cavern, unraveling wards, checking their scrying mirrors, or tossing some of kind of ancient stones that looked like runes; and the freakiest of all...*eyeballs!* Dozens and dozens of large, almond-shaped, blood-red eyeballs peering out through the various stony ledges and rocky membranes of the cave.

Niko had actually walked up to those creepy, unpleasant things, waved his hand over each scarlet pair, and closed the craggy lids.

No...

Just no, Saber thought.

An eerie chill crept up his spine as memories of living in the Dark Ones' Colony and his occasional—inevitable—interactions with Salvatore Nistor crossed his mind. The dragon, which was the name Vanya and most of the house of Jadon had taken up calling Saber, didn't mind fighting an enemy, any enemy, no matter the rival's strength or power, but toying around with magick, sorcery, a vampire who could wield unseen energies in ways even the best of soldiers—and warriors—could not?

Nah...

Saber would rather let sleeping dogs lie.

Speaking of sleeping dogs, or sleeping girls as it were, according to Jankiel Luzanski, Gwen was still out like a light, curled up on a woven-grass pallet toward the back of the cavern, next to a pile of weird, sundry items stacked atop a plastic grocery bag: a comb, a brush, and a used bar of soap—nothing too strange about that—a bottle of chewable vitamins, a can of V8, and a half-eaten packet of beef jerky. *Okay...* That might make some sense too, all things considered, but the carton of Tic Tacs, the fingernail file, and the unused Bic pen?

What the actual—

Saber shook his head.

Didn't matter.

What mattered to the sentinels and to the king, to Napolean, was the fact that Gwen was asleep by compulsion, and according to Jankiel, there were no cryptic spells or magical potions involved, just a typical vampire coercion, inducing the female to remain asleep for at least a couple of hours.

Saber could only hope it was a sign, a positive omen, that it meant Fabian intended to be gone for at least that long. And based on the pile of assorted crap piled beside her, they all had a pretty good guess where the Ancient had gone: likely to *feed* and to forage for Gwen.

No sooner had the thought cleared his mind than Niko's voice echoed from the back of the humid cavern. "The cave is clear."

Jankiel's sonorous tone followed in quick succession, even as the five-hundred-plus-year-old vampire swept his hand through his unkempt hair—he had clearly crawled straight out of bed before transporting to the cave. "The girl is good to go as well."

Julien Lacusta snorted and gave Ramsey Olaru a nod. "Let's get this show on the road, sentinel. The sooner we're out of this cave, the better."

"No shit, Sherlock," Ramsey quipped back, giving a nod to his oldest brother, Santos.

Since vampires could not dematerialize carrying an object over fifty pounds in weight in their arms, the sentinels had already decided to let Santos carry Gwen out of the cave, then hit the skies with his black-and-blond wings. Julien would fly point, in case Fabian showed up. Ramsey and his twin, Saxson, would take up Santos' flanks, and Saber would get the rear. Niko and Jankiel would follow the vampiric formation as ghosts, hovering and flying—haunting the team as it were—in the background. The goal was short, sweet, and simple: no confrontations, no messes. Just get the damn girl and take her back to the manse!

Santos made a beeline to the pallet where Gwen was sleeping, eyed the bag of sundry items warily, and promptly decided to leave them. He lowered his six-foot-three, 190-pound frame to the ground and effortlessly scooped Gwen up, careful to cradle her head. Her long, damp locks fell over his bicep and his shoulder, blending into his own unusual black-and-blond tresses, but the female didn't rouse.

Saber felt the hairs on the back of his neck prickle. *Let's go!* he snarled telepathically to his fellow sentinels, the wizards, and the tracker, no longer caring to speak out loud.

Don't have to tell me twice, Julien replied, hustling to take his place in the lead.

And then just like that, all seven vampires, along with a sleeping human girl, dove through the raging waterfall and into the night, their large magnificent wings expanding and taking flight.

* * *

Drawing deep swallows of blood in greedy, feral gulps, both fangs firmly lodged inside a thick, fleshy throat, Fabian Antonescu still managed to hiss like a viper, expelling air between his canines as his burnt-copper eyes shot open.

Fog...spiders...watchful eyes...

Alerting his spirit from over twenty miles away.

Wizards...warriors...*vampires*...

Interlopers, desecrating Fabian's cave.

Darkness flooded the Ancient's heart, and rage swelled in his breast: Someone had transgressed the cavern, gotten through Fabian's wards, and someone was touching—*no, taking*—Fabian's *destiny*.

Panic calcified in his bones, even as reason gave way to impending insanity.

He ripped his fangs from the human's throat, tearing skin, cartilage, and muscle; and then he tossed the rotund human male to the ground, indiscriminately leaving him to lie—and bleed out —beneath a scraggly cropping of sagebrush. It didn't matter. The man had been a ruffian and a swindler the last thirty-five years of his life...

And Fabian had far more pressing matters to attend to.

No one touched Fabian's *destiny*.

No one!

He would extract their souls from their corporeal bodies and knead them like dough on a baker's block, before twisting their spirits into pretzels and sending them to an unseen purgatory of Fabian's expert and creative making...to rot for all eternity.

He didn't have time to travel, to make hasty use of his wings, nor did he think he possessed the wherewithal to teleport to the cavern and confront all seven interlopers before his own internal fog, the insanity always simmering just beneath the surface, took over and rendered the High Mage useless.

He needed to strike while the iron was hot.

Right here, right now, from Silverton Creek...

Thrusting both palms forward, upward, and out, his eyelids began to flutter, and he drew upon his second sight, scanning... searching...scouring the grotto for Gwendolyn.

Cursed wizards, warriors, and nosferatu, where the devil was his woman?

And then he saw her...

She was still asleep.

Yet she was being lifted from the cavern floor into the arms of a tall, comely vampire, a male with eyes the color of pure blue crystals and hair the color of wheat and coal, with streaks of winter's snow interspersed throughout the sandy winter. And then just that fast—the waterfall!

Great Corona Borealis...

No!

The interlopers were diving through the cascade, one after another! And the last one, the last vampire—*son of a jackal and all things unholy*—the male was a descendant of Prince Jaegar! His wild black-and-red banded hair gave him away—the vampire was a Dark One, and he was flying in formation alongside his purer cousins from the house of Jadon.

What in tarnation?

How the hell...

Rage turned to bile, and bile turned to madness.

Fabian blinked several times in quick succession, and then he narrowed his psychic focus on the banded-haired male, the dark spirit from a corrupt and cursed genesis, the son of Jaegar, flying in the rear, with that damnable "crown of the king cobra." The ancient mage would strike the Dark One first. He would annihilate him instantly. He would tear out his heart, shred it into pieces, and toss it like rotten carrion to the four directions. Fabian would strangle the breath from the bastard's throat before dislodging his head from his body, and then he would go after the wretched, unforgivable beast who was carrying someone else's *destiny* in his arrogant, brawny arms.

CHAPTER SEVENTEEN

C alling forth the most powerful spell he could conjure from the lore of the goddess Andromeda—the rite to channel his entire essence into bloodlust and malevolence, to strike and kill from a distance with his soul—Fabian Antonescu shut everything out, other than the wind, the ether, and the magnetic, cosmic pull of the six directions.

A low, feral growl rose in his throat as he closed his eyes and gave full vent to his psychic, magus powers and reached for command over the laws of nature. Two heartbeats, maybe three, and the High Mage had become undiluted quantum energy in motion: ruler of the force which created worlds.

His drubbing, frantic heartbeat began to stabilize, to slow down, and his breathing grew steady, oxygen now moving freely... and deeply...rising and falling from his diaphragm.

The banded-haired male with coal-black eyes...

Fabian narrowed in on the rear of the aerial formation, vampires soaring like mist through the night, until his temperate heartbeat, his full cognition, and his ancient soul found their target.

Ah, yes, perhaps six feet tall, perhaps six-foot-one—it was hard to tell from a horizontal position—perhaps 185 pounds of hard, taut muscle, and the male's wild hair whipped just beyond his shoulders, conforming in resplendent tone to his silken wings. Yet, there was a hardness in the male's features, a severity at odds with his deceptive, carmine beauty, a cruelness to his mouth. The elements of both ice and fire swirled through his aura like a psychic fingerprint, over eight hundred years ancient.

Fabian hissed, air seeping through his canines, as he entered an even deeper state of consciousness: Thoughts were powerful entities; words carried authoritative vibrations; and pure, unobstructed *intention* could build or destroy cities, nations, civilizations...let alone, souls.

Fabian harnessed all three: He envisioned the male's heart being seized from his body and the breath of life being strangled from his throat. He spoke the commands in native Romanian, as well as in the original dialect of the universe: that which was born from the cosmos...single-celled micro-organisms...that which had taken form over billions of years of evolution. And then he sent his focused intention, spiraling like the shaft of a primordial arrow, across the blackened skies, beneath the haunting moon, and into the chest of the banded-haired male, even as he circled the Dark One's throat with calcifying, constricting ether.

"Wizard!" A feminine shout.

Fabian jerked.

"Fabian, come quick! I need your help!"

He whipped his head to the left, then the right, trying to identify the intruding spirit, to make sense of the angry-yet-lyrical voice. The arrow he had sent into the Dark One's heart-chakra faltered, and the ether began to slip...

"Noooo!" Fabian threw back his head and roared with rage, regaining his focus and strengthening the commands—

"*Nanaşule!*"

This time Fabian jolted.

"Nanaşule..."

He knew this expression! He knew this word! It was the literal Romanian term for *godfather*, but one Fabian recognized as far more personal and nuanced: one who wields the power of the gods, yet behaves as Father; one who is both respected and beloved.

But where was it coming from?

And then, almost as if he were caught between worlds, the visage of the banded-haired male began to fade into the background, even as a hazy desert mirage began to shimmer into view.

A hologram?

A haunting?

A celestial visitation?

"Who are you?" he snarled. "Why are you here? What do you want!"

"Nanaşule." That word again. "Please, godfather, protector, beloved High Mage; you promised my brother Jadon you would ever keep me safe. Fabian, please...help me."

His legs began to tremble, and his hands began to shake.

And then a beautiful goddess solidified before him with long, flowing locks of flaxen hair, waves of golden sunshine, cascading over slender shoulders. Her eyes were the lovely hue of pale spring roses, and her long, curly lashes fluttered with innocence as she gazed up at Fabian with adoration...or love?

He grimaced—the light was too bright, too piercing.

Besides, it couldn't be.

There were only two females who had ever called him Nanaşule: the maiden Ciopori and her younger sister...his ward...the second-born daughter of King Sakarias and Queen Jade—

Princess Vanya Demir...

The name, the words—the rising memory—split Fabian's

skull like an axe, and he staggered backward from the force of the intrusion, losing his balance and striking the ground.

Vanya.

Vanya...

"Vanya?" He spoke her name out loud.

"Help me, Fabian. Come to me, *now*. Turn away from your mission; it is of no importance. You are charged with my safety, and I am in need."

His ears began to ring, his fingers curled inward, and his forehead grew feverish with sweat. Whatever this was, he could not trust it. It was trickery...necromancy...a demonic scourge meant to disassemble and confuse, to seize what was left of his sanity: *the hawk, the raven, the vials of blood...*

Scrabbling along the ground, he raked his fingers through the dirt and bit down on his lower lip until he drew the sweet taste of blood. He shook his head wildly from side to side, now gritting his teeth, and stared at a single dark-brown pebble beneath him, until he could see—and focus upon—nothing else. The ancient wizard tensed his shoulders, balled his hands into fists, and narrowed his gaze, even further, on the pebble until he could make out every uneven ridge, divot, and curve. He held onto his sanity with an iron dictate, willing the apparition—*the trickster*—away, whilst focusing on a singular stone until all the world disappeared.

At last, the memories—and the hallucination of the woman—began to fade.

"Stay out of my head!" he shouted. And just like that, the apparition was gone.

But so were the vampires, flying in formation, and so was the male from the house of Jaegar.

Fabian had lost his only opportunity to strike, his only opportunity to rescue Gwen.

Cursed evil spirits and creatures of night, the interlopers had slipped through Fabian's fingers—the vampires had taken his *destiny*—and Gwendolyn was gone.

As the realization settled in his soul, he hugged his knees to his chest, bowed his head, and made a solemn vow: Nothing—neither dead, nor alive, nor existing in the worlds between—would stop Fabian Antonescu from reclaiming his *destiny*, or punishing the souls who had taken her.

* * *

Saber Alexiares closed his eye and shivered, his heart pounding like a tambourine drum in his heavily laden chest. He had felt the scourge of errant energy behind him like the sudden swell of a sandstorm blasting through a dry, sweltering desert, and he had known in an instant that his immortality had come to an end.

The power.

The sheer velocity.

The unwavering, malignant intention...

The wave had claws, and hatred, and magic.

Not unlike the power solely possessed by Napolean Mondragon, Fabian Antonescu could kill from a distance if he chose to—*the ancient High Mage could take life with his soul*—and every male in the house of Jadon needed to be warned, to be made aware of this fact. But that wasn't the information that had shaken Saber to his bones...

Something had disrupted the mage's murderous rage.

Something had interrupted the kill.

Someone had placed their spiritual anima between Saber's heart and throat, and Fabian's intention to annihilate both, startling the Ancient just long enough to distract him, to thwart his sanguineous plans.

And it hadn't been Napolean Mondragon or Nachari Silivasi...

Someone had placed her own life at risk to make sure Saber lived.

And Saber knew exactly who that *someone* was.

* * *

Vanya Demir collapsed on the bottom stair of the long, winding staircase in the foyer of her custom-built Gothic Victorian home, her hands going up to her heart.

Blessed Cygnus, the swan, goddess of her lineage, Vanya had almost panicked.

She had been following Saber with celestial magick from the moment he got the call from Napolean—watching from a distance, hovering just beyond his spirit—wanting to get a glimpse of Fabian or the cave. She knew she shouldn't have done it, but the temptation had been too great.

And then, her mate had passed through a waterfall; the air had turned foul with malevolence; and she had gotten the glimpse she had only hoped for earlier—only it wasn't the High Mage she remembered.

Oh gods, she had almost panicked, dropped her magick, and lost hold of Saber—and the lethal force that was heading right for him. Fabian could have seized Saber's heart in an instant—such was the strength of that malevolent power—and he fully intended to smother the life from Saber's throat and behead him when he was finished.

Slumping from the bottom stair to the floor beneath it, Vanya laid her arms on the cold wooden step and her head on her trembling arms. And then she wept...and wept...and wept.

Dear goddess, she had almost lost the love of her life.

Saber had almost been extinguished by Fabian.

CHAPTER EIGHTEEN

Deanna Dubois Silivasi stood outside the underground holding cell, staring through the open door and thick iron bars, each imbedded with thousands of inset diamonds, at the sleeping woman on the narrow cot, her previous "house guest," Gwendolyn Hamilton. Deanna had expected Nachari to be at her side when they woke the female up—and he would join her shortly, or at least as soon as possible—but plans had quickly changed.

She glanced at her watch and frowned.

It was a quarter after midnight, and the entire compound was alive with frenetic energy and bustling warriors...sentinels... wizards. And with very good reason: According to Saber Alexi- ares—a male who had been stolen at birth, raised in the Dark Ones' Colony for eight hundred years, and later returned to the house of Jadon to ultimately become a loyal sentinel and mate to one of the original princesses—Fabian Antonescu possessed a rare and terrifying skill. Not unlike the powerful monarch who ruled the house of Jadon, the Vampyr king, Napolean Mondragon, the ancient High Mage could leave his corporeal body and strike other living beings in the physical realm with his ethereal core. The vampire could kill from a distance with his soul.

And this had been a game changer to be sure.

While rescuing—or abducting—Gwen (it depended on one's point of view), Saber had barely escaped Fabian's ghostly attack, his malicious assault, and now the king wanted the sentinel to go back to his Gothic Victorian home, fetch Vanya and their son, Lucien Sabino, and bring both to the manse for safekeeping... perhaps for assistance with celestial magic. The king did not believe Fabian would become indiscriminately homicidal or strike out at random warriors, healers, and vampires in the house of Jadon just to display his prowess or vent his rage, enact vengeance, but the king was concerned that the High Mage might zero in on those who had stolen his *destiny*: the sentinels, most specifically Santos, because the male had carried her out of the cave; Julien Lacusta, the tracker who had located Gwen and tracked her through the forest; and Niko Durciak, plus Jankiel Luzanski, the wizards who had unraveled Fabian's wards and assisted in Gwen's removal. The king still did not believe Fabian would ever—could ever—harm Vanya or Ciopori, but the distraught High Mage might just seek them out. Who knew what a feral, half-mad, ancient vampire might do in the throes of desperation and a Blood Moon? Who knew how much Fabian had seen from afar in terms of what had happened in that cave...?

Deanna sighed, and then she shivered: She would never forget what the Ancient had done to Nachari, when her mate had tracked Gwen's essence to the first, original cavern—Fabian had lacerated Nachari's jugular and torn his aorta, leaving the male only heartbeats removed from permanent expiration.

The final death...

She blinked away the thoughts—she couldn't go there now. She had too much on her plate, and so did Nachari...

Along with the other Master Wizards, Nachari had been tasked with creating an energetic suit of armor, a psychic-yet-physical impenetrable vest that could be worn over a vampire's body—one which would cloak and shield the anima—to protect the sentinels, Julien, and themselves until the situation with Fabian was resolved. Needless to say, they were all in uncharted territory, since up until then, Napolean was the only vampire who had ever posed such a threat, and even he was winging it, so to speak, in terms of explaining to the wizards just what took place when he left his body, searched out the soul of another, and struck from an ethereal state.

Gwendolyn stirred on the cot and rolled over on her side, commanding Deanna's immediate attention. *Oh boy, so it was time.* The female would either wake up on her own, or Deanna would release the compulsion: Having been converted just over sixteen months ago, she had more than enough skill to do so at this juncture, and it was up to her to comfort the woman, to answer Gwen's questions, and to teach the likely shell-shocked human all she needed to know in the short term.

It was up to Deanna to ignore the chaos all around her and focus her full, compassionate attention on Gwen, even as the warriors cordoned off several vital areas, surrounded the king's mansion, and prepared to use the same aggressive, strategic tactic they had once used on Napolean Mondragon to subdue and contain him...way back when.

During the monarch's Blood Moon with his queen, Brooke Adams...

When Napolean had been possessed by the Dark Lord Ademordna in the form of a caustic worm, and the warriors had confronted him—surrounded him—with nothing more than a vial of chloroform emptied into a convenient silk handkerchief in order to cover the king's mouth and nose; a speedy injection of one of Kagen's most powerful sedatives, those the Ancient Master

Healer often used with his vampire patients before performing delicate surgery in the Dark Moon Clinic; and a heavy black velvet hood embroidered with dozens of carefully placed, studded diamonds to render the king and his powers impotent, if only for a limited duration.

"If it ain't broke, don't fix it," Deanna murmured beneath her breath.

If it's good for the goose, it's good for the—no; that made no sense...

If it was good for the ancient king, it should be good enough for the ancient High Mage.

And the way Napolean saw it: If the sentinels could isolate Fabian long enough, his lethal powers made inoperative, the king —or even the celestial princesses—could surely bring him up to speed and get through to him. Worst-case scenario, they would try again and again...and again...bringing him in and out of sedation, using Napolean, the princesses, the wizards, even Gwen to make inroads, foster trust, reach his recalcitrant spirit. And if all their efforts failed, then the Blood would deal with Fabian and eliminate his threat to the valley, once and for all, in twenty-nine days.

In the meantime, it was up to Deanna to ignore the fact that somewhere in the valley, roaming loose right now, there was an ancient and powerful High Mage who could light up the heavens with neon lightning and a thunderous blood echo; send wave after lethal wave of energy coursing sideways through the air like a burning scythe; and maim, kill, or annihilate from a semi-corporeal state...from a distance.

It was up to Deanna to set aside her awareness that this same vampire was *pissed as hell*, headed in Deanna's direction, and probably bound and determined to retrieve the beautiful human woman sleeping on the cot in front of her.

* * *

One fist wrapped around each ornate cast-iron handle, Saber Alexiares flung the Victorian entryway doors open, stormed into the familiar, grand, open foyer, and scanned the vestibule, the formal sitting room, and the immediate hall for Vanya. Stepping forward toward the majestic winding staircase, flanked by the most elaborate custom railing and iron spindles, he bit down hard in an effort to subdue his rising emotion and projected his voice to the ceiling: "Vanya!" Despite his best efforts, the word filled the hall like a small crackle of thunder, echoing all the way to the upper landing and rattling the beams in the attic.

The princess strolled calmly into the long, narrow hall, a delicate porcelain teacup cradled in her elegant left hand—she must have been in the kitchen—and by all the gods, she looked enchanting...stunning...too beautiful to be mere flesh and blood. And the sight of her stirred something dangerous and dark inside Saber: something primordial, protective, and territorial...

Something instinctive, dominant, and elemental.

And just like that, Saber saw red. "Princess," he hissed like a true, immortal vampire, "*what did you do?*"

She set the teacup down on a long, aged, mahogany console-table and flashed her mate a loving smile. "I saved your life, dragon."

His heart skipped a beat in his chest, and the organ nearly curled inward.

Just seeing her like this...hearing her voice...standing before her, once again, in their foyer: *Thank all the gods—and even their dark, twin hosts, if necessary—Vanya was alive and well.*

And then the buried, dormant fear—the kind of terror that can only be masked and contained as rage—began to rise like a morning tide swelling from a bitter, hidden ocean. Once again,

Saber did his best to control his tone as he spoke in a dry, even cadence: "What. Did. You. Do?"

Her expression grew solemn, the arch in her brows straightening. "You do understand," she initiated, "that I am an original female, also from the time of the Curse, and that it was—*and is*—the women who hold the secrets of our celestial progeny." She sighed as if shifting a heavy burden from one shoulder to the other. "You do understand that, together, Ciopori and I are likely as powerful as Fabian?"

Saber bit his lower lip, trying to restrain a scowl. "Vanya, *what did you do?*"

She shrugged her slender shoulders and angled her jaw upward in defiance. "I followed my mate, more or less psychically. I stayed in close contact with your energy, and when I felt the intrusion...no"—she waved a graceful hand through the air —"when I felt the murderous, lethal *energy* focused upon your heart, your throat, your very soul, like a rattlesnake ready to strike, I called out to Fabian. I projected my image and my light into a hologram, all the while knowing I would only have a split-second to intervene with celestial magic before the High Mage's malevolence hit home. I repeat, I saved your life, dragon."

Saber nodded wearily, then angrily. "Yeah," he snorted, "I got that memo. I was kind of referring to the tagging along, to the placing *your* spirit, *your* soul, and *your* immortality in Fabian's path, to the fact that the vampire could've reached you, snatched you through the psychic connection, targeted *your* heart, *your* throat, and *your* soul instead. He could have killed you, Vanya." At this, the beautiful, elegant princess took several steps forward, and Saber backed away. "*Don't.*"

She raised her eyebrows again, and her soft, pale, sensuous lips curved down into a frown. "*Dragon—*"

"We already had this conversation."

"I realize," she murmured, "but, Saber, I didn't have time to—"

"I told you if something happened to you, I wouldn't survive it."

Vanya's shoulders curled inward. "Dragon, please; you must understand—"

"You told me we would do this *together*. You told me that should the time come when either you or Ciopori had to face that wizard, you would do nothing without consulting me first." His voice began to rise with passion. "And since when do you tag along...*psychically*...on sentinel business?"

At this, Vanya blanched, and a spark of anger flashed in her pale rose eyes. Both hands shot to her hips. "I have never...before. I knew it was Fabian, and I felt... I could tell... You are behaving like a child." Her words were as angry and disjointed as her thoughts, and something foreign, latent, bitter, and cold welled up in the corners of Saber's eyes: unbridled fear...

Barely leashed rage...

Teardrops, perhaps...

He couldn't make sense of it.

He only knew that Vanya was his life, his entire world—the very air that he breathed—and earlier, this night, she could have been extinguished. The light could have gone out of Saber's world. The sun could have disappeared, once again, from the sky, casting his immortal soul back into endless darkness, just as it had been in the Colony.

And for what?

For him?

Vanya could have died...*for Saber?*

And what about Lucien? Their son!

All that was going to be righteous or worthy in that remarkable child was going to come from his mother, not his sire...

Saber swallowed his bile, and his voice turned cold as ice.

"You gave me your word, Vanya." She froze for the space of several heartbeats as if she were finally beginning to grasp the depth of his angst, yet to Saber's way of looking at it, she was nowhere near understanding.

Nowhere near it.

"Saber," she whispered soothingly, stepping forward to reach up and cup his cheeks in her hands.

He batted her hands away. "You gave me your word."

She stared down at her open palms in bewilderment—and a little disgust—then shook her head adamantly. "Dragon, I did not have time to think...to consider...to consult you. Are you as mad as Fabian? Please try to understand, my love. That vampire would have killed you."

He smirked and shrugged his shoulders. "And?"

She blanched. "And you are my...my everything."

He swallowed hard—his heart felt like it was rending. "My life? My existence? Never equate it to yours!" He shook his head in disbelief and indignation. "I can't believe you would make such an error in judgment, such an...*inaccurate*...calculation."

Now this just ticked Vanya off. She was positively stupefied. "Saber, you don't get to define your worth to me. You don't get to—"

"Yeah," he interjected. "I get that now. You made that pretty clear."

"What the hell are you talking about?"

"I get it. You don't need me to help make decisions. You don't need to consult with anyone. You're an original princess. Your magic is equal to—or at least in the ballpark of—Fabian's. And if something is about to happen to me, you *will* step in. That's your free will. Yeah, I've got it, Vanya."

She threw up both hands in exasperation. "Saber, now you're twisting my words and taking this way too far. I did what I had to do. I didn't have time to think! Have you even stopped to consider what this night was like for me? What I went through? What I felt? My own devastation and terror?" The pitch of her voice rose with her anguish. "Don't you understand that I love you, too?"

"You gave me your word," Saber said icily. He could not let her compassion—or her love—reach him. Not now. Not when the stakes were so damn high. Not when she had acted so recklessly.

"I didn't have time to think!" she repeated coldly.

"You gave me your word, Vanya." Saber glanced away; his eyes cast upward, toward the top of the stairway, in the direction of the landing. "Lucien's asleep?"

Vanya's gaze followed his, and her expression was distressed, her countenance, a mess. "Yes, of course. It's nearly twelve thirty or one o'clock in the morning."

Saber nodded. "Okay. I'm needed at the manse, obviously. And so are you. I think it would be best for you to drive my Viper—more bells, whistles, tricks and wards on it—and I'll follow you in the Outback."

She visibly drew back. "You don't care to ride with me and Lucien?"

His throat started to constrict. "When I..." He steeled his resolve and began again. "I'm gonna be busy with the sentinels and Napolean for the duration; doubt I'll have a chance to take a break. And I may need my car—you never know—you may need yours as well." He cleared his throat and pressed on. "Either way, I'm not going to stay with you and Lucien in one of the guest suites. If and when I get a chance to break free—should Napolean demand that we *feed* or get some sleep—I'm gonna grab a room at the Dark Moon Lodge. If you need me for something, you'll have the information, and it's not like we can't speak telepathically."

Vanya's knees appeared to buckle beneath her, but she quickly caught her weight, straightened her spine, and drew back her shoulders. "You're leaving me, Saber? Over this?"

TESSA DAWN

He shook his head in exasperation—and resolve. "You heard what I said, Vanya."

She blinked away a volley of pressing tears, her eyelashes fluttering wildly. "So, you're going to start living at the Dark Moon Lodge, instead of with me at the manse? And what about when this nightmare is over, when it's time to come back home?"

He didn't reply.

She bristled. "I see."

He tapped his foot against the floor, impatiently. She didn't see. She didn't understand. She didn't even *begin* to get it, but Saber was all out of time...and words. The dragon was finished with the conversation.

"You're being selfish, close-minded, and hateful, dragon." She hurled the words like daggers, then proceeded in an openly bitter tone. "No, you're just being *cruel*."

He waited, knowing there was nothing more he could say, no way to explain or console her. She would never understand, and why should she? How could she? She hadn't lived his life; she hadn't been lost for eight hundred years to a corrupt, insidious darkness; she had no idea what life, completely absent of light, looked like. Felt like. Had been like. She didn't understand that his worth paled in comparison to hers, and she never would. Vanya was exactly who she was: strong, brave, proud, and independent. And as long as she was tethered to Saber, she would risk that which was too precious to risk...again and again...and again.

"Saber..." His name was hardly audible on her tongue. "You do realize that your solution to not wanting to lose me is to walk away...and lose me? That this is *your* brilliant judgment at work— your *accurate* calculation?"

He shrugged one shoulder, feigning all the indifference he could muster. "We gotta go, Vanya."

She laughed then, a hollow, empty, tinny sound. "Just so we're clear: You are aware that Fabian is still out there, right?

154

Roaming, desperate, *planning*...somewhere in this valley? You do understand that not only is the male highly unstable, but that Ciopori and I are the only two souls he knows, even if he doesn't quite remember...or get it yet?"

This time, it was Saber who laughed out loud, only his chortle was cold and satirical. "So...*what*? Are we pretending to be afraid of him now?" He allowed his upper lip to curve into that familiar, characteristic scowl. "I'm not leaving you and Lucien unprotected, Vanya. Napolean is going to be at the manse, along with half the warriors in the house of Jadon. Marquis and Ciopori will be close by as well, and that's to say nothing of Nachari and the Master Wizards." He stopped. She was baiting him, leading him down a rabbit hole, and he was no longer willing to go there. "You need to pack a bag, wake up our son, and grab the keys to the Viper—"

"*You* wake up our fucking son and pack his bag, yourself," she snarled.

He drew back and appraised her warily. "A'ight."

She simply glared at him then, her bottom lip trembling. "You're a real jackass, Saber."

"Yeah," he quipped. "A fire-breathing dragon."

She narrowed her gaze in contempt, then smoothed the front of her nightgown, and he almost faltered—he almost gave in.

But he couldn't.

He wouldn't.

Clearing her throat, she glanced askance, staring at anything but him, and spoke in a carefully controlled, emotionless tone. "And if there's a decision to be made between the two of us, right away? Should Napolean require my intervention, or Ciopori's, with Fabian?" She pressed her eyelids shut, took a moment to maintain her composure, then slowly reopened her shadowed pupils. "Despite what you think, I did mean what I said when I promised I would consult you. Saber, *I did not have time earlier*, as the mage was about to *kill* you, to end your life forever. However, I still would not do anything hasty...or ill-advised... should it affect my mate negatively."

Saber's own legs felt like they were made of jelly...or spaghetti...so he locked his knees, barricaded his heart, and placed a hard, impenetrable barrier between his soul and Vanya's, reminding himself, once again, why his decision was so imperative: As long as Fabian was haunting the valley, the princess would continue to monitor her mate like a hawk, to follow Saber in battle if necessary, to use any power or magic at her disposal to intervene if she felt Saber was in danger.

Vanya would continue to expose herself and risk her life...

Maybe it had always been this way.

Maybe he had just failed to see it this clearly before.

But it was as stark as a neon sign hanging in the celestial heavens: Vanya's love for Saber was her greatest weakness right now, and her willingness to protect him was an unthinkable vulnerability...

Channeling eight hundred years of living in the Colony and consulting his long-lost, Dark One's soul, he curved his upper lip into that signature smirk, once again; only this time, he did it on purpose. He had to end this endless push-and-pull once and for all—the banter was too dangerous. "If you need to consult with someone, you can turn to your sister or Marquis. Better yet, you can consult with Napolean—perhaps your ex love-interest will make better calculations than your mate."

Vanya flinched and stepped back like he had physically struck her, her eyes growing wide in shock...and rage. "Wow... okay...that was cold as hell, completely uncalled for, and not to mention, hitting below the belt."

He jacked up both eyebrows, but he didn't blink. "Anything else?"

She took several deep breaths, like she was trying to cork an explosive fury. "Yeah," she finally whispered, icily. "I changed my mind: I will pack for myself and Lucien—you don't need to go near him—and I don't care if you follow us to the manse or not. Do whatever the hell you like. Just get out of my house and get out of my sight."

Nodding his head, Saber vanished from the foyer.

CHAPTER NINETEEN

1:00 AM

Gwen Hamilton felt a firm yet gentle tug on her consciousness, much like a small fish nibbling on the end of a line. *Tap, tap, tap*—the fish continued to tug at her—*wake up, wake up, wake up.* Her eyes fluttered open, and she stared up at the dome of the cave.

No, not the dome of the cave...

She sat up abruptly and rolled over to crawl on her knees, only to fall several feet and slam against a hard, cold floor. Her mind was still cloudy, but the platform beneath her did not register as the damp, earthen ground she was accustomed to. Rather, the floor felt hard and uneven, like it was composed of stone, maybe mortar, hardened and tightly packed earth. Her knees absorbed the bulk of the impact, exposed as they were in the crude, Neanderthal miniskirt, and she grimaced in pain even as she swiped her hands in front of her, waving her arms to and fro, trying to regain her bearings.

"Gwen! Gwen! Are you okay?" A familiar and friendly feminine voice.

What the hey?

A gentle, if not graceful, hand on her shoulder, and a tall woman knelt at her side. "Gwen, I'm so sorry—I didn't think you would fall."

Gwen blinked several times, turned toward the woman, and rubbed her eyes to dislodge the sleep. "Deanna?" The thick ash-brown hair with its long, layered tresses falling to the woman's midback with subtle, yet radiant, highlights of deep brown and gold was unmistakable, as was Deanna's confident, gentle tone. But how the hell had Deanna Silivasi found the cave? And where in the world was Fab—

"*Fabian!* Where is he?" Gwen cried out, scrabbling to her knees and twisting in a semicircle to survey her immediate surroundings.

"Shh," Deanna coaxed. "It's okay. Calm down." She placed one hand on Gwen's tense shoulder and rose gracefully to her feet, drawing Gwen up by the elbow, until both women were off the ground. "Have a seat on the cot—you're okay, Gwen. We found you. We have you. You're still in the vale, but you're back...with us."

Gwen shook her head in confusion and rubbed her eyes again. "What...where...who?" She lowered her butt, slowly and unsteadily, settling onto the...cot?...and Deanna settled beside her.

"Shh, it's okay," Deanna repeated, this time rubbing gentle circles along Gwen's lower back. "I know it's confusing. Just take your time. In fact"—she paused to glance around the dimly lit space—"let me get you something to drink."

Deanna rose from the folding bed, and Gwen almost reached out to snatch her by the hand and drag her back down. Gwen had no idea where she was—why she was in a cubicle, on a cot, or how she had gotten there—but she didn't want the beautiful vampire to leave her side for even a minute.

Deanna's voice!

Deanna's kindness...

The fact that Gwen was sitting next to someone other than Fabian...

For the first time in forever, her heartbeat thumped with a scintilla of hope, and Gwen wanted to grab onto that optimism, however faint, and hold it in two tight fists.

She did not want to let go of her lifeline.

"I'll be right back," Deanna assured her, seeming to sense Gwen's fear. "I'm just gonna step right outside that door"—she pointed toward a heavy, open, iron door, flanked by thick, sparkly iron bars and a cubicle-shaped anteroom on the other side—"grab a glass of water, and I'll be right back."

Once again, Gwen's gaze swept around the sparsely lit chamber, only this time she studied it far more carefully, her sleepy brain and her watchful eyes straining to work in tandem, to make sense of her new surroundings, to put a vague and confusing puzzle together as quickly as possible: two small windows near the top of the room, each welcoming refracted moonlight; thick iron bars all around the cubicle that seemed to shimmer with iridescent sparkles, almost as if they were coated in diamonds. The same held true of the stone walls and the stone floors—yes, they were sealed by some kind of mortar—and the sturdy walls all around her, they had to be at least five or six feet thick.

Gwendolyn was sitting in a cage...a prison...some sort of holding cell or guardroom.

No—

The guardroom was right outside the open door, on the other side of the thick, shimmering bars: a desk, an ancient set of iron keys hanging beside it, and scattered sparse furnishings, a plain, stiff sofa facing two upright chairs.

"Where am I?" she finally muttered, her eyes following Deanna's every move like a vigilant bird of prey, unwilling to even blink—or turn away—from its quarry. "Deanna, where am I?"

Deanna smiled broadly, her bluish-gray eyes sparkling in the moonlight as she returned to the cot with a bottle of water held loosely in her right hand. "Here. Take this. Drink as much as you can and *listen*. Gwen, we don't have a lot of time. I'm going to ask you a string of questions, and I'll probably fire off more information than you can digest all at once—but time is of the essence, and we need to be expedient. I know you have a million questions for me as well. Just try to listen for now, if you can."

Gwen accepted the water, twisted off the cap, and slowly raised the plastic bottle to her parched, thirsty lips. Deanna was right; Gwen had a host of questions, not the least of which were *Where is Fabian, and how quickly can you get me out of Dark Moon Vale?* But in the ten short days that she had lived with Deanna and Nachari at their brownstone, she had learned enough about the level-headed woman to know that Deanna did not mince words or play games. She was honest and kind and a very straight shooter. So, if Deanna said time was of the essence, then it was.

Besides, knowledge was power, and information was golden.

Gwen could not figure out what was happening, decide what she wanted to do next, or formulate a plan to escape the valley without it. "Shoot," she muttered between gulps of water. "I'll do my best not to interrupt."

Nodding with approval, Deanna patted Gwen's thigh. "I know this is hard. I know it's confusing..." Her words trailed off as she seemed to pull them back in order to heed her own advice. "You are at Napolean Mondragon's compound in the northwest region of Dark Moon Vale. Napolean is the king of the Vampyr, and this...this holding cell...is toward the back of his property, linked to his manse by a long, circular, underground tunnel. It's part of a series of ceremonial halls and chambers. Gwen, it's the safest, most secure, most impenetrable chamber in all of Dark Moon Vale." She took a deep breath, and her eyes shifted upward and to the left, as if she were searching for more precise information, a better way to describe it. "Napolean and the Vampyr have traditionally used this room as a jail...or a holding cell...but that's not what is happening with you. For you, Gwen, it's a safe room. A vault. A place to keep you sequestered and safe from harm."

Gasping in surprise, Gwen inhaled too much water. She coughed several times, spit it out, and wiped a trickle of the fluid from the corner of her mouth with the back of her hand. "A safe room, a vault, a place to keep me safe—do you mean from Fabian?"

Deanna smiled again, only this time her reassurance seemed weak, and the expression didn't fully reach her eyes. "Yes; well, sort of."

Gwen twisted the plastic cap back onto the bottle, bent forward, and set the water down on the floor, before turning to face Deanna more squarely—she needed to study those polished-marble eyes more closely. Deanna's gaze usually revealed everything, and when the beautiful brunette unwittingly glanced away, her eyes darting sideways and downward, Gwen nearly shuddered: Of course, Deanna was parsing her words carefully, *very* carefully...

She had said, *Sort of*, not, *yes*...

Because no one—not even Deanna and Nachari—could truly keep Gwen safe from Fabian. The wizard was far too powerful, and the truth was written all over Deanna's flawless, but telling, features.

"So be it," Gwen said. "Go on."

Deanna nodded and met Gwen's stare once more. "From what we could gather—and by *we*, I mean the king, his sentinels, Nachari, the Master Wizards, and a handful of other warriors, including a tracker—Fabian gave you a compulsion to sleep and left the cave for a time. We think it was somewhere around ten PM."

Despite her agreement not to interrupt, Gwen held up her hand: "What time is it now?"

Deanna glanced at the elegant, blush and rose-gold timepiece fastened around her left wrist and frowned. "About one o'clock in the morning."

Gwen shut her eyes. "Then he knows I'm gone."

"Excuse me?"

"By now," Gwen clarified, slowly reopening her lids. "Trust me; by now, Fabian definitely knows that I'm gone."

If Deanna was rattled by the statement, she did her best to conceal it. "We assume that much," she replied dryly. "It's one of the reasons you're here in this cell."

"So, Fabian left me in the cave around ten o'clock, and then what?" Gwen prompted, wanting to get back to the details...to the information she desperately needed.

Deanna's expression softened. "And then Nachari alerted the king; the king alerted the tracker; and the sentinels and Master Wizards did the rest. They got you out of that cave as quickly as possible and brought you back to this cell."

"Why?" Gwen blurted, interrupting yet again. "I mean, how did you know...how did Nachari know...where I was or how to find me? Why is the king of the vampires interested in my fate?" Deanna opened her mouth to respond, but Gwen pressed on: "Why would a vampire king, a bunch of sentinels and Master Wizards, as well as a tracker, all concentrate their supernatural efforts on me, a simple human woman?" She shrugged. "I mean, I know my situation sucks, and I do believe you and Nachari, as well as Braden and Kristina, do care as much as you can—I mean, you have all been as kind and generous as possible since bringing me here to the vale—but Deanna, c'mon; in the bigger picture, I'm nothing to any of you. I'm nothing to your kind. What do you care what Fabian wants with me...what he did to me...what that crazy, ancient vampire has planned for me?'

At this, Deanna visibly blanched, and then she reached out to squeeze Gwen's hand, holding it firmly within her own. "Gwen, listen to me carefully: I know you might not believe me, and I also know this entire ordeal has been horrifying, frustrating, more than a little unfair. Ever since Braden rescued you from The Fortress and brought you back to Dark Moon Vale, it's been one shocking event after another, and you have had no control over your fate or circumstances. I can't even imagine what your existence has been like since that evening at the old stone well, the day when Fabian awakened and took you away from all of us. But—"

"No, Deanna," Gwen said sharply, "you can't even begin to imagine."

Deanna nodded slowly. "And I won't pretend to." She leaned in closer and locked her gaze with Gwen's, her pupils narrowing with purpose. "But I do know what it is like to be living a normal human life, going about one's business, only to be haunted—disrupted—by the existence of vampires. I know what it's like to be held against one's will, ushered into a strange new world, and to try to come to grips with the fact that you belong to a male you've never even heard of before then." She paused to catch her breath. "My situation was different—I had dreams, visions, strange drawings—I came of my own accord, searching for answers. But that doesn't change the fact that I was surrounded by vampires, held against my will, and kept in the valley..." Her voice trailed off as she seemed to gather her thoughts. "Point is: I understand more than you think I do. I wasn't always one of them —one of us—and I do care about you, Gwen, far more than you imagine."

Gwen licked her lips, which were suddenly dry. "How did you come to be with Nachari?"

Deanna waved her hand through the air. "It's a really long story, and we don't have time right now, but I will tell you everything later."

Gwen shook her head emphatically. "No, I'm not talking about the play-by-play, what happened, or how you met. How did you come to *be with* Nachari—*why* did he want you in the first place?"

Deanna furrowed her brows. It was obvious she was trying hard to follow Gwen's line of questioning, that she wanted to be both honest and open, but she was having trouble making sense of the questions. "Do you mean—"

"Why did he want you, Deanna? What were you to him?"

At this, Deanna sighed, sounding mildly exasperated. "Well, Nachari was...he was somewhere else at the time...but his brothers recognized—"

"Recognized what?"

"Me," Deanna said briskly. "The fact that I was his *destiny*."

Now this caught Gwen's attention. "His *destiny*." It was neither a question, nor a statement, but more of an utterance. She had heard that word at the brownstone, and Fabian had also used it. "*Destinul meu*," she muttered, speaking the exact phrase she had heard so many times from Fabian.

Deanna blinked sympathetically, and her countenance softened. "That means *my destiny* in Romanian," she clarified. "So, Fabian has already explained everything?"

Reflexively, Gwen let out a hollow burst of laughter, and then she held out her left wrist, displaying the various enigmatic lines, markings, and celestial impressions. "Fabian doesn't explain anything, Deanna. Conversation is not his strong suit, and frankly, he's rarely sane enough to speak." She pointed at her wrist. "Corona Borealis. His ruling celestial lord, apparently, the one who chose me as Fabian's *destiny*." She paused just long enough to retrieve the memory, revisit the conversation in her mind. "Proof that I was chosen to walk this world beside him. That Blood Moon, the other night; Fabian said it was a sign from the heavens—a signal, like an omen or something—that was meant to let him know he had found his mate. Oh, but he didn't actually need it. It would seem he knew the second he found me, the moment he first heard my heartbeat: Apparently, it awakened him from the bottom of that well."

Deanna drew back in surprise, then crossed both arms in front of her, clearly deep in thought. "Wow." She took a second to turn Gwen's words over in her mind. "Sweetie, I'm going to need you to share all of this with Nachari and Napolean. They are going to want to know every single detail."

Gwen heard Deanna's appeal, but she was too fixated now on the Blood Moon and Fabian to address it—she was too close to finally having some real answers. "And he also said," Gwen continued, "that if a male vampire loses his *destiny* before he appeases the Blood—whatever the hell that actually means—then he dies, that his death is both imminent and unpleasant. Did I leave anything out, Deanna? Did *Fabian* leave anything out?"

Deanna curled her hands into fists and spoke sharply... directly. "Thirty days?"

"No, he never mentioned an exact time frame."

"Conversion?"

"*What?*"

"Pregnancy or the sacrifice?"

Gwen felt her face pale. "No. What...what the hell?"

"The original Blood Curse?" Deanna finally asked.

Gwen buried her face in her hands. *Oh God; this was really, really bad, way worse than Gwen had imagined.* "I think you have an awful lot to tell me, Deanna, because Fabian did not explain shit, and frankly, I'm really freaking out."

Deanna rested her hand on Gwen's forearm. "I promise that I will not leave even one stone unturned, but for right now—this moment—we really need to bring Nachari and Napolean in on our conversation, on anything else you can tell us about Fabian... his powers...or his history. Gwen, as urgent and shocking as the Blood Curse sounds, it can keep—*it will keep for the remaining twenty-nine days*—but as you said earlier, Fabian already knows that you're gone. So, you have to help us protect you. And sooner than later."

Gwen sat up sharply, brushed Deanna's hand off her forearm, and leaned forward, into the conversation.

Holy.

Hell.

Why had she been so slow to put two and two together?

"Ultimately, this Curse...this Blood," she said, "all those crazy things you just mentioned; they're driving Fabian like a computer hard drive. He may as well be a preprogrammed robot. He isn't going to go along with Nachari and your king. And the lot of you, as well as half the vampire-warriors in this valley, cannot protect me, can you?" She raised her chin, and her shoulders stiffened. "You didn't really rescue me as much as commandeer me. Is that correct, Deanna?"

"Gwen..." Deanna sighed, her frustration clearly showing.

"Let's just keep it one hundred, Deanna." Gwen had had enough of sympathy, kindness, and beating around the proverbial bush. This was serious as a heart attack, and she finally got it. She glanced around the holding cell, seeing everything with a fresh pair of eyes: She was in a well-fortified and strategically placed bunker, and the pieces of the puzzle suddenly snapped into place. "None of you understand what the hell happened that evening at the well. None of you know just what...or who... Fabian is. You don't comprehend his powers, you don't know if he's a friend or an enemy, and you're terrified that you can't control him—am I right?" She didn't wait for a reply. "He's not just a threat to me; he may very well be a threat to this entire valley." She chuckled sardonically, although there wasn't an ounce of humor reflected in her voice. "And I'm being kept in this vault, this *safe room*,' as you prefer to call it, as live bait, aren't I?" An angry tear escaped the corner of her eye as she glared at Deanna. "You have no intentions of keeping me away from Fabian or sending me back to my home in Denver, do you? You just need me to lure him out of the wild, and then you'll play it by ear...take it one step at a time...from there. But essentially, you're winging it, and that's why any information I can give you is so vital."

Deanna tucked a thick lock of hair behind her ear, worried her bottom lip, and swallowed a lump of regret. Then she raised her chin in a direct reply and met Gwen's stare, unerringly. "This isn't some Machiavellian plot, Gwen. And no one is here to lie to you or hurt you. I get it. You're scared. We all are, but it's far more complicated than you just laid out. Yes, we are baffled by Fabian. And yes, we do not understand the full scope of his powers. And yes, the Curse and the Blood will draw him to you like a moth to a flame—it already has—and he won't stop coming. But that doesn't change the fact that we care deeply for *both* of you, that we revere and honor the house of Jadon, that we want to protect and save every soul in this valley...if possible." She leaned in more closely. "And for the record, you hit the nail right on the head: Fabian *is* coming for you, Gwen, and all our warriors are prepared to intercept him. Nevertheless, one way or another, we are all going to have to deal with the Corona Borealis Blood Moon and the fact that you are this High Mage's *destiny*. We didn't count on it. We didn't ask for it. But here it is. The question for you is who would you rather deal with...work with... receive help from: horrific circumstances be damned, Fabian Antonescu, back in that cave, or me and Nachari, here in this cell? I don't have another option for you, Gwen—the gods know, I wish I did."

Deanna's words hit Gwen like a two-ton truck crashing into the side of a brick wall.

So there it was...

Deanna was keeping it one hundred, just as Gwen had asked, and the truth was far uglier than any manufactured fiction.

Very well...

"He's crazy as a loon, Deanna," Gwen said bluntly. She sat back on the cot, crossed her half-bare legs beneath her, and folded her arms in front of her stomach. "He rants and raves about ravens, hawks, and vials of blood." She twirled her finger along the side of her temple. "He hallucinates, he attacks me like a wild animal whenever he gets the urge to *feed*, or at least he used to, and he goes in and out of some invisible fog that absolutely consumes him. He only possesses a fraction of his memories, and your house of Jadon is right to be afraid—the vampire is powerful beyond imagining."

Deanna seemed to be somewhere else, lost in concentration, her eyes narrowed and focused downward. "I'm relaying all you've said to Nachari," she explained. "In fact, I'm allowing him an open channel so he can listen directly and process firsthand." She glanced back up and smiled. "Nachari wants you to know that he's very glad we found you, so relieved that you're safe, and he said, *'Please tell her there is nothing more precious in all the house of Jadon than a female* destiny. *You, Gwen, are infinitely beloved. Fabian is incredibly important to all of us, and we want nothing more than to welcome him into the fold, get through to him—and to ease your burden. But at the end of the day, should Fabian declare himself a sworn enemy of this house and refuse to be assuaged, he will be the one who is expendable, not you. We will* protect you at all costs.*'"

Gwen swallowed hard.

For whatever reason, she knew Nachari was speaking the truth—and so was Deanna—all along. They had not asked for this nightmarish situation any more than Gwen had. If anything, they were simply trying to mitigate the damage and learn, become wiser, as they went along.

Gwen understood that.

She really did.

Just the same, she had an agenda of her own, and she couldn't afford to give anything away for free: Something for nothing was not an option. "Tell Nachari I said thank you," she murmured, "and this is what I need. *No*, this is what I require: I want to know everything you can tell me about being a *destiny*, about the house of Jadon and how I fit in. What exactly is a Blood Moon, and why does it happen? What do you already know about Fabian Antonescu? Explain the Curse, the Blood, and conversion. Whatever the heck you meant by pregnancy, twenty-nine more days, and the sacrifice. I need you to spell it out for me in *a-b-c-1-2-3* fashion, including all my options. I understand that time is of the essence, and I have no desire to play around. But tit for tat...quid pro quo...you answer a question; I answer a question. That's how this is going to go, and how fast it moves is up to you."

To her credit, Deanna did not react in anger or with frustration. "I think that's fair," she said, "and so does Nachari."

Gwen tried to conceal the lump in her throat. She knew the vampires could force anything they wanted, and she was a bit surprised, as well as relieved, to see both Silivasis' reactions. "Thank you," she said softly.

Just then, a tall, stately woman with beautiful blue eyes and ebony, shoulder-length hair strolled into the outer guardroom and wound her way toward the holding cell, carrying a small silver tray with a conical lid in one hand and pulling a medium-sized case of luggage, the kind one might use as a carry-on bag, behind her.

"Brooke," Deanna said by way of greeting, her eyes lighting

up with unconcealed affection.

"I heard everything," Brooke replied, cutting to the chase. "Nachari broadcast the conversation to Napolean, and Napolean shared it with me." She quickly changed the subject. "Brought some food for Gwen—just some fruit, bagels, nuts, and cheese— and that bag you packed, back at the brownstone: Gwen's clothes, her toiletries, and some personal effects. Figured there was no reason to leave the suitcase upstairs in a guest suite, not even until later this morning."

Deanna smiled with appreciation. "Thank you." And then she gestured toward the gorgeous, ebony-haired woman. "Gwen, this is Brooke Mondragon, Napolean's mate and our queen." She repeated the gesture, indicating Gwen. "Brooke, this is Gwen-dolyn Hamilton."

"Nice to meet you," Brooke said, leaving the luggage just inside the holding-cell door and setting the tray on the edge of the cot.

"You, too," Gwen replied. *What else could she say?*

"I'm sorry it's under such awful circumstances," Brooke added, stepping back and away from the cot.

Gwen nodded.

"Oh, and there's a small pad of paper and a pen on the tray as well. If you want or need anything, maybe something different to eat or an item Deanna forgot to pack, please don't hesitate to write it down. We'll get it as quickly as possible."

Gwen glanced at the tray and nodded, but she didn't reply aloud—time was still of the essence...

The queen cleared her throat, even as she turned on her heel and headed out of the cell. "Can't stay," she muttered to Deanna. "Napolean wants me, well, somewhere else. But if you don't mind me asking..." Her voice trailed off; she turned back around and pointed loosely toward Gwen's bare, exposed legs. "Your skirt. What happened? I mean, ten words or less."

Gwen chuckled dryly. "Why not." She stood up and patted the material, smoothing it out so the women could see it more clearly. "This is about as revealing as one can get in terms of Fabian's mindset...and logic." She took a deep breath and just blurted it out. "This custom-made Fred Flintstone skirt was crafted by Fabian Antonescu, sometime after midnight, the second night after he captured me. He took my clothes, washed them in a stream, then tore my jeans into ribbons so he could weave a proper skirt." She met each set of shocked, seeking eyes—first Brooke's, then Deanna's—in turn. "He figured my family—*the Hamiltons*—was indigent, or my father wouldn't have dressed me in trousers. So, he fixed my jeans into a miniskirt, promised to outfit me like a lady in the future, if we ever got back to civilization, and then he threw a dead, crusty rabbit in my lap. For breakfast. The cold, dead, unskinned rabbit was supposed to be for breakfast."

Brooke gasped and covered her mouth.

Deanna bit her lower lip and closed her eyes.

"Well," Brooke finally muttered, "sometimes silence is golden. I would hug you, Gwen, but you don't know me from Adam, and right now, I imagine you hate all vampires." She shook her head and strolled out of the guardroom.

"*Gwen...*" Deanna said. She closed her mouth, then opened it again, along with her ebony eyes. "I...I—"

"Don't bother," Gwen said. "Besides, we don't have time."

Deanna nodded sympathetically. "Just...just...did he ever skin the rabbit...or at least cook it?"

"Eventually," Gwen answered.

A moment of silence hung between them. Then Gwen sat back down on the cot, removed the lid from the silver tray, and glanced sideways at Deanna. "Tit for tat. Your turn. What exactly is the Curse?"

CHAPTER TWENTY

Nachari Silivasi stood beside his sovereign lord, studying the deep lines of worry in the king's typically placid expression.

"I can feel him. He's close," Napolean said, glancing skyward.

"Yeah," Nachari agreed. "So can I."

The king's massive compound sat back in a lush grove of mountain foliage, beyond a lengthy, looped driveway in the northwestern quadrant of Dark Moon Vale, flanked about ten miles on the left by the Dark Moon Mineral Plant, another twenty miles behind the Dark Moon Academy, and not far from the Valley of Shadows, about fifteen miles to the south. What afforded the large complex privacy was the thick forest that dotted its northern edge and the accompanying large pine, spruce, and evergreens that loomed like giant sentinels, shrouding the intricate, interwoven structures. As the house of Jadon's ceremonial halls and chambers were connected to the manse by a long, damp, circular tunnel that ran north to south, underground, from the back of Napolean's living quarters to the heavy, arched wooden doors that opened to the Hall of Justice and the

Chamber of Sacrifice & Atonement, respectively, the king had placed several Master Warriors in the heavily treed courtyard that lined the tunnel, above ground, and he had asked his sentinels to surround the western end of the rear-most structure, the six-foot-thick wall that enclosed the holding cell. The way the king saw it, Fabian would either approach from above or below the tunnel, or he would come, unerringly, directly to the jail.

Nachari could not disagree.

And now, as the moon banked low in a dark, ominous sky, reflecting an eerie yellow glow across the valley floor, the Master Wizard felt a ghostly chill prickle along his spine. When the large trunk of a huge nearby evergreen began to creak and bend in an unseen wind, Nachari's shoulders stiffened, and his stomach lurched. He took a deep, calming breath to settle his nerves. Yes, Fabian was close—his powerful energy was practically electric in the air.

The youngest Silivasi took an unwitting step back and surveyed the present warriors' horseshoe formation, the way it virtually curved all around the jutting end of the holding cell where Gwen was waiting, locked inside, with Deanna, Ciopori, and Vanya. The quartet was being guarded by Julien Lacusta, Kagen Silivasi, and the two attending Master Wizards, Jankiel and Niko.

Outside, Napolean stood beneath one of the two narrow holding-cell windows, while Nachari stood beneath the other. To Napolean's immediate left stood Ramsey Olaru at the horseshoe's left quarter, with Saxson to the front, approaching the toe. The same formation occurred to the right, with Saber at the right quarter and Santos near the toe. On the other side of the jutting stone structure, outside Nachari's line of sight, he knew that his eldest brother, Marquis, was watching and waiting on the side of the building, at the horseshoe's far left heel, and his other brother, Nathaniel Silivasi, was positioned at the far right heel. Furthermore, Keitaro Silivasi and Rafael Dzuna, Saber's father, were perched atop the roof. Fabian could not approach the cell from any direction without encountering a Master Warrior, in many cases, an ancient. He couldn't get into the manse, and he couldn't enter through the connecting tunnel without encountering a dozen more.

"Ready," Napolean murmured, projecting his voice just enough to reach all highly attuned vampire ears. "He's practically on top of us now."

The air sizzled with energy.

The night fell deathly quiet.

The surrounding trees began to shake, bend, and moan; the ground beneath the vampires' feet began to tremble; and a small flock of birds, including a dark majestic nighthawk, scattered.

Then just like that, as if out of nowhere, a terrifying yet awe-inspiring apparition appeared in the sky: half man, half falcon, a dozen shimmering shades of copper, bronze, and gold.

Nachari inhaled sharply.

He couldn't take his eyes off the apparition hovering in the air above them, with outstretched wings, at least ten feet wide, in a glorious, silken span, and eyes shaped like almonds, rimmed in black, glowering unforgiving daggers through the waiting warriors on the ground.

Fabian Antonescu was magnificent.

Pure and simple.

He was equal parts regal and feral. He was terrifying in his presence, bearing, and unabashed arrogance. He was adorned in some sort of indigenous clothing—an aged ivory tunic, cinched trousers, and the conspicuous absence of undergarments—and by the look on his harsh copper features, the vampire had not come to play games.

Napolean raised his chin, drew back his proud, broad shoulders, and broadened his stance, leaning ever so slightly forward like an alpha wolf, instinctively displaying dominance before its pack, his own long silver-and-black locks beginning to lash behind him, even as his body emitted a faint golden glow.

Blessed Andromeda, the male was pulling energy from the hidden sun...

Not enough to sap his power, not enough to attack with pure, undiluted radiation, but enough to show the approaching vampire—enough to manipulate the formidable cosmos all around them—that he was not an ordinary male, and his powers were as lethal and far-reaching as Fabian's.

The peacock-like display had its desired effect, as Fabian's shimmering, burnt-copper eyes locked unerringly on the king's onyx-and-silver irises, and the former's chiseled, tunic-clad body floated backward a couple of feet. Fabian angled his head to the side and sneered. "You channel the very sun in the midst of a dark, moonlit night." A statement, or a question, Nachari couldn't tell, but the High Mage's voice was like thunder crackling in the sky, and Nachari couldn't help but remember the power that had come out of the aged stone well, the power that had nearly leveled—and ended—them all. He couldn't help but remember what Fabian had done to him, personally, the last time the two had met in the ether.

Nachari strengthened his own invisible psychic suit of armor, even as Napolean stepped forward between Saxson and Santos—the king was not going to hide behind his regents like an inferior beta male. "And you can take life from a distance," he said calmly, still holding the ancient one's gaze. "As can I."

A harsh, wicked smirk curved along one corner of Fabian's mouth. "Who are you? What is your lineage?"

"I am Napolean Mondragon, born in 810 BC under the reign of King Sakarias, descended from the goddess Andromeda and her human mate, Demetrius Mondragon. My sire was Sebastian Mondragon; my matron was Katalina Constantin."

"Mondragon?" Fabian echoed, appearing surprised. "From the house of Andromeda." He snorted. "Huh! I knew of your father, Sebastian, back in Romania—you were but a poor, grimy child back then."

Napolean took no offense. He nodded warily, never letting down his guard. "Yes, I was just a boy, ten years old at the time of the Curse, and now, I am no longer a child, but a king. Come down from the sky, Fabian Antonescu, descended of the celestial god Hercules and his human mate, Arylia, chosen by Corona Borealis; and son of Fortino Antonescu and Koryn Anne Rosa... High Mage to King Silvano and his eldest heir, King Sakarias. Descend from the clouds and speak to me, eye to eye, vampire to vampire, ancient to ancient...mage to king. There is much we need to discuss."

Gwen had described Fabian's state of mind as precarious at best.

She had called him *crazy as a loon*, describing frequent bouts of confusion, recurrent hallucinations, and word-salad rants about ravens, hawks, and vials of blood. She had depicted his memory as fragile—or absent—yet up until this moment, Nachari had found Fabian to be focused, lucid, and keenly aware of both self and surroundings.

That changed in an instant.

His nostrils flared, his gaze shifted from Napolean to the back of the jutting stone building, and the tips of his wings lit up with red-and-orange flames that matched the sudden molten rage in his murderous stare. "Release my *destiny* at once and return her to me," he bellowed, darting to the ground like a falling comet, folding his wings into his back, and hunching forward into a feral posture, ten claws extended from two curled hands.

Napolean did not back up.

In fact, the aged king took a haughty step forward. "Gwendolyn is safe in our care."

"You have no right!" Fabian thundered. "She is my *destiny*, promised by the gods!"

Napolean shook his head. "No one disputes this, mage. Yet, I have every right." He waved his right hand to the side, indicating Nachari, while never taking his eyes off Fabian. "You almost killed our Master Wizard, and you threatened one of my sentinels by attacking the male from a distance, while he was defenseless. I cannot let you harm those who are both under my protection and innocent."

Fabian's burning gaze shot to Nachari, and he scoffed with blatant derision. "What is this...this *Master Wizard*? I know of no such designation."

Napolean sidestepped between the ancient and Nachari, careful to maintain an arm's-length distance between himself and the agitated vampire. "It is hard-won designation, bestowed upon males in the house of Jadon who complete four hundred years of study in wizardry. It is one of four disciplines attained at the Romanian University."

Fabian smiled then, appraising Nachari from head to toe. "Four hundred years?" He laughed openly. "'Tis child's play to me, Napolean of the house Andromeda." He whipped his head back, front, and center. "Give me my *destiny*. Now."

Napolean held both palms in the air in a calm, cool, non-threatening posture. "The two of you will be reunited very soon, once you cooperate. Fabian, surely you can appreciate the delicacy of this situation. You have been gone...lost to us...for so many centuries. There is much we can share with you. Let us assist you, as well as your *destiny*, Gwen. Let us give you proper lodging and time to rest. No one is threatening your female, and we have no intentions of keeping the two of you apart."

Fabian prowled forward, and this time, Napolean stepped back. "You have ten seconds to return Gwendolyn to me," the High Mage growled, "or I will annihilate every living thing in this orchard." He oscillated his fingers in the air, twirling a dark, inky film in and out of his claws, even as sparks fell like raindrops from his palms. "Nine...eight..."

Napolean released his own claws—and his fangs—and began to round the ancient vampire like a prowling lion. "Gwendolyn will not be released until you cooperate. We cannot let this situation remain as it is."

The two proud males circled each other for the space of several heartbeats, even as the sentinels began to close in...four... three...and then Fabian lunged at the king's jugular.

Napolean disappeared, vanishing into thin air.

Fabian twirled his pointer finger in the king's general direction, and a lasso-like vortex appeared around Napolean's invisible essence. The High Mage tugged on the unseen rope, drawing the king closer and closer.

Napolean flashed back into view, his eyes glowing crimson red, and using two focused beams of light, he burned through the invisible twine and backed away again. "Let's end this, wizard. I do not wish to fight you."

"Give me my *destiny*."

"Cease this madness, and you shall have her in due time."

Fabian curled his upper lip in disgust and flicked all ten fingers in the king's direction, sending splatters of what looked like volcanic lava spewing into the king's dark eyes.

Napolean drew in a quick, harsh breath, closed his lids, and became a shimmering, pulsing mirage of smoldering gas. The lava passed right through him.

And then Fabian did something wholly unexpected: He leaped into the air, vaulted over the king, and landed inches away from the outer holding-cell wall. He slammed both palms against the thick, stony barrier, murmured an archaic phrase in Latin, and sent stream after stream of a dense red fog into the mortar, swirling about the stones and seeping into the cervices, until the structure appeared to be drenched and bleeding.

The sentinels continued to close in, carefully concealing the vial of chloroform, the black velvet hood, and the syringe filled with a powerful sedative. Marquis and Nathaniel rounded the building, and Nachari drew from the surrounding elements, calling his magick into the tips of his fingers while whispering the first stanza of a paralyzing spell, softly beneath his breath.

"Gwendolyn!" Fabian shouted. "Come to me, now! Follow my voice."

Despite the six-foot-thick, diamond-embedded fortification, which should have rendered the High Mage powerless, the outer cell wall began to undulate...then open...like a portal.

"Gwendolyn! Come quickly."

Nachari gaped in surprise as the portal morphed into a tunnel, and the elements of carbon, silica, and oxygen began to swirl in revolving spirals, along with iron, magnesium, and calcium. The tunnel continued to spin at a speed no human eye could have followed, and Gwendolyn Hamilton, with her shoulder-length blond hair and wide, frightened green eyes, scurried into the tunnel...the hands that were pulling her back more like ineffective liquid than flesh-and-blood retractors.

If Julien, Kagen, and the Master Wizards couldn't restrain her, then neither could Deanna or the princesses.

Holy.

Shit.

The ancient vampire's powers were inexplicable...phenomenal...*foreboding.*

And by the way the sentinels picked up the pace and intensity, it was clear that Saber and the Olaru brothers had gotten the same memo as Nachari: Ramsey withdrew the hood from behind his back, spread it open, and lunged at Fabian, even as Saber and Saxson closed in on both sides—Saxson's fingers splayed wide with a silken handkerchief, already doused in chloroform and nestled in his palm—both warriors laser-focused and poised to strike.

Santos was right behind the other two.

Syringe in hand, like a dagger, he aimed at Fabian's jugular, and that's when Gwendolyn—bless her heart, because she had to be under an implacable compulsion—emerged, wide-eyed and terror-stricken, from the supernatural tunnel and shouted a warning to Fabian:

"Wizard, look out! *Behind you!*"

CHAPTER TWENTY-ONE

Gwendolyn had no idea what she was doing...or saying. It was like some foreign entity, without a functioning frontal lobe, had possessed her, and she no longer had access to complex thinking or reasoning: From the moment Fabian had called out to her, to the way she had wrestled the huge, imposing tracker and the powerful Master Healer for her freedom—each male's hands becoming like useless smoke and fog, slipping right off her, passing right through her—to the absurd, idiotic, *what-the-actual-hell* warning she had just given Fabian, Gwen was behaving irrationally.

Somehow, Fabian had managed to punch through the holding-cell wall, to open the supposed impenetrable barrier of stone, mortar, and diamonds with psychic power alone, and when he had called to Gwen—*Come to me, now! Follow my voice*—his command had been irrefusable.

But it was more than that...

More than just a compelling demand...

Gwen had *felt* the ancient wizard's desperation and need; she had heard the frantic beating of his heart in the swirling tunnel walls; and the tug on her own heart, the pressure on her chest, had felt like a fifty-pound barbell about to crush her sternum.

She didn't care for Fabian—

Did she?

And she certainly did not want to return to the wild as his captive human flunky!

But at the same time, she was certain that her physical, mortal heart would break into a thousand pieces if she didn't find her way back into his keeping, such as it was, back into his arms —*back into his possession*—before Napolean's sentinels could capture or harm him.

And that was why she had warned the vampire: *Wizard, look out! Behind you!*

Now, as she reached for Fabian's outstretched hand, leaped out of the swirling tunnel, and tried to insert her body between the ancient wizard and the sentinels, she felt an equally powerful force slam into her: A stunning male, with onyx eyes and silver slashes throughout the irises, waved his hand in a regal, authoritative gesture, and Gwen's palm slipped out of Fabian's. She flew backward through the air, as if she were virtually weightless, and landed in another vampire's embrace.

He closed his arms around her shoulders like a vise, and she began to struggle in earnest. "Let me go!" She stomped at his feet. "No. *No!* Fabian!" She twisted and turned. She raked her nails across his flesh. She tried to kick backward at his groin, to no avail, and then she bit him, sinking her teeth deep into his forearm.

She had to get to Fabian.

She had to get to Fabian!

"Gwen, be still. Stop fighting."

She knew that voice—it was Nachari Silivasi...

Yet and still, she could never stop resisting.

She. Had. To. Get. To. Fabian!

And then Nachari did something as shocking as it was unexpected: He fisted her hair in his large left hand, bent her head to the side, and bit her, sinking what had to be his incisors, based on their sharp, frontal position, deep into her jugular.

She cried out in pain as a momentary burn, like the sting of a scorpion or the insertion of acid, flowed into her vein, and then just like that, Nachari Silivasi was inside Gwen's mind, manipulating her thoughts and controlling her body. As he retracted his fangs, a stream of serenity flooded her consciousness, and her body fell lax against him. Her head lolled back on Nachari's broad shoulder, and she turned her attention back to the scene playing out before her; only this time, she watched it unfold with calm indifference.

She was a spectator now...

No longer an interloper.

And Fabian was fighting like a banshee.

He was spewing Romanian curses at everyone present and lashing out wildly, even as a fearless vampire, maybe six-foot-two or six-foot-three, with wisps of light-ash hair falling forward into his eyes, encircled Fabian's convulsing throat with one arm and shoved a silken cloth over his mouth with the other, straining to hold it in place.

Another male—one with chin-length hair, the striking features of a supermodel, and the body of a Mack truck—slipped some sort of black sack—no, a hood—over the ancient wizard's head, wrenched both of Fabian's arms behind his back, and held both wrists, steady, in two iron fists.

Yet another vampire—a wild thing with black-and-red hair, not unlike the tresses on the two teenagers who had confronted Gwen that second night in the forest—grasped a fistful of Fabian's wild mane through the hood, shoved his head forward, and struggled to hold it steady. A tall, handsome warrior with pearly white teeth, fangs fully extended in the moonlight, raised the hem of the hood and stuck Fabian in the neck with a long, thick needle. The warrior immediately depressed the syringe, reached into the upper right pocket of his duster, retrieved a second, matching plunger, and stuck the ancient wizard again.

Gwen felt like she should protest...

Or scream...

Do something—*feel something*—but Nachari must have muted the sensation, as well as the memory, because the scene and Gwen's inner turmoil faded into the background like a lost, hazy dream, stolen upon wakening.

Fabian's knees began to buckle, and he moaned another curse.

His arms flailed outward—seeking, grasping, failing to find purchase—and then he crumpled to the ground. *Was he finally defeated?*

Despite Nachari's magick, Gwen gasped and choked back a sob.

And then it was like the night responded with stillness, silence, the calm before a storm...

In a low, almost muted whisper, Fabian began to chant in Latin, beneath the hood, even as his body remained prone, sprawled on the ground. The wind in the hollow all around them picked up. The moonlight turned a dim, dusty gray. And particles of dirt, the earth beneath the ancient wizard—leaves, pine needles, and stones—began to shake and shimmy and ascend into the air.

"Step back," the powerful one commanded, brushing his long black-and-silver locks behind his shoulder. "Nachari! Jankiel! Niko! Can you contain whatever this is?"

Nachari lowered Gwen's limp, fluid body to the ground and rushed forward, along with two other vampire males—the Master Wizards who had been in the guardroom with the tracker and the Master Healer. The air began to hum, and the hairs on the back of Gwen's neck stood up, even as the multicolored manes on the heads of the watching warriors began to glow and rise.

"He's going to level this entire orchard," Nachari said, "despite his weakened state, even half passed out."

"And everyone in it," a second Master Wizard agreed.

"Can you stop him?" the powerful one asked, addressing all three wizards at once.

Nachari shook his head.

"No, my king," the second Master Wizard replied.

"We're sorry," the third one offered. "We've never seen anything like this."

The king lowered his head, pinched the bridge of his nose, and took a slow, deep breath, ostensibly to regain his center and focus his thoughts. "The spell he is conjuring...what *exactly* is he calling forth? Can any of you tell?"

A moment of silence, then Nachari blanched. "*Great Perseus, the Victorious Hero;* Napolean, he's going to behead us all. And I believe he *can* do it."

The king's onyx-and-silver eyes grew wide, before flashing feral red. "Marquis! Nathaniel!" he shouted, glancing toward the edges of the jutting structure, each one in turn. "Sentinels! Wizards! Julien! Kagen!" He bellowed the names into the air. "Get Gwen and the rest of the women; take Brooke and the children; clear out the manse and get the hell out of dodge. Now! I want every vampire within a mile of this compound at least fifty miles away in the next thirty seconds. Move!" With that, the powerful king leaped across the grove, straddled Fabian's prostrate body, one powerful leg on each side of the ancient wizard's torso, threw back his head to face the sky, and raised both palms, out and up, in some form of supplication. His rugged body began to glow a molten orange and red as what appeared to be helium, perhaps hydrogen gas, began to swirl all around him—above, below, beneath, and through him—and then the king drew the fiery radiation into his fingertips and turned his hands over, palms now facing down, and directed all ten fingers at Fabian.

* * *

Gwen's heart lurched in her chest as one of the sentinels—she couldn't tell which one—grasped her from behind, hefted her by the waist, and released a pair of loud, furious wings, prepared to take off in flight.

"Ancient powers, dark and light; fire and fury, which fill the night...retreat from this peaceful glen."

Where had the beautiful women come from?

"Cease this madness!"

"Desist, revenge!"

"Protect both king and faithful friend."

Ciopori Demir Silivasi, the raven-haired princess who had waited along with Gwen and Deanna in the holding cell, stood across from her sister, Vanya, each chanting a separate line of the refrain while standing on opposite sides of Fabian's supine body.

"Step back, milord." Ciopori spoke evenly to Napolean. Her tone was respectful, but it brooked no argument.

The king blinked twice, raised his head, and took a cautious step in retreat, pulling—then banking—the sum of his power in the palms of his hands, even as a dark-haired brute of a vampire, with long black hair and phantom, blue-black eyes, took a wary step forward, approaching Ciopori. His posture was careful... restrained...but his expression was fierce. "Ciopori, my love—"

"Not now, Marquis. We don't have time." She flicked the backs of her fingers in the brute's direction, ushering him back, and to Gwen's surprise, the fearsome male paused, surveyed the trio—as well as the proximity of the king—then backed away.

The wild, black-and-red haired vampire, the one who had held Fabian steady for the syringe, did not appear as reasoned or calm. He also spun on his heel, approached the women, and glared at Princess Vanya, but the flaxen-haired beauty stopped him short with a harshly raised palm. She didn't even bother to make eye contact. "Get back, dragon, before you ruin us all."

"Vanya..."

"Get. Back."

Without waiting for the *"dragon"* to retreat, the women shuffled even closer to Fabian, the toes of their feet on either side of his supine body. They raised their arms in the air, creating a bridge above him, then placed their hands palm to palm, enshrouding the ancient wizard beneath them. And then they began to speak in unison:

"Great goddess Cygnus, from which we hail,
defend each soul within this vale;
extinguish fear and rage...
Heart of the lamb, spirit of the dove;
peace, serenity, hope, and love...
come dwell within this mage."

The princesses released their hands, squatted down beside the ancient wizard, and gently removed the hood from his head. "Fabian," Ciopori whispered softly.

"Nanaşule," Vanya echoed. "Do you know who we are?"

The black-and-red haired vampire tensed, his biceps twitching, and he fingered what looked like the pommel of a dagger concealed beneath his waistband, but he did shuffle a few inches back.

Fabian paid him no mind.

The ancient wizard snatched the hood from the women's hands and tossed it aside into some nearby sagebrush, and then he rolled to his side and settled his weight on his elbow. His sculpted lips turned down into a scowl as he surveyed the woodland—the surrounding vampires who had stayed to watch—and then turned his attention back on the women. His groggy, half-lidded eyes narrowed on Vanya, studying her features intently, and then they shifted to Ciopori—and his jaw fell open.

He squinted.

He drew back.

He shook his head slowly from side to side.

"It cannot be," he mumbled, manifestly slurring his words. Whatever the sentinels had injected into the wizard had clearly taken effect, despite the fact that it had failed to diminish his terrifying command of magic.

Ciopori's golden eyes lit up, sparkling like brilliant, sun-drenched diamonds. "Nanaşule, it's me, Ciopori, and *sister* is right here beside me." She reached out to take Vanya's hand. "You did it, Fabian; you saved us both. Your sleeping spell kept us safe, warm, and dry until such time as we were finally awakened."

Fabian blinked several times as if he had an obstruction in his eye, and then he cocked his head to the side and slowly sat up, this time, bracing his mass on his lethargic forearms. Time stood still in the meadow, every vampire-warrior holding his breath, as Fabian continued to appraise both women—slowly, methodically...cautiously—before sluggishly nodding his head. "Ciopori... Vanya... Daughters of Sakarias...the last of a dying race. Is it really you? In North America? Did Jadon come, after all?" He looked so confused, so forlorn, that for a moment, Gwen thought he appeared more like a bewildered, lost child than an all-powerful alchemist vampire.

He reached out with a tentative hand and stroked the side of Ciopori's cheek, and a sprinkle of teardrops fell from her eyes like a crystal string of jewels. He stared at her so intently, so long, that it seemed as if he were afraid to blink, afraid that she might be an apparition or perhaps disappear.

"I'm here, godfather. It's really me, and I've missed you so. Vanya and I can never express our regret, or apologize enough, for not searching, for not thinking...for not just instinctively knowing that your heart was still beating."

At this, he finally blinked. And then he shifted his attention to the flaxen-haired princess, reaching out to twirl a handful of Vanya's silken locks between his fingers. "Vanya..." The word was spoken like a prayer.

Unlike Ciopori, Vanya did not restrain even an ounce of her relief or her jubilance. She leaned forward, wrapped her slender arms around his shoulders, and burrowed her head in the crook of his neck. She opened her mouth to speak, but words failed her. And then she wept.

Fabian stroked her hair for several heartbeats. He nuzzled his chin against her like an adoring, protective lion, and then his eyes began to glass over—and not from sleep or sedation—as the familiar fog set in.

Instinctively, Vanya pulled away, and Ciopori scooted back.

Gwen sighed...

Despite her hesitance and trepidation, Gwen knew better than every vampire in the vicinity what was about to happen to Fabian...how quickly the fog could take him. "He needs to *feed*," she said aloud, addressing no one in particular, "or there won't be any more questions asked, let alone answers, and there won't be any more lucidity."

At the sound of Gwen's voice, Fabian whipped his head to the side, his canines punched through his gums, and his eyes flashed, fiery red. "Gwendolyn!" He practically snarled her name. "Draw nearer. Come to me."

He didn't use a compulsion.

He didn't have to.

Gwen knew the wizard would remain restless, grow ever more distraught, unless and until she was right by his side. And if she ignored his command, he would simply draw her to him with his powers.

She made fleeting eye contact with Ciopori, then Vanya, appealing to both women with her eyes: pleading for protection, offering cooperation, hoping to let them both know, with a gaze, that she was placing her trust in their kindness and praying that they were truly in control.

"Dear God, please let their spell hold," she whispered beneath her breath, and then she slowly padded across the forest floor to take her inescapable place beside Fabian Antonescu.

CHAPTER TWENTY-TWO

Being a gifted sorcerer in the house of Jaegar as well as an esteemed member of the Dark Ones' Council had its perks. Not only did black-hearted, high-strung males—who were generally prickly, arrogant, and easy to anger—genuflect when Salvatore passed by, but having use of centuries-old black magic as well as access to a clairvoyant, oracle cube was a significant advantage to boot.

So, there was that...

However, Salvatore Nistor did not care to use said magic to shape-shift, not even on the few critical occasions when he was actually able to pull it off.

Shape-shifting was hard.

He was a vampire, not a lycan.

It required a shit-ton of energy, even more concentration, and unlike Nachari Silivasi—the pretty-boy, green-eyed wizard who strutted around the house of Jadon like he was one of the celestial gods themselves—Salvatore couldn't actually conjure anything as magnificent or bad-ass as a black panther. In truth, he couldn't even morph into a cobra or a black mamba, which would have been fitting for one of his ilk.

While it was common knowledge that most adult vampires could shape-shift into the form of a bat if they chose to—*what the hell was the point of that?* A small, webbed, ugly-looking, rodent-like creature with a furry back and an eight-inch wingspan...

Wow...

Impressive.

If Salvatore wanted to hang upside down all night, he would simply purchase an inversion therapy table from a local fitness shop—way more comfortable than grasping some potentially slippery surface with one's webbed talons, and then clenching them tightly, all night long.

Who the hell could sleep in that position, anyway?

Nope, that was for the birds, or the mammals, per se.

And speaking of actual birds, that was also the reason Salvatore had chosen to shift into a nighthawk, just shortly after midnight. That, and the fact that his crystal cube had been acting batty all day long. He chuckled at his own clever pun: *acting batty!*

How apropos...

Yet what was going on in the house of Jadon—what was going on in the entire Dark Moon Valley—was neither appropriate, nor cute. The finicky crystal cube had continued to flash and glow since early Wednesday morning. It had continued to exhibit nonsensical revelations of falcons, hawks, and ravens; vials of blood and ominous copper eyes; and ancient settings, from a time long gone, sceneries only found in the Southern Carpathian Mountains.

As if the cube's disjointed displays were not enough, Salvatore had remained troubled, or at least perplexed, by what had happened to the three teenage vampires—Anton, Sven, and Ozzie—in the forest nearest the Red Canyons, the night of the

Corona Borealis Blood Moon: the night someone—or something—had fed from Ozzie's throat, nearly draining the adolescent completely dry without ever making contact with his throat. The night another powerful vampire had imbibed on the fledgling from a distance, using sorcery, alone, to subdue and sap his prey.

In short, the cube would not shut up.

The flashes were insistent and incessant.

And something very, *very* odd—even preternatural, bewitching, and electric—had permeated the air of Dark Moon Vale, saturated the atmosphere with ancient mysticism.

Something super creepy was going on, even by Salvatore's standards.

And having had enough of lying awake, staring at the stalactites hanging from the ceiling—while the cube just *chattered, chattered, chattered*—Salvatore had finally crawled out of bed around midnight and opted to explore.

Now, as he returned to his luxurious underground lair, his heart was still racing, and his head was still spinning: Indeed, he had used his considerable sorcery to shape-shift into a seemingly innocent nighthawk, and he had perched silently in a tree behind Napolean Mondragon's mansion, banking all but a scintilla of his considerable powers. He'd had no choice. Even hidden away in the body of a bird, if Salvatore had shown up on the eastern side of the Red Canyons, beyond the invisible dividing partition of the Valley of Shadows, with his numerous dark vampiric powers radiating outward, the king's sentinels would've picked up his presence in a heartbeat.

He had not been willing to take that chance.

So, as it stood, he had hidden like a cowering foe, shrouded amongst a flock of ordinary birds, and then he had waited...and listened...and watched. And what an eyeful...an earful...what a stunner of a mind-fuck he had gotten.

Alas...

Salvatore finally understood what was going on with his cube, why the damnable thing was so agitated.

Alas...

He finally knew what had happened to the three young vampires!

A flock of falcons that breathed fire and blood had rained down on the adolescent Dark Ones before coalescing into a powerful vampire, and a half man, half falcon had descended from the sky, at the rear of Napolean's grand compound, making unapologetic demands of the king and his sentinels to release a human woman into his keeping!

The Corona Borealis Blood Moon...

Gwendolyn Hamilton was the falcon's *destiny.*

And the vampire who had fed from Ozzie's throat—from a freakin' distance—the one with such great sorcery that the valley's air had become electric, was none other than the long, lost legend Fabian Antonescu: an ancient Romanian reincarnation, a fabled alchemist to kings and princes.

The son of a bitch was still alive.

And he was wreaking havoc in Dark Moon Vale, upending the house of Jadon, despite the fact that the celestial gods had seen fit to give him a human *destiny.*

Salvatore rubbed his jaw as he strolled lazily, yet thoughtfully, toward the raised platform in the middle of his limestone lair, approaching his enticing iron bed and the glowing crystal cube beside it: "Well done, my faithful friend," he murmured. "You were factual, after all, and I owe you an apology: I should've never grown weary of your...*loquacious*...chatter. Now then, what of these ravens, these hawks, and these mysterious vials of blood?"

CHAPTER TWENTY-THREE

I n all his centuries ruling the house of Jadon—bringing the light Vampyr together and confronting numerous threats and enemies—Napolean Mondragon could not recall a more difficult challenge, nor a time when his every decision was so incredibly consequential, when every choice he might possibly make could have such irreversible consequences for the long-term future of the Vampyr and all his beloved subjects.

He sighed and leaned back against a stiff wooden pew in the back row of the Ceremonial Hall of Justice, where he, Fabian, Vanya, Ciopori, Gwen, Nachari, and Deanna had been held up for the last two hours.

There had been no point whatsoever in trying to bring Fabian back to the holding cell.

Yes, they could have kept the powerful High Mage sedated.

And yes, by adding diamond-embedded shackles and leg-irons to the equation, a secondary set of restraints within the already heavily fortified structure, they may have managed to contain the ancient vampire, minute by perilous minute, dodging and weaving as they attempted to stay one step ahead of Fabian's lethal magic, but what would that have accomplished? Treating the indomitable male like a prisoner of war would hardly have endeared him to the house of Jadon.

As it stood, the princesses had been the king's saving grace: Their celestial magic, as well as the inexplicable calming influence they had over their long-ago fatherly caretaker, had likely saved Fabian from ruin. Had the females not stepped in when they did—had they not interfered in the forested garden at the rear of the compound—Napolean would have surely incinerated Fabian.

The High Mage had left the king no other choice...

Napolean exhaled again, rubbing his hand over his aching chest: *Thank the celestial gods and goddesses it hadn't come to that.*

At least not yet.

As for now, and in place of the holding cell, Napolean had chosen the Hall of Justice as an acceptable compromise: a non-threatening way station of sorts, a peaceful yet fortified area that was still close enough to the iron-barred chamber, should it still become necessary to move or restrain the High Mage. Consequently, they had spent the last two hours gently questioning Fabian, while applying as little pressure as possible—they did not want to put the volatile vampire on the defensive as they debriefed him, shared as much of the past twenty-eight centuries as possible, and did their level best to bring the Ancient up to speed on the modern house of Jadon, all in hopes of forging a tentative trust.

Napolean's goal was simple.

Uncomplicated...

Make the barest inroads with the ancient vampire; hope like hell that Gwendolyn and the ensuing Blood Moon would be enough to hold him, entice him to stay within the compound; then offer him free use of the estate's main guest house—so the sentinels and Master Wizards could keep a close eye on him.

Then pray.

Yeah, Napolean thought, *to the four directions, to the celestial gods, to the spirits of the ancestors, and especially to Prince Jadon.*

Just pray...pray...*pray.*

"Shit. Just shit," the king mumbled beneath his breath. Hope and prayers aside, he would have to play this one by ear, take one hour, if not one minute, at a time. He doubled down on his concentration, determined to reexamine the last couple of hours in a more systematic, analytical fashion. He folded his hands in his lap, cleared his mind, and began to sort through the most recent sequence of events...

Thus far, Gwendolyn had offered to feed the agitated, half-feral vampire, and bless her valiant heart for doing so—it was nearly 4:30 in the morning, and the human female had to be exhausted and emotionally spent. Yet to her enduring credit, Gwendolyn pressed on. Behind those frightened, exotic, light-green eyes, she was as strong as any warrior, and she possessed the courage of a lioness, whether she knew it or not. Moreover, she was also the only soul in the room that Fabian truly trusted or would allow to remain that close to him. Certainly, he had shared a handful of isolated, tender moments with Vanya and Ciopori, instances when he seemed to remember—and openly cherish—his enduring bond with both females, but those moments were few and far between. To be certain: Gwendolyn was the glue holding the whole tentative exchange together.

And to their credit as well, Vanya and Ciopori had managed to strengthen their spell, even going so far as to weave a faint golden web of peace, security, and lucidity all around the walls and the ceiling of the ceremonial hall in hopes of catching and sustaining Fabian's sanity long enough for the king and Nachari to make inroads. Knock on wood, but so far, the spell had been working. Gwen had followed through on her offer—she had fed Fabian—and in turn, Deanna had made sure Gwen was both fortified and rehydrated. Meanwhile, the king and Nachari had carefully...thoughtfully...brought the ancient mage up to speed on what had happened since Marquis Silivasi awakened Ciopori in early September, nearly two years earlier.

And while it frustrated the king that Fabian had not disclosed more information in return—he had not relayed his own history or shared any personal memories, shed any light on what troubled him so deeply—Ciopori had stepped in, once again, with her usual grace and aplomb, repeating the familiar backstory for Fabian's benefit: Nine months after the Curse, *Nanaşule* had secured passage for the princesses on a ship to North America. He had fed them, protected them, and taken excellent care of them, all the while awaiting Prince Jadon's return. But when the prince had not shown up, when the obligations and dangers had become too numerous—including the rise of Fabian's own feral nature— the High Mage had placed the females in an enchanted sleep in order to await the return of their brother in both safety and slumber. Since the present was so uncertain, Fabian had chosen to enshroud and preserve the women for the future.

In truth, it was a sad and harrowing story.

Unfortunately, it had not prompted Fabian to share additional facts about his own mysterious past, nor had he filled in any blanks about the time immediately thereafter. Whatever had taken place in the valley—whatever had happened to the ancient vampire, once the princesses were out of the equation—still remained a mystery. According to Fabian's guarded contribution, he had simply grown weary of waiting and fashioned a similar elixir. He had conjured a very difficult but powerful spell to place his own immortal body in slumber.

No explanation about the origin of his shadows or the fog that now haunted him.

No expounding on whether he traveled or stayed put.

No clarification on how he ended up at the bottom of a well, other than to insist that the ground was dry and unencumbered when he burrowed into it. As far as Napolean could tell, Fabian shared the common suspicion—the well must have been built sometime later by the valley's human inhabitants, who had no idea whatsoever they were digging atop a powerful, ancient creature.

Ah, Napolean thought, *but the gods knew where the humans were digging, and if past was prologue, the wise deities had orchestrated the entire coincidence.* And with that in mind, the king had felt confident enough to make three early, if not tentative, determinations:

First, he had no illusions that the celestial females could maintain control over such a powerful, unpredictable being as Fabian Antonescu, at least not long term—their spell would not hold forever. Fabian was a wild card at best. His powers were immense and unmeasurable, and at the end of the day, he was simply not a vampire to trifle with or turn one's back on. Thus, why the guest house remained the best option.

Next, the intimate setting Napolean had chosen—a small grouping of vampires in the ceremonial hall—had indeed been the right choice for debriefing: The formal nature of the gallery had afforded the esteemed High Mage the proper amount of etiquette and deference to feel he was being respected; the relaxed nature of the interaction had allowed the princesses sufficient time to reunite with their beloved nanaşule; and the presence of the females, as well as Deanna and Nachari, had provided Gwen with the impression of safety, a temporary sense of well-being, however illusionary and transient.

Last, but not least, Napolean had managed to avoid a battle for dominion, two rams locking horns in a confrontation for supremacy. He had been able to move in and out of a primary role, to join in the questioning—or conversation—and retreat just as easily, turning the room back over to the females and Nachari.

And knowing those three things, believing them to be true, Napolean had made a singular wager: He had explained both the process and the benefit of a mind-to-mind transfer of information to Fabian and asked the ancient mage to allow such an intimate intrusion for his own personal benefit. And he had ordered Nachari Silivasi to perform the transference, while Napolean retreated to the back of the hall and took a seat in the last row of pews.

To Napolean's way of thinking, the ancient mage was as ready—and as sane—as he might ever be, the knowledge was desperately needed, and Nachari Silivasi was more than capable of transmitting 2,800 years of language, history, and customs directly from his hippocampus, cerebellum, and prefrontal cortex into Fabian's. While the latter vampire had been reluctant at first, Fabian had finally agreed to the psychic procedure. After all, he was a powerful, sagacious, and supremely skilled magician, not to be outdone—or intimidated—by another, subordinate wizard. Napolean had wagered—and relied upon—the elder alchemist's pride when he had made the seemingly innocent suggestion, and in all fairness, Fabian was also wise enough to know that his lack of current knowledge left him at a disadvantage.

So far, Napolean had played his cards just right.

And now, as he waited toward the back of the hall, watching as Nachari conveyed the last remaining vestiges of present-day knowledge directly into Fabian's mind, Napolean could only hope that Nachari had read between the lines, intuited his king's full intentions, and would manage to pull off a magnificent feat of sorcery all his own...

Nachari Silivasi may not have been High Mage to anyone.

Unlike Fabian, the green-eyed wizard had not been born

beneath the power of an Autumn Equinox, and he had not walked the earth for 2,855 years...

But he had spent four hundred years at the Romanian University in the rigorous study of magick, an accomplishment that was not to be underestimated. He had also spent four months and one week in the Valley of Death & Shadows, outlasting and outwitting both demons and Dark Lords alike, and he had stolen the Blood Canon, the ancient book of black magic, from Salvatore Nistor, just shy of one year and nine months ago, and memorized every page.

No...

Nachari was not as powerful as Fabian Antonescu, but that didn't make him the lesser wizard. The two vampires were simply different—and thus, the king was betting on Fabian's inherent sense of superiority as well as Nachari's keen, intuitive instincts: Napolean fully expected the younger Master Wizard, who was known for having the touch of a butterfly when he entered or exited another being's mind, to retrieve something extra when he finally retreated: to seamlessly implant a host of memories, while carefully salvaging the same from Fabian, on his way out the "cerebral door."

* * *

Ten minutes.

Fifteen...

Maybe twenty passed, before Fabian had finally had enough. "No more!" he snarled, sounding both overwhelmed and irritated as he drew back abruptly from the transference, severed the skin-to-skin connection between Nachari's fangs and his own punctured wrist, and stood up from the pew at the front of the hall, taking several generous steps back, away from the milieu. "I get it," he emphasized tersely. "Much has changed. Much has transpired." He shook his head in bewilderment. "Airplanes, cell towers, and solar panels. Microwave ovens, computers, and endless noise...wars...dissension amongst the humans." He waved a dismissive hand through the air. "Yet they are our prey, not our priority." Still seated on the pew where she had been planted beside him, Gwen winced, but Fabian didn't seem to notice. "You live in grand houses, like the castles of old, only with every conceivable convenience...luxury. And while you can still transport through space and time—while you can still fly if you choose to—you often prefer to...*drive*...around in vintage calypso coral Ford Mustangs."

Napolean rose from his perch at the back of the room and began to make his way to the front of the hall, leveling a sideways glance at Nachari Silivasi as he passed the green-eyed wizard. "Automobiles," he corrected, "many different kinds." Nachari had obviously over-emphasized his own cherished Mustang during the transmission.

Nachari flashed a million-dollar smile and shrugged, owning the slight error in judgment, and then he punctuated the gesture with a firm, affirmative nod—and Napolean knew. Indeed, the Master Wizard had read his king unerringly, and he had managed to retrieve some of Fabian's memories—or thoughts—without ever being detected.

Fabian cleared his throat. "Enough. I get it. If there are further details I need to absorb, I will take them from Gwendolyn later." Once again, Gwen grimaced, but Fabian was far too focused on Napolean to notice, the High Mage's gaze both piercing and unsettling, as if he were trying to read the king's very soul. "Ruler of Prince Jadon's descendants?" he asked.

Napolean stopped in the center of the aisle, about six or seven feet in front of Fabian, and spoke with unconcealed confidence, perhaps a hint of dominance. "Yes."

Fabian smirked. "And you brought all those who pledged

allegiance to our liege, as well as their sons...*and their sons...* together in this vale?"

"I did," Napolean answered matter-of-factly.

"And you created the laws and customs of the *current* house of Jadon?"

Napolean nodded, allowing his silence to speak for him, this time.

Fabian harrumphed. "Noble." He sighed. "Industrious." He nodded. "Wise and well executed." He surveyed the rest of the room. "Better a ruler who lived before the time of the Curse than someone with no knowledge of or experience in our ways...our customs...our mores."

Napolean did not respond.

He didn't even blink.

He did not need Fabian Antonescu's consent, nor his stamp of approval, and it was imperative that he remain dignified and seemingly in control.

The tips of Fabian's fangs slipped down beneath his upper lip, whether in a show of supremacy, an involuntary reflex, or a sign that he was about to become feral again, Napolean couldn't tell. Nonetheless, the king waited in silence, allowing the powerful Ancient to take the conversation wherever he saw fit. As long as Fabian was speaking openly and coherently, as long as he appeared moderately sane and displayed a modicum of respect, Napolean would allow him to vent, complain, or wax poetic for as long as he needed to.

"It would seem you have honored our customs," Fabian said in a more thoughtful tone, "but this, I must ask directly: You still honor the Autumnal Equinox; you still recognize the Harvest Moon; but do you remember...*do you revere*...the sacred Millenia Harvest?"

Napolean frowned, a bit taken aback.

Now, that was out of the blue...

He tilted his head slowly to the side and opened his mouth to speak, but Fabian cut him off before he could utter a word—

"*The Millenia Harvest Moon,*" Fabian barked. "There is to be another in less than three short months." The mage's hand twitched at his side. He was becoming agitated, Napolean realized, even as he was trying to hide it.

"I'm well aware of this," Napolean said. "September sixteenth. We plan to celebrate."

"Ah," Fabian replied, "but do you *revere* the custom? Do you remember what the first Millenia Harvest Moon meant to our people, so long ago?"

Napolean wasn't certain if Fabian was testing him, teaching him, or berating him in some subtle manner—it really didn't matter. The king drew back his broad, proud shoulders and angled his jaw just a little higher, standing to his full six-foot-four stature. It wasn't lost on the monarch that he and Fabian were the exact same height, or that the only difference in their bearings was one of Napolean's inherent nobility versus Fabian's unfailing pride, a posture that would've been bred into one of Fabian's elevated stature, especially in ancient times.

"It was 988 B.C.," Napolean replied, "the first Millenia Harvest Moon celebrated by our people. It was told that King Silvano's grandfather, an only child and sole heir to the throne, was born at the exact moment the Harvest Moon ascended, ushering in a new Autumn Equinox and a millennium of peace and prosperity for the progeny of celestial gods and men. *Our progeny,* Fabian, *our* illustrious ancestry. Yes, I remember; and yes, I revere..."

"Good," Fabian muttered. "Then you also know that the first Millenia Harvest Moon was celebrated 143 years before I was born, and that I was also—"

"September twentieth," Napolean interrupted, feeling the need to take back command of the subject. He had to demonstrate his mastery of the past if he was to be trusted to lead the future. "You were also a child of the Autumn Equinox. And it was told that your powers were made that much greater by the lingering Harvest Moon."

At this, Fabian cocked his brows, seemingly impressed. "You remember much, Napolean Mondragon, son of Sebastian and Katalina, descended of the goddess Andromeda. Yet, as you admitted earlier, you were only a boy at the time of the Curse. Ten years old, was it?"

"A child then," Napolean agreed humbly, humoring the ancient one a little longer. "However, as I also conferred—and I will repeat it now—rest assured, I am no longer a boy."

Fabian studied the king carefully, eyeing Napolean from head to toe, but he didn't visibly react. "The *next* Millenia moon was celebrated in 11 A.D.," he said, returning to the subject at hand.

"And the next in 1011," Napolean added.

This time Fabian nodded. "Every thousand years, when the Millenia Harvest Moon appears, the celestial gods—"

"Drench the earth with power," Napolean cut in, "and they open a channel between the celestial sphere and earth, allowing their offspring access to pure, undiluted energy from all six directions."

"As do the Dark Lords," Fabian said ominously, "Prince Jaegar was our progeny as well, and his forebearers also celebrated the Millenia Harvest Moon in antiquity." A deep, haunted shadow eclipsed his eyes, and Napolean drew back in caution.

The king was well aware of the common ancestry, Prince Jadon and Prince Jaegar sharing one history; although it suddenly occurred to him that he had never thought to ask Saber Alexiares if the Dark Ones also acknowledged the sacred millennial moon—

No matter.

He could ask the sentinel later...

Sensing a much deeper wariness, a much more foreboding concern in Fabian's dark, black-rimmed, copper gaze, he spoke evenly and with caution. "Why do you ask about the coming Harvest Moon, Fabian? What is its added import to you?"

Fabian swiped his brow with the back of his hand, and his features grew taut with tension. "I do not know, *King Mondragon*. I do not...understand...nor can I remember why this coming moon is so vitally important, but make no mistake, it is." As if a switch had flipped in his head, or he was scrambling to stay in front of the "fog"—the ramblings and lapses in sanity Gwen had warned Deanna about—Fabian took another step back, raised one palm in the air, and crooked his fingers at his *destiny*. "Gwendolyn, my dove; come to me."

He did not make further eye contact with Napolean...

Or anyone else.

He was not asking for permission to command his female.

Napolean sighed, but he did not interfere, as Gwen rose wearily from the front pew and made her way to the foot of the platform, where she stood before Fabian, looking so small and marginalized by comparison. She didn't bother to seek interference from one of the Vampyr females. She didn't bother to ask if she *had* to go to him, if they were simply going to allow Fabian to take her, perhaps back into the wilds, and she certainly didn't try to argue or resist. Whatever horrific lessons the ancient one had taught her, Gwen had learned them well.

Napolean's stomach clenched—he hated to see her like that.

She was so smart.

She was so resourceful.

And the king of the Vampyr had no doubt she was biding her time, waiting for an opportunity to escape, going along to get along—*for a time*—so to speak. But dearest gods, she looked so tired, so drained, so overwhelmed.

Napolean hated to let the interplay between them continue as it had been, but alas, the situation was delicate, and the choices were not black and white: Fabian Antonescu was a valued elder; a nearly indomitable foe, should he continue to oppose his vampire brethren; and a powerful potential asset to the house of Jadon, if they could bring the High Mage into the fold. Beyond that, he clearly harbored secrets of some sort—secrets, the king could only hope, Nachari would later shed light on—and the entire interaction had become a perilous game of chance.

It was a chance the king had to take.

So yes, Napolean would allow the ancient vampire to command his *destiny* as he saw fit, within reason, and he would offer Fabian use of the compound's guest house, although he would certainly make sure the structure was heavily guarded by his sentinels and Master Warriors—not to lock the High Mage in, he reasoned, but to alert the house of Jadon right away should anything go amiss, should Fabian choose to threaten the valley again. The king could only hope and pray that he could flash to the scene in an instant, if necessary, before the lethal mage could annihilate any of Napolean's invaluable and beloved warriors.

Napolean sighed inwardly—if he had to channel the sun, he would.

If he had to destroy Fabian Antonescu, so be it.

But he would move heaven and earth to salvage one of the greatest treasures the house of Jadon had ever recovered before he would let that happen.

The gods were not stupid, nor were they blind.

They had led young Braden to Gwen at The Fortress, and they had brought the human female to that aged stone well...for a reason. They had awakened Fabian, using Nachari's power, and not a century earlier—or a decade later—but now.

Right now.

Eleven weeks before the Millenia Harvest Moon.

All might seem random, but the king knew better.

And it was up to him to walk the fine line between trying to control fate and exercising faith, allowing the gods to lead him as he knew they inevitably would.

"Is the fog approaching?" Gwen's steady, but weary voice breached the silence as she gazed into Fabian's eyes, ostensibly searching for signs of neurosis, checking to see if the High Mage was slipping away...becoming feral. She shuddered. "Do you need to *feed* again...so soon?"

The mage scrubbed his face with his hands, locked his gaze with hers, then gently reached out and cupped her cheeks in his hands.

Ciopori and Vanya audibly gasped.

Deanna shuffled anxiously beside Nachari.

And the king watched in shock and fascination as the ancient one fell to his knees, buried his face in his hands, and bowed his head before Gwendolyn Hamilton. "By all the gods, I beseech you, my dove—my heart, my future, my *destiny*. I have been so ignorant, so lost, so out of touch with the world you live in, so out of touch with your pain and your fear. I have been wild—*I am wild*—confused and overwrought, so I will not lie to you now: My mind is not sound, my heart is not whole, and my memories are as broken shards of pottery, scattered about a barren ground. Were it not for the magical web spun by the princesses, I would not be speaking these cogent words now, and I fear that even such a powerful spell will soon slip away as the shadows creep in, evermore." He reached to take her hands in his, and while she flinched at his initial touch, she did not pull away. "The tenderness you deserve, the compassion you have earned, may yet be met with harshness or severity in the future—I cannot promise to be what you need, to give all you require, or to become worthy of this claiming...worthy of you. But with the gods as my witness, and before this ancient king, I swear to you I will try, that I will do my best to reclaim the broken pieces of my memories. For you, Gwendolyn Marie Hamilton; I will do this for you. And while I can, before I become a monster once again, look into my eyes and search my true soul—I beg your forgiveness, *destinul meu,* for I have truly treated you abominably."

CHAPTER TWENTY-FOUR

G wen sat on the edge of an oversized distressed-leather sofa in an otherwise serene, well-appointed great room, beneath a high wood-beamed ceiling, staring at Fabian like he was an alien from another planet as the ancient vampire tried to acclimate himself to the modern guest house and all the foreign, contemporary conveniences.

He looked like a giant on the matching burnished walnut sofa, directly opposite of Gwen, and if it weren't for the black metal and reclaimed wood, industrial coffee table dividing the space between them, she would have felt far more trapped than she had in the caves.

Far more trapped and far more stunned.

At least in the wilds, Fabian had been feral and unpredictable—he may have vacillated between trying to be some sort of prehistoric hunter-gatherer-protector and a batshit crazy mage, constantly disappearing in and out of a mental fog, but at least Gwen had known what to expect...

What to fear.

What to try to avoid...and endure.

This male, this vampire, this tender, devoted, if not amorous suitor was a complete alien being, and Gwen had no idea how to handle him or his shocking, unexpected confession. The princesses had woven an incredible spell, affording Fabian the longest period of sanity he had experienced since Gwen had met him. Between that and Nachari's memory transfer, which had brought the archaic wizard into the twenty-first century—at least in theory and information—the striking, perhaps temporary transformation had left Gwen in uncharted waters...up shit creek without a paddle...

Or a boat.

She stared at the coffee table more closely, studying the knots and lines in the wide wooden planks, wondering how old the trees were, where they had come from, what secrets were held in the reclaimed carbon, oxygen, and hydrogen. After all, everything on earth was *One*, the same basic elements, the same energy in motion, not only reclaimed, but rearranged, repurposed, moved from one form and function...one place...to another. Again and again.

"Your mind wanders, *destinul meu*." Fabian's coarse, yet sonorous voice filled the great room, seeming to rise to the vaulted ceilings and slowly float back down. "These observations you make, they are not..." He paused, as if searching for newly acquired words. "They are not magic, nor an understanding of celestial ways—energy, the six directions, the interplay of cosmos. Rather, they are—how would you say?—science. The study of physics, chemistry, biology. Was this something you learned in the large university, the one with the red tiled roofs? Interactive—no, integrative—physiology, the ranking you achieved?"

As far as Gwen was concerned, the alien had just grown a second head. "The degree," she corrected, her shoulders stiffening. "The degree I earned at Colorado University was in Integrative Physiology." The base of her neck stiffened to match her shoulders, and her muscles felt sore. *Blessed Mother of Mercy*, it was 5:30 in the morning, and between the questioning, debriefing, and memory transfer in Napolean's ceremonial hall, they had been at this all night.

Gwen didn't want to have a cordial conversation with the alien being.

She just wanted to go to sleep.

However, she didn't dare inquire about the sleeping arrangements in the guest house—at least in the caves, she'd had her own pallet, opposite the fire. There was no way—*no way*—she was going to curl up in a luxurious bed, atop a modern mattress, with Fabian the Neanderthal. Not even if he had traded in his club for a metaphorical long-stemmed white rose.

"Ah," Fabian commented, seeming tired and uneasy himself. "A *degree* in Integrative Physiology..." He shifted awkwardly on the leather sofa, his tattered ivory tunic looking archaic by comparison.

Gwen shook her head.

Napolean Mondragon, being the same height and approximate size as Fabian, had loaned the ancient wizard a boatload of clothes—jeans, sweats, T-shirts, boots—yet the ancient wizard was still wearing the old, tattered tunic, at least for now. By contrast, Brooke, the king's mate, had apparently gone to the brownstone at two o'clock in the morning and packed the rest of Gwen's things, bringing them back to the guest house along with that first carry-on-sized suitcase, so Gwen's familiar garb would be there when she arrived—and Gwen was dying to slip into her soft, familiar, faux fur robe.

No more ripped, hand-woven, Flintstones miniskirts for her!

But she wasn't about to lounge around in an otherwise naked body, covered only by a robe and a pair of scant panties, in front of Fabian.

Fabian's dark, burnt-copper gaze narrowed in both fatigue

and scrutiny as he watched Gwen like a hawk. "You fear getting undressed, becoming more comfortable around me? You fear sleeping beside me?" He cocked his head to the side. "Sleeping with me?"

She gulped. "Please don't read my mind."

He frowned. "You are projecting, my dove."

She squirmed. "I'm...I'm not used to you being...this mentally present...this long." She immediately averted her gaze, yet she kept the vampire in her peripheral vision.

He sat up straighter on the parallel couch. "You are not used to many things." Despite being the resident fish out of water, he still spoke with that unconcealed pride, the subtle arrogance that just seemed to be part and parcel of who he was, all the way to his broken core. "I have not shown you affection...tenderness... romantic interest." His eyes shifted downward to her shoulders, then to her waist, to her knees and her thighs.

She crossed her arms over her chest and pressed her back into the cushions behind her, as if she could disappear in the seams of the couch. "You...*you haven't shown me...*" Her mouth felt suddenly dry, and she forgot what she was about to say—the exact wording of her protest eluded her, and her jaw dropped open, instead.

"Shall I come over there? Sit beside you?" He gestured toward the empty space beside Gwen on the twin sofa.

Gwen shook her head adamantly and held up her hand. "No," she insisted. "Just...just...*no.*"

He shifted again. "What do you wish from me?"

She almost coughed. "Excuse me?"

"As a token of my affection. What do you wish from me, Gwendolyn? How can I please you going forward?"

She almost started to cry. "You can't...I don't... Fabian, this isn't going to work."

His eyes shifted upward and to the left. "Um, do you..." He

seemed to be concentrating hard, like he was trying to retrieve a memory that was not his own. "Do you like chocolates, scented oils...flowers?"

Gwen clenched her eyes shut in dread. "Fabian..." She blinked them back open. "I think you meant chocolates, *perfume*, and flowers—and you're kidding me, right?"

He sat there in silence for the space of several heartbeats, and then he crossed his arms at the wrists, grasped the tattered hem of his aged tunic, and drew it over his head, tossing it aside on the couch.

Gwen almost jumped up and ran.

"What are you doing!" she exclaimed as an intensely vivid memory flashed into her head: that night, beneath the roaring waterfall, when Fabian had lathered his hair, turned his back on her, and flashed a view, so stunning, of...male perfection...he had caused her to backpedal right off a ledge; the sight of all that naturally tanned, copper skin coating such hard, defined musculature; and the way he had projected such ownership of Gwen—her person, her body, her very *being*...

The mere recollection made her queasy—uneasy—and as much from fear as anything else.

The male was simply overwhelming.

Intimidating.

Despite her earlier protests, Fabian rose languidly from his seat, took a pair of steps forward, and brushed the palm of his hand sideways against the edge of the coffee table, sending it sliding across the great room and no longer between them. He took several more confident steps forward, dropped into a squat in front of Gwen, and knelt between her knees.

She flinched and shrieked.

He smiled—*smiled*—and then he chuckled, deep in the back of his throat.

He appraised her openly—his eyes combing over her hair, her

cheekbones, her lips—before tracing the slope of her shoulders, the curve beneath her arms, and the small of her waist.

She gasped, and her eyes opened wide as saucers.

He grasped both sides of her waist in his palms and felt for the contour of her ribs, pressing inward with his thumbs in a massaging motion, almost as if he were measuring the size and shape of her rib cage.

One row at a time.

Slowly moving upward.

Feeling her curvature like a potter molding clay.

"Stop!" she finally barked, slapping at his wrists. "Fabian, what are you doing?" She knew she sounded desperate. Trapped.

He looked up then, holding her gaze in a burnt-copper stare that seared heat right through her. Then he reached out and traced her lips with his thumb—and not so gently.

She almost bit him. *No, Fabian.* She mouthed the words. "I don't know you that well."

The corner of his wicked mouth turned up in a smirk. "Have we not showered together, shared the same cave? Does your blood not flow through my veins?" His pupils softened until they were nearly hypnotic, and Gwen suddenly feared the use—*no, the abuse*—of magic.

He wouldn't.

He couldn't.

"Don't you dare," she whispered.

He reached up abruptly—assertively—entwined his fingers in her hair at the nape of her neck, and drew her head forward, even as he encircled her waist and did the same with his other hand. He bent so swiftly, so unerringly, to her lips that she never saw the harsh, passionate kiss coming. He simply covered her mouth with his and claimed her like she had always been his for the taking.

She started, balked, and tried to draw back, even as a current of warm, electric energy stunned her. *Oh, gods...what was happening?* She felt dizzy. His hand moved at the small of her back, and just like that, he drew her forward and flush against his hard, bare chest.

She whimpered.

He deepened the kiss.

And heaven help her because it didn't make sense—she didn't like this mage; she didn't care for this vampire; she did not want Fabian Antonescu, and she still hoped to escape her destiny—but that kiss...those lips...*what the hell was he doing?!* Her back arched, her stomach clenched, and her hand found its way to his jaw involuntarily. She was stroking his cheek!

She was drowning in an overwhelming current of pure, undiluted sensation.

And pleasure.

And everything she thought—everything she believed she knew—everything she had felt, up until that moment, flew right out the window. That kiss. That mouth. Those lips...

He broke the contact gently, fingered several strands of her hair, and slid the backs of his fingers downward, along the slope of her neck, before letting them fall away. "You are my true *destiny*, Gwendolyn." His voice was hoarse and commanding. "Our passion is promised. The lust has always been there."

Gwen snapped right back into reality.

The lust?

The lust!

Oh shit, this male was wild, untamed...often feral. She would've never used the word *lust*, nor did she want it. "Fabian, please..." She was about to beg for mercy, for her virtue, when her sharp, quick-witted mind came back on board. "Ravens," she blurted. "Hawks! Vials of blood. Did Napolean or Nachari help you remember?" She knew it was a low blow, a desperate hail Mary, but she would rather have him crazed and mad—disappearing back into the fog—than consumed by lust and just arrogant enough to take her, right then and there, in the king's secluded guest house.

He stiffened and shuddered.

"Do those things have anything to do with the Millenia Harvest Moon?" she persisted. "Anything to do with the Curse?" She swallowed hard and waited, half expecting the ancient wizard to reach out and strike her in anger...or to drag her from the couch by the hair and toss her onto the bed in the master guest room.

Who knew what Fabian was capable of when he was feral?

"Do not!" he warned in a deep, guttural growl.

She swallowed hard and grew quiet.

His head fell forward, and he swiped his hands through his long, wild, golden hair. "The raven...the hawk...the blood of the ancients..." His pupils dilated, and Gwen knew she had gone too far—she was playing with fire, and she was about to get burned. "Sleep...endless sleep...but I remained aware. At times, I had to escape." His words were growing short and clipped now, unsteady and rushed. "I became the hawk, Gwendolyn. I became the raven." His fingers curled inward, digging into his scalp as if he could retrieve the lost memories—somehow make sense of them—by physically rooting them out of his head. "I traveled through the darkest nights, my disembodied soul in the breasts of birds."

His butt hit the floor, and he scampered back, shuffling his feet in front of him and pushing away from the sofa. He whipped his head to the left, then the right, as if he were scanning for something nefarious...seeing something that wasn't there.

"Fabian?" Gwen called cautiously.

His gaze shot back to hers, only this time, it was absent of sentience and reason. "Two vials of sacred blood," he continued rambling, "held fast within my talons. Light cleaves to light, and darkness cleaves to darkness."

Gwen had heard those words before, but what did they mean?

And would Fabian finally be whole, capable of obtaining —*and maintaining*—his sanity, once he fully understood? Once he remembered? She didn't want his carnal attentions—or, God save her soul, perhaps she had pushed his fragile buttons because somewhere deep inside, she *did* want them...desperately.

She had responded to the mage's touch...and his kiss...like he had offered her life-giving water after a lifetime wandering through the desert.

She had never felt anything like him.

His presence.

His passion.

His *perfection*.

Yet she had pushed him over a psychotic edge in order to escape her own confusion—her body's almost certain reaction—should the vampire have continued his...seduction.

"Fabian," she whispered. "I'm sorry. Should I call Brooke or Deanna? They could call the princesses. Maybe Vanya or Ciopori—"

"Be quiet," he admonished, though there was no anger in his tone. "Can you hear it?" He held out both hands, as if feeling for something directly in front of him, and his eyelids fluttered shut.

Gwen gazed all around the room and tried to concentrate. "Hear what?"

"The whispers in the wind. The power stirring in the ether. The Millenia Harvest Moon is coming, and the Blood is excited. Ancient rivalries rousing. Ancient hearts beating, once again, within the breasts of the innocent...*and the guilty*."

The hairs on the back of Gwen's neck prickled, and while still remaining on the couch, she leaned forward, toward Fabian—

she couldn't help herself. "The Blood?" she asked, remembering everything Deanna had told her. "Do you mean the females who cursed the houses of Jadon and Jaegar? The blood of the slain?"

"No!" he nearly shouted. "The blood of the ancient ones... when the Harvest Moon reaches its zenith, and the celestial gods open the channel." He grew deathly quiet then, once again listening intently and leaning into...something that wasn't there. Something Gwen couldn't even fathom. And then just as suddenly, his eyes blinked open, and he stared right through her. "It will not be a time for weakness...for human frailty. It will not be a time for hesitation or indecision. Our mating must be sure. Complete."

Gwen did not like the sound of that last sentence—at all!

What the hell was he talking about?

He rocked forward then, onto his hands and knees, and prowled as much as he crawled toward her. "*Destinul meu*, my beautiful dove; you can no longer remain as you are. The gods have placed you in my care, under my protection, and I have failed to act decisively. For your benefit." He glanced absently toward an eastern window. "The sun is steadily rising, and by noon, it will be at its meridian." His countenance hardened and his jaw stiffened. "By then, you will be as I am: Vampyr."

Gwen didn't have to understand all the ramblings of a madman to catch Fabian's drift—or his intentions. Deanna had explained it all quite efficiently, and Gwen knew full well that the ancient mage was talking about conversion: *By then—by noon —you will be as I am.*

Vampyr.

Oh, hell no!

This party was definitely over!

She didn't know how she did it, but she virtually sprang from a seated position onto her feet, rocked back and forth, from the balls of her heels to the tips of her toes, and placed one leg about twelve inches behind the other, flexing her rear calf muscle while preparing to leap over—and beyond—the mage.

To run.

"Fabian!" She cried his name in a piercing, desperate tone, hoping to snap him out of the madness. "Don't you remember what you said...before?' The pleading in her voice was pitiable, and she despised it. "You said I deserved more tenderness, more compassion. You said you would try...*for me*. You asked me to forgive you for treating me so harshly and to give you another chance."

His burnt-copper eyes glazed over, and his fangs began to descend from his gums.

Not his canines...

His incisors.

Gwen drew in a harsh breath of air and watched as the predator continued his way across the floor, eyes focused forward, ears almost twitching, lips turned back in a feral display of dominance. She sprang when he got within six or seven inches of the couch and hurdled over his head—her bare feet hitting wide-planked wood floors; her ankles and calves bending, springing, flexing—and then she took off running as fast as she could toward the guest house front door.

The wizard sprang as well, transitioning from hands and knees to nimble feet in an instant, landing in front of Gwen and blocking her passage. Wrapping his strong, iron arms around her waist, he hefted her off the floor like she was virtually weightless, and held her high in the air as he carried her back to the sofa, kicking, screaming, and punching.

"Gwendolyn," he snarled, a small hint of sentience still remaining in his predatory brain. "You do not understand what's coming—nor do I, not fully—but trust when I say this is compassion. This is a second chance. *Destinul meu*, this may be the only hope you have for survival."

She pounded her fists atop his rock-hard shoulders, squirming to get away. And then the tears began to flow freely. "Please, Fabian," she whimpered. "Please, I'm begging you, okay?" She sniffed and burrowed her head in the arch between his neck and his shoulder, feeling hopeless and defeated, yet still desperate for a reprieve. "I know what conversion is. I know how it is done. I know the pain and suffering. Don't do this to me, Fabian. Please, please don't do this now. Any bond we might ever have, any inroads you might ever make...you will sever them for good."

He paused, and her words seemed to wash over him like spray from a gentle shower, yet he didn't relax his hold. "Ah, *draga mea*, my darling, my precious, beautiful dove—you still fail to realize who I am. What I am. The span of my powers. Under duress, and with pure intent, I can feed from another being without physically touching them. I can strike to kill from a distance with my essence alone. Earlier, in the forested glen behind the king's manse, I could've slain every warrior there with a spell. And I can convert my *destiny* without causing her to suffer. I can send your conscious mind somewhere else, enchant the impulses as they travel along your nerves, tell your brain to interpret something else entirely. Submit to me, *destinul meu*; this thing I do cannot be delayed."

CHAPTER TWENTY-FIVE

NOON

By the time Nachari Silivasi strolled onto the king's veranda, the outdoor terrace toward the front and side of the manse, the princesses and their mates were already there: Marquis and Ciopori were sitting side by side, their backs to an iron railing, their feet facing a central firepit. Napolean was seated across from the Ancient Master Warrior and his royal *destiny* on one of two large outdoor ottomans. Princess Vanya sat to Napolean's left on the second ottoman, and Saber Alexiares, her sentinel mate, stood on the opposite side of the terrace, behind Marquis and Ciopori.

Okay, that was a little weird.

But...*Saber.*

Enough said.

Nachari took a seat on the three-cushioned, dark-wicker lounge with Marquis and Ciopori to his left, the king and Vanya to his right, and the lurking dragon sentinel still accessible in the background by means of Nachari's peripheral vision.

"Greetings, brother," Marquis grunted formally.

"Greetings, Master Warrior," Nachari replied, both

respecting the Ancient Master Warrior as an elder in the house of Jadon and acknowledging the weight of the meeting, the seriousness of the situation, at the same time. His voice softened just a bit as he made eye contact with Ciopori. "Sister."

The princess inclined her head. "Nice to see you, Nachari."

Nachari turned his attention to Vanya. "Princess."

Vanya took a long, nasal breath, her nostrils twitching—*or were they flaring?*—glared in Saber's direction, then drew her shoulders back and shrugged it off. "Greetings, Master Wizard." Her voice was perfectly even. "You look especially handsome today."

Nachari jerked back, caught off guard, and then his eyes immediately shot to Saber, who scowled, but didn't otherwise react. Not a cool thing to do...or say...at least not in the company of dominant male vampires. Nachari gently cleared his throat. "Well, thank you. Very kind to say." He immediately turned his attention to the king. "Apologies for being the last one here, milord. I had to—"

Napolean waved his hand, cutting Nachari off. "You're fine. You're still a few minutes early."

Nachari pursed his lips together, remaining silent.

Okay...

So, the tension on the veranda was thick enough to cut with a knife, and the king did not have time for pleasantries: *well noted and good to know.*

As if he had read Nachari's thoughts, Napolean leaned forward on the ottoman, braced his elbows on his knees, and regarded the Master Wizard circumspectly. "As anxious as I have been to question you, Nachari, to find out what—if anything—you learned during the memory transfer, I felt it was best to wait until the current company was present so we might all discuss the facts and findings together."

Nachari waited a moment to comment, making sure the king

was done speaking and he truly had the go-ahead. When no other invitation was forthcoming, he cleared his mind of all other distractions and quickly organized his thoughts. "So," he began, his attention focused solely on Napolean and the subject at hand, "as you might surmise, I had to be careful. *Very careful.* Fabian wasn't looking for—or expecting—a retrieval of his memories during the process, but he would've felt anything other than the gentlest tug. That said, I was able to retrieve some scattered, long-term memories, but I wasn't able to search the entire cortex."

Saber snorted in the background, and both the king and Nachari trained their eyes on him.

"You have a question or a comment?" Napolean asked the sentinel.

Saber shrugged.

"Speak up," Marquis barked, seeming to be mildly annoyed with the vampire looming behind him. *What in the heck was going on?* A fleeting exchange of rather intense eye contact flashed between Marquis and Ciopori. The princess raised her eyebrows in disgust and then, just as quickly, relaxed her features. It was the kind of wordless conversation that passed between couples all the time—a private, inside parley, taking place without words—a *reference* to a discussion that had likely taken place earlier, long before they joined the others on the veranda.

Hmm, Nachari wondered, trying to think of anything controversial that could've passed between Saber, Marquis, and Ciopori —he had no idea. But then again, Saber was mated to Ciopori's sister, so it could've been anything under the sun.

Saber spared Nachari a half-hearted glance. "No questions. Only one comment: We all take memories from the minds of others, usually humans of course, but to me, it never seemed that complex—you kind of feel your way through it...sense it...latch onto it. Just didn't get the whole *entire cortex* thing."

Nachari nodded thoughtfully. "That's true," he acknowledged, "but we aren't usually wading around in over 2,850 years' worth of information. The frontal lobe of the cerebral cortex plays an instrumental role in all memory, both short and long term, especially in how we process either one. But while the hippocampus acts as the catalytic agent for long-term memory, those actual traces are encoded at varying locations in the cortex. In other words, if someone runs their fingers along your arm, you feel it—you know they're touching you. But if someone pokes with one finger and starts to dig, you begin to suspect something else is going on." He paused to search for a way to tie his explanation and his analogy together. "When I was withdrawing from Fabian's mind, I couldn't dig around in the hippocampus and still remain undetected. However, I could lightly graze—draw my psychical fingers back—in what felt like a wider, more random pattern, as I withdrew from his cortex. Thus, why I came away with a scattering of long-term memories, but relaxed my touch as I grazed, and exited, the prefrontal lobe."

Saber shook his head. "TMI," he muttered, meaning *Too Much Information*, but he punctuated the comment with a nod of approval. "Sorry for the interruption."

Nachari nodded, and Vanya rolled her eyes—this time, both the king and Saber took notice. To his credit, Saber shifted in his lazy stance, crossed his arms over his chest, and simply glanced away, but the king studied Vanya for at least ten uncomfortable seconds. "Is there a problem?" he finally asked her.

Vanya blanched, appearing suddenly mortified. "No," she answered quickly. "We're just..." Her words trailed off. "Apologies, my lord; I wasn't aware I was being so obvious. Please continue with the matter at hand."

Napolean hesitated, then sighed. "Well..." He was clearly making an in-the-moment call, whether to pursue the obvious friction or move on. "Well, these are delicate times, and things get terse behind closed doors. Just make sure you take the time to attend to both houses." His eyes sought Saber's. "The house of Jadon and your own home." He turned his attention back to Nachari. "Now then, what were you able to draw out of Fabian's mind?"

Before Nachari could answer, Ciopori flipped her long, raven hair behind her shoulder and twisted around in her seat, eyeing Saber like he had cow dung on him. "Kind of hard to do when one makes his home at the Dark Moon Lodge." She swiveled back around in her seat as if she hadn't just interrupted the king and Nachari, as if she hadn't spoken a single word.

Saber looked exasperated and, frankly, ticked off. "Stay in your lane, sister," he drawled.

Nachari winced, as sure as shit, and Marquis glanced over his shoulder and leveled a phantom-blue glare that could've frozen fire. "And you in yours, dragon," he snarled. "How you speak to your mate is one thing. How you speak to mine—that's another."

Saber's nostrils twitched, but he didn't say a word.

The king took a slow, deep breath, stretched his neck, and turned his attention back to the Master Wizard. "Nachari, continue."

Nachari tried to follow suit—he drew several deep, cleansing breaths, both inhaling and exhaling slowly, concentrating on moving negative energy out and positive energy back in.

Alrighty then...

"So," Nachari said evenly, "Fabian's mind is fairly scattered, just like Gwen explained. Nothing is in clean, linear order, just lots of random recollections, and some are blotted out; it's almost like he's blocked them...repressed them." He refocused his train of thought. "At any rate, we were wondering about his time in Romania, what happened leading up to and after the Curse, and while the princesses have been able to fill us in on all they recall, there were a few isolated impressions that stood out."

Now this caught Napolean's full attention: "Go on."

"As we all know, Prince Jadon rescued Vanya and Ciopori from the castle in December 801 B.C., yet they didn't sail for North America until February 799 B.C. They arrived sometime in May."

"'Tis accurate," Vanya supplied.

"Well," Nachari continued, "during those first five months leading up to the Curse, Fabian kept in contact with Prince Jadon, mainly through messengers, while the band of rebel warriors and mercenaries remained hidden in the Transylvanian Alps."

"I remember that time," Ciopori said. "You have no idea how hard it was to stay warm throughout the winter in those mountains."

"Had it not been for Fabian's magic," Vanya added, "we would've all surely died."

Nachari nodded. "Yet he disappeared for a time, didn't he? His entire band disappeared that spring, probably one night, right before sunset."

Vanya visibly shivered, rubbed her arms for warmth, and it wasn't lost on Nachari that Saber's steely gaze followed the motion unerringly. "Yes," she all but whispered. "May sixteenth."

"We didn't know it then," Ciopori said, "but we certainly found out later."

Even with Fabian's broken memories floating around his head, Nachari couldn't imagine what that day—that hideous night—had been like, nor the immediate weeks to follow. The Blood Curse. "It would seem that even as Prince Jadon was scrambling to alert his loyalists, to have each and every one pledge their loyalty to his house in perpetuity, before the sun set and the Curse became irreversible, he still had the presence of mind to send a homing pigeon to the mountains...to alert Fabian.

He warned the High Mage and his rebel band about what was coming."

Napolean's dark, onyx gaze grew cloudy, the silver slashes in his irises blending with the sky, and Nachari knew the king was remembering that fateful night. After all, Napolean's father had been murdered by Prince Jaegar, while the evil monarch was swept away in bloodlust, and Napolean had lived through the agony of the First Change. He had only been ten years old.

"We were hurried into a fortified cave," Ciopori offered, "and all the males gave us their rations—their portions of our communal food supply—their weapons, and their heaviest furs. We were told to stay inside, to remain sequestered until Fabian returned, but we didn't understand why."

"No," Vanya agreed, "not until the High Mage returned to the cavern several weeks later, a completely different and dangerous creature."

Ciopori shut her eyes. "How he struggled to maintain his... composure...to remain protector, instead of predator." She opened her eyes and locked gazes with Vanya, and an unfathomable remembrance passed between them.

Marquis placed his heavy, muscular arm around Ciopori's shoulders and drew her against his chest, but he didn't offer words of sympathy or ask her any questions. In truth, she had probably shared the memory with Marquis many times before, and even the hardened Ancient Master Warrior had enough sense to know when words were simply inadequate.

Napolean sighed, ostensibly burying his own personal tragedy—now was not the time. "So, Fabian learned of the Curse from a homing pigeon." He frowned. "How did he pledge his loyalty to Prince Jadon from so far away?"

Nachari's eyebrows shot up. "He couldn't. I mean, there was no way he could return to the castle...to the village. But from the bits and pieces I glimpsed, he fell to his knees and prayed. He made the pledge to the gods themselves, hoping they would spare him from the Blood's cruelest wrath—"

"Becoming a son of Jaegar," Saber cut in. And this time, it was Vanya who glanced his way.

"Yeah," Nachari agreed. "Being totally and completely damned, without benefit of the *four mercies*."

Saber clenched, then relaxed his fists. "Yep, doomed for all eternity, like my father, Damien, and my brothers, Diablo and Dane." He shifted his full arctic attention on Vanya: "To think: Way back when, May sixteenth, if the Alexiares patriarch had only kissed Jadon's ring instead... There are some things that just aren't worth dying for, that aren't worth risking one's life. Sometimes, we don't understand that our individual souls—our safety, our survival—affect the ones who will come after us more than any heroic choice made in a treacherous moment. There are some risks you just don't take, not if you're thinking of the ones you're supposed to love, not if you're considering the future."

Vanya gulped. "*Dragon...*" She shook her head slowly, and her eyes clouded with tears.

Napolean scooted to the edge of his seat. "Ah," he pondered aloud. "I see." His eyes shot back and forth between Saber and Vanya several times before settling on the sentinel. "The princess intervened when Fabian would've surely killed you that night as you left the cave, the night when you and the other sentinels rescued Gwen with the help of the Master Wizards."

"He could've killed her," Saber snorted.

"He would have killed you!" Vanya chided.

Napolean held up his hand. "First of all, Saber, whether or not the first vampiric sire of the Alexiares line would've pledged his loyalty to Jadon or Jaegar would not have affected you one iota. You were born to Rafael and Lorna Dzuna, not to Damien Alexiares. You are a true son of the house of Jadon, and the only difference would've been—you would not have been stolen in the first place." The king narrowed his gaze on Saber in emphasis. "Beyond that, I think you know, deep in your soul, that your true brothers yet live: Their names are Ramsey, Saxson, Santos, and yes, even Julien Lacusta, and any one of them would die for you. Kill for you." He glanced toward Nachari, and his eyes reflected his respect. "In fact, if I recall, when Diablo came for your heart—to slay you—it was this green-eyed Master Wizard sitting right here, as well as Ramsey Olaru, who showed up to get your back. Ride or die. And if I further recall, that was even after you had attacked Deanna. Correct me if I'm wrong, but I believe that's called brotherhood. Loyalty. *Honor.* Much like the vows we make in our mating ceremonies."

Saber barely stifled a snarl. "I know that, milord. I get that more than you know." Anger flashed in his coal-black eyes, and the fear behind it—the terror clearly fueling it—was palpable. "Don't forget, I have the insignia HOJ literally inscribed on my heart. At least when it comes to the house of Jadon, I know where I call home...where I hang my hat." He gestured, surly, toward Vanya and sneered. "But I'm just not so sure about my other home because anyone who knew me...really, truly got me...would get that there are certain losses I could never survive, would get that *I* am the last thing on this earth worth risking their life for."

Napolean allowed Saber's words to linger, and Nachari wondered if the king had seen it too: Long-term and short-term memories be damned, there were those gray areas, the memories traveling back and forth along neuropathways, assisted by the hippocampus, that opened a bridge between the two. And Saber was stuck right in the middle—his feet may as well have been encased in cement—because he was projecting a memory so clearly, so strongly, that no one had to enter his head to view it: The *dragon*, as everyone in the house of Jadon referred to Saber, was standing in the Red Canyons on a frigid night, frost coating the nearby trees, and by this point, Napolean Mondragon was to his left, and Ramsey had taken Nachari's place to Saber's right...

Achilles Zahora, also known as The Executioner, was standing across from Napolean, a wicked tattoo of a black mamba with jeweled red eyes and daggers crossing along its scales stamped like an armband around his right bicep, and he had led Damien Alexiares—the father figure who had raised Saber for eight hundred years in the Dark Ones' Colony—to the fore of the semicircle, right next to Dane, Saber's younger brother. In an instant, just a flash, Achilles had flanked Damien on the right and reached to secure his shackled wrists, even as Salvatore Nistor had flanked Dane on his left and restrained his wrists as well. Both Achilles and Salvatore had released their claws, drawn back their powerful arms, and punctured their respective prisoners with dizzying speed, splintering their backs and extracting their hearts.

The moment was seared into Saber's memory like a brand.

The horror...the loss...the utter helplessness.

And while few in the house of Jadon could truly understand Saber's attachment to males without souls, Achilles and Salvatore may as well have ripped out Saber's heart too. For a lack of a better descriptor, the dragon still had some form of PTSD, and Vanya coming so close to Fabian Antonescu, bearing her heart and her soul to rescue Saber, had catapulted the male right back to that canyon. He was stuck in his brain stem, and he couldn't let go.

Despite his obvious love for Vanya, the male was not going to budge on this one.

Both wise and observant, as he always was—yeah, the king had seen it too.

Like a dominant wolf displaying its prowess, Napolean's chest swelled and his hackles rose. His shoulders hunched forward, like he was about to lunge, and his dark pupils narrowed

—locked with Saber's—like two piercing lasers: a direct, eye-to-eye, frontal challenge from an alpha male to a lesser member of his pack.

Nachari scooted back on the lounge.

"Okay," Napolean snarled, "so you don't want to lose the princess, and she should've known confronting Fabian like that, exposing herself in the ether, was too much for you to handle. How selective of you. How fucking self-aware. How absolutely and utterly selfish, dragon."

Saber's top lip twitched, even as his fangs descended of their own accord, but he didn't take the bait.

"So now, you're the only vampire allowed to feel fear; you're the only player in this game—in your family—allowed to defend what they love."

A soft growl rose in Saber's throat. "With all due respect, my king"—he spoke the last two words with borderline contempt—"why don't you stay..." The sentinel's words trailed off.

"Stay in my lane?" Napolean grunted. "You mean, like Ciopori?" He rose from the ottoman and squared his shoulders to Saber. "Why don't you make me, dragon?"

Nachari recoiled, his heart thumping wildly in his chest.

What the actual hell?

Napolean was pushing every one of Saber's buttons, inciting the dragon like a fifth-grade bully on a human playground, and he was doing it on purpose.

Saber chuckled uneasily. And to his credit, he took a cautious step backward, pressing further against the rail behind him. He was showing deference—if not submission—to his alpha leader, but the truth was always in the eyes...and the energy. The dragon's fingers were twitching at his side. His shoulders had inched forward, even as his body had moved back, and his gaze was still locked with Napolean's, as opposed to averted or turned to the side.

The beta wolf was not submitting; he was simply doing his best to avoid a fight.

And just like that, the alpha struck.

Napolean shot over the firepit and across the veranda so quickly, his motion was a blur. In an instant, less than that really, he had Saber's throat in his claws, and he was forcing him backward, down, onto his knees.

Saber whipped his head to the side, snarled like a rabid animal, and sank both his upper and lower fangs into the flesh of Napolean's palm, rearing back against the king's dominant pressure.

Resisting.

Rebelling...

Marquis snatched Ciopori by the arm and scrambled to the other side of the firepit, even as Nachari jumped up and stood in front of Vanya. Whatever the hell else the king was doing, he was intentionally spurring Saber to violence, and the confrontation was about to get vicious.

Napolean ripped his hand out of the dragon's mouth, tearing both skin and tendon as he retrieved it, and then he pinched the dragon's jaw, squeezing it shut from either side, forcing Saber's inverted cheeks to mold around his teeth.

Saber snarled like he was frenzied—or possessed.

And that's when the king released his own enormous, jagged fangs, allowing them to slowly descend from his upturned mouth. He lowered his head to Saber's neck—slowly, deliberately demonstrating dominance—then twisted the sentinel's head by the jaw to further expose his jugular.

The dragon bucked like a wild bronco.

He snatched the king's wrist and tried to pry the talons from his face.

He snarled and spit and gnashed his teeth, but Napolean just kept pressing him down—lower, lower, then lower still—until

Saber's jugular was entirely exposed and his face was mere inches from an otherwise bare, soil-filled planter recessed into the deck.

Nachari sucked in an anxious breath.

He knew Saber Alexiares fairly well.

And any moment now, the vampire, who had grown up as a Dark One, was going to come up swinging, even at his king. Saber was as likely to go for Napolean's femoral artery as the king's family jewels, and he would definitely try to flip the monarch over his back before he allowed him to press his face into the dirt.

"What is he doing?" Vanya asked anxiously. "Nachari, can't you stop this?"

Nachari shook his head.

"Marquis!" She turned to her brother-in-law in desperation, but her entreaty was met with the same response. "*Sister!*" she finally pleaded, her wide eyes locking with Ciopori's.

"Shh," Ciopori cautioned, "don't interfere. Just wait, Vanya. Trust the king."

Saber was trembling from head to toe now, an autonomic, crude reaction to the internal battle between his mind and his instinct: his overwhelming impulse to fight back—much harder—and his fragile, but still-apparent restraint.

And then Napolean relaxed his grip on the vampire's neck, just a smidgeon. "This is the posture you would put your mate in?" he snarled in Saber's ear. "Is this the submission—the humiliation—you wish to wring out of Vanya?"

Saber wrenched his head back, finally breaking free from the king's feral grasp. He spun around like a wildcat, twisting in the air; crouched down like he was ready to pounce; then leaned forward, squaring off to the king, all ten claws brandished and ready. "It's none of your business!" His voice was guttural. "She's *my* mate now, Napolean; not yours!"

Saber's head snapped back like a rubber band.

He staggered, then regained his balance.

Holy shit, the king had just rebuffed him with a backhand; only, he had done it so sharply—so swiftly—no one had seen the monarch move.

"Yes, sentinel," Napolean replied, "Vanya is *your* mate, and gods forbid, should something, someday, happen to her...or to you...or even to Lucien, your souls will move beyond this plane, and you will reside in the Valley of Spirit & Light forever. *Together*." He flicked his wrist in Vanya's direction. "Look at her, soldier! She is not Damien Alexiares! She is not your brother Dane, and she is not that wretched Diablo! Dragon, she is not doomed, and the two of you will never be separated, forever—*you cannot be separated forever*. This is not the same thing. This is a different place and time."

Saber tilted his head to the side and blinked two times, still trembling, still panting, still stowing his rage.

"Look around you, son—this is your king's veranda, not the Red Canyons! And Fabian is not Achilles Zahora."

Before Saber could react, or process the king's words, his head snapped back three times—*smack, strike, thwack*—as Napolean corrected him, again and again, each time in such quick, exacting succession, the strikes were virtually invisible.

And finally, Nachari understood...

Vampires were akin to men in many ways, but first, they were predators—always predators—instinctual, primal animals. And Saber was more primitive than most because of his upbringing. His mammalian brain was literally stuck, and it had nothing to do with logic, or reason, or vindictive emotion. As much as he had been the alpha leader of his brothers in the Colony, he was now the alpha leader of his family—protector of his mate and his son— and he had never felt more helpless than when Vanya had confronted Fabian in the ether. He no longer knew how to defend his pack, and his hindbrain had simply...gotten stuck.

Nachari watched on in morbid fascination—how well he understood. When the primal brain was engaged in a sympathetic response, the modern brain, the frontal cortex, just didn't work so well. And Napolean Mondragon was bound and determined to snap Saber out of the former and into the latter, even if he had to take him to task from one end of the veranda to the other.

The king wasn't having a cerebral conversation with the dragon.

He was having a primal, basic, almost mammalian interchange.

And by the look of recognition that flashed through Saber's eyes, it was working: The dragon's trembling lessened, his panting slowed down, and his rage began to subside.

Saber scrambled back on the veranda.

He held both palms in the air, stared at Napolean in a moment of bewilderment, then slowly—perhaps reluctantly, at first—lowered his head.

The king nodded and waited patiently.

And then Saber shifted his weight to one knee, bowed his head even lower, and waited in silence.

The king tapped Saber's left shoulder with his mauled, bleeding hand, and Saber accepted the offering. He bent to the crest ring on the fourth finger of Napolean's right hand and kissed it with reverence.

Napolean nodded. "Speak freely."

Saber raised his head, but he kept his eyes respectfully averted. "I would humbly ask my king, a fellow descendant of Jadon, an Ancient Master Justice, and chosen son of the goddess Andromeda, for his forgiveness. I meant no offense, Napolean."

Napolean's demeanor immediately softened. "I know you didn't, dragon. And for the record, you also never attended the Romanian University—you had no occasion to practice the formal apology—yet, here you kneel, a true son of *Jadon*, instinctively knowing the ritual. Apology accepted, son, but I do believe your true regret belongs to the female you love."

Saber closed his eyes, bit his lower lip, then slowly reopened his lids and searched for Vanya. The princess was standing on the other side of the firepit, and her pale rose eyes were glistening with tears. "Vanya..." He breathed her name, more than he spoke it.

As if no one else in the world existed, she made a wide arc around the firepit, strolled across the veranda, and kneeled in front of him. "I had no idea this was so raw, so vulnerable, for you."

He searched her eyes like he was seeking the secrets of the universe in their depths. "Princess..." He struggled to contain his emotion. "I don't...I don't even know how...where to begin."

She waved her hand through the air. "Shh. 'Tis not necessary, dragon; I saw all you couldn't say."

He sighed with relief...and regret. "I would never want to subvert you...control you. I just couldn't fathom a world without you, and I made all the wrong damn choices. I said things I should've never said, and I did things I should've never done. Can you forgive me?"

She smiled then, and her pale rose eyes practically shimmered with compassion and kindness. "I will not disagree: Moving to the Dark Moon Lodge was beyond any insult I could have ever imagined, even in our darkest hour, but"—she cupped his face in her hands and traced the lines of his angular cheekbones with her thumbs—"but pride is not a wise counselor."

"Neither is fear," he murmured.

With that, she nodded and pressed her forehead to his. "All is forgiven. I love you, dragon, more than life itself."

He shuddered and closed his eyes.

"Saber." The king's imperious voice interrupted the tender

moment. "Apologies. I know you and Vanya need time...a moment for healing...so we will wrap this up quickly. But there are yet a few more questions to ask Nachari and one, specifically, intended for you."

Saber's mouth moved silently, and Nachari figured he was speaking the words to his mate on a private telepathic bandwidth, so no other vampires could hear. As soon as the dragon opened his eyes, and his lips stopped moving, Vanya rose with the grace of a swan, padded across the veranda, and took her seat, once more, on the ottoman. Only this time, Saber followed. He stood behind the princess with one loving—and very territorial—hand on her shoulder.

"Pardon our domestic disturbance," Vanya said sweetly, as if they had simply interrupted the meeting with an inside joke or an offhanded comment.

Nachari sat back down and chuckled softly. *Domestic disturbance, indeed.* He turned his attention back to Napolean. "Milord?"

Napolean took his seat as well, waiting while Marquis and Ciopori did the same. "I appreciate the risk you took on behalf of the house of Jadon. Filling in the missing pieces—the time immediately before and after the Curse—has given me much to think about. Was there anything else you garnered from the mage's memories? Perhaps a glimpse into the vampire's vexing shadows...whatever it is that haunts him so deeply...the origin or the catalyst behind the madness?"

Nachari folded his hands in his lap and studied his fingers intently, thinking. "It was so jumbled, so murky; I couldn't really latch onto anything. However, there was something, and it felt important. It felt connected, like perhaps a thread weaving all else together."

Napolean raised his brows.

"He rambles about a hawk and a raven: It was clear to me that during his long, nearly endless slumber, the wizard left the dream weave—a piece of his disembodied soul traveled in the breast of a hawk...and a raven...almost at will. And while it was blotchy, unclear, it would seem that early on, centuries ago when the mage first engaged the sleeping spell, the hawk and the raven carried something in their talons: small apothecary glasses, what we would call vials today, corked with the bark of a tree and filled with a very dark, sanguine substance. My eyes would say wine, but my nose, my vampiric senses...the vials were filled with blood."

Napolean rocked back in his seat, even as Marquis leaned forward.

"My brother, Prince Jadon," Ciopori said, "he made a pact of some sort with the mage before we sailed for North America. Being newly Vampyr, I do not believe they communicated well—or perhaps not at all—telepathically, though I honestly don't remember. We never thought to ask such things. But I do know —*I do remember*—the occasional messengers and homing pigeons, the fact that the newly made vampires could sense each other's blood." She shrugged her elegant shoulders. "I don't know if they were tracking, *feeding*, or what, but the surviving males in the rebel band all exchanged blood with one another, long before Fabian, Vanya, and I left Transylvania. The vampire mercenaries drank from each other's wrists."

"Yes," Vanya concurred. "Fabian once said they could find each other, much like a hound on a hunt, through the blood."

Ciopori nodded, enthusiastically. "Exactly. Which brings me back to my initial point: Long before the Curse, when Sister and I were yet children, I remember watching Fabian move throughout the castle, in and out of the apothecary. The mage could heal and cast powerful spells with blood, and he often carried various vials of the substance, containing the essence of the patients he was treating or enchanting."

"Yes," Vanya said, holding up two fingers. "I remember that as well, but the blood of the monarchy—my own, Ciopori's, that of our parents and our brothers—was considered sacred because it afforded such power to those who could wield magic. When we became ill, Fabian would let our blood personally, then destroy all vestiges once we were healed."

"Indeed, sister," Ciopori agreed, meeting Vanya's pensive stare, "but that's what I've been trying to say: Fabian did not imbibe from our brother, Prince Jadon. The High Mage was too well trained; brother's blood was too sacrosanct; and Fabian's respect was inviolable. Rather, Jadon gave the High Mage a vial of his blood for safekeeping—or perhaps for tracing—before we sailed to this land. Nanaşule used to wear it around his neck as an amulet. I believe he was not to absorb it unless things became desperate, a worst-case-scenario arrangement should Jadon have trouble finding us."

"Oh...whoa," Nachari cut in. "That rings true for me as well, in terms of what I saw, just small, splintered flashes of memory: Fabian going below deck on a large wooden vessel, that ivory tunic, his golden-bronze hair." The Master Wizard shook his head. "I was paying such close attention to his clothing, to his expression, that I didn't zero in on his neck, but Ciopori is right— he was wearing a vial of blood as an amulet, only he wasn't wearing just one. He was wearing two."

The king drew back. "Who else's blood did he have? Who else's blood did he need?"

"Could've been two vials of Prince Jadon's blood, milord," Saber offered. "You know, just to be safe in case something happened to the first."

"Hell," Marquis snorted, "could've been anyone's: King Sakarias', another mage's; shit, might've been Fabian's own plasma."

Napolean nodded circumspectly. "Anything else, Nachari?

Anything at all?"

Nachari furrowed his brows in concentration.

The hawk.

The raven.

Two vials of blood.

And then his head jerked up. "Light cleaves to light, and darkness cleaves to darkness," he blurted.

"Excuse me?" Marquis asked.

"Don't know," Nachari said. "Just a phrase spooling around in Fabian's head…over and over…like a broken record. That, and my own overwhelming impulse to run that phrase by Braden."

"Braden?" the king asked, blinking in surprise. "Why Braden?"

Again, Nachari didn't have an adequate answer. "No idea," he offered. "Just an odd, but insistent, impulse. Maybe because the boy is so psychically connected to the house of Jadon. Wouldn't be the first time he's provided answers."

Napolean appeared to think this over. "Very well," he finally said. "I will trust you to follow up with your instincts, and perhaps we can revisit this again with Fabian, now that we know the right questions to ask of the mage." He flicked his wrist in the air, as if dismissing the subject, then twisted at the waist, to regard Saber more directly. "Dragon, one last question for you: Did the Dark Ones—*will the Dark Ones*—celebrate the Millenia Harvest Moon?"

"Oh yeah," Saber drawled without hesitation. "But I don't know if you would call the house of Jaegar's interpretation *sacred*. From what I was taught, when the powers of the Dark Lords drench the earth on the night of the Harvest Moon, there's a lot of…*feeding*…going on: youngest brothers satiating their fathers and their siblings, a lot of dead bodies left in their wake, and a whole lot of human women getting pregnant, then dying forty-eight hours later. It's more like an orgy than a holy rite. The Dark

Ones will commemorate all the sacrifices that led up to the Curse, not the millennium of peace and prosperity that followed the birth of King Silvano's grandfather."

Vanya cringed. Her shoulders stiffened and curled forward, and she gazed down at the ground. "It still pains me to think of things you may have been forced to do. I am hesitant to even ask what ceremonies you have been required to participate in, dragon?" Her voice was both strained and regretful.

Saber sighed. He placed a second hand on the other side of her shoulder and gently massaged her muscles with all ten fingers. "Princess..." His tone spoke volumes. "Fortunately, I am not old enough to have seen a Millenia Harvest Moon yet. As for other ceremonies, over eight hundred years? You know I was never *forced* to do anything. For all intents and purposes—and as far as I knew—I *was* a Dark One, angel."

She didn't respond.

She didn't look like she could...

His voice dropped to a low, careful whisper. "Princess, you already know my hands are unclean, but I've never molested a human woman—can we just leave it at that? Keep the past in the past?"

She reached up, placed her right hand over his left, then squeezed it; and nothing more was said.

Napolean surveyed the tender interaction before gently clearing his throat. "I think we've had enough for one day. Time to adjourn this meeting." He leveled his gaze on Nachari as he rose from the ottoman to see his guests off. "Wizard, I want you to hang around for a few minutes so the two of us can mull this over. And also"—a faint light sparked in his pupils—"when you do go back home and check in with Braden, I want you to ask him if he's had any interesting dreams lately, if anything strange, or seemingly random, has disrupted his sleep. In fact, when we next question Fabian, I think Braden should attend."

CHAPTER TWENTY-SIX

Gwen stepped gingerly into the deep, sunken whirlpool tub in the guest house's master bathroom, allowing her sensitive skin to adjust to the heat of the water. The oversized, rectangular tub was wide enough for side-by-side bathing and was built into a raised wooden platform beneath panoramic windows that offered a stunning, treed view of the valley floor. Last she had absently counted, it had at least thirty-eight jets in total and an adjustable underwater mood lamp.

Fabian must have played with the buttons when he ran the bath, because the mood lamp was set on a soft, mellow green; the basin was filled with scented oils—smelled like lavender and perhaps vanilla—and bubbles from the generously applied, all-natural bubble bath were rising to the rim of the tub.

As she reclined against the back rest and let the massaging under-jets take her over, Gwen exhaled deeply.

Fabian...

What was she going to do about her predicament now?

There was no turning back.

She was already a vampire, although she didn't feel that much different.

At least not yet...

She arched her neck, rested her head against a built-in pillow, and tried to make sense of the past forty-eight hours: the conversion, Fabian's constant caretaking and attention, and the mage's improved, or at least semi-stable, state of mind.

The wizard had been true to his word, at least as far as the conversion had gone. When he had first bitten her in the neck with those sharp, piercing incisors, Gwen had wished for death: the strength of the venom, the intensity of the pain, the way it had snaked through her veins at high velocity, like an unseen arterial serpent seeking to destroy her from the inside out... But then, the pain had ceased almost as quickly as it had started. Fabian had cradled Gwen in his lap, his arms shackled around her waist and shoulders, while pressing her head gently, near his heart. And he had stayed in that position for all three hours of the conversion, completely focused and determined, lost in a trance.

According to Deanna Dubois Silivasi, conversion was supposed to hurt.

Like a bitch!

There was no way around it.

The female *destinies* could not be unconscious during the process. The venom was indeed destroying the mortal body in order to compel The Change, and unlike the forty-eight-hour process of pregnancy and birth, the males couldn't block their mate's excruciating pain. But then, Fabian had insisted that he hadn't blocked it. He had simply taken Gwen someplace else, along with him—he had traversed the veil between life and death, crossed from the mortal to the immortal plane, and hovered on the outskirts of the physical world where spirit, not the body, had dominion over sensation and reality. He had literally stepped over from this world into the afterlife, without severing the connection, perhaps the silver cord, to the former, and it was there in the world between worlds that Fabian Antonescu had converted Gwen.

According to Fabian, he lingered there often; perhaps it was how he had known she was his *destiny*, even before the Blood Moon had revealed it.

Gwen had known the wizard was powerful.

She had known he could cast incredible spells.

But to command the portal, or the bridge, between planes... even now, Gwen could hardly comprehend it.

The motor inside the tub purred in a soft, droning hum as the jets switched over to another cycle, and Gwen switched her attention to Fabian's surprising devotion, the way he had cared for her after the conversion. At first, he had checked all her vital signs, her reflexes, her new vampiric powers, carefully explaining each and every one in turn, giving her an opportunity to try them out and acclimate to them. And then he had fed her—*so gross at first*—insisting she learn how to take from both his wrist and his throat. And finally, he had insisted that she rest, sleep deeply, every two or three hours, following his waking tutelage.

And so the past forty-eight hours had passed, more like a dream than a nightmare, with Fabian talking to Gwen, asking her questions, teaching her about her new, enhanced body, and touching her...caressing her...massaging her at every turn, before insisting upon—or helping—her sleep. And the only thing more stunning, more unexpected, than the wild wizard's sudden tenderness and caring was that fact that he had the presence of mind, albeit still a little shaky, to commit to either one.

Gwen had no idea what had happened.

It wasn't like someone had given him a lobotomy, and it wasn't like he was altogether sane, but there had been a marked transformation: Napolean had sent human servants to the guest house, several whose families had willingly served the house of

Jadon for centuries, to feed the High Mage at regular intervals, and Fabian had reluctantly accepted the gift.

Thank goodness, Gwen had slept through each *feeding—that was something she didn't care to watch...or see...maybe never.*

And slowly, but surely, Fabian had begun to request ancient books, texts, records from the king's library and the Hall of Justice. It was like he was supplementing the memories Nachari had implanted with research of his own—Fabian had wanted to know every step and event in the progression of the house of Jadon, and he had devoured the information like a starving man devouring food. The wizard had swallowed it whole.

And the more he learned, the more he contemplated, the more he seemed to connect missing dots, until his ramblings and bouts of feral consciousness began to give way to a tentative trust: The wizard was slowly allowing the king into his inner sphere, but not for himself, for Gwen.

For Gwen...

She shook her head and adjusted the dials on the jets behind her neck.

Gwen didn't believe for a minute that Fabian had been magically healed, or that anyone would be safe to turn their back on him, expect "the fog" to vanish. But she did believe that the ancient princesses had woven a powerful spell in the ceremonial hall, and moreover, she believed what was grounding Fabian, anchoring him to Dark Moon Vale and keeping him in the guest house, was not the desire to embrace the modern house of Jadon, and not any burgeoning friendship with the king, but a deep, abiding, if not unconscious love for those two magical, beautiful females: Vanya and Ciopori.

Old habits die hard.

And Fabian was their *nanaşule,* their godfather, one who wielded the power of the gods, acted as Father, and one who was deeply respected and adored.

That adoration flowed both ways...

Finding the females safe and alive, realizing they had families, children, responsibilities to Prince Jadon's descendants, had made all the difference to the mage. It had allowed him to at least *be still* for a time. It had kept his demons at bay.

The large, heavy, rustic barn door to the master en suite slid open, and Fabian strolled in, padding silently and gracefully toward the tub, as seemed to be the predatory gait of his kind.

Their kind.

Gwen stifled a gasp.

At this juncture, she had seen Fabian in regular street clothes before, but the visage still seized her heart: The ancient wizard was wearing a pair of faded blue jeans, a plain white T-shirt, and his feet were bare. His long, layered, golden-bronze hair was still damp from a recent shower and falling near his eyes, the blond and burnt-red highlights stark against the black, almond-shaped rims of his burnt-copper gaze. Even when he wasn't trying, his stare radiated heat and projected mystery, and right now, he was staring straight into the bathtub, admiring Gwen.

She glanced down at the bubbles, making sure everything that should be covered was amply obscured from his gaze. So far, he had not tried to initiate sex again—*our passion is promised; the lust has always been there*—but Gwen knew it was just a matter of time.

"Did you realize that one can conjure fire from that large, heavy silver contraption in the kitchen?" he asked randomly. His voice was deep and gruff. "Just by pressing down, then twisting those...um...those dials."

Gwen blinked several times. "You mean the stove?"

He tilted his head to the side, which she now knew was a sign of memory retrieval. "The...not an oven or a...grill...the cooktop. Yes, the gas range."

Despite herself, Gwen smiled faintly. "Those come in electric too. Electric and convection."

He frowned, and the creases around his mouth only accentuated his full, sculpted lips. "Why do vampires have a...an appliance for the purposes of cooking food?"

Gwen shrugged impulsively. "I don't know. Maybe because this is a guest house, and sometimes, they have human guests?" The words *human guests* brought her right back, front and center, to her current plight: *Dear gods,* Gwen was no longer human, and she was no longer a guest of these Vampyr. Like it or not, she was part of the house of Jadon now, sired into vampirism by an ancient, enigmatic wizard, and her life was never going to be the same.

Things would *never* go back to normal.

And there was virtually zero chance that she was going to click her heels three times and end up back home, in Denver.

He harrumphed, still thinking about vampires and appliances, apparently. "No, I don't believe it has anything to do with this being a guest house. Nachari and his mate have one too. A gas range, that is." He shook his head to dismiss the thought. "But there is something else troubling you...shadows in your eyes. That is usually my domain, so tell me: What troubles you, Gwendolyn?"

She held her palms under the water, against two soft jets, dividing her attention between the soothing pressure and the puzzling vampire. *That is usually my domain? Was Fabian making a joke? Or at least trying...* "Just thinking about my family," she said. "I haven't called or texted them in over a week." She straightened her back and pulled her knees toward her chest, careful to make sure the bubbles came with them. "They know I'm staying in Dark Moon Vale; they believe I'm enjoying the lodge, the horseback riding, the whitewater rafting, but if they don't hear something from me soon... Well, don't be surprised if they just show up. We're a very close family."

Fabian closed the distance between the sliding barn door and the luxurious tub, kneeling beside Gwen's shoulders; then he dipped his hand in the water and swirled it around.

She jumped and stiffened.

"Shh," he coaxed. "I've bathed you before."

She shook her head in bewilderment. "No, you washed my hair with a bar of soap, beneath a frigid waterfall. That's not the same thing, Fabian. Grownups don't bathe grownups."

The corner of his mouth curved up in a grin. "And if I recall, I kissed you right here." He ran the backs of two fingers along the nape of her neck, just above the curve in her shoulder.

She brushed his hand away.

Undaunted, he scooted a couple of inches over, placed both hands on her slender shoulders, and began to massage her tense muscles.

"I already have thirty-eight jets," she told him.

"Mm," he murmured, "but do they feel like this?" He kneaded her trapezius muscles, drew a deep line with his thumbs along the zone between her rhomboids and her scapula, and nuzzled his chin in her hair. "You may contact your family this evening or tomorrow, as soon as I learn more about them and we figure out, together, how we intend to handle their interference going forward."

Gwen's shoulders hardened.

Massage over!

"Their *interference?*" she snapped.

He drew back in surprise. "Their questions, their presence in your life...their *role* going forward."

She raised her chin and angled her jaw, locking her gaze with his, unapologetically. "Their questions will be answered *by me.*

Their presence will be as often as they want. And their role will be...my mom and dad!"

Fabian studied her expression intently, then reached for a bar of almond-and-vanilla soap, lathered it against his palm, and began to apply long, even, deep-pressured strokes, up and down her arms, once again, using his thumb to trace every striation in her muscles. "Your parents will never know how you truly came to be in this valley. They will never know about the aged stone well, and they certainly will not know that you are mate to an ancient mage and vampire—they will know nothing about the Curse or the Corona Borealis Blood Moon. Some memories must be implanted, even as others must be erased." He cupped her cheek in his large, rugged hand and brushed his thumb over her upper lip. "But yes, Gwendolyn, my dove; I will welcome your guardians with open arms, and in time, I will come to both love and respect...Mark and Mary...just as you do. That is a husband's duty."

Gwen shivered from her head to her toes.

A husband's duty...

She could think of a dozen words for Fabian Antonescu and how he might approach life, but *husband* wasn't one of them.

He studied her expression again, then returned to his soapy massage, this time moving his hand to her upper thigh, her knee, and her shinbone, finally focusing his thumb on her ankle. "You miss them?" he asked.

"Very much," she whispered.

He nodded. "I have been so long without family or friends, I no longer experience the pain of their absence."

Now this brought Gwen up short. Fabian's family and friends —the thought had never occurred to her, but of course, he once had them. It wasn't like he had hatched from an egg. "I'm sorry," she whispered, not truly understanding where the words or the sympathy was coming from.

A mournful smile curved along the edges of his mouth, but it didn't spread any further. "You are my family now," he reminded her.

She closed her eyes.

"Gwendolyn..."

She kept them shut.

"Gwendolyn, look at me, dove."

She didn't obey—she would never be obedient.

Fabian sighed. "Last night, before you fell asleep, I asked you about your life before we met, and you told me of your studies, your friendships, those things that brought you pleasure, such as your family's cat, Matilda; eating cuisine from the peninsula of Italy; traversing up and down steep mountains from a chair in the sky so you can fly down very quickly on two long, colorful sticks. And as you spoke of such memories, I had the impression of a scent...a long-ago memory of my own...the bark of aspen trees, the smell of wildflowers, the distinctive aroma of a particular meadow, high up in these Rocky Mountains. But I cannot understand why your memories invoked my own. And I must admit, I'm curious to learn even more about you."

Gwen slowly opened her eyes, and when she glanced askance at Fabian, his expression was so clear...so guileless...so sincere. It was like she was seeing a completely different vampire, one who came from a family, who had friends, one who also had fond memories and past times of his own. Speaking of past times: "The colorful sticks are called *skis*, the hill is called a ski run, and flying down it really fast is called skiing."

He pondered her words for a moment. "And you miss this... this skiing...very much?"

She laughed softly—she couldn't help it. "Well, yes and no. It just turned July, so ski season is over, but yes, in the winter, if I didn't get to ski, I would miss it very much. But mostly, I would miss my girlfriends...*my besties*... Skiing was something we did together."

He furrowed his brow. "When the Blood Moon has concluded, and we make a home together, mayhap I will ask Napolean to build you such a...ski run so you and your...besties... can have your own special mountain."

Despite herself, Gwen was stunned. She turned her head to regard him directly, and for the first time since she'd encountered the ancient wizard, she really looked into his eyes, into the soul behind the vampire, not just the color of the orbs. "You...*you*..." Now she was the one stuttering and pausing. "You would do that...*for me?*"

His dark gaze grew even darker still, and his beautiful copper complexion nearly glowed, framing flawless features. "Ah," he sighed, "to you, I am yet a monster, and truth be told, I may always be. But yes, Gwendolyn, I would clear a mountain for you." He leaned forward, lifting his hand from her nearest leg and switching to the inner thigh of the other—careful to keep his attentions just above her knee, along the back of her calf, and around her ankle. "If you asked me for the moon and stars, I would get them for you."

She gulped. "Why?" She couldn't help it, but she wanted to know. The gods had made Gwen Fabian's *destiny*, and he was as stuck with her as she was with him. The two had very little, if anything, in common, and the last five days had been anything but romantic or endearing. Despite the caves, despite the claiming, despite Fabian's recent and insistent caresses, the two did not have an intimate relationship.

And they likely never would.

Fabian withdrew his hand from the water, stood to his full, proud height, and wrenched the T-shirt over his head. With a dexterity he should not have possessed in such little time, he released the button on the fly of his jeans and swiftly undrew the zipper. And then he slid the denim down his taut, muscular pelvis, allowing the pants to fall to the floor.

Gwen jerked in surprise and immediately looked away.

As usual, the male was going commando…

She guessed some old habits died harder than others; either that, or Napolean had been unwilling to share his underwear.

The ancient vampire walked, unashamedly, to the far end of the bathtub, gestured for Gwen to scoot forward—a motion she could still see in her peripheral vision—and climbed in behind her, like they had been doing this very thing together for a dozen years. Her heart raced in her chest as he sidled up against her: his chest to her back, his pelvis to her rear, his strong, brawny arms wrapping around her and hovering just above the swell of her breasts.

He waited for Gwen to settle down and lean back, and it took all the composure she had to do it—but what else could she do? Where else could she go? Besides, sitting up straight was the wrong position if she hoped to remain covered by the white, frothy bubbles.

And then something else occurred to her, something Fabian had said: *Last night, before you fell asleep, I asked you about your life before we met…and I had the impression of a scent…a long-ago memory of my own…the bark of aspen trees, the smell of wildflowers, the distinctive aroma of a particular meadow, high up in these Rocky Mountains.*

"I've been here before," she blurted.

He leaned forward, if that was even possible. "Pardon?"

"Dark Moon Vale. I've been here before, but I never connected the dots…until now."

He swept a wet lock of her hair behind her right shoulder and bent down to kiss the trail of the water. "Tell me more," he whispered into her ear, his voice growing husky and slightly hoarse.

She shivered yet tried to maintain her concentration. "Over

the years, my friends and I have visited so many mountain towns in Colorado—also a favorite pastime—and one of them was a couple towns over from Silverton Creek. Anyhow, we hiked a lot, and one afternoon, in the Roosevelt National Forest, we came across the most stunning grove of giant aspen trees. And when I say giant, I mean supernatural...impossible...perhaps a hundred, a hundred fifty feet, with trunks so wide at the base, they were almost the width of a small car. I had never seen anything like them."

Fabian froze behind her, and his ever-roaming hands grew still.

"Long after that afternoon with my girlfriends, I would come back on occasion and hike to that grove, especially during autumn when the leaves were changing, and I would just bring a blanket and lie beneath this one particular aspen, the largest one in the bunch, directly in the center of the orchard. It was massive, amazing, one of the most beautiful things I had ever seen, and I'm sure you're not going to believe this, but about five feet up from the base of the trunk, someone had carved a perfect likeness of a hummingbird into the bark of the tree. And I don't know how they did it, but the colors on its primaries—the turquoise, purple, and orange—those hummingbirds aren't native to Colorado, so it had to have been a tourist from somewhere else." She sighed, almost wistfully, the memory bringing temporary peace. "I guess I just never made the connection between the national forest, how far we had hiked, and the proximity to Dark Moon Vale." When at least a minute had passed and Fabian hadn't responded —or moved—Gwen rotated her head to the side to glance over her shoulder. "Fabian?"

His head fell forward against the back of her hair. "Do you remember the bird's head or his eyes?"

"Oh, yes," she said, enthusiastically. "Just beyond its beak, toward the crown, was—"

"A gentle slope of orange, rising to pale yellow," Fabian supplied.

This time, it was Gwen who grew silent.

"And along and beneath its dark chestnut eyes," Fabian whispered, "on the side of its throat, there was a vivid ocean blue. The orange reappeared as a spattering below the gorget, between the blue and the crest of its wings, its chest and flank a magnificent turquoise and green."

Gwen nodded slowly. "You can see my memories—this memory—that clearly?"

He shook his head and tightened his arms around her. "No. I am not reading your memories, Gwen. Nearly 2,810 years ago, give or take a year, after arriving in North America, I discovered the most beautiful, captivating grove of tall, quaking aspen trees, and I became so enamored of that orchard that I cast a spell of enchantment over the foliage, making all within eyesight immortal. The trees must have been massive when you found them because they are practically ageless, and the hummingbird on the center tree, I carved it from the fine edge of my dagger and colored it in from the palette seen throughout my travels, fixing the color to the bark with magick. And then I cast a spell of brilliance to enhance its beauty and ensure that it never faded." His voice dropped to a low, silken purr. "It would seem that thousands of years later, my *destiny* found my artistic rendition."

There were a few rare, timeless moments in life when everything just suddenly shifted.

When the axis one was standing upon tilted, and the entire landscape was just somehow changed.

This was one of those moments for Gwen.

She had spent countless hours lying beneath that aspen tree —*Fabian's aspen tree*—and she had studied that hummingbird in earnest, wondering endlessly about its creator.

Feeling a soul-level connection with the artist...

She twisted further around and met his seeking gaze, her lips gently parting as her jaw fell open. *My God*, she thought. *I know this man—I know this vampire—I've seen his soul a dozen times in those majestic colors; I've seen his intelligence in that attention to detail; I've seen his love of life, and his reverence for nature, his adoration of simple beauty, in that singular, astonishing creation. And he was with me in all those moments...*

And I was with him.

I know who he is beyond the shadows.

Her eyes welled up with tears.

And his matched hers.

He reached across her shoulder, grasped her jaw between his thumb and forefinger, and tilted her head back to expose her lips. And then he kissed her with a passion, intimacy, and hunger unlike anything she had ever believed possible.

She breathed life...

Love...

Longing...into his mouth...

And kissed him back with abandon.

CHAPTER TWENTY-SEVEN

F abian was instantly swept away in the moment.

He couldn't believe this was happening—that his *destiny* was welcoming his passion; that she had found the artistic carving on the old, enchanted aspen tree, so many centuries later; that the gods had drawn Gwen to Fabian long before the two had encountered one another at the well.

And this changed everything.

It meant the deities had never left him—they had always been aware of the mage and his plight...his slumber...his confusion. And fate had been working on his behalf.

Always...

On his behalf.

Yes, Fabian was meant to be exactly where he was, in Dark Moon Vale, in Napolean's guest house, communing with the modern house of Jadon...

Beside Gwendolyn.

The gods had foreseen it.

Nay, they had *arranged* it.

He tunneled his fingers in his *destiny's* thick, damp hair, reveling in the powerful sensation, the pure feminine allure of it —it had been so long. So long since he had worshipped a woman.

The hot, swirling water in the jetted tub may as well have been a cauldron of fire as Fabian's body erupted in flames. He kneaded Gwen's waist, then her ribs, then the underside of her full, heavy breasts with his free hand, and groaned into her mouth.

She shuddered, but she did not pull away.

Rather, she twisted around, even further in the tub, and wrapped her arms around his shoulders.

He trembled from head to toe.

And then his fangs exploded from his mouth in feral ecstasy, and he kissed—and nipped—a trail of fever from behind her ear, along the slope of her neck, and over her wet, soapy shoulder until she trembled with him.

His arousal shot up in the water, swelling to full engorgement, and he slid both palms beneath the globes of Gwen's ass, kneaded the muscles with hunger, then lifted her from the bottom of the basin, repositioning her on his lap: face-to-face, breasts to chest, mouth to sensual mouth. "I cannot stop," he groaned in her ear, his hands tracing and grasping at every tantalizing curve, his fingers exploring her hips and her thighs, her stomach, her nipples, then her mouth...again.

He placed two fingers over her tongue, encouraging her to suckle, and then he moved them slowly in and out of the wet, moist cavity, before withdrawing the digits and exploring her lips —roughly, erotically—with his sensitive fingertips. "Oh, gods, Gwendolyn," he rasped in a deep, heady drawl. "I want you, every inch of you. To give you pleasure like you have never known."

She gasped and unwittingly rocked her hips.

Fabian's erection jerked, and he felt all the blood—all the reason—leave his brain and flow down through his body.

He kneaded her breasts.

He laved her nipples, grasping his female by the small of her waist and arching her back to expose both full mounds to his full exploration. Then he tasted them, grazed his fangs along her areolas, and drew her deep into the warmth of his mouth.

He bit down, pricking her skin, and sat back up, grasping a fistful of her hair.

He was past the point of no return.

He slid his fingers between her trembling thighs, felt her, explored her, memorized every furrow and curve, then tunneled inside her—testing, feeling, stretching her core—preparing her for his passionate invasion.

Her eyes were glassy, her nipples were hard, her lips were gently parted, and she was panting.

Oh gods, yes.

Yes, yes, yes...

He wanted to take his time, explore her further, bring her to a half-dozen orgasms before he entered her, but the desire was at a fevered pitch. Fabian was lost in the rapture of all things Gwendolyn, and his body was aching to take her, command her, claim her. At last.

Her tousled hair...

Her feminine moans...

The perfect flesh on her thighs...

The hawk, the raven, the vials of blood...

Light cleaves to light, and darkness cleaves to darkness.

"No," he barked, snarling at the fog. "Not now; not now!"

Not now!

Gwendolyn stiffened—and not from passion—and Fabian's heart skipped a beat.

He was going to lose her...

He could not lose her!

Not when they were this close to finally becoming one.

He growled into her ear, a bestial warning, clutched her waist in both hands, and lifted. With the grace of a swan and the predatory instincts of a lion, he shifted her forward, spun her around, and placed her behind him, facing the back of the basin, sprawled on her hands and knees.

He quickly sidled up behind her, and she twisted her neck to look past her shoulder, locking her gaze with Fabian's: Her exotic, light-green eyes were wild with fear, confusion, and lust.

The hawk, the ravens, the vials of blood...

The coming Millenia Harvest Moon.

No!

No!

He would not allow this! The fog would *not* take him over right now.

He only needed to *feed*...

Yes, first, he needed to feed.

His fangs grew even longer as he palmed Gwen's ass, massaged each globe in a harsh, circular motion, then spread the flesh nearest her core with his thumbs, exposing her heat to his hungry, feral view. He moaned in ecstasy, bent over her back, and held her still by both shoulders.

Gwendolyn squirmed and resisted, starting to panic. "Fabian, no! Don't do this." She tried to twist away from him, move from beneath him.

He tightened his hold.

The hawk, the ravens, the vials of blood...

Only the strong, the dominant, will overcome.

He bent his head and made a seal over her jugular.

"Fabian, no!" She arched her back toward him, trying to buck him off, then strained to wrench her neck away from him. "Let me go! I don't want this."

He rocked his pelvis against her globes, even as he homed in on the scent of the addicting fluid, Gwen's rich, platelet-thick, crimson blood—he could already imagine the pleasure as it snaked down his throat.

"The hummingbird, the one you carved in the tree. It was beautiful, peaceful...acquiescent."

He blinked three times.

"Fabian, this is the twenty-first century. I am your equal, not your property, and I am telling you, *no*. No *feeding*. No sex. No more. Get off me!"

He jerked as if she had struck him with a club.

No feeding.

No sex.

No more.

Get off me!

Her words were clear, unambiguous, and striking—no matter the century in which they were spoken. No male of character, as far as time immemorial, could fail to discern their meaning.

The coupling was not wanted.

The hawk, the raven—her blood called out to him.

The coupling was not wanted!

Fabian flew back in the tub, propelling his body so hard with his wings, he slammed against the opposite wall and sent water in violent waves, splashing across the bathroom floor. "Gwendolyn," he panted. *"Destinul meu..."* He combed his hands through his hair, inadvertently scoring his scalp with his claws.

He didn't care.

It didn't matter.

The pain, the blood, the wake-up call were exactly what his animal needed.

He scrambled across the bathroom floor and turned around in feverish circles, searching the tiles for his clothing, dripping water in random puddles, and heaving in air. "Forgive me," he barked, snatching the jeans off the floor and quickly shrugging into the T-shirt.

It clung to his wet, heaving body.

Instinctively, he knew it was 12:30 PM, and the sun would still be at its zenith—Fabian was an ancient, a vampire, a descendant of celestial gods—he could *feel* time and the position of the sun and stars in his very bones and spirit.

But he couldn't flee into the night, nor could he become one with the shadows, not at noon, not when all were awake and busy going about their daily lives. Nonetheless, he *had* to escape the frenzy...the fog...he had to outrun the madness.

He would go to Napolean Mondragon.

He would consult the wizard, Nachari.

He would humiliate himself among the males of his kind, by begging the princesses for mercy...for assistance...for intervention.

There had to be at least one soul—one damnable, powerful vampire—in Dark Moon Vale, in the house of Jadon, who could free Fabian from this scourge, once and for all.

Blessed Hercules and curse the darkness—he had almost ravaged his female.

He had almost taken Gwen by force.

He was not fit for this world, let alone this modern existence.

Gwendolyn scrambled out of the tub, reached for a large white towel, and glared at Fabian like she resented him, *despised him*, and the look on her face—the hurt in her eyes—Fabian's stomach turned over in waves of nausea. He wanted to break something. Hurt someone. He wanted to kill, and he *needed* to feed.

His head jerked up as he skimmed Gwen's thoughts: fear, disgust, despair...and loathing.

Fear for the future.

Disgust with the...*fog?*

Despair both for herself...*and Fabian.*

Dear gods, her loathing was not of the mage, but of a human man, long ago, who had taken such advantage of her mother, when her father had been lost in a gambling addiction. A man who had not been crazed or insane, but calculated, deliberate, and evil.

Gwen did not hate Fabian.

She hated the demons that haunted him.

The demon of a human man who almost destroyed her family, who still on occasion haunted her, too.

And in that moment, Fabian knew—*he knew*—this female was truly his *destiny*. For compassion such as hers could come from no other than a deity. To despise Fabian fully would be akin to rebuking her own eternal soul. To completely turn her back on him, she would have to forfeit her...*self*.

He shook his head, dumbfounded, and then he snarled.

He would humble himself before Napolean and the king's wizards. He would slay these demons if it killed him, but first —*but first*—he would unleash his rage and his vengeance and feed until there wasn't a drop of blood left in his victim.

And he knew exactly where he was going.

He tunneled, just a little deeper, into Gwen's frontal lobe, then followed the bridge of the hippocampus back to a specific time in her childhood, and then he closed his eyes, gave full vent to his mystical powers, and became quantum energy in motion... ruler of that which created worlds.

He slowed his heart rate and deepened his breathing, exploring Gwen's memories further.

A human man in a black limousine: his hair color, his eyes, his psychic footprint...

His date of birth.

And the distinct cosmic imprint—the alignment of stars and planets—that occurred when the son of a whoring jackal was born...

He had it.

He had him.

All that was left was to follow the individual vibrations—the thought patterns, the unique and distinct energy, nature, and stamp on the cosmos—the dark man in the limousine had left in the universe: to follow it backward with Fabian's ethereal body, and this time, to bring his corporeal form along for the ride.

Glancing once more at his *destiny*, Fabian Antonescu dived into a speeding tunnel, where neither time nor space held dominion, and he vanished just as swiftly from the guest house bathroom.

* * *

The man's name was Paul McNeil.

He was in his late fifties or early sixties, and while Fabian knew very little of the modern world, how wealth was displayed in the current century, or what hamlets were considered affluent in Colorado, Paul's sprawling estate was spread out over what had to be at least a ten-acre parcel of land, surrounded by several lavish outbuildings and secured within an opulent...*neighborhood*...which housed a gate and several guards. A magnificent city skyline towered behind his back terrace—from Nachari's memories, Fabian assumed this city was called Denver —and he had a large, geometric swimming pool beneath a high-domed solarium.

The bastard was living a lavish lifestyle.

No matter.

Fabian had not come to have tea or to discuss the local economy.

He emerged in the dark man's parlor as nothing more than a funnel of mist and smoke and immediately merged with his corporeal body, flashing into view in an instant: eyes, no doubt, gleaming red; claws, fully extended; fangs elongating even as he prowled toward his prey.

Paul was sitting in a tall, upholstered armchair in some sort of library, his greasy, thin gray hair combed straight back with some sort of oil. His dull, dirt-brown eyes were focused on some sort of ledger nestled in his lap, and his cracked, reedy lips were pursed together in concentration.

"Paul." Fabian whispered his name, and the male jerked back in his chair, sending the ledger flying to the ground, before instinctively grasping the lapels of his tailored shirt and trying to jump out of the chair.

"Remain seated," Fabian drawled, and the human fell back down, his feet planted like the roots of an oak to the fabric-covered floor.

The human frantically scanned the room with wide, frightened eyes—the desktop, the credenza, the tall rows of bookshelves—his gaze momentarily fixing upon a horizontal mallet and a scattering of nails lying beneath a large, rectangular oil painting. Apparently, Paul had not yet had an opportunity to hang one of his lavish treasures.

Fabian extended his finger toward a tall, wing-backed chair, situated between the desktop and the credenza, and drew it across the library floor, from a distance, until it came to rest, facing Paul's armchair. Then the vampire strolled slowly, and with confidence, to the neatly upholstered seat, bent to scoop the ledger from the floor, and sat down, lazily, before leaning back.

He crossed one leg over the other.

He opened the ledger and perused the entries. "What do we have here?"

He flipped through several pages. "Ah," he purred in a low, lethal rasp. "A wealthy man who spends his days counting his money." He glared at Paul with murderous disgust. "Feeling rather self-satisfied, weren't you?" Fabian's pupils narrowed into two tiny slits, and the mage bathed his sclera in fire...as backlight.

Paul squirmed in his seat, too terrified to even cry out.

He scooted as far back as he could, trying to blend his narrow, bony ass-cheeks with the base of the armchair, in an effort to gain even a few inches of space between himself and the menacing vampire. "Who are you?" he stammered. "*What* are you?" he whimpered. "Why are you here, and what do you want?" His voice was quaking like a leaf.

Fabian wasn't sure how to answer...

The grim reaper?

Your worst nightmare?

Or Justice, finally calling...

"The question is," he finally hissed, "what will *you* be tomorrow?" He reached forward like an apparition and slid a ghostly hand in, then back out of Paul McNeil's chest, twirling several inky strands of the man's black spirit between his own curved and clawed fingers. "A dark, worthless soul who preys upon the frailties of others?" He blew on the sticky web, and it lightened...just a little...from dark, sable black to dull, fossil gray. "Or a reformed soul who has given all his money to the poor and the needy, one who will forever live as a wanderer...a pauper...rummaging for food in fetid alleyways?"

He shrugged one shoulder and thought it over:

What to do?

What to do?

What did Paul McNeil truly deserve?

Sometimes there were punishments worse than death—sometimes, crossing over to the spirit world was a gift, a blessing... And then Fabian remembered Gwen's eyes—his *destiny's* fear and her loathing—her hatred of the demons that haunted them both.

He flicked the dirty, soiled tendrils of Paul's lost soul onto the floor and snarled: "Or a dead man's corpse rotting in an unmarked grave?" And then he tunneled so violently into Paul McNeil's gray matter that the human's head snapped back like someone had punched him.

Paul jerked in the chair like he was having a seizure, but Fabian kept right on excavating...scanning...searching for a very specific set of memories and feelings, or the lack thereof: If he left the human's mind shattered or ruined, *so what*. If the mongrel died, right then and there, from fright or a sudden hemorrhage, *so be it*. Fabian had to know, if only to satisfy his own sense of morbid curiosity, whether Paul McNeil had ever experienced a moment of regret, shame, or remorse. And the vampire did not have time to play tiddlywinks with the terrified Homo sapiens.

The urge to *feed*...

The desire to kill...

The impulse to shred, maim, and annihilate was too overwhelming.

Fabian wouldn't last much longer.

And then he found *the absence* of what he was looking for in the human's long-term memory: Indeed, Paul had no discernable recollection of Gwendolyn or her mother. The man had extorted so much money in his lifetime, taken advantage of so many helpless women, that he didn't even remember Mary Hamilton or her husband. They were nameless, faceless scraps of meat, unsalted and tossed in an overcrowded silo.

Fabian withdrew from the human's mind. "I am here to right a wrong, to settle an old, outstanding score, and to see that you leave this earth with at least one memory intact." He retrieved *Gwen's* memory, her description of Paul's perversion, from his own short-term memory bank; transferred the story and impressions into the human's skull; and illuminated each one so violently—so vehemently—Paul's eyes began to bleed. "Do you remember now?" Fabian snarled. "Do you remember the little girl?"

Paul's bloody eyes rolled back in his head, and he began to foam at the mouth.

"Do you remember what you took from her mother?"

A glob of frothy spittle dribbled from the corner of Paul's mouth, down his chin, and onto his tailored shirt.

"Do you have any idea what you did to that family?" Fabian watched the piteous creature continue to suffer as he let his ominous words linger in the room...

Silence.

Choking.

Grunting.

The man was on the verge of death.

"Not now," Fabian murmured. "Not yet." The High Mage still needed to feed. And Paul still owed Gwen an apology.

Fabian brought his own hand up to his mouth, released his incisors, and filled the fleshy part of his palm with venom. Then he reached forward and pressed the poultice over Paul's eyes, until the bleeding...choking...and grunting had stopped. The High Mage leaned back in his chair and ripped one of his own talons free from a forefinger—watching as the nail grew back. He snatched Paul by the collar, tore his tailored shirt open, and swiftly punctured the human's heart with the severed claw.

Fabian swirled it around in Paul's blood, before sealing the human's wound with a drop of venom. "We can do this as many times as we need to," he hissed, reaching down for the ledger, flipping it open to a full, blank page, and tearing it out of the book. He placed the page on top of the register, spun it around, and slid it onto Paul's lap. Then extended the dripping, blood-tipped talon forward. "Start writing," he growled.

Paul gasped in horror and began to stammer: "What...*what*...I don't under—"

"No!" Fabian shook his head. "Do not speak, not a single word. Just take the quill I have provided for you and scrawl your apology on this page—in blood—to Gwendolyn."

If Paul's dull-brown eyes opened any wider, they were going to pop right out of his skull. "Please," he pleaded in fevered angst,

"I can't write right now...*I can't*...I swear it." His entire body began to shake. "I'm sorry. Tell her I'm sorry. I didn't mean to harm her—or her family."

Fabian lowered his lids and sniffed. "What does *do not speak* mean to you?" Without awaiting Paul's reply, he stretched his arm in the direction of the unhung oil painting, crooked his fingers inward, and drew the mallet and a nail into the palm of his hand.

Paul urinated in his custom-made trousers as Fabian palmed the underside of his jaw with one hand and shoved the nail a few centimeters into the body of his mandible. He reached for the mallet and lightly tapped the remainder of the dark gray spike home—any greater pressure, and Fabian would've shattered the entire jaw, perhaps driven the nail into the human's cranium, rendering Paul unable to write...or think.

"Now then," Fabian drawled, making a concerted effort to maintain his fragile composure, "let us try this again. *Dear Gwen*..."

Tears of agony streamed down Paul's face as he snatched the bloody, makeshift quill and struggled to lean forward, over the page.

Dear...

Gwen...

He sprawled the words in a nearly illegible hand, but Fabian figured it would have to do—and then the blood dried up on the tip of the talon.

Fabian sighed in exasperation.

Then he struck a second time: a puncture to the heart, a swirl of the quill... He healed the wound with venom. "I would write much, *much* faster if I were you." He extended the talon to Paul, once again, only this time, he enchanted the bloody tip with magick so it wouldn't dry out—Paul didn't need to know this.

Dear Gwen, I am so, so, so, so sorry!!!

Paul McNeil.

"Good enough," Fabian grumbled, realizing it was the best the man was going to do under the circumstances. He took the page, folded it into the palm of his hand—again, using magick—then slowly crept forward in his winged-back chair and snatched Paul by the neck.

Finally...

And with unrestrained savagery, Fabian drew his prey to him and feasted on Paul's throat—he drank until there were only mere drops of blood left and the weak human's heart was failing.

Thump-thump.

Thump...thump.

Thump.

The heartbeats were slowing to a paltry crawl.

And that's when the High Mage plunged all five claws into Paul McNeil's chest, fisted the barely pulsing organ, withdrew it from the cavity, and left it in the human's lap. "I would say have a care—*have a heart*—in the future, but there is no future for you."

The human expired with his eyes wide open, gaping at the organ that once gave him life.

And Fabian retreated, back into the ether...

Spinning, tunneling, speeding back to Dark Moon Vale.

It was time to meet with Napolean.

CHAPTER TWENTY-EIGHT

S alvatore Nistor did not consider himself a maestro of world literature or a nerdly scholar of all things past. Nor was he apt to spend days on end in the Colony's library, perusing the historic annals for more than a couple of hours at most. Certainly, the Blood Canon, the ancient book of black magic which Salvatore had possessed for centuries, before Nachari Silivasi stole it right from underneath him, had been an exception.

No matter.

He had memorized every word of it.

Still, histories, fact, and figures were not the vampire-sorcerer's cup of tea. He preferred a more hands-on approach, which is why he enjoyed his divination and discerning information from his glowing crystal cube.

Until now, that is.

He hung his head, massaged his brow, and leaned forward toward the nightstand beside his enormous iron bed in order to cup the cube in two venerable palms. It was 6:00 in the evening; the sun would be setting at precisely 8:32 PM; and Salvatore would be able to leave his lair, stroll beneath the moonlight, and catch a fresh breath of air, which he desperately needed.

Perhaps he could even discern a bit more from the moon, stars, and chaotic energy swirling around the vale: *Great Dark Lords and whores of the Abyss, what the actual fuck was going on in the house of Jadon?* One minute, the skies were filled with lightning; the next, the air was positively electric with anxiety; and still the next, there was a faint golden web of peace, security, and lucidity floating about the ether, emanating from the direction of Napolean's compound. And all of it—every last scintilla, iota, and trace—was because of Fabian Antonescu, the legendary High Mage of monarchs, risen from the dead.

Salvatore sneered.

Indeed, the second coming of Jeepers Creepers.

He released the cube, twisted to stare at the heavy golden duvet blanketing his bed, and frowned at the utter nonsensical mayhem before him: notecards, sticky notes, a box of fine-tip, black Sharpies. What would his brothers of darkness think of him if they knew the Colony's greatest sorcerer—a deceptively handsome and brilliant dark witch, verily, an illustrious member of the Dark One's Council—was holed up in his chamber like some mentally affected dolt, scrawling random notes, visions, and divinations on small yellow squares of paper?

He harrumphed and glared at a random scattering of illogical scribbles...

King Silvano's grandfather, 988 B.C.

Maiden voyage. North America. 799 B.C.

Hawk—circled twice!

Raven—underlined with an explanation point.

Achilles Zahora, blood, blood, blood...

Salvatore jerked back, then seemingly out of nowhere, a human child's jingle flashed into his brain, and he hummed an infantile tune about things that were different...things that didn't belong. Great Ademordna, and curse his own immortal soul, Salvatore Nistor was now channeling *Sesame Street*! Had every trifle of drivel he had ever encountered, seen, or witnessed in a feeble human mind been stored in his long-term memory?

He shook his head.

That wasn't the point...

The point was: *Achilles Zahora, blood, blood, blood...*

He reached for the crumpled sticky note and held it up to the lantern light, noticing how the shadow from a nearby stalactite played across the yellow paper. Then he twisted back around to show it to his cube—as if the damn thing had eyes with retinas.

The cube began to glow, and he held it closer.

The glow began to flash!

Interesting...

He stuck the sticky note against the crystal—*because why the hell not?*—and watched as the damnable thing began to shake, tremble, and hum. And then one vision after another appeared in the biosphere behind the cube:

Achilles Zahora, "The Executioner," in all his magnificence and strength—seven feet tall, pale citrine eyes, a bronze complexion, and chin-length, black-and-red hair—the circular band around the male's upper right bicep, a black mamba with jeweled red eyes...

Achilles Zahora, "The Executioner," bathing in an ancient tub of blood, imbibing the viscous substance through his mouth, his ears, his nostrils—nay, his very pores—whilst swirling it around his tongue.

Achilles Zahora, "The Executioner," rising from a shallow grave like a mythical phoenix ascending from ash...

What. The. Actual. Fuck.

The cube went dark, like it was exhausted, expended—like it had just ravaged a worthless woman and finally spent its load.

Salvatore removed the sticky note and stared at the cube. He glanced behind his shoulder and stared at his bed—at all the random notations scattered about the duvet—and he sighed.

There was something there...

In all these haphazard scrawlings...

Something incredibly important.

And whatever it was, it had everything to do with history and Fabian Antonescu—it had everything to do with Achilles Zahora.

Perhaps it was time to inform Oskar Vadovsky, as well as the other esteemed members of the Dark Ones' Council, that something was afoot in Dark Moon Vale, and it did not just affect the house of Jadon.

CHAPTER TWENTY-NINE

The sun had set by the time Fabian returned to Dark Moon Vale, by the time the ancient High Mage had finished toying with—and killing—Paul McNeil, by the time he had hunted and fed upon a score of other human prey, at last drinking his fill.

He had not been in a hurry to return to Gwen, and not because he didn't care for his sweet, beleaguered *destiny*—her ardent kiss, the fear and disappointment in her eyes; both still lingered in his memory—but because Fabian knew Gwen needed some space, some time alone to both decompress and to weigh the gravity of all that had happened between them...all that had happened in her life over the past five days.

And truth be told, Fabian needed some time to clear his head as well.

Gwendolyn would not try to escape.

He was certain of it.

Surely, even Napolean had to know the High Mage was aware of the sentinels and the vigilant warriors, the fact that they were watching the guest house from a respectful distance, ostensibly to make sure Fabian did not flee the valley with Gwen...

The fact that they were guarding the fragile couple from afar.

If Gwendolyn ran off, they would have to corral her, yet again, and no one wanted to capture, entrap, or lure Fabian to the king's manse a second time—the first time had been too dangerous...too volatile. No, Napolean's loyalists would keep Gwen right where she was until Fabian returned, and if the High Mage was being candid, someone would've also followed Fabian to Paul McNeil's residence if they had known how to track an immortal spirit traveling through the space between worlds, neither traversing the earth, nor navigating the cosmos, but somewhere in between.

Alas, Napolean Mondragon himself was the only vampire in the vale who could do such a thing, and Fabian doubted that the king had been given ample warning, nor could Napolean have foreseen Fabian's intent.

Now, as the High Mage reached for the heavy black iron knocker on the front door of the king's private residence, he took a slow, deep breath and reminded himself of what he was doing—and why he was doing it.

For Gwendolyn.

He had to banish the demons once and for all.

He had to finally sift through the fog...*for Gwendolyn.*

He had come far too close to harming his female, if not physically, then emotionally—spiritually—and while Fabian may have been a brutish male, lacking in several refined qualities, he was not a wild beast in the fields, nor was he a defiler of women.

He grasped the knocker in a firm right hand, but before he could use it, the ancient king opened the door. "I've been waiting for you," the monarch said solemnly, the silver slashes in his dark, ominous eyes radiating concern; his banded black-and-silver hair falling to his waist. And then he took several generous steps backward and just stood there for a moment, appraising Fabian intently. Studying him. Waiting for him to enter the grand foyer of his own accord.

Fabian nodded, for words were not needed.

He followed the king into the manse and immediately noticed several striking, round art niches, each adorned with the most exquisite, harmonious renderings of landscapes from the ancient homeland. Fabian recognized each and every Romanian pictorial—he had known the places well—as he followed the king beyond the foyer and into a private rectory.

Again, the magnificent art on the high, domed ceiling caught the High Mage's eye: intricate, hand-painted detail in a mythical scene from an ancient Greek myth, featuring the powerful god of thunder and lightning, Zeus, and his son, Apollo, god of music, poetry, light, prophecy, and medicine. Fabian paused for a moment to study the resplendent mural, even as the king took a seat on an exquisite, deep royal-blue sofa and gestured silently with an open hand, inviting Fabian to occupy the tall, wood-and-red upholstered chair cattycorner to the antique coffee table.

Fabian sat in silence, his eyes still sweeping the room. Every corner, every window, every nook and cranny was also a piece of art—the windows coated in frosted glass, adorned with scenes of battlements and likenesses of the gods; the art niches festooned with either custom inlays or priceless, timeless mementos from Greece, Persia, Egypt, and beyond. Truly, the provocative ruler of the house of Jadon had lived a long and textured life.

Fabian raised his chin, at last regarding Napolean squarely, and folded his hands in his lap. "I am not one to mince words, Napolean, son of Sebastian, and it is as odd to me as it must be to you, to meet with another Ancient of my kind in this distant valley...to have come here of my own accord. There is no point in pretending that the two of us are friends...or allies...at least not yet. And I do not deny, nor make any apologies for all that has happened prior to this moment, this unexpected, rather desperate, impromptu meeting. Nonetheless, we are where we are. We are *who* we are: both ancient sons of Jadon whose immortal paths have crossed, the past and future intersecting in this valley, and alas"—he waved his hand through the air, indicating the rectory —"in this exquisite parlor. You are aware of the Corona Borealis Blood Moon. You are acquainted with my *destiny*, and you are privy to the demons...the shadows...the madness that haunts me. You fear my powers, as well you should." When Napolean shifted forward in his seat, his dark onyx eyes flashing with a hint of red, Fabian held up one hand. "Just as I am keenly aware that you are a warrior who can also strike and kill from a distance. You are a conjurer who can channel the very sun. Your powers are vast and unknown to me, and as a natural-born leader among his peers, you have risen to your rightful role as king: both for a reason and, I believe, with the gods' favor."

Napolean relaxed, and Fabian pressed on. "I served King Silvano as well as King Sakarias, as a byproduct of their lineage... and my own. I do not know if I can *serve* another, one who did not descend from the same royal blood." He flicked two fingers facetiously, but not in rebuke or with disrespect, and rubbed his chin, deep in thought. "That is not a personal affront, nor is it meant as an insult. Like you, I am from a different time and place. But time will tell, as it always does. And if the gods are merciful, it will also heal." He cleared his throat. "I imagine you know why I'm here—not to challenge your reign, nor to question your rule— but to seek your assistance with the...*fog*...that engulfs me. Perhaps we may all move forward together."

Napolean sat back in his chair and stared at Fabian for the space of several heartbeats—the monarch had to know what Fabian's words had cost him in pride, in candor, and in vulnerability. When the king finally spoke, his voice was calm, noble, and determined. "The gods have led all of us to this beautiful valley, and in time, they will reveal their wisdom as well as our roles. I am pleased that you are here, and I am intimately concerned—and committed—to the outcome of this current Blood Moon. Fabian, son of Fortino, you are a free vampire in this valley, a gifted High Mage in the house of Jadon, and always welcome in my home." He nodded once to emphasize his words. "Now then, Nachari Silivasi, the youngest living son of Keitaro and Serena, has in his possession a book known as the Blood Canon, an ancient text of black magic."

Fabian smirked. "I am well aware of this tome. Prince Jaegar was rather obsessed with it in his time."

Napolean's eyebrows shot up. "I can only imagine. Then you've seen it, read it? Had occasion to study it?"

"Some," Fabian said. "I studied many manuals, but most of my teaching was passed down through my lineage and acquired through hands-on practice over many, many moons."

Napolean briefly lowered his head in appreciation. "Of course. Fortunately, for us, Nachari has studied it well, and over the past two days he has revisited the spells dealing with confusion...madness...and memory loss, the spells dealing with inner demons and their exorcism. And he has come across a possible path forward for you and all the house of Jadon."

Fabian waited silently. There was no point in denying that he was confused, mad, or severely affected by memory loss—after all, it was why he was sitting in that parlor.

"Since you have given me the courtesy of both honesty and bluntness, I will afford you the same," Napolean said. "There is a spell that requires the recipient to merge his or her mind with that of another, a mind of equal strength and power, so that the two become as one consciousness. I believe—and Nachari agrees —that my own mind is the only one old enough, strong enough, powerful enough to merge fully with your own. And in this state, should you choose to allow it, my own awareness...my sanity and my lucidity...can shore up your own. In other words, together, we may defeat this fog, glimpse through all the smoke and mirrors, and recover both the memories that are lost to you as well as your soundness...your correct state of mind. And trust me when I tell you, High Mage, that Nachari Silivasi is a wizard of untold talents—he is an incredibly powerful sorcerer in his own right, and I believe he could bring us both through this conjuration, whole and unharmed. In addition, there is another, a fledgling vampire, sired outside the Curse as an existing son of a human *destiny*, under the power and protection of Lord Pegasus. The boy is named Braden Bratianu, and he sees things he should not be able to see; he knows things he has no logical way of knowing; his heart beats in both time and rhythm to the very soul of the house of Jadon. He has translated spells from the Book of Black Magic in the past, and he has dreamed important matters, which affect the entire house of Jadon and my subjects. We would want this young vampire to be present as one can never tell what he might divine during the conjuring."

This time, it was Fabian who stared at Napolean, studying the king's eyes intently: his mannerisms, his integrity...his very soul. Finally, when time seemed to stand still, the High Mage nodded. "Very well, descendant of Andromeda—a celestial house of mystics and magic. I will open my mind and my spirit to you so that we may both exorcise these demons that haunt our common houses: for me, the domicile which houses my body; for you, the modern house of Jadon and the secrets which may very well affect its future. And I will allow the wizard, Nachari, to perform the ritual—don't forget, I saw what the green-eyed vampire could do when he entered my cave from the ether. I also encountered his panther, a magnificent beast indeed. As for the boy, this Braden Bratianu, I am reluctant to have one so young witness such a personal and powerful event, but I will defer to your judgment, King Napolean Mondragon. You do not strike me as a rash or a reckless male, and I believe you understand the stakes at hand."

Napolean's dark brows softened as he regarded the High Mage thoughtfully. "Very well. I will summon the wizard and the boy right now; there is no reason to wait to move forward."

CHAPTER THIRTY

N apolean slipped easily into the bond of minds...
His and Fabian's.

It felt as if he were floating on a cluster of soft, fluffy clouds. Fabian was floating right next to a him, and a million strands of a cosmic spiderweb were binding...weaving... their conscious and subconscious minds together. As if the king and Fabian were one consciousness.

In truth, they were still in Napolean's rectory, each seated side by side on the royal-blue sofa in a semi-reclining position: arms resting gently at their sides with wrists in their laps, palms facing up; shoulders gently touching; and feet elevated on matching ottomans. Prior to Braden arriving about thirty minutes late and slipping into the room quietly—the boy had been on the opposite side of the valley, visiting Niko and Jankiel at their shared white-granite manor house in eastern Dark Moon Vale when he had first received the summons—it had taken Nachari about thirty minutes to cast the spell and solidify the conjuring.

Napolean had been easy enough to relax, to hypnotize. After all, he had unfailing trust in the green-eyed wizard, but Fabian had been antsy, reluctant, harder to subdue. Despite his desire to go through with the seeking, the High Mage had not given over his control—or his agency—easily. But Nachari had slowly managed to ease Fabian into the light gray mist of the trance, take him deeper into the smoky gray depths of hypnotic sleep, and finally settle him, firmly, into the dark, mystic depths of the spell, his mind fully merged with Napolean's.

Now, as Nachari led both ancient vampires through a maze of hopes...dreams...fears ...*memories*, Napolean tuned in acutely to the Master Wizard's serene, yet commanding voice: "Come closer to the fog, Napolean," Nachari instructed. "Fabian, what do you see?"

The High Mage shifted ever so slightly—ever so uncomfortably—on the sofa, but he remained in a deep delta state of awareness. "I see nothing but bramble," he grumbled, his annoyance evident, even in his enhanced, suggestible state of awareness.

"And you, Napolean? What do you see when you glimpse into the fog?"

Napolean took a deep, diaphragm breath, moving air fully in and out of his lungs and slowing down his heartbeat. It was difficult, yet vitally important, to stay focused while traversing the internal landscape of Fabian Antonescu's mind, for truly, the High Mage's psyche reminded the king of the humans' seven natural wonders of the world: Fabian's mysticism, magick, and the clairvoyant energy flowing through it reminded Napolean of Victoria Falls, powerful, raging, streaming brute force, unrestrained and constantly repeating. Fabian's base of knowledge, the breadth of his studies and his wisdom, reminded Napolean of the Great Barrier Reef, thousands of ridges, reefs of data, hundreds of islands filled with lore and legends. And the way the High Mage wielded it all, accessed it or turned it over, reminded Napolean of an aurora, brilliant, flowing, vivid lights in every neon color, mixing and streaming together—and that was just to name a few.

Straightaway, as Napolean gazed into the fog, the centuries that denoted Fabian's slumber in Dark Moon Vale, the king was reminded more of a haunted forest—thick, dense, tangled, gray brier—Fabian was right to describe it as bramble. Still, there were intermittent patches of serried, dark green leaves, times when the High Mage had rested peacefully, interspersed with soothing rivers and meandering tributaries that indicated the mage's mind, his soul, seeking outward. And alas, that led to the thickest of bramble, when the mysticism, magick, and clairvoyant energy that reminded Napolean of Victoria Falls had demanded release...and travel.

When the mage had unknowingly, unwittingly, sought the breast of a hawk or a raven to pour all that energy inside, to escape the crypt of the earth, and to soar beneath the valley's peaceful heavens.

Only, the mage had not found peace, at least not every time...

Napolean's eyelids fluttered as he squinted to see deeper inside the fog.

The hawk had embraced the light, but the raven had indeed cleaved to darkness. And each—Napolean gasped—each bird always carried an amulet in its talons, one of the two sacred vials of blood.

A shiver ran up and down the king's spine, and Fabian jerked on the couch.

"Shh, be still," Nachari whispered to the High Mage, the former's voice both thick with compulsion and bewitchment. "Release your fear and your unease, High Mage. Allow Napolean to enter this memory for you."

Fabian panted.

At first, the breaths were quick and shallow, but as Nachari continued to chant, they grew deeper...more even. And some way, although he didn't know how, Napolean knew that Nachari was weaving powerful magic, like the threads of a rope—tugging, pulling, staking the memories down—refusing to let them slip away or remain obscured by the madness in the bramble. A light shone into the haunted forest, and Napolean's palms begin to sweat—he recognized the spirit, the soul of that light, the very essence of the house of Jadon.

Without even knowing it, Braden Bratianu was lending his power, his strength, and his sentience to both the High Mage and the king, and his light had entered the forest.

Fabian began to growl.

But why?

For the first time, the High Mage was seeing Braden Bratianu's face, his now six-foot-two, muscular frame; his placid burnt-sienna eyes with those golden pupils; his chestnut-brown, shoulder-length hair; and more important, the luminosity of the youngster's spirit. Fabian had not had occasion to formally meet Braden, to look him in the eye or to shake his hand, before Nachari had begun the conjuring. And now, the fledgling's presence—his visage—was troubling the High Mage greatly.

But why!

Several dense, obtuse branches of bramble parted, and perched atop a craggy, forked limb sat the most magnificent hawk: wings of golden bronze, stripes of white and blond on its breast, and eyes the color of deep, dark burnt copper, shaped like almonds and rimmed in black.

"Fabian!" Napolean spoke the High Mage's name aloud even as his own soul entered the breast of the hawk and took off in flight, a vial of...*a vial of*...yes, blood, in its talons. "This isn't... ancient," Napolean murmured. "The memory that set off the madness; it's fairly recent."

He was spinning now.

Falling.

Diving.

Then shooting back up, into the clouds.

Scouring Dark Moon Vale for a...*host?*

"No!" Fabian shouted from his repose on the couch, beside Napolean.

"Stay with it, milord!" Nachari commanded, even as he began to chant something in Latin, then Romanian, anchoring Fabian even deeper into the fog. "What do you see, my king?"

Napolean shook his head briskly, not so much from dread or fear, but from the sheer power of what the hawk was doing, the energy crashing from those "Victoria Falls." "I'm restless. I'm troubled," Napolean mumbled, channeling Fabian's vexing recollections. "Prince Jadon hasn't come. Are the females still sleeping, or have they passed away? Were they set upon by a wild animal or an errant spiritual energy, an entity hovering too close to Earth's realm? I can't remember. *I can't remember!* But the vials are no longer safe! If something happens to me"—if something happened to Fabian—"all will be lost; there is no other to take up this mantle. Who else knows where the women were interred? I must pass on my only fail-safe—the princesses' only hope of being found or awakened—for surely, I shall never rise again from this slumber."

"No!" Fabian shouted, again from the sofa, this time grasping Napolean's forearm in a desperate, iron grasp. "Back away, my king."

"Stay with it, Napolean." Nachari was now hovering over them, and Braden's light began to flutter.

"Light cleaves to light, and darkness cleaves to darkness!" Fabian snarled angrily.

"The universe demands balance," Napolean chimed in. "I cannot conjure light without also conjuring darkness—the contrast is needed for equilibrium." He was still channeling Fabian's thoughts. "This gift I have held onto, protected, secured for all these centuries, the blood of a righteous prince who begged mercy for his followers; the blood of a wicked prince who brought his civilization to its knees—one given to me freely by a wise and benevolent brother; one stolen from the castle's apothecary, violating the other brother's free agency—a vial of blood I was asked to keep safe...a vial of blood I was never meant to keep."

Fabian dug his claws into Napolean's flesh, and the king felt himself slipping from the spell scape, the tethered bond between himself and Fabian.

"What do you see?" Nachari demanded. "My lord, look quickly, look now! *What do you see?*"

Napolean strained to hold onto the vision, to peer a little longer inside the fog.

And just like that, the air left the rectory.

Centuries and centuries after the High Mage had fallen into the deep, endless sleep—and five weeks *after* Ciopori had been awakened by Marquis—Fabian had felt a distant stirring, the presence of the living, breathing females, sentient in the valley. But *dearest gods, have mercy*, the High Mage had been so focused on the vials and consumed with madness, he hadn't realized the princesses were alive, awake, and well.

He had feared for their safety, instead.

And consumed by desperation and fear, he had entered the breasts of the hawk and the raven, the bird of prey and the scavenger, each one in turn. And now, Napolean watched as the golden-bronze fowl dove down from the sky, hovered above a sleeping vampire, and removed the cork from the vial held in its claws with the hooks from its other talon: The golden hawk emptied the contents, *the blood of an Ancient*, into the mouth of a sleeping boy...

Braden Bratianu.

Dearest goddess Andromeda. Napolean jolted. In a fit of terror, desperation, and insanity—whilst in the body of a hawk—

Fabian had placed Prince Jadon's blood in Braden's young, nubile body for safekeeping.

"Drink this blood and welcome life..."

And he had commanded it—*no, conjured it*—actually bonded the blood itself to the next Millenia Harvest Moon, when it would ripen, fully awaken, and activate—so the lad might find and save the princesses.

Princesses who had already been found.

This time, it was Napolean's mind that was reeling!

That fourteenth day of October, two years back, during the king's Blood Moon and the ensuing Blood Possession, Braden Bratianu had tapped into Napolean's plight: The day before, he had almost given a young human girl, named Katie Bell, a psychic lobotomy—such was the sudden surge in the boy's powers—and on that Wednesday, October 14th, he had gotten deathly ill, doubled over, and vomited on the side of the road because he had *felt* the invasion of Napolean's soul.

The hawk had visited Braden the night before.

And the Dark Lord Ademordna's possession was not the only reason—or cause—for the child's sudden swell in psychic abilities.

Napolean gasped aloud...

No wonder the boy had so many visions.

No wonder he could see things, dream things, that no one else could perceive or interpret...and translate spells from the Book of Black Magic.

No wonder his heart beat in both time and rhythm with the very soul of the house of Jadon.

The prince's blood was alive in his veins.

And despite the surge in the boy's psychic powers, the blood had not yet become fully active—*not yet*—not until the Harvest Moon, when the spirit would no longer lie dormant.

"The second vial," Nachari prompted, his voice betraying his own shock and bewilderment, as the king continued to project both thought and word to the Master Wizard. "Milord —*Napolean!*—what happened to the second vial?"

"No! *Do not!*" Fabian shouted, rising from the couch, twisting around in a frenzied motion, and grasping Napolean by the throat.

The king snapped out of the bonding, severed the connection, and broke the spell.

But not before he saw a flash of one last image: a midnight-black raven—also with burnt-copper eyes rimmed in black—seeking, tunneling down, down...*down*...deep beneath the earth, through a tunnel in the old sacrificial chamber, the one once found in a musty cave burrowed within the Red Canyons, the arroyo that led to the Dark Ones' Colony. The raven was seeking a compatible vessel—a worthy host—whose vibration would be strong enough, vile enough, wicked enough to host the blood from the second flask.

Light cleaves to light, and darkness cleaves to darkness.

The universe—*nay, power itself*—demanded balance.

The High Mage could not conjure one without evoking the other—it was ancient, shamanic law.

Napolean didn't see the entire contents of the second vial emptied, but he did see the raven's talons; he did see the vial uncorked; and he also saw the giant, hulking male with a tattoo of a black mamba banded around his upper right bicep, lying beneath the laser-focused raven.

"*Drink this blood and welcome death.*"

The ancient blood of Prince Jaegar was fed to a sleeping Achilles Zahora, The Executioner for the Dark Ones' Colony.

CHAPTER THIRTY-ONE

THE VALLEY OF SPIRIT & LIGHT ~ TWO HOURS LATER

In the blink of an eye, less than that really, the celestial god Corona Borealis vanished from the high, starry balcony outside his shimmering palace bedchamber, his celestial castle set between the heavenly citadel belonging to Lord Hercules and the divine bastion owned by Lord Bootes. He donned The Northern Crown and sent his essence streaming to a brilliant fortress in a huge, spiral galaxy—elongated, tilted at an angle to the earth, and 2.5 million light-years away—where the resplendent celestial goddess Andromeda made her home. As expected, Andromeda stood outside her own bedchamber, on the terrace, leaning against the balcony railing, her kaleidoscope eyes reflecting a hue of turquoise as she gazed into a surrounding cluster of stars; her long, flowing auburn hair cascading about her graceful shoulders like living waters; her snow-white wings folded gently behind her back.

"Ah, so you are drawn to the earth as well?" he intoned, landing gently on the ivory balcony.

Andromeda looked up and smiled. "Corona. What a pleasant surprise."

He inclined his head gracefully.

"Indeed," she continued. "They have been at it for hours—the Vampyr, that is—the sons of Jadon. And now, Napolean paces restlessly beneath the moonlight, alone, often gazing up at the stars."

Corona Borealis nodded. "Of course he has much to consider."

She sighed. "Much to consider and many questions, as does your child, Fabian."

Silence settled between them for an immeasurable amount of time as, together, they replayed the night's events and peered, as one, into the sparkling cluster of stars, watching the varied events on Earth unfold beneath them:

The Master Wizard, Nachari Silivasi, utilizing a spell from the Blood Canon to merge Napolean and Fabian's minds.

The stunning revelation, the secret held within the fog.

The shock, fear, and uncertainty now plaguing Braden Bratianu, and Nachari's noble attempts to comfort the lad he so dearly loved, to settle the gifted boy's restless mind.

Ah, and Fabian's guilt over a mistake he could not have avoided, a choice made in error during a moment of desperation and madness—the High Mage would have to work through the guilt, embrace his species' frailty, and make peace with his imperfections as well as embrace his powers...eventually.

And then there were Napolean's incessant, endless questions...

The wise and noble king of the Vampyr ran his fingers through his long, black-and-silver hair before absently rubbing his neck. Nachari had managed to pry Fabian's fingers from the king's throat, but not before the two coincidental events—the revelation and Fabian's feral reaction—had been seared into the king's somatic memory, forever imprinted and intertwined as a psychosomatic souvenir which would evoke a sensation of choking whenever the king recalled this fateful night in the future: the night the house of Jadon learned that the blood of an ancient prince flowed in the veins of one of its youngest, most beloved fledglings.

"Shit. Just shit," Napolean whispered beneath his breath, and Andromeda couldn't help but chuckle.

What in tarnation does all this mean? the king wondered.

He gazed at the moon.

What will happen in just under three months' time when the Millenia Harvest Moon rises? Will Braden remain as he is, a curious, albeit sometimes insecure, burgeoning seer who has the heart of a warrior within a pure, untainted soul? Will he continue to develop into the fine young vampire he is rapidly becoming, or will he transform into something altogether different...something far more ancient...something far more powerful? Will he become the ancient prince or some amalgamation of the two?

The king pinched the bridge of his nose.

And whose memories will he possess?

What powers will he wield?

Will he take his place as the rightful ruler of the house of Jadon —nay, as the very lifeblood and origin of the same—*or will he retreat into the shadows, lost to the house he loves, to Nachari...to his family...to* Kristina, *unable to find his place in such a strange new reality...as a dual being?*

"Holy hell..."

Gracefully, almost imperceptibly, Lord Corona glided to the side and placed a firm, strong hand on Andromeda's shoulder. "Such questioning goes hand in hand with a life lived on Earth. Your king will find his way."

Andromeda covered Corona's hand with her own and gave it a gentle squeeze. "Yes. *Yes*, I'm certain he will, but moments like these test the fortitude of gods, men, and vampires alike. The temptation to simply answer all the king's queries, to infuse his noble mind with answers...upon answers...is nearly over-whelming."

"Free will, beautiful goddess," Corona whispered in her ear. "Free will and self-determination—we crafted the laws at the beginning of time. Life is meant to be lived, not circumvented."

She lowered her long, heavy lashes and sighed. "Of course, Corona; I understand." And then Napolean sank to his knees, and her heart constricted.

"Great goddess Andromeda," Napolean whispered, almost absently and out of habit, "what exactly is carried in the blood of a noble, celestial progeny—an ancient prince turned vampire by a curse—anyway? Power, essence, mysticism? The desire to rule and conquer? Will Braden finally be able to solve the ancient mystery? Will he know how Prince Jadon died?" *If he died*, the king thought next. "Keep it together, Napolean," he murmured. "Of course Prince Jadon died. How else could a piece of his spirit live in Braden now?"

A crystalline tear fell from the corner of Andromeda's eye. "'Tis truly heart-wrenching to watch," she whispered. "This night, Napolean seeks my counsel; Fabian seeks your forgiveness, as well as the pardon of the vampires around him, especially Braden Bratianu's. And the child, himself; he is plagued with uncertainty. He—"

"Braden Bratianu is no longer a child," Corona interrupted softly but sternly. "He has long since become a powerful young man...a powerful Vampyr."

"Yes," Andromeda agreed. "I realize this—we all do—but those closest to him still see his duality, the child within the vampire." She waved her hand through the air, and swirling star-dust followed the motion. "It is of no matter; the *young male* still questions the gods. He wonders if he is going to die, if he will lose the part of him that makes him Braden, the soul he has always been. Oh, Corona, the vampire indeed wonders if he will have some odd connection or bond with Achilles Zahora, a Dark One. Will he remember The Executioner as a brother? Will Achilles remember him?"

"He asks wise questions," Corona said.

"Yet all the king can tell him, all Fabian can say, is *only time will tell.*'"

Corona shrugged a strapping shoulder. "They will not lie to the young one—falsity is not their way. It is not who we created them to be, long before the Curse assailed them. Nachari loves Braden dearly, and he has already assured him that he will not traverse this path alone. Braden's parents and his brother; the sentinels and his mentor, Julien; the king, Kristina, and all the warriors in the house of Jadon, as well as the powerful High Mage will walk him through this, remain at his side."

"Yes," Andromeda agreed, "the Master Wizard has a compassionate heart, but he is also worried and seeks guidance from his ruling lord, Perseus."

Corona paused to consider Andromeda's words. "Much power, much magic, will be loosed upon the earth with the rising of the Harvest Moon, and Lord Perseus will draw nearer to Nachari—he is one of his favorite sons. Yea, we shall all watch over our children, Andromeda. And you and I both know that Napolean, the king, will embrace Fabian, the High Mage, as a brother of the same beloved house—the two will work together as equals going forward, and the Fellowship of Wizards will both accept and elevate the ancient mage as leader...*teacher*...one who has much living history and authority to bring to their collective practice of magick." He chuckled softly. "In no time, Fabian will be questioning Nachari about the time he spent in the Abyss—about his ability to transmute into the body of a panther—and Nachari will be eagerly seeking Fabian's centuries of intimate knowledge, wanting to know each and every spell...the ancient ways of shamanic power. Our sons are loyal brothers at heart.

They will gravitate to one another, and together, they will be stronger."

Andromeda pushed away from the balcony and turned to face Lord Corona directly. "Forgive me, my lord; I have been quite selfish in my musings. I have not yet asked you about the wizard, Fabian...about your beloved one's Blood Moon...about his *destiny* or his path going forward. Surely my heart is not the only one tied in knots this night."

Corona appraised Andromeda's spectacular, singular beauty, and he *felt* the starlight sparkle in his own bluish-white eyes. He reached inside his golden tunic and retrieved two glistening strands of moonlight, fragments from the actual silver cords that tethered Gwendolyn and Fabian's souls to their bodies on Earth, and then his powerful celestial wings extended, elongated, almost in an unconscious show of power...and pride. "As you know, Napolean has urged the High Mage to return to the guest house —to see to his *destiny* and attend to his Blood Moon above all else. The Millenia Harvest Moon will appear soon enough and take care of itself; they have plenty of time to study its history, consider this new revelation, and formulate a plan before September sixteenth. They have ample opportunity to comfort and counsel young Braden. And in the meantime, I have not so much interfered with but perhaps refined these cords."

He ran the pad of one nimble finger along the slimmer, silver cord. It was brilliant, resilient, and soft to the touch. He ran the same finger along the second cord: rougher, stronger, and slightly frayed at the edges, yet glowing with power and mystical light. "Gwendolyn's soul is troubled, but aware. She is awakening to Fabian, even as she fears him, but the love infused in this cord burns bright. Should Fabian unravel the tough, fearful edges, he will find what was always intended for his pleasure...his claiming...his infinite protection and care."

He held up the second cord, turned it over in his hand, and

caressed it between his thumb and his forefinger. "And Fabian's soul, rest assured, is no longer fractured. The High Mage will no longer be haunted by the fog." He held up his other hand to dissuade any protest. "To be clear, I did not meddle with his fate, nor his choices, but his soul has been asking to be healed. His female draws him like a powerful magnet, and her willing, ardent kiss was a stronger force than the madness. Secrets...demons... that which haunts the soul in darkness cannot maintain its power once exposed to the light. The ancient wizard will still need to acclimate to the current century—he will still need to integrate into the house of Jadon, mend many fences with his *destiny*, and find his place in Dark Moon Vale—but he shall do all three with a sound body, mind, and spirit, going forward." With that, Corona ran his fingers, one last time, over the rougher silver cord, and all the frayed edges sealed back together.

Andromeda smiled, teasingly. "You walk the fine line between interference and gentle intercession quite well, Lord Corona."

He bowed his head. "Thank you."

She turned back toward the railing, extended an elegant arm outward, and grasped a handful of stardust in her fingers. Then she tossed it into the galaxy and sent it spiraling to the earth. "Napolean, Nachari, and even young Braden will sleep soundly tonight, their anguish lessened. And they will allow Fabian the time and space he needs to attend to his most pressing matter, fulfilling his Blood Moon with Gwen, before drawing his attention back to the coming Harvest Moon."

Lord Corona folded his wings behind him, sidled up behind Andromeda, and wrapped his strong arms around her in a tender, appreciative embrace. "Thank you, goddess. I see I am not the only deity capable of walking such a fine, thin line with equal grace and ease."

CHAPTER THIRTY-TWO

DARK MOON VALE

I t was just past midnight when Fabian finally returned to the guest house.

Freshly showered and wearing a pale green pair of flannel pajamas, a heavy beige robe, and thick, fuzzy socks, Gwen stared into the steam-coated mirror in the master suite's bathroom. Needless to say, she had not been able to sleep and had hoped a long, hot shower would do her some good. She placed her palm against the glass and rubbed it in a circle, staring into her reflection, her tired, light-green eyes.

Did she even recognize the woman looking back at her anymore?

It had been so long since she had felt like herself.

It had been too long since she had been free...

Although the sound of the front door opening and closing was hardly perceptible, Gwen heard it clearly with her new, enhanced vampiric senses, and she knew it was Fabian who entered the foyer because she recognized his scent: sandalwood, a masculine earthiness, and for lack of a better term...*power*.

She flinched, and then she shivered.

And then she slowly flipped off the light, padded out of the bathroom, and headed to the great room to meet the ancient wizard, who could certainly hear, scent, and sense her too. There was no point in running—or hiding—trying to avoid the confrontation. Hell, Gwen had thought about escaping dozens of times since Fabian had left her alone, earlier that afternoon.

But what was the point?

Yes, Gwen was faster, stronger, even more nimble and quiet now, but she was still no match for Napolean's sentinels. She was still no match for the vampires of Dark Moon Vale, nor for the Corona Borealis Blood Moon.

She was still no match for Fabian Antonescu.

Rounding the hall into the rustic parlor, she couldn't help but wonder who would be there to greet her...or assail her...this time. The feral, savage creature who had leaped from the well? The starving, brutish vampire who had once fed from her at will? Or the softer, kinder caretaker—protector—who had brought her food and provisions; soaped her hair beneath a waterfall; rescued her that night in the forest?

Or the dominant, passionate lover who felt he could take whatever he pleased...

By force if necessary?

She sighed and kept her eyes averted downward, even as she strolled quietly to the same distressed-leather sofa she had sat upon before, and waited, holding her breath, without moving a muscle as Fabian, thankfully, took a seat on the opposite burnished-walnut lounge.

The wizard was quiet.

He didn't say a word.

Until finally, Gwen felt compelled to look up at him.

One glance, and she knew something was different.

Very, *very* different.

Something had definitely changed.

First, there was a solidity, a strong, grounded presence behind his burnt-copper eyes. They were no longer blank or vacant, glazed over with hints of shadows. And his countenance—his back, his shoulders, his bearing, even the angle of his jaw—it was confident as always, but it was also now...relaxed...calm. Yet there was a heaviness all around him, something weighing on his mind. Gwen cleared her throat and waited for her captor to speak.

"Captor..." He stole the word effortlessly from her mind. "Yes, I suppose that is what I have been. I *regret* that may be all I have been." He glanced up at the high wood-beamed ceiling as if he might find his next words in the rafters, and then he leaned forward and captured her gaze, held it like a magnet sustaining a charge. "Gwendolyn, my dove, my *destiny*..." He allowed the words to settle. "I mean you no harm, and I will not come near you. I will not touch you again, unless and until you welcome my nearness. I do, however, have something to give you."

He stood to his full, imposing height, took several purposeful steps forward, and laid a piece of green- and black-lined paper on the coffee table in front of her, before gliding back and resuming his place on the couch.

Gwen glanced down at the paper, a ledger of some sort.

And then she jolted, as much from the overwhelming smell of blood as the desperate crimson scrawls scribbled hastily across the page.

"It is a letter, a note of apology," he said evenly, "scribed by Paul McNeil, the human male who took advantage of your family and extorted unwanted sexual favors from your mother, so long ago. It is an apology to you, written in his own blood, moments before he expired."

Gwen's stomach clenched, and her heart constricted, even as the breath momentarily left her lungs.

An apology written in blood...
By Paul McNeil.

How?

When?

Why?

"You are my *destiny*," Fabian nearly purred. "The female given to me by the gods to honor, protect, and love. This man's insult to you—to your loved ones—could not remain unpunished. No one who harms you in such a deliberate, foul manner will ever be allowed to draw breath again."

Gwen pressed her hand to her heart.

Good Lord...

She glanced at the page a second time: *Dear Gwen, I am so, so, so, so sorry!!! Paul McNeil.* The terror jumped from the page, as did the fact that the author was dying...

Fabian had found the man who had all but ruined her family, tracked him down, and killed him—*for Gwen*—and she didn't know what to think about that, how to feel about that: *Capital punishment was a bit extreme!*

Yet, Fabian was not a human man, nor was he bound by human laws or systems of justice. He was an ancient, nocturnal predator to his very core: wild, territorial, and clearly systematic in his thinking and actions. This was way too much to process right now. "Can we visit this later?" she asked. "I mean, if I feel the need to revisit this at all? It's too much to absorb right now, Fabian."

He sighed as if something in her question, perhaps her tone of voice, upset him. "Of course," he said. "You are a woman of free agency."

At this, she found her spine: "You mean, like I was in the bathtub? Before you left."

He closed his eyes and grimaced, and when he opened them again, they were burning with a glow from a hidden fire. "No." He spoke sternly. "Not like that. Never again like that." He waved his hands in front of him, making a loose figure eight, and a brilliant, shimmering crystal dagger, with the head of a falcon carved into the crossguard, appeared in his palm. "Before I returned to the guest house, I fashioned this blade from spirit and stone, from earth and ether, and I placed the strongest spell I could conjure into its razor-fine edge. Rest assured, Gwendolyn Hamilton, when you wield this blade, your powers will supersede my own. Should I ever force myself upon you again, thrust this blade into my heart...or run it across my throat. Hell, cut off the hand that offends you, if you desire, and I will be powerless to stop you." He rose once again, slid the dagger onto the coffee table, then took his place back across the room.

Gwen stared down at the knife, the enchanted dagger, and simply gaped at it in awe.

Holy shit...

This was a game changer.

She gawked at Fabian, even as her heart began to race: For the first time since she had met him, she had something sitting right in front of her that she could use to gain her freedom, to end her captivity...to level the playing field between predator and prey. And Fabian had created it on purpose—*for her.*

He had just handed Gwen her equality.

Her eyes filled up with tears, and she exhaled slowly.

She didn't know what to say.

"I would like to tell you a story," he pressed on as if the dagger wasn't even there. "Will you listen, Gwen? Will you hear my tale?"

She blinked three times: *What the hell was happening? Who was this vampire?* "Yes," she stammered, not knowing what else to say. But in truth, she wanted to listen; she wanted to hear whatever Fabian had to tell her. She needed to better understand the High Mage.

He nodded ominously. "You already know about the Curse and the Vampyr, so I will not start there. I will not repeat answers

BLOOD ECHO

to questions you have already asked of Deanna, and I know what they are because they were implanted in my mind, along with Nachari's...*understanding*... during the memory transference."

Gwen chewed on her bottom lip. "Okay."

"I would take you back to a village in Romania, to the family and circumstances of my birth," he began. "I would have you understand the generations of magick and sorcery from which I hail, the duties the males of my line performed for the monarchy, and how I came to be in North America...how I ended up sleeping beneath that well."

Gwen listened in rapt fascination as Fabian recounted his father, Fortino, and his mother, Koryn Anne; as he spoke of a king named Silvano and another named Sakarias; as he described the ancient Romanian palace, the castle's undercroft, a vaulted crypt in a cellar where he practiced his craft, and finally being elevated to the royal oratory and position of High Mage. She was practically on pins and needles when he recounted those perilous days in the Great Hall, as Prince Jaegar steadily rose to power and Fabian forged a secret alliance with his twin, Prince Jadon...when Fabian fled to the Transylvanian Alps to await the arrival of the fleeing princesses...and when the wizard and his rebel band of warriors and mercenaries underwent The Change, following the Blood Curse.

And then the hairs on the back of her neck stood up as he told of boarding a large, wooden, seaworthy vessel in 799 B.C., while wearing two amulets, filled with blood, around his neck for safe-keeping, and caring for the princesses in a strange new land.

Her heart couldn't help but go out to him as he described his struggles, his fears, what finally led him to make an agonizing decision—to place the women in an enchanted sleep and to eventually follow them in slumber.

The endless nights of silence.

The restless nights of dreaming—and traveling—in the breast of a hawk or a raven.

The anguish and madness that slowly set in: *Light cleaves to light, and darkness cleaves to darkness...*

And finally, Fabian told Gwen what he had learned earlier this night at Napolean's manse, along with Nachari, Braden, and the king: what the High Mage had done with the blood of the Ancients, the power that was coming with the looming Harvest Moon, and why he believed he had blocked it all out...why he believed his mind would not fracture in the same way again.

Silence hung over the great room like coastal fog in the early hours of dawn as Gwen stared intently at Fabian, glanced down at the blood-scrawled page from the morbid ledger, and eyed the crystal dagger once again.

She didn't have words.

She could barely take it all in.

Fabian's life...his history...the origin of his madness.

Everything that had happened since the moment she had met him.

This vampire in front of her was a lot of things, but he wasn't a monster—or a rapist—or a one-dimensional beast. He was wise, and educated, and highly skilled. He was both savage and refined; domineering, yet caring; reflective, thoughtful, and deliberate. He was equal parts nobleman and wild beast. He was a wizard—a High Mage—a vampire, and a caretaker.

And he was baring his soul before her.

"*Nanaşule...*"

She turned the word over on her tongue, taking it both from his story and the forested glen behind Napolean's compound, and tried to grasp its full meaning...

Godfather.

One who wields the power of the gods, yet behaves as *Father;* one who was both respected and beloved...*for a reason.*

"Say something, my dove," Fabian prompted.

Gwen was at a complete loss for words. The male sitting across from her may as well have been a stranger—*or was he?*

Hadn't she seen each and every nuance, each side of the vampire, throughout their five-day ordeal? Hadn't she met the mage and the monster; the nobleman and the vampire; the father and the protector in fleeting moments as they'd hidden in the caves? "I don't know what to say," she murmured, being as honest as she knew how to be.

He nodded, and then he smiled wanly. "I understand."

She blinked several times again, and for the first time since he had returned from the vampire king's mansion, she really took him in: his stunning burnt-copper eyes rimmed in raven black; his almost glorious, layered bronzed hair falling to chiseled shoulders, with highlights of blond; his tall, proud bearing and muscular frame; the way he held her gaze without apology. The male was simply and undeniably...magnificent. And Gwen had never been more caught off guard, unsettled, or confused in her life. "Thank you," she finally blurted, the words just falling out.

He raised his sculpted eyebrows. "Pardon me?"

"Thank you," she repeated, more quietly. "For seeking Napolean's help; for confronting your demons; for bringing me back this truth. *Your truth.* I don't know what it changes—if or how it will make a difference—but at the same time, I feel like it might just change everything." Her eyes grew moist with tears once more. "For the first time, I feel like...like...there may be something more than just fear—or captivity—between us."

Fabian exhaled slowly.

He rose from the couch to come to her side, and she immediately shook her head. "No."

He retreated instantly and sat back down. "Gwendolyn..."

"Yes?"

"Take the rest of this night and the whole of tomorrow to

consider all you have learned. To consider all that has transpired. Contact your family if you still desire"—he paused to retrieve the correct words—"phone them? Text...or email? Whatever you prefer. And I will come to you again, tomorrow night. I wish to take you somewhere more personal. We will talk then. Confront this together."

Her mouth may have fallen open—she wasn't sure. "I'm free to contact my family?"

He smiled and shrugged his shoulders, and this time there was warmth in his eyes. "You are wise beyond your years, Gwendolyn Hamilton. Wise, and strong, and perceptive. You know what can—and cannot—be shared with your loved ones, for their well-being as well as your own, for the protection of all those who inhabit this valley. You know what the Blood Moon entails and what it means for both of us. Before this night, I was so mired in fog, I could not see the light in the one right in front of me. I could not discern her heart or her soul, so I led with brute strength, with dominance and force, as opposed to...fostering trust. Do not get me wrong"—he waved his hand through the air —"all you have seen of me represents my true person, my carnal and bestial natures, but I am not incapable of learning or growing. I am not incapable of trying...*for you*. You may contact your family because yes, you are free, and also, because I trust you to do so with care. Will you meet me tomorrow night, my dove? Will you allow me to take you back into the wilds...just for a time?"

She wasn't sure if she nodded or just stared at him blankly. "Where will you go tonight?" And she couldn't believe she had just asked him that question, as if she cared where he went.

She closed her eyes and shivered as the truth sank in like a rock dropping to the bottom of a pond: *She cared...*

Very much.

Oh, dear Lord, when had that happened?

How had that happened?

"It is not unusual for a descendant of celestial beings, a mage or a vampire, to wish to commune with nature, to seek solace beneath the moonlight," Fabian said. "This night, I will also seek to reflect and...process. I will sleep beneath the stars and hope that my lord, Corona Borealis, will offer favor and forgiveness to his prodigal son."

This time, it was Gwen who wanted to get up from the couch, cross the room, and provide some sort of comfort: Fabian was a lot of things, but he wasn't prodigal. He wasn't reckless, irresponsible, or negligent.

Still, she didn't dare.

Everything was too new, too fragile, still too shocking and unexpected. She wasn't sure if she could trust it—if she could trust Fabian.

Just yet.

If she could trust herself.

"Yes," she finally answered. "I'll go with you tomorrow night."

CHAPTER THIRTY-THREE

THE DARK ONES' COLONY

"Sorcerer."

"Executioner."

"What brings you to my lair this night?" Achilles Zahora asked Salvatore Nistor, as the giant of a vampire backed away from the heavy wooden-and-iron door and allowed his councilman to enter his private underground chamber.

Salvatore strolled in noiselessly and glanced around the lair, taking in the lantern light, the uniquely formed stalactites and stalagmites scattered about the craggy ceiling and floor, and the prominent pool of bubbling, steaming water that sat in the farthest corner of the abode, a natural hot springs that smelled of sulfur, one the colony guardsman liked to use as his personal jacuzzi.

"Well?" Achilles grunted, sounding more than a little bit irritated—he had probably been sleeping.

Oh well.

"Well," Salvatore drawled, slinking to the edge of a black walnut dresser; appraising an unusually old and wicked-looking dagger sitting atop the heavy chest of drawers; and fingering the smooth antique hilt with open appreciation. "Well, I think I would like to get to know you better."

Achilles eyed Salvatore warily, his pale yet rich citrine eyes narrowing in suspicion. "With all due respect, my liege. It's almost one o'clock in the morning."

"Yes," Salvatore said, "but then you are a nocturnal creature, are you not? Nighttime is when we come out to play."

Achilles raised his thick, dark brows and sauntered to a nearby custom-upholstered divan, sinking deep into the fine, soft leather cushions, and placing his feet up on the opposing granite footstool. He waited in icy silence as Salvatore continued to stroll about the room, taking in the scant decorations, the solid gold candelabras, and the rare, priceless display of wall décor: The Executioner's personal collection of obsolete medieval weapons, accumulated over many centuries.

"You have appeared in many of my visions lately, Achilles," Salvatore said. He waved his hand in the air as if he desired to erase that statement and start over. "No, you have appeared in many of the images reflected within my crystal cube, and I am wondering why that is?"

Achilles grunted, shifted uncomfortably, but he didn't say a word.

Salvatore turned around to face him, leaning back against a particularly rugged pillar about five feet away. "I see you bathed in blood, executioner. I see you imbibing the glorious elixir through your mouth, your ears, your nostrils. It seeps through your very pores, and you swirl it around your tongue. I also see you rising from the ashes of a shallow grave like a blood-drenched phoenix, drunk from the wine of carnage. Can you tell me why that is?"

Achilles barked an insolent laugh. "How the fuck would I know," he rasped. "You're the sorcerer, the maleficent sage—you tell me."

Salvatore scowled. "If I knew, I wouldn't be here." He pinched the bridge of his nose to compress and constrict his rising impatience. "Nonetheless, I was hoping we might find out more... explore the possibilities...together."

This time, Achilles sneered openly. "Can it wait 'til morning?"

Salvatore scowled. "No, executioner. It cannot."

Achilles held up two massive hands in both exasperation and disgust, but he didn't utter another disrespectful word. At least not then.

"Blood, blood, blood," Salvatore reflected aloud. "Why do you think that is?" He furrowed his brows in consternation. "Why *are* you so unusually bloodthirsty, Achilles? Come to think of it, you always have been."

Achilles ran a brutish hand through his chin-length hair and snorted. "I dunno, sorcerer. Maybe because I'm a...vampire?"

Salvatore chuckled out loud. "True. Very true. We are all predisposed to blood. But..." He linked his fingers together and rotated his thumbs in ruminating circles. "You kill more than some; you feed a bit more often; you were eager to become a member of the Colony Guard, to punish and extinguish your wayward brethren when occasion calls for it—you revel in the slaughter almost like a dark lord, a hellhound...a savage barbarian. Don't get me wrong—your talents have served our colony well, and I am not in any way displeased with you. Just trying to solve a mystery, my friend. Just hoping for added insight."

The circular band of a black mamba, wrapped around Achille's right arm, flexed and relaxed as his bicep twitched. "I'm sorry if your cube has been keeping you up at night, but can I speak freely—may I be honest?"

"Of course," Salvatore purred. "I would wish for nothing less."

"I have zero shits to give about your visions or your cube,

Salvatore," Achilles began. "It's one o'clock in the blasted morning, and nocturnal or not, I was up all day and I need some sleep. I have no fucking idea what you're talking about, even less desire to answer any of these random, pointless questions, and my fangs are beginning to throb, which just makes me pissy and uncomfortable. So, if you don't mind..."

Salvatore gazed into the steaming hot natural pool, not so much because it drew his attention, but because he needed to use a focal object to restrain his temper. His own fangs descended from his gums, and a deep, guttural growl rose in his throat. "I am your councilman, Achilles, one you are sworn to serve. And I am also a rather...talented...sorcerer. I could turn your heart to stone or curdle the blood in your veins with the cast of a spell from across the room. Perhaps you would be wise to remember who you're speaking to."

Achilles laughed even louder this time. "Point well taken," he barked. "And I could snap your illustrious, talented neck before you could mutter the first three words of that spell." He sank even deeper into the divan, crossed his arms in front of him, and shrugged his giant shoulders. "So, we are both males of varied talents. Kudos to us. But I don't think you wish to challenge an ally, a dark brother who is indeed sworn to both serve and protect you, and I have no desire to test a sorcerer. So, I guess that brings us back full circle. I kill because I'm an executioner. I *feed*, maybe more than I need to, because I revel in the taste and feel of blood. And if I come across as a dark, savage barbarian, well again, back to where we started: I'm a vampire. *What the fuck!?*"

Salvatore drew in a deep, measured breath.

They weren't getting anywhere with this line of questioning, and the conversation had become openly hostile. This was not what Salvatore wanted, and truth be told, why would Achilles have any knowledge of Salvatore's cube or the visions? The male was rather single-minded, primal—he was simply a bloodthirsty killing machine, and he always had been. Although, one would be prudent to never underestimate him: Achilles was also very wily. He was intelligent, clever, and incredibly methodical in his thinking. In his killing.

It was up to Salvatore to figure this out.

It was not Achilles' puzzle to solve.

"Very well," Salvatore drawled, spreading a graceful hand in the direction of The Executioner's huge brass bed. "Go to sleep, Achilles. Pardon for interrupting your repose. If you don't mind, I will simply have a seat on your divan and watch you in your slumber."

Achilles blinked three times. "You're gonna sit on the damn couch and watch me sleep?"

Salvatore nodded winsomely.

Achilles frowned and cocked his head to the side. "I don't swing that way, councilman...just in case you were—"

"Shut up!" Salvatore snarled. "Neither do I."

Achilles harrumphed. "S' all good. No judgment. Just making a point of clarification for the record."

Salvatore closed his eyes.

Let it go, sorcerer, he told himself.

The male is tired—he's grumpy—he means no disrespect.

He bit a hole in his bottom lip and swirled the tip of his tongue around the ensuing droplet of blood. "Of course," he replied coolly. "Go to sleep, vampire. I will let myself out when I've had quite enough."

CHAPTER THIRTY-FOUR

The past twenty or so hours had done Gwendolyn a world of good.

She had managed to finally get some sleep. She had actually spoken to her mother, Mary, and placed both their minds at ease with a false, concise, but necessary story about extending her time in Dark Moon Vale and being out of cell phone range while camping in the forest with friends—she couldn't exactly tell her she had been abducted by an ancient vampire, claimed beneath a Blood Moon, and converted to another species. And she had taken the opportunity to digest *all* that had happened between herself and the ancient mage since the moment he had taken her from that well.

It didn't mean she had made peace with it.

And it didn't mean her heart and mind were open to a future —*no, a very long lifetime*—of being Fabian Antonescu's mate.

But she had to admit, the reflective mage who had returned from Napolean's manse intrigued her. The beautiful six-foot-four male who had sat across from her on the distressed-leather sofa made her heart beat just a little bit faster. And the thought of seeing him again—looking into those haunting eyes and absorbing the way he looked at her, spoke to her...wanted her—had her mind practically reeling.

With possibility.

And trepidation...

With excitement and caution.

Now, as she stood in front of him, her back to his chest, his hands over her eyes, she took a moment to catch her breath from the whirlwind flight. Fabian had whisked her into his arms at the guest house, spread his wings, and shot into the sky like the falcon he could become, the falcon he had been the night he had saved her in the forest and the night he had first appeared at Napolean's manse. He had soared effortlessly beneath the moonlight until, at last, they had softly landed at his intended destination.

"Turn just a bit to the right," he whispered in her ear, his voice thick with anticipation.

Gwen shivered, both from the cool night air and the vampire's nearness, as she angled her body as instructed.

"Now." He removed his hands from her eyes, and she blinked them open.

She gasped.

They were standing in a very familiar orchard, filled with thick woodland foliage and enormous, jutting aspens, the grove from Fabian's past...the serene retreat from Gwen's. And nestled neatly before the giant quaking aspen, in the center of the grove, was a simple white wooden table—carved out of aspen wood—and covered in an elegant linen cloth. Atop the table sat a pair of heavy candlesticks, flames flickering at the apex of two silver candles, beside a chilled bottle of wine, a single red rose, and a container—no, a crumpled plastic package—of chocolate doughnuts.

Gwen stifled a giggle—she couldn't help it.

The doughnuts looked as old as Fabian. He had obviously

lifted them from 7-Eleven, and truth be told, the gesture warmed her heart: Hadn't he recently asked her if she liked chocolates, scented oils, or flowers? He must've gotten his wires—*Nachari's memories*—crossed.

"Are you not pleased?" he asked, reacting to her laughter.

She took several tentative steps forward, padding along the uneven ground, even as the scent of pine and sage wafted to her nostrils, and stared beyond the gentle flicker of the candle flames at a silhouette she knew like the back of her hand: a brilliant, flawless hummingbird carved into the trunk of the tree, with vivid turquoise, purple, and orange on its primaries.

"It's beautiful," she whispered. "I love it."

"The table? The rose, wine, and chocolates? Or the bird?"

She bit her bottom lip—*she would not laugh again.* And as long as she lived, she would never let him know that his *chocolates* were actually stale, cheesy doughnuts.

Her breath caught in her throat.

Where the hell had that thought come from?

As long as she lived...

With Fabian?

Now *she* was the one caught in a fog—Gwen was losing her mind!

He placed the pads of two fingers along her neck and pressed them against her jugular. "Your pulse," he rasped. "Your heart is racing."

She gulped and tilted her head, trying to twist away. "Fabian, don't."

He pressed even closer, his imposing chest brushing her back, his broad, powerful shoulders framing her smaller frame. "Don't what?" he murmured, running his fingers down the length of her neck, along the slope of her shoulders, and over her trembling arms.

She caught his hand with hers. "That. Don't do that."

He nuzzled the back of her hair. "Very well." And then he rotated his hand, placed it over hers, and extended her arm until they were touching the tree together, his forefinger over hers as he began to lightly, delicately trace the outline of the hummingbird.

Gwen exhaled slowly, studying the magnificent carving, instantly caught up in its beauty and the moment. "How did you do this?"

"Do what?"

"This, right here. Create the illusion of his wings, almost fluttering?" She traced the rise and fall of the glorious feathers. "And this; the spotting on its chest. I remember counting the circles—they're like half-moons."

"Ninety-nine, to be exact," he said. "Some turquoise, some dark blue, others rimmed in black."

"Yes," she commented. "Sixty-eight in turquoise, twenty with dark blue, and eleven rimmed in black."

He bent forward and pressed a slow, lingering kiss along the hollow between her shoulder and her neck, and then he quickly reached for her hand, once again, and brought it back to the tree. "Place your fingernail here, Gwendolyn." She pressed her nail against the tree, and her finger began to glow. "Move it downward," he husked in her ear, and she felt a surge of power, like a fine, cool mist, descend from the spot on her neck where he had kissed her, down through her arm, and into her hand. His fingers covered hers, exactly, and magic streamed through them as, along with Gwen, Fabian began to trace the outline of another bird: metallic violet on its throat and chin; a golden halo on the crown of its head; silver and pale green on its chest and wings; and all four colors blended together in its tail. "His female mate," Fabian whispered, and Gwen closed her eyes.

She knew her voice was quivering. "But he doesn't know her," she said softly. "They've only just met, perhaps just tonight."

"Ah," Fabian mused, placing the full palm of his hand over the newly carved bird and infusing the colors with light. "But he's always known her in his soul."

Gwen froze in place, listening, tuning in, every cell in her body drawn to the ancient vampire's voice...and his words.

"She turns her pillow over," Fabian continued, "several times each night, in order to flush the cool side of the fabric against her cheek. It is the same reason she loves to...*ski*...the cool wind in her hair, the snow beneath her feet. She is never more alive, more awake, or more aware than when she is soaring down a mountain with only mountain air—crisp, cool, invigorating—kissing her frosted skin." He blew a cold wisp of breath over the back of her neck and pressed a kiss along each vertebra, slowly working his way down...

She spun around to face him—and evade him. "You've been reading my memories."

"I've seen your soul."

She shook her head, nerves and desperation getting the best of her. "But I haven't seen yours."

"You have," he countered, cupping her jaw in his hand. "*You have.*"

"Fabian, I can't do this. Any of this. The Curse...the Blood Moon...our mating." She cringed at the very sound of that word: *mating.*

"You can," he countered.

"No, I really can't."

He stepped back, captured her gaze, and smiled wolfishly, his burnt-copper eyes warming with heat. "You wore a dress."

She drew back in surprise. "What?"

"You wore a dress, Gwendolyn. This night...for our date...you wore a beautiful dress." He traced the low, lightly hemmed bodice of the black-and-green sundress Gwendolyn had chosen from her suitcase, the pads of his fingers brushing against the swell of her breasts. "My beautiful, exotic dove, who prefers to wear trousers like a man." He chuckled. *Was he making a joke?* "You knew I was taking you somewhere special...private...that I long to be with you, and still, you wore a dress." His eyes drifted downward to the pleated skirt that barely fell to mid-thigh.

"It's...it's the custom now," she stammered, feeling completely off balance. "Girls don't wear long dresses like they used to. I just wanted to—"

He leaned into her, grasping her jaw between his thumb and forefinger, and lightly depressed the sides of her cheeks. "You just wanted to...*what?*"

She shivered.

Oh, shit; did he know something she didn't?

Was he reading something she wasn't trying to...reveal?

He bent down and kissed her, and his mouth was like golden, liquid fire, burning the protest from her lips.

She tried to pull away—or at least she thought she did.

Which way was up, anyhow?

He deepened the kiss, and his tongue was like lava: testing, tasting, seeking...

She would bite him!

That's what she would do.

She would use her new fangs to draw blood, and he would finally get the message...

What message was that?

He swirled his tongue around the tips of her fangs, traced the backs of her teeth, and then nipped her bottom lip, before drawing it into his mouth to suckle on it.

Her knees grew weak and started to buckle.

She moaned into his mouth...

And that was it.

All the invitation he needed.

His slid his strong, sure hands along the outside of her thighs

—up and underneath the skirt of her dress—hooked them beneath her bottom, massaging the globes as he explored—then lifted her, effortlessly, off the ground. And heaven help her, she wrapped her arms around his neck and her legs around his waist, as he carried her across the grove to the table with the blood-red rose and white linen.

He made a shelf beneath her bottom with the length of one forearm, freeing his other hand, and then he waved it in the air, pointing his fingers toward the candlesticks—and they rose from the table top, drifted to the sides, and hovered above the setting like antique, romantic lanterns.

The bottle of wine floated into his hand, and he removed the cork with his teeth, even as he gently set Gwen down on the edge of the table, then traced her lips with his thumb. He raised the bottle, tilted it toward her, and she opened her mouth to taste the fermented grapes.

He coated her lips with the wine, instead.

And then he devoured her mouth in earnest.

Gwen gasped when he passed the bottle into his other hand and grasped her throat, caught her windpipe between the side of his thumb and the length of his lower forefinger. He was purring, snarling...groaning into her mouth, and she stiffened for a moment—but only for a second—before it hit her, then really sank in:

Fabian Antonescu was not going to harm her.

She could trust him...*completely*...though she had no idea why.

How...

When it had happened.

Yes, he was still the vampire who had emerged from the well.

And yes, he was still the High Mage from Romania, the one who wielded magic like others drew breath, but he was also the artisan, the craftsman, the soul who had carved the humming-birds into that tree.

Both his and hers.

He had been right—she knew him, very well...

And he wasn't trying to hurt her or control her—he wasn't trying to impose his will.

He was trying to love her, to give her pleasure...

He was trying to share a part of his soul.

And more than that, he belonged to her.

Fabian Antonescu belonged to Gwen.

And she belonged to him.

She tunneled her fingers into his glorious golden-bronze mane, marveling at how the colors sparkled in the candlelight... beneath the moonlight...and then she breathed his name out loud on a wing and a prayer, wanting something she could barely comprehend.

He growled, deep and low, from the back of his throat; reared back long enough to hook his hands beneath her arms and lift her —slide her—further back, toward the center of the table, brushing the rose and the *chocolates* aside; and then he lowered the straps of her dress from her shoulders, exposed her breasts to his gaze and the cool night air, and lifted the wine, tilted it again, coating her breasts in the rich, warm fluid.

Fabian drank until he had his fill.

Swirling his tongue along wine and raised nipples; laving the swell, sides, and peaks of Gwen's breast; suckling her flesh, her passion, and her hunger along with the intoxicating elixir.

When he tugged the dress downward, over her waist and her hips, beyond her thighs, her knees, and her ankles, allowing it to fall to the ground, she shivered with anticipation. When he raised the bottle, yet again, this time above her quaking stomach, she chuckled beneath her breath.

Yes...yes...yes...

His lips on her stomach; his mouth on the side of her waist; his tongue tracing the curvature of her ribs...and then swirling, nipping, drinking...lower, lower, lower still...until he covered the soft, lacy fabric between Gwen's most intimate pleasure and the night with his perfect, sculpted lips and the heat of his mouth.

He breathed warm air through the fabric, and she arched on the table.

He laved her flesh through the silk and the lace, and she began to writhe beneath him.

And then he finally removed the obstruction, lifted her hips from the table with two powerful hands, and nestled in between her thighs, to tease, torture, and tantalize, until Gwen could no longer withstand it.

"Fabian," she cried, fisting his hair. "Stop...you have to stop." Her voice was thick with ecstasy and need, and he read his *destiny's* every desire as if she had transmitted what she wanted—what she needed, most—directly into his mind.

And truth be told, she probably had.

Fabian rose from the edge of the table, unbuttoned, then unzipped the jeans Napolean had given him, and he let the denim fall to the forest floor. Commando, as always, his erection sprang free, and it was as hard, thick, and exquisite as Gwen remembered. For a moment, she couldn't even imagine taking that much of Fabian inside her, but the gods knew what they were doing—and clearly, so did he.

She let her head fall back and her legs fall open as he covered her body and nestled against her, and then she moaned in ecstasy and tried not to hold her breath as he filled her, slowly rocking back and forth, until he was fully lodged inside her.

Yes...yes...yes...

As Fabian Antonescu finally claimed his *destiny*, Gwen claimed the vampire right back.

And then the High Mage, a son of Jadon—the wild predator

who had leaped from a well—took Gwen to the celestial heavens with him, and back down to Earth in Dark Moon Vale. And all the while, Gwen could've sworn that the vampire illuminated the sky with fireworks—neon orange, green, and red—their bodies intertwined on a white linen-covered table as brilliant girandolas, comets, and skyrockets exploded, their souls mingling in a timeless grove of giant aspens, shimmering willows, and dazzling roman candles...

Their fate sealed beside a magnificent, timeless aspen, pageanting a turquoise hummingbird and its metallic-violet mate.

CHAPTER THIRTY-FIVE

SEVENTY-TWO HOURS LATER

"He is stunning, so alert...strong," Princess Ciopori commented.

"Positively perfect," Vanya added, scooping the newborn babe, barely a half hour old, into her arms.

Gwen stared at the beautiful child nestled in Princess Vanya's arms, hardly believing the infant was hers. Her son. Hers and Fabian's...

Falcon Fortino Antonescu.

Born—well, called forth from his mother's womb by his vampire father—on July 7th at eight o'clock PM, nearly seventy-two hours to the minute from the night Gwen and Fabian had made love in the aspen grove.

The fourth of July...

Gwen chuckled beneath her breath—she really had believed Fabian had created all those fireworks in the sky. With so much going on, she had completely forgotten the annual US holiday; and truth be told, she had seen the explosions again—at least in her mind's eye—when she and Fabian had made love again the next morning...and the next afternoon...and later that night as well, July fifth being the night he had commanded her pregnancy.

"Someone cannot stop smiling," Ciopori teased, eyeing Gwen sideways, even as she reached for Falcon's tiny hand. "Then I take it Nanaşule has finally won your heart?"

Gwen blushed and looked away.

"Well, based upon the presence of this babe in my arms," Vanya quipped, playfully, "I would say he certainly won *something* from you." She chuckled beneath her breath.

Gwen answered the teasing with a sheepish smile, but she shifted uncomfortably on the now familiar distressed-leather couch in Napolean and Brooke's guest house. She didn't know Ciopori or Vanya all that well, and everything was still so new. Fabian had wanted to go forward with the pregnancy right away, to fulfil the demands of the Blood Moon and the House of Jadon's ceremonial conventions with a very simple and unassuming naming ceremony in the presence of only the princesses, the king, Deanna and Nachari—and Gwen had not objected. After all, things were changing...moving...so quickly, and there was so much more to come.

While Gwen would have preferred her *besties* from college over Ciopori or Vanya, she understood why that wasn't possible... just yet...and she also understood why Fabian wanted the noble females there: They shared a long and intimate history, a deep and abiding love.

As it stood, Gwen was simply grateful that Fabian had agreed to include Deanna and Nachari—at least she knew the vampire-couple a little better—and in truth, Deanna had always gone out of her way to extend her hand in friendship to Gwen. She had stood in the gap, so to speak, from the moment Gwen had arrived in the valley.

Beyond the logistics of the pregnancy, naming and mating ceremonies, Gwen was also eager to return to some semblance of normal life, to incorporate her family and friends into her *new vampire normal* in Dark Moon Vale as soon as possible. And the sooner she and Fabian got settled, the sooner they could invite Gwen's clan—*all her people*—to the vale, the sooner they could alter the same's memories to include a recollection of Gwen and Fabian's relationship, which now included a child...and the sooner she and Fabian could settle into a place of their own.

Fabian intended to build a custom home in the peaceful grove of aspens, a home with a large wraparound balcony that overlooked—and directly faced—the tree with the two mated hummingbirds carved into its trunk. The wizard was determined to watch the moon rise behind the ancient relic, every night going forward, to carve out their own private, peaceful sanctuary on the familiar mountain.

Napolean had already agreed to give Fabian the land, materials, and resources to make it happen and to allow the High Mage and his *destiny* to remain in the guest house as long as needed, until the home was finished, and Gwen still felt like she was caught up in an ancient nightmare-turned-modern-fairy-tale...

She could hardly catch her breath.

Still, once things settled down, she fully intended to broach a delicate subject with Fabian, who was, for all intents and purposes, hopelessly old-fashioned, to put it mildly: She would find a way to speak with him about going back to school, using her degree in Integrative Physiology to become a physical therapist. It had always been her dream, and maybe she could work in the Dark Moon Vale clinic—surely Nachari's older brother, Kagen, would not object to her coming on board.

In the meantime, she waited with Ciopori and Vanya—and the little miracle named Falcon—for Fabian and the king, Nachari and Deanna, to show up for the semi-formal ceremonies.

"How long does it take, anyways?" Gwen asked Ciopori, eyeing the large decorative Roman numerals on a nearby wall clock and the front foyer, each in turn. "I mean, the sacrifice in the chamber. Shouldn't they be back by now?"

Ciopori smoothed the skirt of her long, flowing midi dress, leaned forward on the sofa, and placed her hand over Gwen's. "All is well, Gwendolyn. I assure you. Napolean has entered the Chamber of Sacrifice and Atonement to make the required sacrifice more times than he could count, and he has always emerged unscathed. He will walk Fabian through it; they will appease the Blood together, and Fabian will return to you—and Falcon—just as he should." She glanced at the baby and smiled, then turned back to Gwen. "The real question is: How are you doing with it all? How was the birth, the...emergence...of the Dark One? I know that we do not have a history of our own, at least not yet, but Vanya and I are here for both Fabian and you, and there is nothing you cannot speak with us about."

Gwen squeezed Ciopori's hand. "Thank you. I think I'm doing fairly well, all things considered. This custom"—she held her hand in the air because *custom* was not the right word—"this *curse* is barbaric, to say the least. I'm still having a little trouble wrapping my mind around it."

At this, Vanya's eyebrows arched upward. "We are all of the same mind, Gwendolyn. The punishment visited upon the sons of Jadon, for so many centuries beyond the original sin, was ill-conceived and malicious at best, hardly suggestive of justice. Honestly, I don't know what my slain sisters were thinking—perhaps they were not thinking at all."

Gwen nodded, but she didn't speak.

There were no words to express what she was feeling.

Ciopori released her hand and slid an elegant, slender arm around her shoulders, instead. "Do you wish to talk about it—what you saw, what you heard—to share more of the experience with women who understand?"

Gwen smiled then. "Honestly, I don't remember that part.

Fabian's magic is so incredibly strong. It's like one of those dreams you have, where everything is so vivid and overwhelming, and then the moment you wake up, you lose it all. You can still sense it, remember having it, but you can't recall what the dream was about—the details are somehow lost to you. I remember the sound of a rushing river...lights and colors, swirling through the room. I remember a feeling of lightness in my chest and power hovering over my stomach, and Fabian saying those words...*some words*...when he called the first twin forward, into the night. And then it's black. It's blank. Empty for a time. The river, the lights, the colors swirled again, and I was holding Falcon in my arms."

She glanced at the babe, now sleeping, his head nestled against Vanya's chest, and grinned, remembering her first glimpse of his light-green eyes, golden-bronze hair, and unmistakable copper coloring. Like his father, he had a heart-shaped birthmark imprinted on his tiny right shoulder, and like his father, his wide, watchful eyes were rimmed in black with a faint golden glow sparkling behind them, projecting generations—if not millennia— of inborn power, the line of his gifted mage ancestry. "I remember thinking he was the most beautiful being, the most perfect creation I have ever seen. I remember my heart filling with love. And then Fabian helped me get dressed, the two of you arrived, and he left the guest house with Napolean and a bundle in his arms. Again, I can't see the bundle, just a shadow next to Fabian."

Vanya pursed her lips together, apparently deep in thought. The princess was weighing her words quite carefully. "Was that your wish, Gwen?"

"What do you mean?"

"To forget...to have no memory of the firstborn son?"

Gwen swallowed her unease and slowly nodded. "Yes. I don't know if it was right or wrong, but I asked Fabian to take it all away if he could. I told him I wasn't sure if I could grasp it...live with it...make peace with it."

Vanya nodded respectfully. "Very well. Then we shall all look forward, for life is not lived in the past. And there is so much to embrace with each new sunrise; you and Fabian have forever to look forward to, and piece by piece, one by one, you will work out all the details, together."

Gwen was just about to reply when a heavy knock on the guest house front door interrupted her thoughts and halted her words. The door opened slowly, and Nachari Silivasi stepped in, ushering Deanna in front of him, his hand placed gently on her hip. "I hear there's a vampire and a lovely *destiny* who want to be mated as soon as possible, and a baby who needs a formal name." His voice was light, airy, and playful.

Deanna rounded the corner and rushed into the room, going immediately to Vanya and Falcon, bending over to study the child, then sidling over, just as quickly, to hold her arms open and out to Gwen. "Oh, my goodness, Gwen, he's precious! Amazing. Stunning. Wow, he's going to look just like his father."

Gwen stood and hugged Deanna. "Thank you. I still can't believe he's real. I still feel like I must be dreaming."

Deanna laughed, light-heartedly. "Trust me; I get it. Once it all happens, it happens so fast." She gave Gwen an extra squeeze, then stepped back and turned toward the princesses. "Hi, Vanya. You look like you have your hands full. How are Saber and Lucien?"

Vanya's smile and her features were stamped with pride—and love—as her dusty-rose eyes lit up. "They are both well; thank you for asking. And yes, this little one is glorious, is he not? Fabian's coloring and Gwen's exotic eyes..." She gently brushed a lock of golden-bronze hair away from the infant's forehead, careful not to wake him, as she smoothed the same silken tresses into the rest of the child's downy crown. Falcon stirred, cooed, and his eyelids fluttered like he was he dreaming.

"Couldn't be more handsome if he tried," Deanna pointed

out again, before turning her attention to Ciopori. "Hey, sister. How are you? How are Marquis and Nikolai?"

Ciopori stood and stretched her back. "Ah, Nikolai just gets bigger and bigger. Heavier and heavier. We need to get all the boys together soon. And as for your brother-in-law, Marquis is a tad bit grumpy, doesn't understand why I am here, and he is not."

Deanna laughed conspiratorially. "Mm...sounds like Marquis. Well, I'm sure Nikolai will keep him plenty busy until you get home—he won't have much time to stew about it."

"One can always hope," Ciopori said, playfully rolling her eyes.

Just then, the front door opened, once again, and Napolean and Fabian strolled into the foyer, a heavy silence trailing behind them. Falcon immediately woke up, began to cry, and Gwen hurried over to Vanya and reached for the babe.

"Shh," Vanya whispered to Falcon, lifting him gently and placing him on her shoulder so she could pat his back. "I've got him, Gwen. He's fine. Go ahead and greet your mate."

"Are you sure?" Gwen asked, studying Falcon carefully: the way he settled, the way he nestled, the way his tiny fists relaxed.

"Absolutely," Vanya assured her.

Gwen stood up straight, glanced across the room, and immediately made note of the heavy lines of worry etched in Fabian's brow. She padded softly across the great room, eyes fixed straight ahead, and stepped into his arms, linked her hands behind his back, and enfolded the wizard in a warm embrace. "Are you okay?" she whispered, drawing back to study his burnt-copper expression.

He glanced down, and his countenance softened. "I'm fine."

"How did it go?" she asked, cautiously.

He shook his head. "It's done." She nodded, and then she turned around and leaned back against him. This time, he enfolded her in his arms. "I am swiftly gaining a newfound respect and a broader perspective with regard to the king," he murmured in her ear. "The male has seen much in his lifetime. He has sacrificed much on behalf of the house of Jadon. I truly had no idea."

Gwen thought about his words and his burgeoning relationship with Napolean. "I think, in time, the two of you will probably become close friends."

Fabian shrugged. "Mm, perhaps. I hope in time, the two of *us* will become even better friends." He nuzzled her hair and inhaled her scent. "As well as life partners and insatiable lovers." He brushed the underside of her breast with his thumb, and she jerked, giggled, and restrained the digit in her fist.

"Later, wizard," she chided.

He purred like a lion, his chest rumbling behind her. "How is Falcon?" he asked, changing the subject.

She smiled. "I think Vanya has permanently adopted him."

Fabian glanced across the room. "That is good to see, although she may not have him indefinitely." His voice became both whimsical and thoughtful at once. "I fear the four of you command my heart: you, Falcon, and the beloved princesses. Vanya has a quick wit and a razor-edged spine; she is strong as well as noble. Those who don't know her well might find her a bit...off-putting...at times or even distant, perhaps reserved. But beneath that grace and unfailing nobility, beneath that carefully controlled demeanor is a heart spun from pure gold. No one loves deeper or more loyally than Vanya—she will make a wonderful guardian angel for Falcon. They both will, Vanya and Ciopori. For truly, the raven-haired princess is fiercely loyal as well—gods save any who cross her or the ones she loves."

Gwen listened to his words, wondering at the true meaning of *guardian angel* to Fabian...what it meant to an ancient Romanian mage...but she would ask him more about it later.

For now, she was just happy—and relieved—to have him back home.

To have *him*—Fabian Antonescu, the wizard, the vampire, and the sane, lucid male—back home. His memories were coming back, becoming easier to retrieve, and his personality was beginning to show...his spirit was beginning to shine.

She stroked his forearms lovingly and glanced downward at her jeans. "Are you sure you don't want me to wear something nicer, like a skirt or a dress, something more formal, for the ceremonies?"

He chuckled, and the sound of it still brought her up short. "Would I like you to wear something other than trousers?"

She laughed. "Yes. Anything other than that Flintstones miniskirt you made me."

He growled in her ear. "I thought it looked lovely on you, my dove."

"You didn't."

He paused as if thinking it over. "No, I suppose I did not. But it looked better than those worn, tattered trousers."

"Blue jeans, and they protected my legs."

"I protected your legs."

"Fabian, I skinned my knees, and I froze at night."

He grumbled and shook her side to side, playfully. "You did *not* freeze, Gwendolyn. I made you a fire. And the only one who skinned anything was me, when I brought you that rabbit, the second night in our cave."

She laughed again and spun around to face him, green eyes seeking burnt copper, rimmed in black. "It was *your* cave, and you didn't skin the rabbit, wizard. It was crusty, the skin was rotting, and I believe rigor mortis had already set in."

He frowned, and his dark eyes filled with mischief. "I *did* eventually skin the rabbit, my dove. And why must you continue to call me wizard when High Mage is so much more appropriate?"

She rolled her eyes. "Fabian, my jeans! Would you like me to change?"

He cupped her cheeks in his hands and smiled wolfishly. "Don't ever change, my dove. I adore you just the way you are."

She sighed in exasperation. "You're impossible." He smiled, and Gwen could've sworn the moon and the stars settled in his dark, mysterious pupils. "Fabian, the king and the princesses are growing restless. Would you like me to go put on—"

He bent low to kiss her, a chaste brush of ardent lips. "No, Gwendolyn. You look as you did when I found you: innocent, beautiful, captivating. I do not wish for you to change your blue jeans—or anything about your personality." He gestured toward the great room. "This ceremony—both ceremonies—they are ancient rituals in the house of Jadon, important rites of passage for the king and our species. I understand why Napolean felt the need to implement them so many centuries ago, and I will be honored to stand beside you and our son as the king walks us through them. However"—he tapped her on the tip of the nose—"I am also from another time and place. Descended from celestial gods and men, yes, but also the son and grandson, many generations extended, from a great house of mages. Our second mating ceremony, Falcon's final naming, will both take place at midnight, tonight, under a blanket of stars, a deep blue sky, and a watching white moon: the three of us together in our aspen grove with only the gods as witnesses, with only the earth for a chapel. Wear whatever you like for the ceremony now—that is fine. Whatever you wear tonight will be swiftly removed, as I intend to make love to you until the sun rises, tomorrow."

Gwen gulped. "What about Falcon?"

"What about him? He's a baby."

"Fabian!" His name was spoken in unison, both by Gwen and Napolean, as the king ushered them forward into the great room.

"Are you ready?" Napolean asked.

Fabian inclined his head. "We are."

* * *

"What name have you chosen for this male?" Napolean's deep, melodious voice seemed to fill the rafters in the guest house, causing everyone present to stand to attention.

As there was no eldest living male from Fabian's family present, the High Mage held Falcon in his strong, muscular arms like he was carrying the lost tablets of Sakarias and the slabs were made of porcelain. Every time he glanced into the child's light-green eyes, his own burnt-copper orbs grew misty. "Should it please you, my king, and find favor with the Celestial Beings, the son of Aquarius, our water-bearing lord who makes his home six hundred light-years away in the Saturn Nebula, is to be named Falcon Fortino Antonescu."

"The name pleases me, mage, and there is no objection from the Celestial Beings."

Fabian raised one eyebrow in question, and Gwen almost giggled.

Deanna had walked her through the ceremony, just before it started, explaining the customs, the verbiage, and what was to be expected—how the ancient rite might be adapted for Gwen and Fabian in the absence of having any close family members present—but the beautiful brunette failed to take into account the fact that Fabian was more ancient than Napolean. The mage glanced around the great room. He looked up at the rafters, then back at the king, and Gwen nearly held her breath, waiting for him to ask, *How do you know what the gods are thinking?* But to his credit, Fabian held his tongue.

When Falcon stirred in his father's arms, and his tiny, heart-shaped mouth curved into a faint, wistful smile, Gwen knew she was in for a very different experience—vampire babies were not like human infants. She could only hope her son had a more... modern...sense of humor than his father, or she was going to be in trouble.

As the sovereign lord of the house of Jadon bent his head to Falcon's wrists and his fangs began to elongate, Fabian took a cautious step back. "Is this really necessary, Napolean?" he asked, his eyes boring into the monarch's.

Napolean smiled graciously. "It is, Fabian. I carry the blood of every male and female in the house of Jadon in my veins. Falcon's will not be an exception."

The room grew quiet as Fabian considered Napolean's words.

Nachari shuffled in place and took Deanna's hand.

Vanya leveled a sideways glance at Ciopori, and both princesses raised their brows, waiting.

Gwen watched her vampire mate like a hawk, wondering if this would be the moment, if *now* would be the time when Fabian finally challenged the king of the Vampyr for authority.

Yet again, Fabian seemed to let it roll off his back; the High Mage was not threatened by the king's position. "Then I suppose you will still need mine...and Gwendolyn's...as well."

Napolean exhaled a deep breath of relief.

So, the king had been wondering, too...

"Taking Gwen's blood is part of the ceremony," Napolean said, matter-of-factly, "but yes, you and I will need to complete the process soon, as well."

Fabian snorted. "The process," he echoed. "You mean the exchange?"

Napolean furrowed his brows. "Excuse me?"

"With my blood flowing through your veins, you can find

me...track me...know far more about me. With yours flowing through mine, I can do the same. You are my sovereign lord, Napolean, and I will honor you as my king. But I remain the highest mage in the house of Jadon, and we shall comport ourselves as equals."

Whoa...

Okay.

So Fabian was not threatened by Napolean, but neither was he ceding his rightful rank and position as the oldest living vampire in the vale.

Once again, the room filled with nervous tension as this time, Napolean appraised the wizard. Finally, the king nodded his head. "Very well. We will attend to the matter after the ceremony."

Nachari squeezed Deanna's hand, and the princesses murmured something beneath their breath.

Fabian declined his head in a noble gesture and held Falcon out to Napolean.

The babe did not recoil in alarm, nor balk in any manner, as the king swiftly scored his tiny wrist with his fangs and imbibed the precious, life-giving fluid. Rather, the child kicked his feet, then yawned, while Napolean sealed the wound with venom—*yep, he was truly his father's son.*

Napolean took Falcon into his arms. "Welcome to the house of Jadon, Falcon Fortino Antonescu. May your life be filled with peace, triumph, and purpose. May your path always be blessed."

He gave the child to Ciopori next, because she was the eldest of the two ancient females and the closest thing to family in the guest house. Ciopori kissed Falcon on the forehead. "Welcome to the house of Jadon, Falcon Fortino Antonescu. May your life be filled with peace, triumph, and purpose. May your path always be blessed." Her eyes met Fabian's, and the look of love that passed between them was timeless.

The princess passed the child to Vanya, who repeated the refrain, and then spoke softly. "You belong to Nanaşule; thus, you belong to me. I will love you as I love my second father...dearly, unconditionally, and until the end of days."

Fabian's eyes glazed over, he looked away, and he had to catch his breath.

He opened his mouth to reply, then shut it, for clearly, there were no words.

Finally, he locked eyes with Vanya and nodded, and Falcon's eyes began to glow, reflecting his father's wordless love, on the ancient wizard's behalf.

Truly, he possessed a piece of both Fabian and Gwendolyn's souls...

Vanya passed the child to Nachari, who repeated the refrain, and Deanna, at last, blessed and greeted the infant, before handing him back to his father.

Napolean cleared his throat and turned his attention back to the newly mated couple. "By the laws which govern the house of Jadon, I accept your union as the divine will of the gods and hereby sanction your mating. Gwendolyn Marie Hamilton, do you come now of your own free will to enter the house of Jadon?"

Time stood still as Gwen paused to process the question: *Did she actually come now*—of her own free will—*to enter the house of Jadon?* The past ten days flashed through her memory like a terrifying, surreal, and enchanted movie, set on triple fast-forward: the fear, the dominance, the fog and the insanity; the desperation, the progression, and the passion; and finally, those dark copper eyes and those strong, brawny arms—those hummingbirds carved into the giant aspen...

"Yes," she said emphatically, "I do."

Fabian lowered his head, shut his eyes, and Gwen saw a single tear escape from the corner of a lowered lid. The High Mage had been uncertain about her answer; a part of the vampire still felt regret—felt unworthy—and for the first time, his humility shone above his arrogance.

Gwen reached out to place her hands on his forearms, even as he continued to cradle Falcon, and Fabian opened his eyes and stared at her.

Stared through her.

Stared all the way to her soul.

"I love you, Gwendolyn Marie Antonescu," he whispered, softly. "And I will spend the rest of my life earning the trust you just bestowed upon me."

Gwen's heart went *pitter-patter* in her chest, and her own eyes filled with moisture.

The mage was speaking the truth.

He did love her...

And he would spend the rest of his life, not just honoring her, but making up for that first week together. *Talk about a diamond in the rough...*

One of the worst things that had ever happened to Gwen had turned out to be her greatest blessing. "I think a part of me has always known you, always loved you," she said openly, "the soul of the one who carved that bird in the tree. And in time, I will come to see him, to know him, to love him even more deeply. If he'll let me."

Fabian smiled unabashedly, and Napolean cleared his throat again.

Gwen laughed and extended her arm to the king—it was time to seal this mating and get on with living—living with Fabian and Falcon.

Napolean took her wrist with exquisite gentleness, then paused to study the beautiful, enigmatic markings along her skin, the stamp and seal of Corona Borealis etched into her flesh... forever. As he pierced her vein cleanly, sank his fangs deep, and formed a tight, unbreakable seal over the wound...as he took several deep pulls of her blood…Gwen reveled in the sensation of complete and utter peace that enveloped her.

She reveled in Fabian's presence and marveled at Falcon's light.

The king released his hold, removed his fangs, and sealed the wound, all in one smooth motion. "Congratulations," he said, backing away.

It was then that Fabian passed the babe to Vanya, cupped Gwen's cheeks in his hands, rotated his thumbs along her jaw, then released both palms with a flourish: Two bright, brilliant, fluttering hummingbirds exploded into the air, shot like rockets toward the ceiling, then dived down—spinning, looping, dancing —as they fell, a dazzling turquoise male and a metallic violet female. They shot up toward the ceiling a second time and disappeared into a puff of smoke, even as every vampire-witness in the room vanished along with Fabian's magic birds, leaving Falcon resting quietly in his mother's arms.

Gwen gasped and smiled. "How did you do that!"

Fabian enfolded his *family* in his arms. "It is only the beginning, my precious dove. I hope you are prepared for a life filled with wonders."

EPILOGUE

B raden Bratianu paced restlessly, back and forth, in front of the floor-to-ceiling windows in Kristina's lavish penthouse apartment on the top floor of the Dark Moon Casino, feeling more like a restless tiger than a seventeen-year-old vampire male. He swept his hand through his shoulder-length, chestnut-brown hair and shook his head in disbelief.

He couldn't believe it was actually happening.

The Millenia Harvest Moon would rise tomorrow, and only the gods knew what the omen would bring.

And as for what Kristina Riley-Silivasi had just offered to give him...

Shit...

Just shit...

Braden knew she didn't mean it.

They had been back and forth, covering the same territory again and again: What would happen tomorrow when the celestial gods poured their power down upon the earth, when the dormant blood of a prince roused inside Braden's young body—quickened, stirred...awakened?

Would Braden still know Kristina?

Would Kristina still know him?

Would Napolean continue to enforce his decree—insist upon seeing the unusual couple mated, two vampires who were both exempt from the Blood Curse? Or would the soul, the spirit—the *what the actual fuck?*—of Prince Jadon be so strong that it ultimately took over? And if so, would Braden actually have a Blood Moon one day, a blood *destiny*, a female chosen by the gods, whom he had to claim, cherish, and mate?

What would happen to Kristina then?

Could Braden still potentially sire female offspring after tomorrow night, or would the Curse placed upon all the sons of King Sakarias—Prince Jadon's progeny and Prince Jaegar's alike —usurp the rare, singular circumstance of Braden's siring?

Braden was *made*, not born, to vampirism.

And thus, he was immune to the punishment—and the required sacrifice—demanded of all biological sons...and their sons...*and their sons*, for all perpetuity, of the original celestial progeny.

If Kristina and Braden made love tonight—if the young, fledgling vampire commanded a pregnancy—then he would have two, not one, offspring to bring to the house of Jadon, possibly rare, precious, coveted female children, and they would belong to him.

To him...

To Braden and Kristina.

Not to Prince Jadon and not to some yet unknown *destiny*, not to some horrible dreamtime mistake made in a fit of madness and desperation by a sleeping High Mage.

"Shiiiit," Braden murmured beneath his breath, glancing over his shoulder to study Kristina's features for the umpteenth time. His head was beginning to spin, and her expression was just as confounded: Her beautiful, normally bright blue eyes were dark with shadows, thick with fear, nearly glazed over with uncertainty...and desperation. Why else would she have offered to do something so personal, so intimate, so permanent? Something she had never been willing to do before?

To couple with Braden before their mating.

To give herself to a seventeen-year-old boy...

Because isn't that how she really saw him?

Always had...

Likely always would.

Despite the fact that Braden had finally stopped growing at six feet, two inches tall; despite the fact that he was now 200 pounds of hard, sinewy muscle, all strength and cords packed around rock-hard abs—strong as an ox and fast as a cougar; imbued with powers, insights, visions, and wisdom well beyond his years—Kristina Riley-Silivasi had always seen him as a kid, someone she might have to wait a decade to be with.

"Say something, Bray," Kristina nearly whimpered, twirling a curly lock of red hair around her finger, nervously, even as she sank back into the cream-colored cushions on the large, plush sectional beneath several soft, glowing, recessed lights, and crossed her ankles in front of her, interlocking the spikes of her stiletto heels.

Damn, Braden thought. She looked so damn beautiful. So damn vulnerable. And what could he say?

He wanted her.

He always had.

And yeah, screw being a seventeen-year-old neophyte in the house of Jadon; he had no doubts whatsoever that he could give her pleasure, make her call out his name, make love to her like a grown-ass male with passion, skill, and dominance.

The instincts were in his blood.

The vampiric passion had always been there, stirring, waiting...rising.

He may have been made by a sire, as opposed to born of the

Curse, but he was still a fully matured male vampire. "You don't mean it, Red," he finally murmured.

She crossed her arms over her chest and shivered, probably hoping Braden didn't notice the latter. "Bray, *I do.* I mean, tomorrow is no longer promised, and we've always been really close, you and me. We've always been great—"

"*Friends,*" he interjected.

She shook her head sadly. "I was going to say: 'We've always been great together.' More than friends, Braden." She took a deep breath for courage, or at least that was the way Braden read it. "The way you look at me...that time you kissed me, that time you stole my breath...we've always been more than friends."

Braden angled his broad shoulders to face her squarely. "And what if I change so much tomorrow that I no longer remember you, Kristina? What if I really do end up promised to another, and meanwhile, you have two of my kids?"

Kristina blanched at his bluntness, then quickly recovered. "Would that be so terrible?"

Braden shrugged. "For me? No. For you, yeah. *Shit yeah*, Kristina, that's not who you are. You could never share me or anyone else. The situation would drive you crazy."

Kristina stared at her hands, studying her bright-pink, manicured nails. "I guess I would learn to live with it," she muttered beneath her breath.

Braden stared at the crease in her eyebrows, the deep lines of worry etched into her frown—did she even know she was frowning? She was sitting on her couch, wearing a nearly see-through white silk blouse over a killer, hip-hugging pink-and-white skirt—smooth, bare legs and painted toenails slipped into a designer pair of stiletto heels—trying to appear calm, ready, and certain, even as her soft, sculpted lips were curved into a frown.

One thing Braden knew for certain: The female truly loved him.

She had to.

Because what she was offering was *everything*.

Her whole heart, her body, the rest of her life.

And for a moment, just a fleeting second, Braden wished he were selfish enough to take her up on it.

He strolled across the living room floor to where she sat on the sofa, braced one heavy knee on the cushion beside her hip, and leaned into her, grasping her high, angular cheeks in his palms, his thumbs anchored beneath her jaw. And then he bent down to kiss her, and he let years of pent-up frustration... restrained desire...flow into the kiss.

She gasped and reached for his shoulders, but he just as quickly pulled away.

He still had to meet with Nachari, the rest of the Silivasi brothers—the sentinels and Julien, the king and Fabian, the High Mage—at Napolean's manse.

Time was running out.

Without looking back, he headed to the elegant sliding doors that led to Kristina's wraparound balcony, brushed them open with two stiff fingers and a backward flick of his wrist, then strolled across the decking, leaped over the banister, and shifted into a glorious eagle the moment his body hit the cool night air.

Because yeah, he had gotten better at that shit too...

Even though, with the exception of Nachari, who could shift into a panther—and now, Fabian Antonescu, the great High Mage, who could probably do all kinds of miraculous crap—most vampires were restricted to only bats or mist.

As he tilted his outstretched wings in the direction of the Vampyr king's compound, Braden did his best not to think of the complicated, confused, beautiful redhead still seated on her couch.

* * *

Achilles Zahora, the Dark One otherwise known as The Executioner, was feeling restless, twitchy, amped up and loaded for bear...

But he had no idea why.

Salvatore Nistor had been right about one thing: Achilles had always been a bloodthirsty savage, a giant of a vampire, and a killing machine...a force to be reckoned with.

He reveled in the slaughter.

He luxuriated in the taste and feel of fresh blood on his tongue, the thick, sticky fluid snaking down his fangs, and he could never get enough carnage, destruction, or bloodshed.

Maybe it was just as simple as that...

Achilles hadn't fed in a while. He hadn't left a string of brutalized human bodies in his wake for at least two or three moons, and he hadn't executed a rebel or a sinner in the house of Jaegar for just as many months. Still, tomorrow night marked the coming of the Millenia Harvest Moon, and the house of Jaegar would be busy, indeed: busy *feeding* on human hosts so younger siblings could feed their fathers...their brothers...in the ancient familial rite; busy satiating carnal appetites of every bent and perverse imagining; busy impregnating beautiful young women who would give birth to two dark sons forty-eight hours later, and die a wretched death as the younglings, the evil offspring, clawed their way out of their sensual, fertile bodies.

Achilles wanted no part in the latter, to become a father...just yet.

True, it was every male in the house of Jaegar's ultimate duty to procreate, and Achilles' offspring would be a coveted prize to his dark brethren. Yet and still, he wasn't ready. It was as simple as that.

Two years back, when that brutish son of Jadon, Marquis Silivasi, had discovered one of the last remaining females of a proud and ancient race—Ciopori Demir—and managed to claim her as his own, seduce her, even as he was caught up in a wicked, deceitful love triangle, believing Kristina Riley to be his true *destiny*, chosen by the gods, Salvatore had managed to abduct the careless princess and bring her back to the Colony: The promise of heated nights, thrusting inside that royal womb; the mystery and allure of a female who might not die—who *might* still have access to celestial magic and *might* be able to circumvent the Curse, thus give birth to female offspring?—had been too strong for Salvatore to pass up. Salvatore had needed to know more. So much remained a puzzle. And he had pulled the trigger, taken the princess, a bit too soon.

He had been reckless, selfish, a bit premature.

And as a result, the sons of Jadon had invaded the Dark Ones' Colony, entering the underground settlement from a tunnel in the back of the sacrificial cave under the cover of night to rescue the missing princess, and they had slaughtered—annihi-lated—*fifty* sons of Jaegar, malevolent infant offspring who had just begun their eternal reigns of terror. In reply, Oskar Vadovsky, the new chair of the Dark Council, had ordered every male over the age of five hundred to go out and reproduce, to replace the lost, slain souls, until at least 250 new demon spawn slept in new cribs.

Achilles Zahora was over a thousand years old, but the Colony Guard and the illustrious council were exceptions to the edict, as were many other males whose seed was not ultimately needed, as 250 women were impregnated rather...quickly.

As far as Achilles was concerned, it was just as well.

He had always craved something better...different...worthy of his rank and file.

Perhaps a female human, corrupt to her core, who would relinquish her immortal soul for the promise of everlasting life on Earth—immortality—a woman drenched in iniquity: a dark, soul-less vessel who could bear Achilles offspring, again and again.

Or perhaps, a blue-eyed redhead who was already Vampyr...

A cherished daughter to the Silivasi clan; a loyal servant of Napolean Mondragon; a hot, ditzy, prime piece of ass who strutted around in stiletto heels, and whose soul would taste like honey, whose innocence...goodness...ultimate light would supersede and overshadow the familiar taste and taint of an already immoral soul.

Yeah...

Achilles would rather claim a female from the light than convert a soul already lost to darkness.

He was perverse that way.

The thought of defiling her innocence...again and again... forcing her to bear children for the house of Jaegar, taking her away from those arrogant, worthless, mother-fucking half-wits from the house of Jadon was just too damn tempting...

First, he would take her away from Nachari Silivasi, a bastard who had once almost bested Achilles in battle, outside Saber Alexiares' cave, when Diablo had shown up to kill the "*dragon.*" Achilles had stabbed the Master Wizard with a ten-inch-dagger; Nachari had shifted into that detestable black panther; and the cat had nearly eviscerated Achilles' throat.

And second, he would take her away from Braden Bratianu, who had eluded Ian Lacusta's nefarious plot to kill the youngster at River Rock Creek: Ian had managed to grasp Braden's heart, and he had almost extracted it from the kid's adolescent body, but not unlike Nachari, Braden had shifted just in time, leaving Ian with a fistful of eagle feathers, instead.

And last, but not least, Achilles would take the female from Napolean-freakin'-Mondragon's collection of faithful servants, from the monarch who had singlehandedly slaughtered eighty-seven dark soldiers during that first Colony raid...

Using only his eyes and his power...

So yeah—*shit yeah*—it would be worth having a ditzy bitch

for a consort, just to irritate, insult, and outwit the house of Jackasses...

And that's why Achilles had no intentions of siring offspring tomorrow night.

While he would join his dark brothers in celebrating all the bloody sacrifices Prince Jaegar, their forefather, once performed in Romania—while he would take his fair share of innocent lives in the most brutal and imaginative ways possible, slaking his itch and assuaging his restless, brutal nature—he would opt out of the procreation...

For now.

He would wait to claim a richer prize...

Kristina Riley Silivasi.

COMING NEXT: BLOOD HARVEST

JOIN THE AUTHOR'S MAILING LIST

If you would like to receive a direct email notification each time Tessa releases a new book, please join the author's mailing list at...

www.tessadawn.com

BOOKS IN THE BLOOD CURSE SERIES

Blood Genesis (prequel)
Blood Destiny
Blood Awakening
Blood Possession
Blood Shadows
Blood Redemption
Blood Father
Blood Vengeance
Blood Ecstasy
Blood Betrayal
Christmas In Dark Moon Vale
Blood Web
Blood Echo
Blood Harvest ∼ Coming Soon

A SNEAK PEEK FROM ZANAIKEYROS

SON OF DRAGONS

(Book #1 – Pantheon of Dragons Series)

He continued to take the stairs, two at a time, until he had passed her without incident, and then he suddenly stopped in midstride and spun around to face her.

She sensed it more than she saw it.

She could literally *feel* his domineering presence behind her, and despite her immediate impulse to *run*, she turned to face him instead.

The stranger tilted his head to the side and emitted some strange, feral sound. It was almost like a snarl, and Jordan's heart began to race. They locked eyes a second time, and she almost let out a yelp: He was glaring at her now, like she had stolen his first-born child, his dark, sculpted brows creased into a frown.

She unwittingly took a step back, clutched the rail, once again, for stability, and stifled a terrified gasp. Determined to appear calm, she stuffed her free hand into her pocket, hunched her shoulders in some instinctive, submissive gesture, and slowly backed away, feeling carefully for each stair beneath her.

He took a casual step toward her, and she almost bolted.

He halted, almost as if he dared not frighten her any further, and then he did the oddest, most animalistic thing: He inhaled deeply, sniffed the air, and he *groaned*.

Whether it was a groan of annoyance, impatience, or anger, Jordan had no idea, but that was the final straw—she had no intention of sticking around to find out.

Releasing the rail, she spun around in a whirl, leaped the four remaining stairs—almost twisting her ankle—and took off running for her car, all the while digging frantically for her keys as she ran. She could hear the stranger's footsteps behind her, and she cringed at the stupidity of her choice. *Why hadn't she screamed or tried to push past him? Headed back in the direction of the mall, to the safety of other people?*

Rounding the corner of the parking garage, she eyed her forest-green, metallic BMW, only five spaces away, and rotated her key-fob in her hand, pressing the *unlock* button over and over, just to be sure it opened. She glanced over her shoulder to judge the distance between herself and the stranger, and gasped, her feet skidding to a sudden halt.

He wasn't there.

Even though she could have sworn she'd heard his footsteps just moments ago, the man was no longer behind her.

She pressed her hand to her heart and fought to catch her breath, feeling a curious mixture of both relief and embarrassment. She scanned the garage in all four directions, making sure she hadn't overlooked his presence, that he wasn't hiding behind a nearby post or a vehicle, and then she started once again for her car.

Angry tears filled her eyes as she finally reached her BMW, yanked on the door handle, and bent to climb inside.

"*Stop.*" An *invisible* hand snatched her by the arm, slammed her door shut behind her, and pressed her back against the driver's-side panel. And then, just like that, the stranger was standing, once again, in front of her.

What the hell!?

ABOUT THE AUTHOR

Tessa Dawn grew up in Colorado, where she developed a deep affinity for the Rocky Mountains. After graduating with a degree in psychology, she worked for several years in criminal justice and mental health before returning to get her master's degree in nonprofit management.

Tessa began writing as a child and composed her first full-length novel at the age of eleven. By the time she graduated high school, she had a banker's box full of short stories and novels. Since then, she has published works as diverse as poetry, greeting cards, workbooks for kids with autism, and academic curricula. Her Dark Fantasy/Gothic Romance novels represent her long-desired return to her creative-writing roots and her passionate flair for storytelling.

Tessa currently splits her time between the Colorado suburbs and mountains with her husband, two children, and "one very crazy cat." She hopes to one day move to the country, where she can own horses and what she considers "the most beautiful creature ever created"—a German shepherd.

Writing is her bliss.

CPSIA information can be obtained
at www.ICGtesting.com
Printed in the USA
LVHW050326261119
638499LV00001B/28/P